Dangerous to Love

REXANNE BECNEL

St. Martin's Paperbacks

DANGEROUS TO LOVE

Copyright © 1997 by Rexanne Becnel.

ISBN: 0-312-96330-0

Printed in the United States of America

St. Martin's Paperbacks edition/November 1997

10 9 8 7 6 5 4 3 2 1

For Rich
Oscar Richard Becnel, Jr.
1973–1997

and for Sara,
who made him so happy.

Prologue

*T*he headmistress, Mrs. Drinkwell, stared at the boy and wrinkled her nose. "He's awfully dark."

The child's governess kept a tight hold of the boy's bony shoulder. "Gypsy blood. His mother," she added, not bothering to disguise her disgust.

Hardly a shocking revelation. As Mrs. Drinkwell well knew, Burford Hall housed a number of boys of unpleasant ancestry. The school's considerable distance from London and their isolated location made them ideal for boarding the illegitimate offspring of the quality. Still, they'd never before had a Gypsy bastard in their midst.

Mrs. Drinkwell pursed her lips in distaste. It never ceased to revolt her the lowly sort of women men of good breeding were wont to cavort with.

"Have you the first year's fees with you?" she asked. "We make absolutely no allowances for credit—not even with the royal bastard."

The governess's eyes brightened at that. "You have a royal bastard here? Oh, but her ladyship will be very pleased to hear that. Very pleased, indeed."

Mrs. Drinkwell gave an arch smile. "So. The wife knows of her husband's shame."

The governess stiffened and her grip on the boy tightened. "She does not! Nor shall she ever learn of it, not if you expect the Dowager Countess to pay your outrageous— Ow!"

She broke off with a jerk and a sharp cry. "Oh! Oh! The nasty little beggar bit me. He bit me!" she shrieked, shaking the violated limb as if to throw off the pain.

While she wailed, the dark-haired child, freed of her grasp, darted for the door. But Mrs. Drinkwell had been handling troublesome boys for many years, and she knew all their tricks. She reached the door first, and when he bared his teeth to bite her, she smacked him fully across the face.

She was a large woman and she did not make any allowances for the fact that he was a small child. His head popped around and he hit the wall with a crash that seemed to echo the crack of her blow. Like a broken doll, he crumpled to the floor and did not move.

The governess glared at the slight, still form. "Godless heathen!" Then she stopped and peered more closely at the unmoving child. "He ain't dead, is he? You didn't kill him? For if you did . . ."

By way of answer, Mrs. Drinkwell nudged the boy with her toe. When that drew no reaction, she kicked him in the leg. He let out a whimper and she sent the governess a gloating look. "I'll thank you not to advise me how to run my own school. Discipline is my area of expertise. I make you this promise. The next time your mistress sees her grandson, he'll have much better manners. Now, why don't you hand over those term fees?"

The governess opened her reticule and handed over the purse. "I'm to say that you're to keep him between terms too. There's money enough here and more will be forwarded from milady's solicitor."

"Doesn't want to be bothered with him, does she?"

"D'you blame her?" The governess edged toward the door. "How'd you like it if your only grandson were a Gypsy heathen? He's blessed fortunate his grandmother cares enough to provide for him at all."

*   *   *

"My name is Ivan!"

" 'Tis John."

"Johnny boy."

Ivan stared at the three toughs who'd cornered him, and struggled not to reveal his fear. But it was hard. He wanted to go home. Instead he was trapped in this awful place, stolen away from everything he'd ever known. And now they wanted him to change his name. He couldn't explain why, but he knew he couldn't do it. He was Ivan, not John. They'd changed everything else in his life, but he wouldn't let them change his name.

"I told you, my name is Ivan."

The taller of the three boys smirked. "Ivan? That's a foreign name, a Gypsy name. You a Gypsy, Ivan?" He dragged out the name.

Ivan lifted his chin and balled his fists. They wanted to fight? Well, then, he would fight. He tried to remember everything Peta had taught him, and all the moves Guerdon had used in his wrestling matches.

The tall boy stepped nearer. His two cohorts did the same. "So? Are you John, or are you Ivan, the Gypsy bastard?" he sneered.

Like an explosion, something inside Ivan erupted and without warning he tackled the grinning youth. Though much the smaller, he caught the older boy by surprise and they went down in a tangle of flailing fists and feet. The other lad fought back, however, and he swiftly gained the upper hand.

But Ivan would not back down. He'd been rudely stolen from his mother and the rest of their band. He'd been locked up in the attic of a monstrous house, then transported to this grim prison. Now he was subject to the attack of boys like these. It was too much to accept and so he rejected it. He bit and clawed, despite the brutal beating he received.

One blow split his lip and he tasted blood. With another stars exploded behind his eyes. But it only fueled his re-

solve. *Intimidate your opponent. Go for his weakness.*
Peta's words of advice to Guerdon rang in Ivan's ears.
Without thinking he roared out his rage. Then he brought
one knee up and miraculously he found his target. With a
shriek the other boy collapsed, curling into a ball as he
clutched his private parts.

"Get him!" the boy sobbed to his stunned friends. "Get
him!"

The other two hesitated only an instant before tackling
Ivan. His defeat was inevitable, but still he would not give
in. Only when the headmistress and her hired man waded
into the fray did the battle end.

Mrs. Drinkwell scowled at the bloodied boys, and her
colorless eyes narrowed in malicious delight. "Take Mr.
Dameron to the woodshed," she ordered. " 'Tis only fittin'
that a tradesman's son learns a trade," she sneered. "Whip
him with the strap, then put him to chopping wood.

"Mr. Pierce shall have the task of cleaning out the privy
house—after his whipping, o 'course. Fitting, isn't it, that
scum should deal with scum?" Her nostrils flared with distaste.

Then she turned to the tall boy who'd started the fight.
To Ivan's amazement, her face composed itself into a
calmer expression. "Alexander, Alexander. What am I to
do with you? Don't you see that it is beneath you to brawl
with so . . . so lowly a creature as this Gypsy bastard? Still,
you must be punished. So. You will be confined to the
schoolroom with extra lessons until Sunday next. I hope
your father will appreciate that even when I punish you, it
works to further your education."

Her face hardened when she turned at last to Ivan. "As
for you, you will have an equally appropriate punishment."
She smiled, only it was the sort of smile meant to terrify a
small boy. And it did.

"See he gets the worst strapping of them all, Lester.
Then up the chimneys with him. With his dark skin, a little
soot will never be noticed."

Though bleeding and dazed, Ivan fought the hulking

manservant. He even tried to strike the man in his private parts, as he'd done with the boy named Alexander. But all he received for his trouble was a sharp cuff to the back of his head and a bone-crunching grip on his shoulder.

The whipping was fierce. Ten blows with a wickedly long paddle. But Ivan was numb to any pain. He neither cried out nor wept, but only grunted at the blows. They would have knocked him down had the man not held him in place with one beefy hand. Then he was taken straight-away to the parlor and forced up into the chimney, scrabbling and crawling up the filthy flue, leaving skin and blood on the rough stones with every move he made.

"Clean it well, lad. And don't be slow, else I'll light a fire 'neath you," the grinning servant cackled from some-where below.

But a fire had already been lit, a fire deep in Ivan's heart that burned hotter with each cruel word, painful blow, and hateful punishment. It started that day and it built with every injustice done him in the months and years that followed. It burned with an intensity that defied description and demanded revenge.

But though he did not know then how to exact that revenge, or even upon whom it should be wreaked, as time passed he would come to know very well.

One

*I*van Thornton paused before descending the steps, waiting for it to begin. Sure enough, a murmur rippled through the crowded ballroom. A lull in conversation first, followed by an even more earnest buzz of whispers.

"It's Lord Westcott."

"The new Earl of Westcott."

"Westcott's bastard Gypsy boy."

Ivan didn't have to hear the words to know what was being said of him. He'd lived the last twenty years and more hearing far worse than that. From the moment he'd been torn from his mother's arms at the tender age of seven, he'd learned how to fight his tormentors. He'd been fighting them ever since.

But there were better ways to fight them than with fisticuffs, swords, or even dueling pistols. He'd learned that too. And now he was poised to punish them all for what they'd done to him—all these arrogant asses who dared refer to themselves as the quality.

He surveyed the room with the carelessly bored gaze of a very wealthy young lord, a gaze that did not prevent him, however, from noting every detail of this evening's assemblage. The old men had already begun to edge toward the gaming room and its ever-ready supply of brandy and cigars. The matrons and chaperones gathered in clumps around the perimeter of the ballroom, keeping an eye on their young charges but ready to share a bit of gossip with the other self-appointed guardians of good society.

The objects of their watchfulness, this season's crop of white-clad innocents, also stood in small groups. They'd been giggling and using their fans to flirt with the young men of the ton. Now, however, they were staring round-eyed at him.

He fought down the urge to snarl at them, to send the entire pack of ninnies squealing in fear for the safety of their mother's bosoms.

Get a hold of yourself. At last revenge was within his reach. He would not ruin everything on account of a few overdressed, undereducated young chits. Before this season was done he would have every one of them competing for his attention. He would have their mothers fawning over him and their fathers eager to have the Westcott line joined with their own.

And he would have his harridan of a grandmother precisely where he wanted her.

"So, Westcott. Did you ever expect to be the most eligible bachelor in London?" Elliot Pierce gave him a not so subtle nudge. "Go on, man. Let the majordomo announce you. I, for one, plan to drink heavily, gamble furiously, and tumble at least two of the housemaids before this night is done. Unless, of course, I can find two willing ladies."

Not responding to his friend, Ivan stepped forward.

"Ivan Thornton. Earl of Westcott, Viscount Seaforth, and Baron Turner," the haughty servant intoned.

Even the servants disdained him, Ivan thought. But that didn't matter to him any more. It had ceased to matter years ago. The only difference was that now he had the titles and the money to make them dance to his tune.

He tugged on his sleeves then marched down the five broad carpeted steps and into battle. Behind him his three closest friends were announced. His only friends.

Mister Elliot Pierce and Mister Giles Dameron earned no particular notice from the curious throng already arrived at the Stennis's off-season soiree. When Mister Alexander Blackburn was announced, however, another buzz began.

A bastard earl and a bastard prince—the former acknowledged and wealthy beyond all bounds, the latter unacknowledged and poor as a church mouse. Still, everyone knew that might change when the king died.

By association, the two unknowns were assumed also to be bastards, and all from Burford Hall—Bastard Hall, as was the school's more familiar name.

Whether horrified or intrigued, repelled by their improper parentage or drawn by the new earl's fabulous fortune, everyone who witnessed the four young men's entrance agreed on one fact: this year's season would not be dull. No, not dull at all.

And of all those who subscribed to that theory, none was so certain of it as Lady Antonia Thornton, Dowager Countess of Westcott, grandmother to the new earl, and author of this entire mess.

Yet she was not prepared so swiftly to write it off as a disaster. Not quite. After all, he *had* attended the investiture three months earlier. As a young man, finished with Burford Hall and sent straightaway to the Continent to extend his education, he'd stoutly denied that he would accept his father's titles when the man died. But he'd come around, as she'd known he would. Who could possibly resist the titles and the fortune that went with them? She'd won that battle when he'd attended the investiture. She was convinced now that she would win the second battle too, for wasn't he here tonight, meeting this season's crop of eligible young ladies? She would see him wed, and soon. Then she'd see the birth of her first great-grandchild. Only then would she consider this war between them won.

"So that is the boy," said a voice from just behind her.

Antonia kept her eyes on her grandson. "You've seen him before, Laurence."

"Yes, but he was younger then. And angrier. I must say,

Toni, I truly believed him when he said he'd rather be a street sweeper than accept the mantle of his family birthright.''

"That was ten years ago. He's older now and wiser. And his father is dead. But don't be fooled by his respectable demeanor. That is merely testament to the talents of his tailor and his barber—to whom he pays an ungodly sum, I'm told. Beneath that handsome façade beats the heart of a savage. An angry savage.''

Laurence Caldridge, the Earl of Dunleith, who'd outlived four wives and six children, stared at her unforgiving profile, not understanding any of this. "If you believe him a savage, why did you acknowledge him as Jerome's son? Why hand him the title? Why not let it go to your nephew—''

"Because I'd rather the title pass to a street sweeper than to any of those idiot children of Harold's,'' she snapped. "And you know it. Now, if it's your intention to stand here and hand me advice I do not appreciate, you had better alter your plans. Fetch me a glass of punch. Wait, I've a better idea. Go to him and introduce him around. In particular be certain to introduce him to the Countess Grayer, the Duchess of Whetham, and Viscountess Talbert. Between them they have seven daughters, granddaughters, and nieces who are eminently suitable.''

She waved her hand in dismissal. "Go on, Laurence. See he is introduced to anyone he has not already met. Meanwhile, I shall contemplate my headstrong grandson and determine how best I am to proceed with him.''

Laurence went off, grumbling and shaking his head. But she knew he would do as he was told. If only she could be as certain of her grandson. She stared at him, at the striking man he'd become, his hair Gypsy black, his skin Gypsy dark. And wearing that outrageous earring. The gall of him!

She had to admire that gall, however. One thing was certain: he possessed the arrogance of an earl. Unfortunately he also possessed the blatantly seductive allure of his mother's damnable race.

Would he approach her? she wondered. Would he greet his only living relative, the woman who'd rescued him from the life of a heathen and given him a birthright comparable to any in the kingdom? Or would he strike back at her by snubbing her?

She watched as he greeted Laurence. Not effusively, but not rudely either. She studied every nuance of his behavior as he was introduced to Lady Fordham: how he bowed, how long he held her gloved hand, his expression as they conversed. When he smiled at something Laurence said, she frowned. He was more than merely handsome, she realized. Much more. Just now he'd reminded her of his grandfather.

She'd never seen any family resemblance in the boy before, save for his ice-blue eyes which were identical to her own. Beyond that, however, he'd always been a damnable Gypsy, no more, no less. But in that smile, in the slant of his mouth and the even flash of his teeth, she'd had a glimpse of her Gerald. Thirty years gone, he was, leaving her to manage the vast holdings that went with the Westcott family name. How she missed him! Their only child, Jerome, had been useless at business. Worse, he'd left no heir but this bastard son of his. She could only pray now that the education she'd given the boy at Burford Hall had prepared him for his responsibilities.

By the time Laurence returned, she was exhausted from the strain. Ivan was dancing with the Feltons' youngest daughter. She was a busty redhead, but far too silly to make a countess.

"Well? Will he greet me?"

Laurence cleared his throat, patted his pockets for his snuffbox, then thought better of it. He tugged on his luxuriant whiskers. "He didn't say. But I think he will, Toni. I think he will. After all, he hasn't seen you since the investiture in January."

It was long past midnight before the insufferable cad approached her. Long past when she would normally have repaired home. But she refused to do so until he greeted her. She could not go to him. That would not do at all.

That meant she must wait for him—or else give everyone in attendance the satisfaction of knowing he'd snubbed her.

When he finally made his way to where she sat, flanked by Laurence and Lady Fordham, she was ready to give him a good dressing-down. How dare he treat her this way!

One look in his frosty eyes, however, and she swiftly squelched that idea. He was angling for a fight, a very public fight with her. She could see it in the frigid depths of his glare, in the tense set of his wide shoulders.

Just like Gerald, the wayward thought came once again. She'd loved her husband to distraction, but they'd fought like cats and dogs. Still, they'd got on well enough. Perhaps she and the boy—No, he was a man. Perhaps they could somehow find their way to a similar sort of volatile peace.

"Madam." He gave her a curt nod. "May I introduce my companions to you?" He indicated the three men arrayed alongside him. "Mr. Elliot Pierce. Mr. Giles Dameron. Mr. Alexander Blackburn."

To their credit, each of the other young men displayed very correct manners. She stared closely at Blackburn, looking for something of his royal heritage in him. No one saw much of the king these days. But in his younger days he'd spent much time in the social whirl.

" 'Tis said I have his mouth, and his hair." The grinning fellow answered her unsaid question in a whisper meant, nonetheless, to carry to the rest of their small crowd.

Antonia's eyes narrowed. "Really? And here I thought it only the glint of sophomoric humor in your eyes that proved your kinship."

Blackburn's grin increased in delight. "At last. A lady who sees the madness in my eyes and does not demurely look away." He fell to one knee, a hand pressed fervently to his heart. "Say you will marry me, my dear Lady West-cott, for clearly 'tis you I've been searching for these many lonely years."

Before Laurence could struggle angrily to his feet, Lady Antonia caught his arm. She grimaced at mad King George's bastard of a grandson. "Get up, you fool. Get up before I accept your daft proposal,'' she added.

That drew a burst of laughter from the other two young men, followed by nervous chuckles from Lady Fordham and then from Laurence. But her grandson did not so much as twitch his lips. Steeling herself against any display of emotion, Antonia addressed his madcap friend. ''I regret that my grandson has not a portion of your wit, Mr. Black-burn.''

''We often remark on his lack of wit,'' Mr. Blackburn answered. But it was Ivan's answer she waited for.

''Is it my witticisms you want, madam? And here I've been deluded into thinking it was my obedience. My grat-itude. My will. Indeed, my very mind. But no, it is only my witticisms. If I endeavor to be witty and amusing, will you then retire to the country content, and leave me in peace?''

She glared into his vivid blue eyes, so like her own it was disconcerting. ''If that wittiness is accompanied by good manners and better intentions, then yes, I will happily retire from your life.''

''Have I not displayed good manners this evening? I've made certain to charm the matrons and dance with their daughters.''

''And is it your intention to marry one of those daugh-ters?'' she asked, deciding to be blunt.

He held her gaze and in his expression there was no mistaking his intense dislike of her as well as a spark of something else. Triumph? No, that could not be it.

He shrugged. ''I plan to marry one of them. If I can find one who suits me.''

''Does that mean you will remain in town for the sea-son?'' She held her breath, hoping, praying that he would. The plain truth was that she was running out of time. She wanted him married and with a viable heir before she died.

This time he smiled at her, though it was not a smile that was in the least reassuring. ''I wouldn't miss it for the world.''

*   *   *

Not an hour later their conversation was not nearly so civil. They'd returned home separately to Westcott House. He confronted her in the cavernous drawing room.

"I am still the dowager countess," she was saying. "You will not put me out of my own home!"

Ivan stared impassively at his grandmother. But inside he was raging. If she thought she was going to live in the same household with him, she was sadly mistaken. If she thought any portion of her life would remain as simple as it formerly had been, she was mad as a hatter.

He allowed himself a faint smile. "I believe I am the one invested with the title and, therefore, possession of this hideous heap of bricks. Not you. I am the one all of the family property is entailed upon. And I am the one who will make the decisions regarding the ultimate disposition of those properties."

He knew that would silence her, and it did, for the disposition of the Westcott title and estates meant everything in the world to the coldhearted bitch who had sired his equally coldhearted parent. As much as she despised him, she despised her brother-in-law's side of the family even more. So long as Ivan did not father a son, the chance remained that the property could revert to her dimwitted nephews, or that he would entail it upon one of them. She simply could not abide that idea. Most of all, she could not abide the fact that she was powerless to control Ivan or, as a result, the vast family estates. It was the power he'd waited twenty years to wield over her.

He gave a grim chuckle at the sight of her choking back her fury. How ironic that his sexual activities should control her life. Despite his father's indiscriminate behavior with everyone but his own wife, he'd apparently sired only one child. Now, however, that bastard son held control of both the titles and the obscene amount of wealth that went with them. In contrast to his father's loose morals, Ivan meant his own behavior to be so discriminating as to be sure no one succeeded him to the same titles and wealth. At least not during *her* lifetime.

It was clear, however, that while discussion of the entailment might restrain the autocratic old woman somewhat, it would not silence her entirely. Were she not such a thoroughgoing bitch he might actually have admired her tenacity. She'd outlived her husband and her son. But she was not likely to outlive him. He would triumph over his grandmother if only by attending her funeral.

"Westcott House is quite large enough for the two of us," she stated in what, for her, was a conciliatory tone. "I keep mostly to my own apartments, which are in an entirely separate wing—"

"You will be more comfortable at the country house," he interrupted. "While I am in town I do not care to see you at all."

"And what will you do? Put me out? I should just like to see you attempt that. Yes, indeed. I would." Her bony hands gripped the crystal-topped cane she sometimes used, while her sharp blue eyes glared shards of ice at him.

But his eyes were just as blue and just as frigid. "I'll maintain a bachelor's household here for the duration of the season. I should think you would approve of that. After all, according to town gossip, I am the newest and most eligible bachelor in town, and sorely in need of a wife."

She peered at him suspiciously. "You will be actively seeking a wife?"

He took great pleasure in the answer he gave her. "Yes."

Yes, he was seeking a wife. But he had no intention of finding one. Let the old crone live on hope. Let her die still hoping.

She leaned forward, unable to disguise her rising excitement. "I know all the good families and most of the eligible young ladies. I can arrange introductions, perhaps even hold a reception."

"That will not be necessary."

"But John, just think—"

"I am Ivan!" he snapped. "I will always be Ivan no matter how you try to make an English lord of me!"

He'd been standing nonchalantly at the wide marble mantel. Now he began tensely to pace.

"All right. All right," she snapped back at him. "I will try to remember that you prefer that Gypsy name. It's just that I've thought of you as John for so long."

He let loose an ugly laugh. "You thought of me as John," he sneered. "The fact is you never thought of me at all."

"I thought of you as the future Earl of Westcott," she informed him in cutting tones. "Now that the title is officially yours you should show me the gratitude and respect I deserve."

"Gratitude!" He exploded. "Respect? Not bloody likely! The only emotion you shall ever have of me is contempt," he swore, forgetting his vow to remain unemotional in her presence.

Ten years he'd stayed away from her and this godforsaken family seat she so valued. Ten years of wandering the world, never happy, never finding the peace he so desperately sought. His mother and her Gypsy band had long ago faded into the landscape. His identity had faded away with them as well, leaving him only his hated ties to the Thornton family tree.

He'd lived like a pauper these ten years since leaving Bastard Hall, letting his more than generous allowance accrue into a tidy sum. Meanwhile he'd worked himself to the bone, taking chances other men would never take, risks that saner minds would run screaming from.

He'd amassed a small fortune of his own along the way, enough to keep him forever independent of his father's family's wealth. So why had he come back? Why had he let himself be invested with those damnable titles?

To spite her.

It hadn't been enough simply to let the cousins he'd never met inherit the Westcott estates. No, that had not been sufficient punishment for what she'd done to him. So he'd come back once he'd heard of his father's death just to spite her. He would become the earl, just as she'd planned all those years ago. She thought she was getting what she wanted, but he would see that she lived to regret it. For despite all her plotting, he would provide her with no heir and she would know that her family line would end with him. She would lose everything she valued to the brother-in-law she so despised—just as she'd caused him to lose everything he valued.

He took a deep breath, fighting for control. "I'm staying with Blackburn until you have vacated these premises."

She perked up at that name. "Oh, yes. Blackburn, the bastard prince."

Ivan gave her a cold smile. "We bastards must stick together, given that our families so readily abandon us."

Her face cooled into a mask of resentment. "If I'd abandoned you, you would be some pathetic Gypsy horse thief, dead or in prison by now."

Ivan clenched his jaw in frustration. The truth of her words was a bitter pill to swallow, but no less the truth. As miserable as his childhood had been, from what he could tell, the other children in his mother's band had fared even worse. If any of them had survived the past twenty years, he'd not been able to locate them.

Still, that did not pardon the old woman for her actions. He poured himself a glass of whisky, tossed it back without savoring the warm comfort of its stinging heat, then set the tumbler down with a sharp crack. "I'm leaving. Send word to Blackburn's house on Compton Square when you have departed."

"I have no intention of leaving my own home," she replied in a frosty tone.

Ivan paused at the door and stared at her. Twenty years ago she'd ripped him from his home, but even then, he would have welcomed her presence in his life. He would have welcomed *anyone*'s presence in his life. But twenty years ago she'd abandoned him, a terrified child, to the cruelty of Burford Hall. To the cruelty of that drunken headmaster and his sadistic wife. To the cruelty of a community of boys, where the bullies reigned and the weak were crushed.

He'd learned one important lesson at Burford Hall, however. One lesson that he lived by still. Might made right.

Now that he had the might—his father's titles and the fortune attached to them—he had the right to do anything he wanted.

He studied the aging crone before him with a cold, aloof gaze. It was too late for her to worm her way into his life now. Far too late. Besides, what she valued most in life— her esteemed position in society and the continuation of her family line—meant nothing to him. Less than nothing.

"You cannot win against me, Grandmother," he said in a derisive drawl. "Stay here if you must, but I warn you, it will not make you happy. You'd be better off in the country, welcomed into the bosom of your family. Ah, but you have no family, do you? At least none that you can abide—or who can abide you. Perhaps your servants can comfort you in your decline."

So saying, he turned on his heel and left, striding purposefully from the elegant drawing room, into the cold marble foyer, and then through the towering doors and down the granite steps. Though Westcott House was as fine a house as could be found in London, he thought of it as an unforgiving heap of stones. It was a magnificent credit to a title handed down for nearly four hundred years. But its only value to Ivan was as a tool of revenge. The ton, the season, the money—it was all a waste of time except insofar as he could use it to strike back at those who had hurt him.

If it brought him no particular comfort to take that revenge, he refused to admit it. For if his goal was not revenge, if his one focus was not to bring low all those who once had looked down on him, then what in hell was he to do with the rest of his life?

Two

*L*ucy Drysdale heard her nephews' angry screams, but she chose to ignore them. Turning her back to the morning-room door, she reread the last paragraph of the letter she'd just received:

> . . . *will be lecturing at Fatuielle Hall during the season. If you are in London I encourage you to attend the entire series of lectures. You will have a particular interest in my theories on the intellectual and moral development of children. Until then I remain sincerely yours,*
>
> Sir James Mawbey, B. A.

Lucy clutched the letter to her bosom and sighed. Sincerely yours. Though she knew it was quite beyond foolish for her to read anything special into that simple closing, she could not help herself. If there was ever a man whose sincere feelings she wished to be the recipient of, it was Sir James Mawbey. Since reading the first of his articles she'd felt nothing but admiration for him.

At long last a man who cared about more than shooting and gambling, and horses and land.

At long last, a man who wondered about the same things she wondered about, and who had taken the next step by putting his ideas all down in articles. Brilliant articles.

She'd read everything she could of his writings in the new field of psychology, and was more than impressed by the depth and breadth of his knowledge. More importantly, however, he'd validated so many of her own half-formed theories about why people behaved the way they did.

When he'd responded to the letter she'd sent him, however, she'd become his most ardent admirer. Since then they'd corresponded several more times, but she had never dared hope to meet him. Until now.

Unfortunately, her brother would never let her go. She knew how penurious Graham was when it came to money. Not to mention his disdain of her intellectual pursuits. He'd absolutely refused to let her attend university, even though a few women were beginning to do so. No matter how she'd pleaded, he'd remained obdurate, stating that she'd already had more education than a woman needed to have.

It was foolish of her to even hope he'd finance a trip to London for her now, simply for the purpose of attending a lecture series—especially when the lectures pertained to subject matters he considered silly and trite. He'd often expressed the opinion that her intellectual interests should be sufficiently satisfied by their father's library and by her role now as the governess to his children.

If anything, Lucy felt more stifled than before. She'd long ago read every book in the library, and as for the children, well, they were children. They could never take the place of well-educated adults with wide-ranging interests.

They did not begin to compare to the brilliant Sir James Mawbey.

She stared down at his letter and fingered its creases, daring to dream the impossible. What if she managed somehow to reach London? What if she met Sir James and he were unattached? Was it so unlikely that an attachment might be formed between them? Nothing so frivolous as passion, of course. Not with the serious Sir James. No doubt he did not believe in romantic love, any more than did she. But the love that could grow from respect and admiration . . . That sort of affection would not be unlikely between them.

Lucy stared around her, feeling a sudden guilt for having such thoughts. And yet the fact remained: she was desperate to find a reason to go to London. If she remained trapped in the Somerset countryside much longer, her mind would surely wither and die.

Another scream broke into her thoughts, but once again she pushed it into the background. Her eldest nephew, Stanley, was an arrogant little monster whenever he wasn't blessedly asleep. As his father's heir, he was treated as the lord and master already. Accordingly, his younger brother, Derek, made it his life's purpose to punish Stanley for being born first. As for her nieces, Prudence, Charity, and Grace, they seemed determined *not* to live up to their names.

Though Lucy had made some inroads relative to their manners since taking on the role of governess to Graham's five children, screaming was something she'd not yet been able to banish from their behavior.

She could hear the voices of the two angry little boys now, and with a resigned sigh she tucked Sir James's letter into her pocket. She would have to go and make peace among them. Never mind that she'd already given the oldest ones lessons this morning, then taken the younger ones out for a nature walk. Surely she was entitled to a quiet moment every now and again. But not today, it seemed.

Then something shattered against a marble floor and she flew from the room.

"Stanley! Derek!" The boys leapt apart, then backed away at Lucy's sharp cry. Though ten and nine respectively, they were similar in size and appearance, and identical in temperament, though no one but she saw the truth in that observation.

"He called me a fart!"

"He called me a horse's arse!"

Appropriate in both cases, she thought, though she wisely kept that opinion to herself.

Like mice out of the woodwork, the three girls appeared. Prudence, at twelve, was old enough to feel much more mature than her brothers, but still young enough to need to torture them about it. "Oh, dear. Are the *children* fussing again?"

"Shut your trap, Pru!"

"*You* shut *your* trap!"

At that moment their mother, Hortense, hurried into the hall. "What in the world—" She stopped in mid-sentence when she spied the pseudo-Chinese vase shattered across the patterned marble floor of the lengthy hall. "Oh, dear. Oh, dear," she murmured, wringing her hands together. "Your father is going to be very displeased. Very displeased." Then she spied Lucy. "Oh, Lucy. How *could* you allow this to happen?"

Lucy chose not to respond to that particular remark. Though she usually tried to be more sympathetic to her whiny sister-in-law—after all, the poor creature was married to Graham, and that was cross enough for anyone to bear—at the moment she had more important matters to deal with.

"Prudence, take Charity and Grace into the rose garden. Now," she added when the girl seemed inclined to argue. "Hortense, if you will leave this to me?" She gave the woman a taut, pointed smile.

"Oh, yes. But . . . but what of the vase?"

"Send Lydia to clean up the mess."

"Yes, but . . . but what will Graham say? About the vase, I mean? He's bound to notice. I mean, it's been sitting in this very spot, on this very table for, well, for as long as I've been coming up to Houghton Manor, and that's a long time—since I was a child—and that would be, well, never mind how long that would be—"

"Please, Hortense." Lucy broke into her sister-in-law's aimless chatter.

"Oh, yes. Of course." Hortense melted away. She was extremely ineffectual, both as a wife and mother. But she was a good breeder, and after all, that was what Graham had wanted. That was all most men wanted, Lucy thought in irritation. No doubt that was precisely what the two hooligans who now stood nervously before her would someday want in a wife. A good breeder with no ideas or opinions of her own.

She fixed the pair of them with a stern stare. "I want the complete truth and in the precise sequence in which it happened."

"It was his fault!"

"He started it!"

"The precise sequence," she repeated. "You shall both memorize heraldic orders all afternoon if the truth is not immediately forthcoming."

The brothers shared a look, one that told her she had bested them, at least for the moment. She usually tried to link the children's punishments to the particular infraction committed. But occasionally she resorted to the time-honored tradition of writing lines. Instead of using biblical quotes, however, she preferred the heraldic orders. It was her own perverse slap at a society so ordered and restrictive as to stifle any creative thought. Though she knew it was unlikely, she hoped that particular punishment would instill in the boys a lifelong dislike for the rigid social orders they'd been born to. Especially Stanley.

"Derek was feeding Sunny," Stanley accused.

"Just an apple!"

"He's my horse, not yours!"

"So then what happened?" Lucy interjected.

"He pushed me down," Derek retorted.

"Well, you threw dirt on me."

"*After* you pushed me down!"

"You deserved it!"

"Did not!"

"Did too!"

"Boys! Boys! How did you end up in here, knocking the vase over?"

"Stanley chased me."

"All the way from the stables? Can I assume that neither of you paused to wipe your feet?"

Derek frowned. "I couldn't stop. He was chasing me."

"Well, he was getting away," Stanley countered. They both peered up at her guiltily.

Lucy stared at them. They were not bad boys. Not really. And to be honest, she was glad that if they'd broken anything, it was that hideous old vase. But that was not the point. They were brothers who were growing up to hate one another, just like so many other brothers of the quality. Younger brothers who would inherit nothing always hated their elder siblings, just as the eldest sons always grew to hate their fathers and waited impatiently for them to die. And all on account of the antiquated system of primogeniture.

"I'll deal with you first, Stanley. I should like to remind you that some day the responsibility for the Houghton stables will fall to you. If you are to rise to your responsibility then you must have a care for every horse there—"

"I do! Nobody can say I don't love all the horses!"

"Do not interrupt. It's rude. No one disputes your affection for the horses. What I want to point out, however, is that you will also have responsibility for all those who tend to those horses. You should encourage *everyone's* affection for the horses, including Derek's. If he would give Sunny an apple, then you should be pleased, not jealous and resentful. Do you understand what I am saying?"

Stanley gave a reluctant nod, as she expected he would. She'd determined long ago that he took his inheritance very seriously. Though his father saw the rank only in the light of the privileges it provided, Lucy hoped to instill in Stanley some sense of the responsibilities too.

"As for you, Derek. Did you choose to be kind only to Sunny, or to the other horses as well?"

His eyes would not meet hers. "I didn't have enough

apples for every bloomin' horse in the stables."

"No, of course you didn't. So you selected Sunny specifically because you knew it would rile Stanley. Am I right?"

He shot her a resentful look but didn't answer. Lucy took a deep breath. Were it not for the broken vase this would not be so serious a matter. But she knew her brother would demand someone be punished for the vase. If she did not give them both a fair punishment, Graham would let all the blame fall to Derek.

When the maid Lydia scurried into the room, Lucy took the broom and dust pan from her. She gave the broom to Stanley and the pan to Derek.

She gave them a stern look. "First you shall clean up this mess. Together." She raised one hand, forestalling their objections. "Then you shall go down to the stables and give every horse, from hunter to draft animal to pony, some sort of treat, whether an apple, a handful of oats, or just a little affectionate light grooming. You shall do that together also, both of you with each horse. When you have completed those tasks, come find me and together we will then go and tell your father what has occurred and how we have resolved it."

All in all, a fair resolution, she decided. Derek knew he had been saved a caning from his father. The swift smile of relief he threw her showed that. As for Stanley, he'd had a new facet of his future responsibilities revealed to him, then been sent to the stables, his favorite place in the whole wide world.

She sighed. As much momentary satisfaction as she received from situations such as this, she nonetheless found it frustrating. She reached in her pocket for the precious letter. There was so much more in life to learn. But she feared she would never have the chance. Rather than experience life, at twenty-eight years old she was already considered a spinster and relegated to raising her brother's children, preparing *them* to experience life.

But not forever, she vowed. Somehow she would find a

way to leave Houghton Manor. She had a very modest income of her own, left to her by her mother's father. But one hundred pounds a year was not enough for her to be entirely independent. If she could only find a way to supplement it, she could afford to leave the stifling circle of her family and move to town.

She heard a scream—this time a little girl's—and she sighed again. She had to find a way out soon. She simply had to!

"She's visiting the Fordhams," Hortense informed Lucy the next afternoon. "Graham says we must all call upon her, even the children. It's because she's a countess, you know, and the Westcott fortune is legendary. Graham says it's a great honor—"

"She's the dowager countess," Lucy reminded her agitated sister-in-law. "I believe I read in the *Times* that one of her grandchildren has recently been invested as Earl of Westcott."

"Well, yes. But Graham says the grandson—her only one—is yet unwed. Graham was very clear in his directions to me. Prudence is to wear her best dress and be careful to ingratiate herself with the countess."

Lucy tried to hide her annoyance but it was awfully hard. Prudence was but twelve and only a child. For heaven's sake, she hadn't even begun her courses. Yet Graham was already hoping to whet the Earl of Westcott's appetite for her? Lucy's stomach clenched in disgust. The new earl was a man fully grown and well traveled, if the *Times*'s report on his investiture was to be believed. What was her brother thinking?

Then Lucy's sense of fairness kicked in. Any man in his right mind would want to marry his daughter to such a wealthy and titled young man. Still, she'd always found the idea of such businesslike matchmaking more than a little repugnant.

"Why is Lady Westcott in Somerset?" she asked, ruthlessly burying her feelings.

Hortense frowned, all the while plucking nervously at her lace-edged cuff. "What if I say the wrong thing? You know I didn't have a proper season. I never had the opportunity to become accustomed to the ton. What if I do something to embarrass Graham? He will never forgive me!"

Lucy took Hortense's fluttering hands into her own. "You are making yourself nervous over nothing, Hortense. Nothing, I say. Just be yourself and you shall be fine."

Hortense heaved a great sigh. "Easy for you to say. Nothing ever frightens you. But I've heard of Lady Westcott through Lady Babcock—you know, over Symington way? She's cousin to Darcy Harrigan whose sister married Viscount Prufrock. They keep a house in town and so are privy to all the latest gossip."

"And what have you heard about Lady Westcott?" Lucy prodded her scatterbrained sister-in-law.

Hortense's eyes grew round. "She is said to be, well, rather severe." She paused. " 'Harridan' was the word Lady Babcock used," she added in a whisper.

"She and Graham shall get along very well, then," Lucy quipped. She regretted her hasty words at once when Hortense gave her a hurt look.

"That's so unkind of you, Lucy. Graham is nothing but good to you. To everyone."

Lucy made a face. "I'm sorry. You're absolutely right. I should not have said that." *At least not in your presence.* "Is Mother going too?" she asked to change the subject.

"Oh, yes. Graham says she must. We must all go, even you."

Even you. Lucy forced herself not to react to the reminder of her status as the least important member of the household. She was the spinster sister, too young to deserve the respect rendered one's elders, and too old to be married off. She had no particular fortune, no title of her own, and though she knew she was considered quite handsome, that was not enough to offset her unfortunate predisposition to speak her mind. But she was expected to go to the Fordhams' to call on Lady Westcott.

She supposed she should be grateful for small favors.

At least it would be entertaining, Lucy decided as she hurried to round up her nieces and nephews. At least she would have someone new to converse with, someone whose opinions and ideas she'd yet to hear. At least there would be a break in the unrelenting routine of lessons and peacemaking and trying to make conversation beyond the mundane.

Please let Lady Westcott possess even half a brain, Lucy prayed. For if she did and if she stayed a while at the Fordhams' home outside Taunton, Lucy might at last have a companion for the scintillating discussions of books and ideas and politics she so longed for. Someone to provide intellectual sustenance until she figured out a way to get herself to London.

The Fordham country house was an ancient ramble of rooms, some dating all the way back to Henry II. The Fordhams themselves were not quite that old, though they looked it. So did Lady Westcott, Lucy decided rather irreverently when they were ushered into that grande dame's presence.

The dowager countess sat in the Fordham seat of honor, a monstrous chair of intricately carved English oak, upholstered with plush Chinese cushions. She wore a gown cut in a severe style, but made of the most luxurious ebony silk Lucy had ever laid eyes on. Heavy as it was, the silk draped as fluidly as the finest gauze.

The woman's only ornaments were a pair of black jet earrings, a heavy watch chain, and an ebony cane with a crystal head. What impressed Lucy the most, however, was that despite her petite stature and birdlike features, Lady Westcott had a most imposing presence. Any other woman would have been dwarfed by that chair and overwhelmed by the rest of the ostentatious room. But not Lady Westcott. Now, why was that?

The dowager countess greeted the visitors with regal civility. Lord Fordham introduced Viscount Houghton first, then Graham introduced the rest of his family. Lucy, of course, was last. But for some reason, the old woman seemed to study her much more closely than she had the others.

When Lucy completed her very correct curtsy, Lady Westcott addressed her directly. "How old are you, Miss Drysdale?"

Blunt, wasn't she? "Twenty-eight. Why do you ask?" Lucy added, deciding to be every bit as blunt as the old woman.

The countess's brows arched in faint surprise. Graham cleared his throat and Hortense began to fan herself, while Lucy's mother, Lady Irene, tittered nervously, as if her candid daughter had only been making a joke.

"No wonder you are yet unwed; you're not the biddable sort, are you?"

Lucy smiled. "I'm afraid not. Do not hold my mother to blame for that fact, though." She sent her mother a consoling glance. "She has tried mightily to instill in me all the feminine traits. While she had success in most areas, there are a few of her lessons, I confess, that did not altogether take."

"My sister has had offers, Lady Westcott. Several *good* offers," Graham emphasized. "But she has not yet found a man who pleases her."

Lucy sent him a sympathetic look. "Were he to be entirely frank, my lady, he would tell you that I always manage to come up with some excuse or another to decline those offers. He would tell you that he has gone through all his acquaintances quite to the point of pulling his hair out. But I remain as you see me: unmarried and likely to continue so."

"And content in that state?"

Lucy stared at the dowager countess. She was small as a sparrow, but with a raven's shiny plumage and a falcon's sharp gaze. For some reason she'd honed in on Lucy as her prey. The question was, why?

The answer came to Lucy with a start. She must be seeking a wife for her grandson, the new earl. But why on earth would she be interested in a spinster possessed of neither title nor fortune? His wealth alone would buy him almost any bride he wished. Throw in the title and he became irresistible, at least by society's standards.

Then an awful thought occurred to her. If his grandmother was reduced to considering spinsters like herself, that must mean there was something terribly wrong with the man. And not just that he'd been born a Gypsy bastard before his father adopted him. The whole world already knew that. Likewise, the whole world would forgive him for it, now that he was the Earl of Westcott. No. There must be something else that made him unacceptable. But what on earth could it be?

"I am quite content," Lucy finally answered the older woman. "I have my books and my correspondents. I fear I am far too set in my own ways to ever accommodate myself to a man's ways."

Lady Westcott studied her another long moment. Had she been younger, or a woman of lesser consequence, the lengthy perusal would have been deemed rude in the extreme. As it was, it made Lucy decidedly uncomfortable, a condition she was not accustomed to and did not enjoy.

It took Lucy's mother and her compulsive need to always keep conversations running smoothly to shift the focus away from Lucy. "Lady Westcott," she ventured, no doubt at the urging of Graham. "If I might be so bold as to suggest, my eldest granddaughter, Miss Prudence Drysdale, though still in the schoolroom, is a most accomplished musician. Would you like her to play for you—ah, for us—I mean for this most esteemed company—"

She broke off when Lady Westcott gave a negligent wave of her hand. "By all means. Have the girl play."

But as the party settled themselves, Lucy was distinctly aware of Lady Westcott's continued scrutiny.

Lucy sat down in an armless chair positioned near the children so that she could monitor their behavior while Pru-

dence played. In the end, however, she did far more squirm-
ing and shifting than did the four younger Drysdales. By
the time Prudence's easy version of a popular air for min-
uets was finished and the five children were dismissed to
take their tea separately from their elders, Lucy decided she
had never met so powerful a personality as Antonia Thornton, Dowager Countess of Westcott.

"Lady Westcott is an old friend," Lady Fordham said
by way of resuming the conversation. She signaled the
maid to place the tea service before her.

"Yes, a very old friend," the venerable old dame echoed. "Old enough to be excused a few eccentricities, eh,
Gladys?"

"Why of course, dear—"

"Then you will not mind if I ask Miss Drysdale to pour.
Miss Lucy Drysdale," she clarified when Graham leaned
forward expectantly.

Lucy repressed her annoyance with her pompous brother.
As if a matriarch like Lady Westcott would ask a girl from
the schoolroom to pour! Poor Prudence would not last two
minutes under Lady Westcott's fearsome gaze.

"Shall I?" Lucy directed this to Lady Fordham.

"Why . . . Why, of course, my dear. Of course. Please
do," she answered. But the confusion on her face was obvious, as it was on Graham's and Hortense's. Lucy's
mother, however, had swiftly grasped the import of the
dowager countess's request, and her round face beamed
with approval. She'd long ago given up matchmaking her
only daughter. In one fell swoop, however, the dowager
countess had revived all those hopes.

Lucy did not know what to think. She'd hoped to find a
boon companion in Lady Westcott, an intelligent conversationalist with an interest beyond the weather, fashion,
gossip, and children. She'd not expected the sort of pointed
interest she was receiving.

She poured the tea, assisted by the maid who handed
round the cups and plates of biscuits. Lady Fordham made
small talk, about her grandson's trip abroad, and the new

variety of Chinese roses that were lately all the rage.

Graham tried to engage Lord Fordham in conversation about a local court case involving a son stealing his own father's horse, but it was quite a waste of effort. Lord Fordham rarely said a word while in the company of ladies. Between his silence and Lady Westcott's, it became more and more difficult for Lady Fordham to carry the conversation. Hortense, true to form, was so intimidated by Lady Westcott that beyond the required words of greeting, she'd clammed up. Lucy's mother, normally quite verbose, only stared expectantly at Lucy, apparently struck dumb by visions of an earl for a son-in-law dancing in her eyes.

It fell upon her, Lucy realized, to revive the dragging conversation. Unfortunately she could hardly blurt out her curiosity about Lady Westcott's poor grandson.

She was saved when the dowager countess sailed back into the conversation. "Have you had a season, Miss Drysdale? I do not seem to recall your presentation at court."

"Mine was not a particularly notable presence in town that year. It was 1819, just before the old king died."

"Ah, yes. I was not in town that year."

"Well, you did not miss much, unless, of course, you are not too friendly with Lady Nullingham. That was the year of her, shall we say, comeuppance."

Lucy's mother gasped, and again Hortense began to fan herself. To mention Lady Nullingham's very public fall from grace was not a subject for polite conversation, especially in mixed company. Lucy meant to shock Lady Westcott, or at least to gauge her reaction.

She was not terribly surprised by the glint of humor in the old matron's eyes. "I've heard many a recounting of that tale, every one of them more than amusing. Yet still I regret not bearing witness to it myself." Abruptly she stood. "I would stroll in the garden a while, Miss Drysdale. Come, give an old woman the benefit of your vigor." So saying, she held out her arm.

Though taken aback, Lucy hastened to accommodate her.

When the others rose, however, Lady Westcott waved them back into their seats.

"Do not bother yourselves to accompany us. I would have a little talk with Miss Drysdale. That is all. Gladys, send for fresh tea. I will want another cup—hotter this time—upon my return."

Then without apology to anyone, the old woman turned and, with Lucy at her side, marched sturdily for the door.

Lucy had hoped for a diversion and it seemed she'd gotten it. Where it might lead, she could not foresee, but for now she planned to enjoy every minute of it.

Three

*A*ntonia was getting desperate. She had to be to even contemplate such an outrageous proposal to Miss Lucy Drysdale. She'd only just met the girl!

But she was not a girl; she was a woman. She was an attractive young woman possessed of a lively intellect as well as a sharp wit and a sharp tongue. Though that was not much to go on, Antonia nonetheless was convinced Ivan would like her. More than that, she was convinced that were he to meet her, he would pursue her.

Not that he didn't appear to be pursuing every other young woman he met. But she knew Ivan would not be landed by some innocent schoolroom miss who melted every time he turned his brooding gaze upon her. These past two months he'd become *the* catch of the season. The mothers coveted his title, the fathers coveted his fortune, and the girls . . . It seemed that the girls coveted everything about him. More tears had been shed and girlish friendships shattered over the so-called Gypsy earl than over any other bachelor since four years ago when Hal Driscoll, heir to the Earl of Lamonte, had finally been wed to that silly Meredith Cavanaugh.

But for all her grandson's intense participation in the social rounds now that the season was in full swing, Antonia sensed that something was not right. He was not sincere in his attentions to the young women. He was not really looking among them for a wife; he was merely toying with them.

Or rather, he was toying with *her*. She let out a muttered imprecation.

"Are you all right?" her companion asked.

Antonia forced her frown away. "Of course I'm all right. Find a bench where we may sit a while." *While I reason out the best way to approach you with my proposal.*

Once they were settled on a weathered garden bench, Antonia fiddled with the crystal head of her cane. Miss Drysdale stared at her expectantly. Not surprisingly, it was the younger woman who spoke first.

"Are you down to visit the Fordhams for very long?"

"A short visit, I'm afraid. A week only," Antonia answered. "I'll be returning to town directly afterward. Are you ever in London?" she added, looking for a way to ease into her subject.

Miss Drysdale sighed. "No, though it's not because I do not wish to be. I expect, however, that until it's time for Prudence's season I shall be confined to a rural existence."

"You will chaperone her when the time comes?" Antonia asked, a germ of an idea beginning to take root.

Miss Drysdale hesitated, as if weighing her words. Then with a half smile, she plunged in. "I am afraid that my dear sister-in-law is not quite up to the role. As a result, I am certain I shall chaperone Prudence. Perhaps I shall be forced to chaperone both daughter and mother. Please don't misinterpret my words," she added. "For I look forward to that day with utter delight. I can hardly wait for the time when I might return to London."

"Perhaps that day is not so far away."

As quickly as that, Miss Drysdale's open countenance became wary. "It would be best, Lady Westcott, if I were frank with you. While your implication is in many ways intriguing, I feel I must tell you that I am not in the market for a husband."

Antonia was relieved that she had never been prone to blushing. Instead she wrinkled her brow and frowned at the girl. "Neither am I, and I spend most of my time in town. If you think I am searching out a wife for my grandson—and you do, confess it—well, you are quite wrong. He is not ready, I think, to marry. Perhaps someday, but not yet. No, I did not bring you out here to matchmake you with my troublesome heir. Rather, I would like to offer you a position in my household for the duration of the season."

That was clearly not what Miss Drysdale had been expecting, and in the brief pause while the younger woman recovered her composure, Antonia studied her. Flawless complexion. Thick, shiny hair the color of mahogany. Vivid green eyes that sparkled with intelligence. Even as she stared into those eyes, Antonia could see the gears turning in the girl's mind.

"A position in your household? What sort of position?"

"I believe you would be an appropriate person to chaperone one of my late sister's granddaughters. Valerie is a lovely girl, but she will be a lamb among the wolves in town."

"What of her mother?"

"I'm afraid Lady Hareton will be of no more use in that regard than would your sister-in-law. She suffers from a nervous condition, as she tells it. As a result she is not up to the rigors of society." *And blessed convenient that is,* she said to herself.

"There are no other relatives that the girl would prefer accompany her? No favorite aunt or older cousin?"

"I *am* her older cousin and her godmother, and I assure you, she would much prefer a younger and more vigorous companion than myself. Come now, Miss Drysdale. You said yourself that you were anxious to return to London. If you are worried about leaving your family, rest assured, they will survive your absence. Besides," she added with a wave of her hand. "It will only be for a few months. After that you are free of any obligation to Valerie."

Antonia could see the excited light in Miss Drysdale's eyes. She had her! To be absolutely certain, however, she leaned nearer and placed a hand on the girl's arm. "I shall consider it a great personal favor if you would agree to my request.''

Lucy could hardly contain her excitement. Here was the chance she'd been waiting for!

When they'd come to visit today, she'd hoped to find an interesting woman who might prove to be a pleasant diversion for the few weeks she was visiting. Never in her wildest dreams had she dared hope for so glorious an opportunity as she'd just been offered. She had to restrain herself from leaping up and dancing a country jig around the iron-willed Lady Westcott.

''I accept your offer,'' she answered, quite aware that her huge grin made a mockery of her perfectly sober words. But she didn't care. She was going to London again! She would be in the company of great wits and even greater minds.

And she would be able to attend Sir Mawbey's lectures!

If she'd ever doubted the power of prayer, she vowed never to do so again, for her every prayer had been answered in the form of Lady Antonia Thornton, Dowager Countess of Westcott!

Lady Westcott rose to her feet. ''Very good. Let us repair to the parlor and inform your family. I should like to depart for London day after tomorrow. Is that agreeable to you?''

As it happened, Lucy's only disappointment was that it took four days, not two, before they finally departed. Two of those days Hortense spent in bed with a sick headache, devastated that ''her darling Lucy'' was leaving. Lucy had never realized how deep her sister-in-law's affection for her ran—though she suspected it was less affection and more neediness. Still, she knew the children ran roughshod over their mother without Lucy there to stop them.

Fortunately, her own mother was almost as excited about Lucy's new position as was Lucy herself, although for entirely different reasons. Irene Drysdale had never completely resigned herself to her daughter's unmarried state. She bemoaned the lack of eligible gentlemen in the Somerset countryside—or rather, the lack of eligible gentlemen that Lucy could abide. London, however, was full of eligible gentlemen.

Lucy had no intention of informing her mother that the only man she had a remote interest in was an intellectual who taught for a living and possessed only an honorary title. As to whether Sir James was a bachelor, she could not say. Just because he hadn't mentioned a wife in his correspondence did not mean there wasn't one. Still, she'd rather believe that there was not.

Lady Westcott's carriage came for her just past dawn. London was a long day's journey and the dowager countess was determined to sleep in Westcott House that night, she told Lucy. Lady Valerie Stanwich would join them within a few days.

That would give Lucy time to find out the particulars about Sir James's lecture series. She might be forced to bring Lady Valerie with her, she realized, but that was all right. As long as she was able to hear him in person, to bask in the light of his prodigious intellect, and try to soak up some portion of the essence of his knowledge she would be content. She heaved a happy sigh to even contemplate such possibilities.

"I take it you are content to be leaving the country."

Lucy smiled at her benefactress. "It's not so much that I wish to leave Somerset, as that I am thrilled to be returning to town. I feel . . ." She paused, searching for the words that would make her feelings clear without casting her family in a bad light. "I am somewhat stifled in the country."

In the close confines of the carriage Lucy felt keenly the weight of the dowager countess's regard. "You are bored to tears, you mean. I assure you, Miss Drysdale, that you will not be bored in London. In fact, I would hazard a guess that you will have your hands quite filled with Valerie."

"Is she strong-willed?"

Lady Westcott snorted. "Strong-willed? Hardly. Rather, she is quiet as a mouse and just as easily startled. She will do anything to please a person." She paused and sniffed. "Except, that is, to put herself forward."

Lucy nodded. "She sounds like a middle child."

"Actually, I believe she is. Yes. She's the fourth of a brood of seven. Seven children. No wonder her mother suffers from a nervous disposition."

Lucy smiled, pleased that she'd been right. "I've noticed that a middle daughter is often the most complacent of children, trying always to please and, in the process, losing her own self."

"Losing her own self?" Lady Westcott gave her a sharp look. "Whatever is that supposed to mean?"

"It's part of a theory about children that I am developing," Lucy admitted, thrusting her chin out in an unwitting show of defiance.

"A theory about children? What do you know about children? You haven't had any, have you?"

"You needn't be a nursing mother to know about children," Lucy replied, more tartly than she ought. "I have been a child and helped raise many other children—not just my brother's considerable brood."

"And *you* needn't take that sharp tone with me, girl. I am not questioning your intelligence. Far from it. If I did not think you of superior mental capabilities, I certainly would not have offered you this position."

The old woman pursed her lips and stared at Lucy from across the narrow carriage space. "Since you obviously have a deep interest in children and why they behave as they do, it might be best if I go into more detail about your duties to Valerie. Because she is so malleable she could easily be led astray by one of those callous young men who pass for gentlemen these days. And unfortunately, they will flock to her in hordes. She is as pretty a girl as you could ever hope to lay eyes upon. Fair-haired and fragile-looking—and with a fortune which, though not immense, is nonetheless more than adequate. Your primary duty will be discouraging inappropriate suitors."

She hesitated a moment and Lucy saw her bony hands tighten on the head of her cane. "And the most unsuitable of them is my own grandson."

Lucy had been all set to question Lady Westcott further about young Valerie. But that last comment about the newly invested Earl of Westcott gave her considerable pause. An unattached earl unsuitable? Her fertile imagination began to spin. Lady Westcott had referred to him once before as her troublesome heir. Could he be one of those dissolute young men given to the baser forms of behavior? She remembered that sort from her own season. The wastrels. The pleasure-seekers. Men who were said to delve in all the vices and participate in the most degrading activities. Wise mamas kept their daughters strictly away from that sort, even if they were from good families.

But an earl? And with the enormous fortune this particular earl was said to possess?

She picked her words carefully. "What precisely is it about your grandson that makes him so unsuitable for a young lady like Valerie?"

The old woman's face settled into a frown. "He is entirely too insincere in his intentions. In the past several months he has engaged the hearts of many a young woman, only to abruptly turn his back on them."

That hardly made him unsuitable, Lucy thought. Fickle, perhaps, but not entirely unsuitable. "Perhaps he fears that they are interested in his title and fortune more than himself. I have heard a little about his history," she admitted. *Who hadn't heard the gossip about the Gypsy earl, born a bastard, no less?* "It may be that this is his way to strike back at a society that for so long held him in contempt— and which would, were he not now titled and exceedingly well off, still hold him in contempt."

"I suggest you save your theories of childhood for a more receptive audience, Miss Drysdale. Ivan is a man, not a child. The fact is, his heritage is a given. Nothing of his birth and subsequent childhood can be altered now. Besides, from the age of seven he has been raised to be an earl. He had a decent enough education, far above the lowly expectations of his birth, I assure you. If he wishes to strike back at anyone, as you term it, neither I nor any of the young ladies of this season is an appropriate target. Nevertheless," she continued, taking a calming breath. "Nevertheless, he has chosen to be difficult. I fully expect him to pursue poor Valerie, and it will fall to you to keep her safe from him.

"And one other thing," she added. "He is not without a certain appeal. You may theorize that this year's young misses flock to him because of his title and fortune. But he would attract young, susceptible females were he a nobody—were he merely a gypsy horse-handler, as he very nearly was."

She gave Lucy a sharp look. "You are no longer young and foolish, else I would not have engaged you as a chaperone. I trust you are also no longer susceptible to the wiles of handsome young men of the ton."

"If I were susceptible to that sort of gentleman, I would have long ago wed. Rest assured, Lady Westcott, your grandson's appeal will be wasted upon me. I plan to be more than diligent in the discharge of my duties toward Lady Valerie. If there is one thing I stand firm upon, it is my disdain of insincere, self-important, would-be rakes."

Lady Westcott nodded her approval, then gave a faint smile. "I am glad to hear it. Very glad to hear it. Now, as we have a long and tiring day ahead of us, I believe I shall attempt to nap a while."

So saying, Antonia closed her eyes and leaned back against the cushion she'd positioned by her head. But beneath her lowered lashes, she kept a close watch on Miss Lucy Drysdale.

She'd set the trap and baited it. It remained now for someone to get caught. Whether it was Ivan and Valerie, or Ivan and Miss Drysdale, was immaterial to her, so long as the damnable boy was wed to someone, and soon. But she confessed to herself that she would rather it be the almost penniless young woman across from her, than her immature godchild.

Ivan had given her fits these last ten years: disappearing without a word; not even responding when he'd been formally adopted and made his father's heir. He'd not come to his father's funeral in the fall. Then he'd waited until the last moment to notify her that he would participate in the investiture this past January. For him to end up with a malleable wife like Valerie would be grossly unfair. He deserved a wife who would give him as much trouble as he would give her.

Antonia felt sure that this Lucy Drysdale was just the woman to do it.

Let him decide upon her, she prayed, though her prayers tended to come more in the form of commands than humble pleadings. *Let him decide on Miss Lucy Drysdale, and let the girl run as fast and hard as she can in the opposite direction. But in the end, let her catch him.*

And let them have her great-grandchild promptly nine months later—if not sooner.

No one had warned her that he wore an earring!

That was the first thought that shot through Lucy's head.

They'd arrived very late at the grand address on Berkeley Square. She'd thought the butler a trifle surprised and perhaps a little worried when he'd bowed them into the foyer. But she'd attributed that more to the fact that Lady Westcott had not sent word ahead that they were coming.

She'd caught the scent of tobacco in the air as she followed Lady Westcott to her suite of rooms, and had suspected, from the lights she'd seen burning, that someone was at home. When the door to the dowager countess's sitting room crashed open and this unannounced male stalked in, however, she knew at once that something was amiss. And also that he must be the new earl.

He was home all right, and he was not in the least happy to see his grandmother arrive.

Still, of all the things she might have noticed about him—his dark, lean features; his glossy black hair; his tall, broad-shouldered silhouette—it was the earring that transfixed her. A gold, glinting hoop that winked back the oil-fed light, and defiantly proclaimed his Gypsy heritage.

She was to protect Lady Valerie from *him*?

Her knees went weak and her mouth went dry. How had his grandmother described him? He is not without a certain appeal? Though Lucy would freely admit that her experience with men had been limited in recent years, there was not a doubt in her mind that this man very likely possessed more physical appeal than half the men in London combined.

Then he opened his mouth and she discovered the reverse side of that considerable appeal.

"Get the hell out of my house!"

Lucy gasped—or at least she assumed it was she who'd made that shocked sound. Lady Westcott merely stared at her coldly furious grandson without so much as blinking an eye.

"I believe we've had this conversation previously. As I told you then, I will not be put out of my own home. You, however, are free to leave, if that is your desire."

"My desire," he snarled, glaring at the dowager countess with eyes as frigid as the winter sky. "My desire is to never lay eyes on you again."

Lady Westcott stiffened. It was only the tiniest of gestures, but Lucy saw it, and her heart broke for the frail old woman. She forced her frozen limbs to life.

"How impossibly rude you are," she snapped, moving to stand beside her hostess. "Lady Westcott has had a long and tiring day. The last thing she requires is to be set upon, and in her own private quarters. Did no one ever teach you to knock?" she finished in her sternest governess tones.

The unconscionable rogue did not do her the decency of even transferring his glare from his grandmother to her. Nor did he in any other way acknowledge that he'd heard Lucy's indignant words. "I am entertaining guests," he continued in the same insulting tones, "none of whom are of the sort you are wont to mingle with. Nor are you their sort," he added, with a mocking twist to his lips.

"I have no intention of greeting your guests," Lady Westcott retorted, holding firm to her position. Still, Lucy detected the hurt in her voice and she sprang once more into the fray. How dare he attack an old woman this way, his own grandmother! And how dare he ignore *her* as if she did not even exist!

This time she stepped in front of the countess, forcing him to recognize her presence. "I'll thank you to depart these apartments. Now," she added. "Right now!"

The glacial stare focused on her. The mocking smile thinned. The furious voice turned low and dangerous. "Unless you are here for some useful purpose, it would be better if you remove yourself from this discussion."

"I am here for a . . . for a very useful purpose," she sputtered. If a body could burn with outrage and yet freeze with unreasonable fear, hers did both. "I am a guest of Lady Westcott's and I—"

"This is my house, not hers. The only guests I will allow are my own." The frosty glare moved over her, head to toe, taking a swift yet alarmingly thorough appraisal of her appearance. Then those bitter blue eyes met hers again. "Dare I hope your purpose here is carnal? And that it involves me?"

She slapped him.

It came out of nowhere. Certainly she did not plan it. But in the ringing silence left in its aftermath, she was not sorry. He deserved it. It remained now only to see how he responded. There was no predicting what a man as cruel and hateful as he might do in retaliation.

He raised a hand to his offended cheek and despite Lucy's intentions to be brave she took an involuntary step backward.

The room shuddered with the silence. From somewhere far off in another wing of the house she heard the faint echoes of music, of a pianoforte playing and a woman singing. But in this particular chamber there was no sound at all.

Then the earl took a breath and Lucy braced herself for the worst.

Instead of lunging at her, however, he bowed—a very

correct though abbreviated bow. Lucy blinked in disbelief, then stared warily at him. What was he up to?

His expression told her nothing, for he'd wiped his face clean of any telltale emotion. His voice, when he spoke, was equally unemotional.

"My apologies, madam. I more than deserved that. I only hope you will find it in your heart to overlook my unfortunate behavior."

It took Lucy a moment to collect her wits. An apology was the last thing she'd expected from this man, this Gypsy earl who was as handsome as sin. She was certain, however, that it was just about as sincere as Stanley's and Derek's apologies to each other usually were.

She drew herself up, tugging angrily at the waist of her wrinkled traveling suit. "I have never—never!—been so rudely treated in my entire life!"

His face remained impassive. But at least he was looking at her now instead of glowering at his exhausted grandmother. It occurred to Lucy that Lady Westcott remained uncharacteristically quiet, but she was not about to give ground by breaking eye contact with the earl. If she was to be dealing with him as often as Lady Westcott had indicated, it was critical that she establish the boundaries of their relationship right now.

As their locked gazes held, his lips curved up ever so slightly. Or at least she thought they did. "Might I inquire who it is that I have treated so rudely?" he asked, one dark brow arched in question.

Lucy assumed the countess would introduce her. After all, it was only proper. When she did not, however, Lucy let out an exasperated breath. "I am Miss Lucy Drysdale of Houghton Hall in Somerset."

"Miss Lucy Drysdale," he echoed, emphasizing the "miss." Again his eyes flickered over her. But before she could take umbrage at his boldness, he executed another bow. "Allow me to introduce myself, Miss Drysdale. I am Ivan Thornton, Earl of Westcott, among other things." He paused. "You said you had a useful purpose for being here?"

Once again one black brow raised in question, but this time Lucy could see the arrogant purpose lurking behind the bland expression he'd adopted. He was no more sorry for insulting her than she was sorry for slapping him, the wretched man!

"I am here to act as chaperone to Lady Valerie Stanwich for the season. Your cousin, I believe? To safeguard her from inappropriate suitors—"

"Like myself, perhaps?" He grinned then, and in that one isolated moment Lucy had a terrible revelation about herself. For with that easy grin, that tiny movement of flesh over teeth—beautiful, strong, white teeth, as it happened—he deflated all her anger. Like a silly, smitten girl, she reacted to that smile, to the appeal his grandmother had alluded to. Her heart began a maddened pace, her cheeks began to heat. And all on account of a smile.

With a silent groan she ordered herself to cease such foolishness. She gave him a severe look. "If this is typical of your behavior, then yes, I would say you are entirely inappropriate for a proper young lady."

This time he laughed, though she'd certainly not meant her statement to amuse him. Before she could muster an indignant response, however, Lady Westcott finally broke her silence.

"Do not bother to argue with my grandson, Miss Drysdale, for you will get nowhere at all with him. His greatest joy in life is baiting me. Since I refuse to participate in his game, I fear you may become his next target. I advise you to ignore him," she finished.

Lucy had kept her eyes trained on the earl while his grandmother spoke and saw the quick veil of dislike that covered his face. When he responded to the countess's comments, however, his words were directed at Lucy. "My grandmother may be right, Miss Drysdale. After all, she has known me longer than anyone else. Now, if the two of you will excuse me? I have a house full of guests. If I do not return to them they may come searching for me. I suspect you would not enjoy that.''

Without further excuse he left, and with him, it seemed, went all the vitality in the room. What an absurd idea, Lucy thought. And yet it was true.

Lady Westcott let out a long sigh, as if she'd been holding her breath. Lucy too exhaled, somewhat unsteadily. She looked over her shoulder at the older woman, who raised a hand, forestalling anything Lucy might have to say.

''You needn't say a thing, my dear. I can see it in your face. He is not what you expected, is he?''

Lucy grimaced. ''I would not state it quite . so . . . so blandly as that. May I sit down?''

''By all means. I'll ring for a tray. There's nothing like a glass of cognac to calm the nerves.'' She gave Lucy a searching look. ''Are you up to this, Miss Drysdale? Can you hold your own with my unpleasant grandson? Or would you rather beat a hasty retreat back to your quiet countryside?''

If Lucy *had* been reconsidering her reason for being in London, the countess's reference to Somerset cured her of it—and she suspected the clever old woman knew it.

''I would prefer to have been better forewarned that he . . . dislikes you so intensely,'' she said, deciding to be candid. ''Also that he has so . . . is so . . . That he has such a presence about him,'' she finally said.

''That he is so damnably attractive, you mean.'' Lady Westcott squinted at her. ''I trust you are not so unwise as to be swayed by his manly countenance.''

''Of course not!'' Lucy retorted. ''But I cannot vouch so easily for your godchild.''

''You will be able to handle Valerie; that does not worry me at all. As for his dislike for me, that is of no moment. No moment whatsoever.''

So she said, Lucy thought as a maid brought in a tray of tea and biscuits, and a decanter of cognac. So she said. But it was obvious that the old woman was as drawn to her brooding grandson as were all the other ladies of the ton.

Lucy suspected the old woman wanted his affection. She wanted his familial love.

Whether she would ever get it was highly debatable, and quite beyond Lucy's sphere of influence. All she could do was make sure that Lady Westcott got what she said she wanted: Lady Valerie Stanwich safely wed to an acceptable gentleman. And safely out of Ivan Thornton's clutches. Beyond that she would not concern herself with the Gypsy earl's personal affairs.

Later, however, once Lucy was settled in her bed, in a very pretty room across the hall from the countess's suite, she found her mind wrestling with the most inappropriate thoughts.

He really was a Gypsy, with his coal-black hair waving over his collar and that hedonistic earring. But he was an earl too, and Lucy understood fully the magnetic pull he would have on any young woman's senses. To even think of those enigmatic eyes gazing into hers, of those strong tanned hands touching her—

She let out a decidedly unladylike oath and turned angrily to her other side. She would *not* think of such things. She could not allow herself to do so. Her role was simple and easily defined: keep Lady Valerie out of Ivan Thornton's clutches.

Still, she couldn't help wondering what female would ultimately fall *into* his clutches. And whether her lot would be awful or wonderful.

Four

*L*ucy awoke some time before dawn to the sound of horses' hooves ringing upon pavement, and noisy, though muffled, laughter. Where was she?

The answer came to her immediately, but not before her heart had clutched in unreasoning panic. She was in London, she reminded herself. At Westcott House. Where the notorious Gypsy earl held sway.

That started her heart thumping all over again, but not in panic—though perhaps, if she were wiser, she would be panicked.

Exasperated by her perverse reaction to Ivan Thornton, Lord Westcott, Lucy threw back the butter-soft coverlet and arose. Behind the heavy damask curtains, dawn was just beginning to flirt with the night, silhouetting the rooflines of good English slate and the rows of fanciful chimney pots that adorned the other houses fronting Berkeley Square. But dawn in the city was not the focus of Lucy's interest, not this morning anyway. Instead she squinted at the carriage pulled up to the front of the house. Four horses stamped impatiently in their traces.

Who on earth would be arriving at such an unheard-of hour? she wondered, peering into the gloom. Even with her cheek against the windowpane, however, she could not quite see if anyone had stepped down from the smart vehicle. That only increased her curiosity. Though she knew it was unseemly, she unlatched the window, then carefully inched the sash up.

Much better, she thought, though she shivered at the rush of cool night air. She leaned out, just far enough to see someone approach the carriage. A woman, with a man escorting her.

Ivan Thornton! She would recognize his wide shoulders and lean build anywhere!

Why that should be true she refused to ponder. But it was he, no mistaking it. And right there, in broad view of anyone who cared to look, he took the woman in his arms and kissed her!

Kissed her? No, when the "kiss" went on and on, until Lucy felt her own cheeks flush, she knew the word "kiss" was wholly inadequate. He was ravishing the woman right there, two stories down and a little to her left. He was ravishing a woman on his own front steps!

Finally he released the woman and helped her up into the dark carriage amidst several more ardent kisses and indecipherable murmuring. Lucy could not drag her eyes away from the scene being played out before her. What sort of woman stayed the whole night at a man's house?

"Idiot!" she rebuked herself. Everyone—even rustics from the countryside—knew the answer to that. Fallen women. Scarlet women. Ladies of the night.

Still, she'd never actually *seen* such a woman.

She peered all the harder, trying to pierce the gray predawn gloom. Just as she leaned out, however, the woman drew back into the carriage, the driver's whip snapped, and the vehicle was off. Disappointed not to have the identity of the woman to link with the devilish Lord Westcott, Lucy pulled back and proceeded to crack her head on the bottom windowpane. She must have let out a cry of pain, for to her horror, the earl's face turned up toward her.

At once she drew back into the room, like a turtle scuttling back into its shell. Oh, dear. Oh, dear. Oh, dear! Had he seen her? Did he know who it was? Would he confront her and accuse her of spying on him?

Abruptly she pulled herself together. What did it matter if he *had* seen her? She'd done nothing wrong. She'd but heard a noise and arisen to investigate it. It was he who should be ashamed of his behavior, not she.

She gave an inelegant snort at that foolish idea. She could predict already that he would not be in the least ashamed. No, not him.

Rubbing the back of her head, she crossed the room and climbed up into the high bed, then sat there cross-legged, contemplating her reluctant host, and trying to root out the source of his considerable discontent.

He'd probably been a terribly lonely child. From what she'd heard and pieced together, it seemed he'd been removed from his mother's care, ignored by his father, and hidden away for years at Burford Hall. For all intents and purposes, he'd been abandoned by every adult he'd ever known.

Was it any wonder he hated his grandmother? She'd never shown him any love. One of Lucy's several theories was that a child deprived of love became an adult who either craved love incessantly, or turned away from it entirely. In which direction had Ivan Thornton's unhappy childhood led him?

Though she told herself it was none of her concern, she nonetheless could not prevent herself from wondering. How had a dark-haired Gypsy child fit into the rigorously structured life of a northern boarding school? What had he done in the years after leaving the school?

The *Times* had said he'd traveled abroad prior to his investiture. But was that the complete truth, or merely a way to gloss over a number of years unaccounted for?

A soft knock at her chamber door sent all her speculations suddenly spinning. She stared aghast across the darkened room at the eight-paneled painted door. A knock, and at this hour. Who could it be?

But of course she knew, and as quickly as that her throat went completely dry.

The knock came again.

She fought a battle between diving under the covers and feigning sleep, and leaping up and bolting the door against him.

One more time the knock sounded.

He was not going away! *So get up, you fool! Don't give him the pleasure of thinking he has intimidated you.*

Even though he did. Even though he scared the wits out of her, with his brooding eyes and intense manner—

She bolted from the bed. He would not get the best of her. No indeed. She stopped an arm's length from the door. "Who is it?"

"You know very well who it is, Miss Drysdale. You need not pretend otherwise."

It occurred absurdly to Lucy that she needed to light a lamp—several lamps—for Ivan Thornton's voice was far too silky and seductive to be allowed free rein in the dark.

She stepped nearer the door. "Go away. I am not about to come out there in my wrapper. Nor am I likely to let you in," she said, clutching her hands and pressing them to her bosom.

"What if I let myself in?"

She gasped. "You would not!"

"You have not known me long enough to know what I will or will not do, Miss Drysdale. Lucy," he added after a brief pause.

"I haven't given you leave to address me so familiarly," she stated, though not nearly so forcefully as she would have liked. "Go away from here before I . . . before I call out to your grandmother."

He laughed, low and husky, and Lucy could picture most disturbingly his face: eyes glittering, teeth flashing, lips curved in a way far too elemental for her comfort.

"Surely you are aware that she is no threat whatsoever to me."

"And surely you know I will not come out nor let you in. So why are you at my door?" she demanded in exasperation.

She heard a movement, as if he'd shifted and now leaned

upon the door. "You seemed so interested in my activities outside. I thought I'd answer any questions you might have."

Questions indeed. Oh, but the man had no shame whatsoever! She sternly overlooked the fact that she was fair to bursting with questions.

"I awakened to a strange noise in a strange house. If I interrupted your . . . your . . . . whatever it was you were doing, I apologize. Now will you please go away?"

For long seconds there was no response. Lucy took the final step to the door and laid her ear cautiously against the crack between door and frame.

"Good night, Lucy," he whispered, right in her ear it seemed. Like a terrified hare, her heart began a maddened thumping, as if his warm breath had caressed her ear and his lips had moved within her hair.

She did not dare respond. Instead she stumbled backward until her calves came up against a slipper chair and she sat down hard upon it.

Good night, Lucy.

He was gone. She knew it though she'd not heard a sound of his departure. She felt it, she decided, in that secret part of her heart that was still a girl's.

In that secret part of her heart that was still silly and foolish and terribly, terribly naïve, she amended.

She remained there, in the gold and cream striped chair, for a long while. The sun broke the hold of darkness and slowly brightened the heavy drapes. The pretty room came into a sharper focus—the mahogany bedroom suite, the gilt-framed floral paintings. But still she sat there, contemplating the weeks and months to come.

Perhaps she should speak to Lady Westcott about taking another house for the duration of their stay in town. For one thing, she did not think she could survive living under the same roof as the violently attractive and unpredictable Lord Westcott. In addition, placing young Lady Valerie in constant proximity to the very man she was most expressly not to become linked with, was not very wise.

Unless what the dowager countess wanted and what she *said* she wanted were two different things entirely.

Was the old woman wily enough to believe that her wayward grandson would seriously pursue only that which he was denied—or rather she whom he was denied?

Lucy sat in the chair a while longer contemplating that thought until she heard an upstairs maid moving about in the hall, and a street sweeper whistling somewhere in the street below her window. She stood up then, feeling more exhausted than she had when she'd first laid herself down. For now she would simply observe her employer and her young charge. Perhaps she'd be better able to deduce the countess's true purpose.

She would also keep a watch on Ivan, Lord Westcott. In the space of less than twelve hours she'd already had two dismaying confrontations with the man. She'd slapped him last night for his impertinence, and should have slapped him again this morning for so boldly rapping at her door.

But it was not those two incidents which most unsettled her. The sad fact was, the man had too much appeal by half. What's more, he'd practiced these many years just how to frustrate and stymie his grandmother. At the least Lucy owed herself time to observe him and figure out how best to deal with him.

But as she poured water from an exquisite porcelain pitcher into its matching bowl to begin her morning ablutions, she knew dealing with him would not be easy. He was smart and clearly bent on making his grandmother's life miserable. And because of her association with the old woman, he seemed set on making her own life miserable too.

Just think of him as an overgrown version of Derek or Stanley, she told herself. *Or Derek and Stanley, all rolled into one. Don't try to thwart him; merely steer him in a slightly different direction. Funnel all that ferocious energy someplace else.*

But what was she to do about her completely inappropriate attraction to him?

Ignore it, was the only answer she could find. *Ignore it. Bury it. Think about Sir James Mawbey instead.*

Yes, Sir James. She seized on the thought of her idol with relief. Ivan Thornton might exude the powerful animal magnetism that any normal, healthy woman would respond to. But he was no Sir James Mawbey, possessed of such deep insights and intellectual gifts. She would ignore Ivan Thornton and think only of Sir James. His first lecture was less than a week away. Surely between now and then she could put a damper on her silly, girlish emotions.

Or so she prayed.

She did not see the earl again that day. Nor the next. Nor the next.

Lady Valerie arrived on Wednesday and they all spent that evening at home, getting the easily startled Valerie settled in. She'd traveled with her maid, a young girl so awed by London and Westcott House and the presence of a real countess that Lucy wanted to groan. Two complete babies, they were. She would have no help whatsoever from the maid Tilly.

A day and a half later the maid's attitude was not much improved. "You will not be required to attend tomorrow's dance, Tilly," Lucy told her. "Lady Westcott and I shall accompany Lady Valerie."

Relief flooded the girl's mousy face. Valerie's exquisite features, however, clouded over. "But . . . but I need her. Tilly has been with me since first I was given a maid of my own. Oh, please. Do not make me go there without her—"

"Don't behave so ridiculously," Lady Westcott interrupted, giving Valerie a sharp look. "A maid in the ballroom? Would you have her hold your hand and prop you up?"

Lucy had determined from the first that Valerie was petrified of the dowager countess. As it turned out, it was a blessing, for the girl clung instinctively to Lucy for comfort. Now Lucy put a reassuring arm around the petite young woman.

"You will have me, Valerie. I will be at your side every minute save when you are dancing." She could feel the girl tremble, and she knew what her next words would be.

"Must I dance?"

Lady Westcott snorted, but Lucy cut her off before she could make another ascerbic remark and frighten Valerie further. "This is an ordinary dance, not actually a ball. There will be dancing, and if you're asked to dance you must accept. It would be considered a great insult to the hapless fellow if you turned him down. You will do fine," she added, giving her a little squeeze.

"Come, let's practice," she continued. "I'll dance the man's part. Just call me Lord Fumblefoot. Will you play?" she asked the countess as she led Valerie into position in the middle of the floor. "Or shall I be forced to hum?"

Ivan followed the unlikely sounds of a discordant piano melody mingled with the singing of a woman of better than decent voice. He'd spent the last few days with Elliot on Regent Street, drinking and whoring within an inch of his life. To his immense disgust, he'd discovered it did no good to behave abominably if the crotchety old bitch did not hear of his actions. Why he'd not thrown her out on her ear was hard to say. His only explanation was that he was bored. If nothing else she and her new companions would be diverting. So he'd come back tonight to torment her in whatever way seemed most appropriate. And to see if he could torment the strikingly lovely Miss Lucy Drysdale.

The last thing he'd expected to hear was music coming from the second parlor.

The scene that met his eyes was equally unexpected. The old grande dame sat at the pianoforte, like a raven perched over the ivory keys, playing a creaky version of one of society's favorite melodies of the moment. Meanwhile, Miss Drysdale danced with an exquisite young blonde, taking the male part to the younger woman's hesitant role.

He stood in the half-opened door, sheltered by the shadows, and watched their antics, fascinated and annoyed all at the same time.

It was Miss Drysdale who was singing. Her voice was throaty and low, not the shrill warble that was currently so fashionable. Likewise she was too tall for the current mode, and her hair too dark. But she was not too tall for him. And dark though her hair was, it seemed nevertheless to catch every light in the room. Her tresses fairly gleamed with streaks of lustrous gold and fiery red.

As he stared at her, he felt the unexpected rise of desire. But it was the younger girl he was interested in, he told himself. Not the chaperone. He forced himself to focus on her instead—his cousin, of course. The girl Miss Drysdale was to protect from him.

What a sparkling little diamond she was, he now saw. With her blond hair she glittered like a silvery jewel. She was small and fair, with blue eyes, he would guess. Only blue would suit that soft, pink complexion.

He grinned at the thought of the game that awaited him. Women had never been much of a problem for him. Even those who'd thought him merely a penniless navy man or an amoral smuggler had not been very hard to seduce. They'd wanted to be seduced and the fact that he'd been a totally inappropriate man had not deterred them in the least. It was even worse now that he was so eminently marriageable—or so able to afford a very expensive mistress, depending on the sort of woman he was dealing with.

This innocent, fresh from the countryside, would present no problem at all—except perhaps to generate some genuine show of enthusiasm on his part. Then again, perhaps this one had a brain in her head. Perhaps this one could speak on subjects beyond the latest French dress patterns and the number of pairs of gloves stacked in her bulging armoire.

Then the song ended. The dowager countess looked up, their gazes locked, and Ivan wouldn't have cared if his cousin was an ugly, tongue-tied imbecile. She was forbidden to the likes of him? By damn, but he would have her.

But not to wed. Never that. No, he would woo her. He would steal her heart. She would cry copious tears on his account and turn down every suitable fellow who offered for her. She would vow to become a Catholic and retire to a nunnery if she could not have her one true love. In short, he would see to it that she made her entire family frantic with her obsession with the man denied to her. Especially her great-aunt, the high-and-mighty Dowager Countess of Westcott. But marry her? Not bloody likely. He would never marry any woman of the ton.

He clenched his jaw and his nostrils flared in anticipation of the battle to come. As for Miss Lucy Drysdale, she'd been lured into the middle of a war she did not begin to understand. If she were wise, she would run straight back to whatever country hamlet she'd come from. If she were not wise, then she would soon learn a bitter lesson. For Ivan Thornton did not abide by her society's rules. He was not of her society nor did he intend ever to be. For now it pleased him to play the role given him as the only offspring of the late unlamented earl. But it was merely a role, donned for a purpose, to be abandoned once that purpose was achieved.

Meanwhile, he had the strangest urge to go dancing.

Lucy saw the dowager countess stiffen, and at once she knew why. Blast, blast, and double blast! she swore to herself. He'd returned!

She swung Valerie around so that she could see her adversary. Valerie had been staring down at her feet, counting her steps under her breath. Lucy's move caught her unawares and after stumbling a bit she raised a frowning face to Lucy. "Was that the place we were supposed to turn? I thought you said . . ."

She trailed off when Lucy did not respond with so much as a glance. That was because Lucy was working so hard to maintain her own composure. Ivan Thornton was here and her battle for Valerie was about to begin. Heaven help her if the girl found him half so attractive as she herself did!

"Good evening, madam." He bowed smartly to the old woman and gave her a beautiful, if utterly false, smile. "Had I known you were entertaining this evening, I would have sent word ahead that I was returning."

He turned that dark, seductive smile on Lucy and Valerie, who still stood in their dancers' embrace. "How nice to see you again, Miss Drysdale." He paused, then went on when she did not respond. "Will you introduce me to your charming dance partner?"

Lucy gritted her teeth. If she was to teach Valerie how to behave in society, she could not very well do so by responding rudely to the man. Especially when he seemed set on behaving politely—for a change. He'd not behaved so well the night they'd met, she fumed. But she could not very well bring that up now.

With an effort she released Valerie and forced herself to give him the barest smile. "Good evening, my lord. I had not realized you'd never before met your cousin. Lady Valerie, this is Ivan Thornton, Earl of Westcott."

Lucy could see from Valerie's widening eyes that though she'd never met Ivan before, she most assuredly knew all about him. And she could see in Ivan's face that he was not pleased with the lackluster introduction he'd been given. Good, Lucy thought. She continued. "My Lord Westcott, may I introduce the Lady Valerie Stanwich. Lady Valerie is from Arundel in Sussex. Her father is Carl Stanwich, Earl of Hareten."

"He knows all that," Lady Westcott interrupted. She'd risen from the piano bench, and now she approached the trio of young people. "He knows who you are, Lady Valerie. And be forewarned, child, that he is very likely the most charming and insincere fellow you are likely to meet the entire duration of your stay in town." Though the countess kept her words light, she was not as successful with her expression.

Following Lady Westcott's lead, Lucy hooked Valerie's arm with her own and forced herself to smile. "Listen to your godmother, Lady Valerie, for she knows whereof she speaks. Your cousin has far too successful a reputation with the ladies to be deemed suitable for so young a person as you," she finished, trying to maintain a lighthearted tone.

Ivan gave her a potent smile. "Why, Miss Drysdale. What an un-Christian attitude toward someone you've only just met. And here I thought I'd been more than charitable, offering to answer any questions you might have about life in town."

He was deliberately taunting her about what she'd seen that night, and about his insulting offer to answer her questions about the goings-on between him and that . . . that hussy.

"Thank you for your offer," she replied through gritted teeth. "Nonetheless, I believe Valerie will be more at ease in . . . in a less worldly sort of company than your own. Isn't that right, Lady Westcott?"

When she glanced at the countess for confirmation, however, the older woman did not appear in the least perturbed. Poor Valerie was trembling in Lucy's arms at so frank a discussion, but Lady Westcott seemed to care nothing at all for the girl's reaction. Could it be that she wasn't really worried about sparing Valerie a broken heart? Lucy suppressed a grimace. Could it be that the entire matter of her employment was a fraud, a deceit devised by the wily Lady Westcott to heighten Ivan's interest in the lovely and innocent Valerie? And Lucy was set most uncomfortably right in the middle of it.

When Lady Westcott finally responded it was with an airy wave of her hand. "Ivan is only flirting with her, Miss Drysdale. It behooves the child to learn to deflect such pleasant, but insincere, attentions."

Yes, it certainly did, Lucy wanted to reply. But she wisely kept that opinion to herself. And the fact was, she could not find it in her heart to blame the old woman. Lady Westcott only wanted her grandson well settled before she passed on. All in all, a reasonable enough desire. But Lucy knew instinctively that young Valerie was not at all the right sort of woman for Ivan. No, Valerie would be de-

voured whole by the likes of Ivan Thornton, and Lucy
could not in good conscience allow that, no matter the unpleasantness that lay between Lady Westcott and her grandson.

She'd been given this position ostensibly to help Valerie
make an appropriate match. Despite Lady Westcott's de-
ception, Lucy decided she would put all her effort into doing just that. For no matter his title and fortune—and his
ferocious good looks—Ivan Thornton was not the right
man for Valerie.

Staunch in her convictions, Lucy faced the earl. "It
would be terribly un-Christian of me not to hope for the
best for both you and Lady Valerie. I pray she will find the
right sort of man for herself, just as I pray you will find
the right sort of woman for yourself."

And they both knew what sort of woman *that* was!

She stared straight at him, daring him with her eyes to
say anything that would reveal the terrible depths of his
depravity, to reveal the wicked behavior he had participated
in during his last night at Westcott House. He could not,
she knew, not if he meant to impress Valerie. Nor was he
likely to declare his piousness, not with any degree of sincerity. So how would he answer her?

What he did was smile at her, a slow, easy smile that
managed to make of him the very image of male beauty.
For a long breathless moment he forced her to see his raw
virility, the essence of his masculinity that was both attractive and threatening to the feminine psyche, both fascinat-
ing and yet a terrible danger too.

He unnerved her quite to the core.

"You are a devout Christian, Miss Drysdale?"

"Why . . . Why, of course. Of course I am. Aren't you?"
she added, hoping to turn the subject away from herself.

That dark, seductive smile remained in place. "Not so
devout as you, I'm certain." Then he somehow seemed to
draw back into himself and in the blink of an eye his focus
shifted to Lady Valerie. "If I might be of some assistance?"

He strode up to the two women and without so much as a by-your-leave, he freed Valerie's hand from Lucy's and drew the girl toward him. "Now, Lady Valerie, if it's dancing you wish to practice, you'll be better served dancing with someone who knows the male portion of the dance—no offense meant, Miss Drysdale. The same tune will suffice," he added over his shoulder to his grandmother. Then without waiting for a response from either woman, he faced the still silent young girl, made her a very correct bow, and readied himself for the dance.

Lucy glared at him, then turned expectantly to Lady Westcott. Surely she would put an end to this . . . this hooliganism.

But the countess had her own agenda. That was plain from the speculative glint in her sharp old eyes. "You are very jolly tonight, Ivan. I don't believe I've ever seen you so completely at ease."

He did not rise to her goading—for that's what it was, Lucy suspected. The countess was goading him, trying to make him react so she could pull Valerie from his grasp—both literally and figuratively. Of course, that would only make Ivan pursue the girl all the more vigorously, which she now could see had been Lady Westcott's plan all along. What a tortured relationship the two of them shared!

"How can I not be at ease in my own home, surrounded by what little family I still retain?"

Lucy heard the faint edge of sarcasm in his voice, and despite her better judgment, she felt the tiniest bit of compassion for him. He'd been deprived of family all his life. Even though her own family could be excruciatingly trying, they did love her and want only the best for her. Ivan had never enjoyed that luxury.

Still, that did not justify his reckless behavior. Most especially it did not give him free rein to terrify a young girl. And Valerie was most definitely terrified. Her blue eyes had widened to huge proportions. Her soft pink complexion had gone pale, and she stood rooted to her spot, her dancing lessons utterly forgotten.

"If you will not play," Ivan continued, speaking to his grandmother, "then perhaps Miss Drysdale will do so." He turned his glittering sapphire gaze expectantly on Lucy and once more she was unnerved, shaken to the core, as if his masculine will fought to overpower hers—and was succeeding.

She blinked, then glanced over at the pianoforte. Once free of his mesmerizing eyes, her mind clicked finally into gear. "Yes, I think I will play," she agreed, as a devious plan took root. "Do you know the galop?" She looked up at him, a challenging expression on her face. "We haven't practiced that yet."

"Of course."

The challenge was taken up.

Lucy seated herself at the handsome mahogany instrument and ran her fingers lightly over the keys, trying to still their trembling. She could feel Lady Westcott's gaze on her and knew, somehow, that the woman was well satisfied with the proceedings so far. But if she thought Lucy would play the part of unwitting aide to the courtship between the cousins, she was quite mistaken.

For Lucy was certain that Valerie was not adept at the galop. Added to the girl's natural nervousness and the way Ivan rattled even the most self-assured young woman—herself, included—Lucy knew the dance would be a fiasco. To ensure it, she meant to play the tune a trifle faster than it was meant to be performed.

"Go ahead, girl. Step up to your cousin. Take his hand," Lady Westcott instructed Valerie, the only true innocent in this convoluted mess.

Valerie cast Lucy a pleading look, and for a moment Lucy hesitated. The child might have been a frightened hare trapped between two competing hawks, so frozen with fear did she appear. More than anything Lucy wanted to rescue her. But in order to be truly rescued from her godmother's plans, Valerie would simply have to endure a little fear.

Lucy began to play.

Within the first few steps it was plain that Valerie could

not keep up with the music. To his credit, Ivan was a very good dancer and he made the steps as easy for Valerie as he could. Still, in the middle of the second verse the girl trod squarely on his toe, then backed away, red-faced and very nearly in tears.

"I'm sorry," she mumbled. "So sorry . . ."

At once Lucy stopped playing and stood up. "No, it's my fault—"

"No. No, it's mine. I'm so clumsy."

Lucy felt awful, even though she knew it was for the best.

"You played it too fast," Lady Westcott accused. "Perhaps a waltz would be better."

"No!"

Everyone stared at Valerie, for that was the single most forceful thing the girl had said since she'd arrived.

"No, I . . . Why don't *I* play and . . . and Miss Drysdale can dance with the earl?"

"I don't think so," Lucy began.

"What a novel idea."

Lucy stared at Ivan, appalled by his remark. "I don't think so," she repeated.

But he had the devil's own glint in his eyes and she had the sinking feeling that she would not be able to escape this awful situation. His next words confirmed it.

"Surely as Lady Valerie's chaperone you have instructed her in all the rules of society, one of which is that to turn down a man's polite invitation to dance is terribly rude."

"Yes, but . . . But we are not out in society at the moment."

"You were practicing though, practicing how to dance. So come, set a good example, Miss Drysdale." He stood before her and bowed. "I would be honored if you would allow me the pleasure of this dance."

Lucy frowned and hoped she was disguising the awful turmoil of emotions that twisted about inside her chest. Why was he doing this? And why was she reacting like a silly, frivolous girl? She'd had her season—two seasons, in fact. She'd danced with any number of earls before, also a marquess, and twice with a duke. Even the king's nephew had danced with her and brought her punch afterward. So why did she find this particular earl so unsettling?

Because he didn't play by the rules, came the answer. Because he was nothing like any man she'd ever met, not in his upbringing nor in his attitude. And that was why so many other young ladies were ready to swoon at his feet too. There was something wild and dangerous about him, and it seemed to draw women like a candle flame drew moths.

"Very well," she muttered, though her anger was directed more at herself than at him. She jerked at her skirts, smoothing them to the side, then tilted her head back to stare mistrustfully at him. "What can you play, Lady Valerie?"

"Oh, anything, Miss Drysdale. A minuet?"

"How about a polka?" Ivan asked, keeping his eyes trained on Lucy.

"I know the 'Frederika,'" Valerie offered.

"That should do very well."

Valerie sat down at the piano while Lady Westcott moved to a red damask settee. That left Lucy and Ivan standing but an arm's length apart, he with a smug smile curving his lips, she fighting back a groan of dismay. A polka. He would have to hold her and she would have to face him the entire time.

This was not going at all as she'd planned. But she would manage, she told herself. She must. She would dance a few turns around the room with him and that would be that. He obviously had a need to conquer every woman he met. But he was quite mistaken if he thought he could conquer her.

She took a determined breath. For a moment—merely a fraction of a second—his gaze flickered down to her breasts. And just as fast as that, her confidence fled. When his eyes once more met hers, she knew the terrible truth— and feared he would read that truth in her eyes. He *could* conquer her, if he put only the least effort into it.

He held out his left hand to her. Shaken to the core, she reluctantly placed her right hand in his. She struggled not to react to his touch, and sternly reminded herself that two sets of gloves separated their fingers. Then his other hand came around her waist, the music began, and she was lost.

He danced very well. Why was she not surprised? But it was more than merely the proper steps and the comfortable rhythm of the music. There was something in the way he moved, some dark, sensuous something that transmitted itself into her so that she danced as she never had. They whirled about the drawing room in an energetic three-quarter time until Lucy's heart was racing and her cheeks had gone pink.

"Dancing becomes you," he murmured, practically in her ear.

"What a well-considered remark that is," she retorted breathlessly. "I've no doubt all the young ladies are quite flattered by it." Even she, who should know better.

He grinned, a faint, knowing expression that made her stomach tighten. "I find dancing with virginal young women a good indicator of their—how shall I say it?—their potential for passion."

Lucy stumbled, but he caught her and kept them going. She stared up at him, both shocked and indignant. Passion? Oh, but he was too outrageous for words!

"Come now," he continued, his eyes glittering with devilment. "We both know you have a particular interest in other people's passions. So confess the truth, Lucy. Haven't you judged many a fellow by his abilities on the dance floor? A clod with two left feet is not very likely to exhibit a bit of finesse in the marriage bed."

"Really!" This time Lucy wrenched herself free from his wicked grasp. At her angry gesture the music came to a crashing halt. Lady Westcott leaned forward scowling, while Valerie seemed to shrink against the piano.

"I believe it is time for us to retire," Lucy said in the haughtiest tones she could muster. "Valerie?"

Wasn't he going to apologize?

Apparently not.

Valerie rose trembling to her feet, intimidated by the furious emotions rocketing around the room. Lady Westcott clearly recognized that some insult had been given and she too rose, cane in hand. "What is this? What? Why do you leave, Miss Drysdale? What offense have you given her, John?"

John? Outraged as she was, Lucy still could not miss the frigid glower Ivan sent the old woman when she called him John. Nor did she miss Lady Westcott's grudging amendment.

"Oh, all right! Ivan. What have you said to her, Ivan?"

From mocking to furious he had gone in an instant, and all on account of his grandmother calling him John. What on earth did that signify?

Then it occurred to her that John was the English version of the name Ivan. Suddenly she could picture him, a darkhaired Gypsy child being forced to abandon everything he'd known in order to become a proper English lord. And yet he'd clung to his name—his true name.

Unwillingly her heart softened toward him—until he turned to her, his rogue's persona firmly in place.

"It seems I made a remark which offended Miss Drysdale's sensibilities. I thought her a more wordly person than she is. For that I apologize."

He was apologizing for thinking her worldly, Lucy noted. Not for the suggestive nature of his comment. Nor for calling her by her Christian name. Once again her irritation with him rose. The fact that he'd been an unhappy child did not excuse the fact that he'd become an impossible man.

Lady Westcott stamped her cane imperiously upon the floor. "Well, Miss Drysdale? Do you accept his apology? I will not abide discord in this house."

Unless it is of your own making, Lucy thought. At that moment she was heartily disgusted with the old harridan's manipulations. Still, she was not about to risk her stay in London. She hadn't been here even a week. If Ivan Thornton thought he could unsettle her to the point that she would abandon poor Valerie so easily, he was more than mistaken. She meant to stay in London as long as she could. She had Sir James's lectures to attend. She had a hundred—no, a thousand—intellectually stimulating conversations built up inside her, just waiting for an outlet.

She had no intention of letting one bad-mannered, ill-tempered earl ruin it for her.

"Apology accepted," she retorted, though without an iota of forgiveness in either her tone or her bearing. "However, it is late and I am tired. Come along, Valerie. We have quite a full day ahead of us tomorrow."

Valerie scurried to Lucy's side. Her pretty face reflected her dismay over any unpleasantness. Lady Westcott had said she was extremely pliable. It clearly came from being a middle child and being caught too often in the midst of family quarrels. Lucy surmised that Valerie would do almost anything to avoid being caught in another one.

Ivan, however, had been an only child. And a lonely child. He stood now, smug and unrepentant, his hands shoved casually in his pockets. Lucy knew he would not let it end so soon.

"You say you accept my apology, Miss Drysdale, but I detect a lingering irritation in your voice. If you will allow me the chance to redeem myself, I would like to do so tomorrow. Perhaps I can take you and Lady Valerie driving in the morning."

"That's really not necessary."

"Valerie must begin to get out." This came from Lady Westcott. Her shrewd gaze caught Lucy's and warned her against countermanding her will. "It will do her good to be seen. It will generate talk about the newest beauty come to town. Be sure she selects something blue to wear," she finished in a tone that brooked no disagreement.

Lucy gritted her teeth. "Very well. But while Lord Westcott provides her with an audience of future admirers, I would ask leave to provide her with a more mature insight into human nature."

Lady Westcott regarded her closely. "A more mature insight into human nature? What precisely is that supposed to mean?"

"There are a series of lectures being given which I would like her to attend with me, regarding human intellect and the influence of upbringing on the young person."

To Lucy's surprise, Lady Westcott agreed. It even seemed she smiled a bit, as if she actually approved of the subject matter, though that seemed rather unlikely.

Ivan smiled too, a lazy, arrogant sort of smile, as if everything were going just as he'd planned. But it wasn't. Lucy would see to that. Let him bait her on the morrow: it would cause Valerie to be all the more terrified by him.

Meanwhile, with Sir James's help she would educate the impressionable Valerie on the value of a balanced relationship between a husband and a wife, one founded, if not on love, at least on respect. Certainly it should not be predicated merely on the consolidation of wealth or titles, or both.

She hooked her arm in Valerie's and with a curtsy to Lady Westcott and a civil nod to Ivan, the two of them quit the room. But later, when she entered her own room and closed the door behind her, she leaned against that sturdy plank of wood and stared at the window opposite it.

Would she hear him through that window again tonight, bidding some shadowy woman adieu?

Though she told herself she did not care at all what he did—last night, tonight, or any other night—she knew it was not entirely true. But it was curiosity, that was all. It wasn't that she cared; she was merely curious, as all reasonably intelligent people tended to be. Granted, it was not a particularly admirable trait, but it was certainly common enough.

She pushed herself off the door and began to pull the pins from her hair. She would ask Sir James his opinion about curiosity, she decided, if the opportunity ever presented itself for her to ask him anything. She would ask him why some subjects excited the mind more than others and, as a result, tempted a person to look closer, delve deeper. But she would present the question in a general way. She would not mention names nor in any other way give the impression she was overly curious about any particular person.

Even though, unfortunately, she was.

Five

*I*van found Giles and Alexander at the Piss Pot, a seedy watering hole that had been a potter's shop in a former age—Pitt's Pottery—but was just the Piss Pot now.

Giles sat over a deck of cards, fleecing a rather tough-looking character of a week's pay. Were it not that Giles was so ferocious-looking himself, he would long ago have had his throat slit in some dark alley, he was that adept at cards.

Alex was the complete opposite. Though tall and of medium build, he had the pretty features of a lad—and languid manners befitting a prince—albeit an unacknowledged one. Now he sat in a corner booth, a pretty bawd in his lap. He had one perfectly manicured hand wrapped around a squat tumbler and the other up the wench's skirt.

Alex was the first to spy Ivan. "What brings you out this dismal night, my friend? Don't tell me your loving grandam has run you out of your own house?"

"Don't think you can go crawling back to Elliot," Giles warned Ivan, never looking up from his cards. "You hurt his feelings when you rejected his humble abode for that excessively large pile of stones you call the family's town house. One would think his three rooms not good enough for an earl."

The girl sitting on Alex's lap gave a little squeal, then a slow sigh.

"What do you say, Tess?" Alex asked. "Can a sweet piece like you tell the difference between a merchant, an earl, and a prince—under the covers and in the dark, I mean?"

She let out a giggle. "Shall we have us a contest, then? I'll close my eyes and give each of you a feel—or p'rhaps take a taste?" She laughed, then rubbed her bottom back and forth upon his lap. "You're beginning to feel very like a king to me, milord."

It was the wrong thing to say to Alex. Ivan could have told the coarse wench that. Any mention of the king, unless in the most derogatory tones, invariably soured the man. But then, what else should one expect? Of the four friends, the three of them who actually knew who their fathers were, despised them. Ivan had often thought Elliot Pierce fortunate not to be cursed with the knowledge of his own father's identity.

"Where's Elliot?" he asked, signaling the tavern master for his usual glass of gin. He took a chair near Alex, ignoring the interested look the girl—now shoved off Alex's lap—was giving him.

"Give us some privacy," Alex growled at the wench, sending her fleeing, her face a mixture of fear, anger, and confusion.

"Elliot is in some gutter or another," Alex muttered once the girl was gone. "His perverse way of celebrating his latest financial coup." He swigged down the dregs of his cup. From the card table came a sharp oath. A fist hit the table. A bottle toppled over, then shattered on the floor.

Ivan glanced mildly at Giles. The other card player had lurched to his feet and stood now, shaking a fist at his still seated opponent—not at all an unusual occurrence. Ivan had learned long ago not to play cards with Giles. Now this half-drunken cooper or draysman or whatever he was, was learning that same lesson the hard way.

Giles didn't move; he just stared at the sweaty brute, stared at him without blinking, until the man let out a string of curses far more inventive than Ivan would have credited the fellow with. Finally he spat, not on Giles, but near enough to make his insult clear. Only then did he leave, shoving over every chair in his path.

"Sore loser," Alex quipped. "What did you take him for?"

"Five quid. You'd have thought it a tenner the way he carried on."

"Where does the likes of him get five quid?" Alex groused. He was forever short of coins.

"By the honest sweat of his brow, if the smell of him was any indication," Giles said.

"He ought to spend his pay on a new set of teeth," Alex remarked, tugging at the long lace cuff that hung from beneath his stylish silver-gray coat. "Or perhaps his tailor. No, good teeth are more important even than good clothes, don't you agree?" Then he focused on Ivan and his tone changed. "You look as though you'd like to knock somebody's teeth in. Your grandmother's?"

Ivan stared at the glass of gin, rolling it back and forth between his palms, watching the liquid swirl. "She has a new ploy, a new game she thinks to play with me. A sweet young thing—you'd like her, Alex. Lady Valerie Stanwich. She's sponsoring her for the rest of the season and has moved the girl, her chaperone, and herself into my house."

"And so you will be moving out again?" Alex asked, joining the other two at the sticky table.

Ivan shook his head. He'd had time to think about his grandmother and her plan—and about the imperious Miss Drysdale—on his ride over to the Piss Pot. "No. Not this time. I plan to maintain my residence at Westcott House. In fact," he said, his eyes glinting at his friends. "I'd like to fill the house with people. Entertain regularly."

Alex yawned. "If you want to run her off, we'd be more than happy to assist you. I can keep the grandmother happy—she likes me, you know. Giles can pursue the girl. No mama in her right mind would let her daughter even look at a merchant's bastard, no matter how much money he has. No offense, old man," he added to Giles with a shrug. "And perhaps, just for fun, Elliot can chase the skirts of the chaperone. Is she hatchet-faced, or a dried-up old prude? Those are the two most popular sorts in chaperones, you know. Or else she—"

"I'll tend to Miss Drysdale myself."

That drew an interested look from both of his friends. Alex's bored expression evaporated and a sly grin lifted one side of his mouth. "Out with it, man. Is she worth pursuing, or do you mean only to aggravate the countess?"

Ivan studied his two friends. Bastards all, they'd bonded during the grim years at Burford Hall. Without them and Elliot, he sometimes thought he might not have survived those hellish years. They were closer than brothers—from what he'd seen of brothers. They'd been in and out of any number of scrapes together. They always looked out for one another, and even had shared women from time to time.

But this was not one of those times.

"I can handle my grandmother and her plotting myself. All I ask of you is that you keep Lady Valerie's dance card filled."

"And what of this Miss Drysdale?" Alex persisted, his clear eyes lit with curiosity. "Shall we keep her dance card filled also? Or shall you tend to that task yourself?"

"Do chaperones *have* dance cards?" Giles asked. Of them all, he was the least familiar with proper society and its maze of rules.

"No," Ivan answered. "But that doesn't mean she cannot dance."

Nor that she, smart and outspoken though she was, could not be made to dance to his tune.

It was almost noon when the Earl of Westcott had a carriage brought around. That was morning by town standards, for breakfast was not served until after ten and morning calls were not actually made until early afternoon.

Lucy had forgotten how silly it all was, for she had learned to enjoy the early morning hours these recent years in the country. Nevertheless, the carriage was here now and they were going out. She could hardly wait.

If only the disconcerting Earl of Westcott weren't accompanying them. To make things even worse, he had ordered the open phaeton brought around for them, a fancy bit of work which necessitated that the three of them crowd in together on the single seat. In order to maintain proper decorum, Lucy settled herself squarely between his lordship and Lady Valerie.

She and Valerie had discussed Ivan Thornton at length before breakfast, and Lucy was quite relieved that the girl was not in the least enamored of the dark, dashing earl. To be more accurate, the girl was positively petrified of the man. He was far too dangerous for the likes of timid Valerie. Far too roguish.

"But he has twenty thousand a year in rents, and even more than that from the funds," Lucy had reminded the girl. "Your family would consider him a brilliant match for you. Aren't you at all tempted?"

Valerie's chin had trembled and her lovely blue eyes had sparkled with the hint of tears. "Oh, please, Miss Drysdale, do not throw me at him. I beg you, do not. He is far too . . . too . . ." She had finished with a helpless little shudder. "He terrifies me. I fear he will make mincemeat of me, if that makes any sense at all."

Indeed, it made perfect sense to Lucy. After reassuring Valerie that she would thwart any possible match between the two of them, Lucy had prepared herself for the trying hours ahead.

"This vehicle is rather small," she began when he seated himself beside her and took up the reins. "Surely you have something larger in your stables."

"I thought the open phaeton a better choice than the closed carriage," he answered as he chirruped to the pair of handsome bays. He swung his head around and met her gaze, and her heart began to thud. Then holding her eyes captive with his, he shifted his leg so that his knee touched hers.

Lucy's heart managed somehow to lodge in her throat.

But then, that was what he wanted, she reminded herself. To unsettle her. To disconcert her.

She refused to let him succeed.

"If you insist on crowding us this way," she muttered, "then at least be good enough to keep your . . . your limbs to yourself."

"My limbs?" He gave a wicked laugh, displaying a flash of white teeth against his dark skin. "That's right. How could I forget? The word 'legs' is far too coarse for ladies of refinement." He leaned forward just a little, and in the process brushed his arm against Lucy's. "Tell me, Lady Valerie. You grew up with several brothers. Do you refer to your lower appendages as 'legs' or 'limbs'?"

Lucy could feel Valerie trembling. Or was it herself? She caught the girl's hand in hers and gave it a squeeze. Though she was glad Valerie's timidity would ultimately be her best protection from the earl's devilish charms, there was a part of her that wanted Valerie to stiffen her spine. She should put Ivan Thornton in his place with a short, pithy reply.

But that was not going to happen, and Lucy knew it. When the silence from Valerie's side of the seat lengthened, when the girl's cheeks grew hot with color and her hold on Lucy's hand turned positively painful, Lucy knew it was up to her.

"Lord Westcott, if you insist on bringing up subjects inappropriate to a young woman of Lady Valerie's sensibilities, then perhaps it would be better if you turn this vehicle right around and return us home."

They hadn't quite reached the end of the square. When they did, however, Ivan proceeded down Berkeley Street, then turned into Picadilly Street, as if he hadn't heard her at all. But he'd heard, all right, and his next words confirmed it.

"You must allow me the opportunity to ascertain my cousin's sensibilities, Miss Drysdale. Athough we are family, we have only just met. If she is not as prone to frankness and candor as you are, you cannot hold me accountable for not being knowledgeable of that fact. I'd be willing to wager that you, notwithstanding your current role as her chaperone, are more likely to call your lower appendage a leg. But if you and Lady Valerie prefer I call it a limb, then very well. I admit it. My limb is encroaching on your space.''

He pressed his leg very deliberately against hers and grinned. Then he pulled it away. ''There. Is that better? My limb is no longer touching your limb.''

If Lucy hadn't been so flustered by the unsettling feel of the strong muscular thigh lying beside hers, she would have dismissed his behavior as merely the teasing antics of a young man. Unfortunately there was a deeper, darker side to his teasing. A threateningly masculine side that she was less sure how to handle.

Praying he was finished with such antics, she resolved to concentrate on getting through the drive as best she could.

Despite her earlier objections, Lucy had to admit that the day was perfect for an open vehicle. The sky was a high, clear blue, decorated with occasional clouds of brilliant white. A light breeze kept the weather mild and she found herself enjoying the ride very much. This was London at its best, free of either fog or smoke.

He handled the pair of bays with a masterful touch. She'd always heard that Gypsies were especially good with horses. His hands were light on the reins, but strong too. She watched them with rapt fascination until she realized what she was doing. Then she tore her eyes away and cleared her throat.

They drove down Piccadilly Street to Park Lane with only the most desultory of conversation. ''That's the King's Palace there, across Green Park,'' she pointed out to Valerie. ''And there, at that fountain up ahead, that's Hyde Park Corner,'' she added, trying to keep her attention anywhere but on Ivan Thornton.

As they neared Stanhope Gate, which led into the park, the busy traffic grew heavier still. Once they turned in at the gate, however, it became little more than a queue lined up through the park, phaetons and curricles and landaus—even a hack or two. And whoever wasn't in a carriage was mounted on a spirited steed.

Valerie was all eyes, staring about like the green girl she was. During her own first season Lucy had been just as impressed by the dazzling display of high society, of the silks and muslins, braid and ribbons, feathers and jewels. Her second season she'd affected a more blasé attitude. Now, however, she found a certain amusement in it. Like children, the ton had come to the park to show off their newest toys. One elegant woman remarked on another's cunning bonnet. One top lofty fellow complimented another's fine mount. And everyone kept a close watch on everyone else, all the while trying to display themselves in the best and most flattering light.

One rather regal-looking couple driving a royal-blue Berlin coach had two enormous cats settled on their laps and three leashed greyhounds following their vehicle, each one wearing a royal-blue cap with a royal-blue feather curving over it.

Lucy coughed behind one hand, trying to disguise her laughter. Valerie did not notice, but the earl did.

"Amused, Miss Drysdale? And by the elitest of our elite society? I doubt the countess would approve of your attitude."

Lucy shot him a sidelong glance. He was teasing, wasn't he? His lips were curved up on one side. Still, she couldn't be certain. "It was only a tickle in my throat," she vowed. Unfortunately, at precisely that moment an overaged roué trotted by, clad in a bright yellow jacket cut much too small. To make matters even more ridiculous, he was riding a pure white steed that was clearly not of a mind to appreciate the crowds on Rotten Row. Lucy could not quite hide the laughter that bubbled up.

"Don't laugh," the earl whispered in her ear. "He's a marquess, recently come into his considerable inheritance from an uncle who lived to be eighty. And he's newly in need of a wife, his three previous ones having died without giving him an heir. No doubt my cousin's family would be overjoyed should you help her snag a marquess.''

Her distaste must have shown in her face, for it was his turn to laugh—and somehow maneuver his leg back against hers.

She answered that not-so-subtle move with an equally unsubtle jab of her elbow into his side. She heard his faint grunt of surprise. But the leg stayed boldly where it was.

''Oh, look, Miss Drysdale. That purple carriage. Is that the king, or one of his family?''

The earl leaned forward to answer Valerie, causing his hip to press against Lucy's. Really, but the man was an out-and-out bounder to take advantage this way! So why was she reacting like a green girl with sweaty palms and racing pulse?

''That is the Duke of Cheltham, Lady Valerie. Or rather his wife, Lady Cheltham. And one of her particular friends,'' he added in a dry tone when the spectacular carriage drew nearer. ''He is rather proud of his familial connections to the royal family. Thus the purple landau.''

An intriguing bit of gossip. Lucy, however, was more interested in removing that hard, muscular thigh from hers lest she lose what little remained of her wits.

''Would you like to walk a while?'' she asked Valerie in a strained voice. Once again she jabbed the shameless wretch beside her, only this time even more forcefully.

''I wouldn't recommend walking,'' he answered before Valerie could. But at least he moved over a fraction of an inch. ''She hasn't yet been introduced into society. To the strict arbiters of our strict society, it would be considered coarse and unrefined.''

He had a point, Lucy allowed, although it was clear by his tone what he thought of that particular rule of society. ''Perhaps you'll provide us with an introduction to some among your grandmother's circle of acquaintances,'' she prompted him.

"Is your charge interested in securing a husband from among the aged and infirm, then?"

"Oh, no!" Valerie gasped, then quickly averted her face.

"The earl is only teasing, Valerie. He knows I have no intention of letting you be paired with an old man."

"Ah, so it's *young* men she wishes to meet," he said. "We're in luck, then, for I believe I see several fine gentlemen of my acquaintance." He raised a hand to a trio of horsemen who sat their mounts in a grassy area just off the roadway.

He'd planned this, Lucy immediately realized. He'd planned the whole thing, and furthermore, his friends, though young and handsome and dashing, would not be of the acceptable sort—at least not for an earl's daughter. Lucy wasn't sure how she knew this, but there was not a doubt in her mind that she was right.

When the three horsemen spied Lord Westcott's carriage, they disengaged themselves from conversation with a group of women in a slightly worn cabriolet and headed their way.

"Good morning, Westcott," said the most elegantly dressed of the three, tipping his hat to the ladies. He was a very handsome fellow, Lucy noticed, exquisitely turned out with his neckcloth tied in an elaborate knot, and lace covering half of his hands. A charming and well-practiced rake, she decided.

"Lady Valerie Stanwich, Miss Lucy Drysdale, may I present Mr. Alexander Blackburn—" The rake's name sounded vaguely familiar. Perhaps she'd read something of him in one of the newspapers her brother took.

"Also, Mr. Giles Dameron—" Tall, dark, and handsome, in a rustic and rather appealing sort of way.

"And finally, Mr. Elliot Pierce." The rogue, Lucy concluded. For Mr. Pierce was every bit as handsome as Mr. Dameron, equally as languid as Mr. Blackburn, and almost as arrogantly dangerous as Ivan Thornton.

The rake, the rustic, and the rogue. They were clearly long-time accomplices of the Gypsy earl.

"We were all at Burford Hall together," Ivan said, as if to confirm her thoughts.

Burford Hall. Also known as Bastard Hall. Of course!

Lucy pasted an appropriately restrained smile on her face. "We are pleased to make your acquaintance."

Mr. Blackburn, the rake, reined his horse nearer to Valerie's side of the phaeton. "How do you find London, Lady Valerie?" He smiled at her, a smile so disingenuous and sincere that Lucy blinked. Perhaps she'd been too hasty in her judgment. Perhaps he was not a rake at all.

"It . . . It is very . . . large," Valerie stammered, blushing to the roots of her fair hair.

Mr. Blackburn shifted on his saddle. If anything, his expression grew more earnest. "I thought so too when first I arrived. But in time I became accustomed to it. Where have you arrived from?"

"From Sussex. Near to Arundel."

"Arundel," he said, nodding. "I've visited very near there. Done some fishing in the Arun."

"My brothers fish there often," Valerie said, gaining a bit of composure.

Well, maybe this wasn't too bad, Lucy thought, letting out a slow breath. They might only be misters, but this one, at least, was exceedingly well mannered.

"Are you from there as well, Miss Drysdale?"

Lucy met Mr. Pierce's gaze. The rogue. He affected a bored sort of grace, yet she detected an avidity hidden somewhere beneath it.

They sat in the early afternoon sunshine another few minutes talking to the three gentlemen about this and that. No, they'd not yet been to Almacks'. Yes, they were invited to the McClendens' dance.

"I hope you will save me a waltz," Mr. Blackburn said to Valerie.

"She is not yet waltzing," Lucy answered before Valerie could. "She has yet to be presented at court."

"Ah, well. Perhaps another set," he said, giving the girl a beautiful smile.

"And one for me," Mr. Pierce said.

"And for me," the rustic Mr. Dameron echoed.

Oh, dear, this might be trouble, Lucy fretted, when Valerie smiled and accepted their offers, just as she'd taught her to do. Mr. Blackburn was charming and had certainly presented himself in the least threatening light. But he was not for Valerie, nor were any of them. Valerie might be a country girl and one of several sisters, but she was nonetheless the daughter of an earl and very pretty at that. Even with only a moderate dowry attached to her name, her looks and title ensured her a very good match—as Lady Westcott had pointed out in her instructions to Lucy. It seemed that she would have to do something about these unsuitable suitors.

She began to fan herself. "I was wondering, Lord Westcott, if you might point out Fatuielle Hall to us on the drive home." She sent him a speaking look.

She was mightily relieved when he chose to acquiesce rather than argue. The three other gentlemen tipped their hats and made their farewells.

Ivan deftly threaded the phaeton through the crowds of riders and carriages, and before long they were free of the congested park and moving at a fair pace homeward. To his credit, this time he kept his leg—his limb, rather—contained in its own portion of the box. As they went along he pointed out particular landmarks: Constitution Hall, the clubs along Pall Mall, and the Charing Cross. Then he turned into Williams Street and slowed before a three-story brick building that wanted a good scrubbing-down.

"This is Fatuielle Hall. Why did you wish to see it? There are very few amusements here any more."

"There are often lectures given here, I understand. I thought I might like to attend one." *Or a series of them.*

"Ah, yes. You mentioned that last night. Tell me, Miss Drysdale. Could it be that you are something of a bluestocking?"

She stiffened a bit. "Not to put too fine a line on it, but

there are any number of ladies who would be insulted by
such a remark.''

''But not you,'' he insisted, studying her with a confident
eye. His gaze held hers so long, and at such near quarters,
that Lucy had to fight the urge to squirm. When she could
bear it no longer, far past the point when his stare had
become rude and all the breath had left her body, she
averted her eyes and stared instead at the slightly shabby
lecture hall, as if its nondescript architecture fascinated her.

He laughed under his breath, then urged the horses on.
But not before Lucy spied a handbill announcing Sir James
Mawbey's next lecture on May nineteenth. That was to-
morrow! She hugged that knowledge to herself and used it
as a shield against her confused feelings toward Ivan
Thornton.

Fortunately, for the duration of the journey home he addressed all the conversation toward Valerie. Even more to
Lucy's good fortune, the girl managed to answer pleasantly
enough, and by the time they arrived back at the grand
house on Berkeley Square, Lucy's alarm had faded—at
least her alarm about Ivan's friends. Perhaps a bevy of admirers was precisely what Valerie needed to bolster her
self-confidence. Perhaps Lord Westcott's friends would do
her more good than harm. After all, it was actually more
important that the girl learn how to handle unwelcome admirers than welcome ones, for the fact was, for such a
pretty young woman as Lady Valerie, there would be far
more of the former than of the latter.

Still, there was that fair-minded portion of Lucy's brain
that thought it more than unfortunate for a man's title and
parents—assuming he *had* parents—to be considered of
greater consequence than his moral fiber. That the richness
of his purse was considered more important than the richness of his intellect.

Oh, well. She could expound on that subject with Sir
James, if she were lucky enough to engage him in private
conversation. Meanwhile, she must steer her young charge
toward men with sufficient title and fortune to satisfy her

family and Lady Westcott. And with any luck, she would find one possessed also of decent character and a fine mind. With luck.

Lucy and Valerie spent the afternoon in Lady Westcott's company. Or more accurately, in her wake. They called at several fashionable addresses, architectural edifices that bespoke wealth and power and heritages traced back to the Conqueror himself. At most of them they simply left their calling cards. But at three they were greeted and offered refreshments. Their hostesses were all of Lady Westcott's vintage and clearly among her dearest acquaintances. The Viscountess Talbert was related to Lady Westcott by marriage. The Countess of Grayer, they were cautioned, was a famous arbiter of town society. The Dowager Duchess of Wickham was, simply put, the Dowager Duchess of Wickham.

Formidable women all, they were cut from the same cloth as Lady Westcott who was, of course, perfectly at ease in their company. But young Valerie was petrified of them.

As for Lucy, she was cognizant of the fact that these ladies could be a huge help to Valerie. But beyond that, her primary reaction to them was fascination. The world was dominated by men, and yet these women had each carved her own place of power within it. Powerful women and how they became that way—that was another topic she longed to discuss with Sir James.

Oh, but she could hardly wait until tomorrow.

Once they returned to Westcott House, Lucy broached the subject of the lectures. "Lady Westcott, do you recall that I wished Lady Valerie to attend several lectures with me?"

"Several? I do not recall anything about several."

Lucy forced herself not to argue. "Tomorrow afternoon the first of the subscription lectures at Fatuielle Hall will be held."

"We have the modiste to see for fittings."

"That is at eleven."

"We've been invited to tea at Lady Hinton's. I particularly wish to see the changes this latest of Robert's wives has made to his town house. Lady Talbert told me she has changed everything his third wife did to the place, and in the process has made it very like it was under his second wife. I am most interested in determining whether or not the new Lady Hinton did so deliberately or not. For if it was accidental, she will be the joke of the season." Her lined face creased in silent laughter.

Lucy pursed her lips and tried to hold back her words, but it was useless effort. "Will you inform her of her mistake—if indeed it was unconsciously done?"

Lady Westcott eyed Lucy shrewdly. "I haven't decided that yet. What do *you* suggest I do?"

Somehow Lucy knew her answer would determine whether or not she would be given permission to attend the lecture tomorrow. That meant she must be every bit as shrewd as the countess. What answer would the woman want to hear, this coldly calculating woman who'd made her only grandchild a pawn in her bid for power?

The answer was obvious.

"What you should tell her depends on her, I should think. If you believe she can be an ally in the future, and useful to you, then by all means tell her that her new decor mimics that of one of her predecessors. Then you can save her from humiliation by spreading the tale that she did the decor that way to please her husband, whom she adores."

Lady Westcott appeared receptive to Lucy's answer, right up to her last words. Then she frowned and pushed her teacup away. " 'Her husband whom she adores'? Bah, but you are as green a girl as Valerie if you believe a wife must adore her husband."

Lucy held her ground. "I did not say a wife *must* adore her husband. I merely said you and she could *imply* that she does."

Lady Westcott considered Lucy with frosty eyes. Then unexpectedly she laughed. Lucy heard Valerie's sigh of relief just beside her.

"You are right in the main, Miss Drysdale. I shall visit Lady Hinton and decide for myself whether she will make a useful friend or not. If I save her from a social *faux pas*, she will most certainly be in my debt."

"Does this mean Valerie and I may forego the visit and attend the lecture instead?"

The countess nodded slowly. Consideringly. "You are a bright young woman, Miss Drysdale. Exceedingly bright."

Lucy accepted the compliment with a smile. She had long ago acknowledged that her intellectual abilities were better than most, although she was not excessively smug about it. But she would have to be more than merely bright if she were to find the right young man for Valerie, one that would suit both the girl's needs and Lady Westcott's plans.

The dowager countess was allowing her to assert her own will only because she thought she was manipulating Lucy and making her an accomplice in her plan to pair Lord Ivan and Lady Valerie.

But when she found out the truth of Lucy's intentions . . .

Lucy smiled blandly at the countess. She would deal with that particular problem when it presented itself. Meanwhile, tonight was the McClendons' ball, although Lady Westcott had termed it merely a dance, as she doubted there would be over two hundred persons in attendance. Still, whether two hundred or four hundred, Valerie was nonetheless terrified at the thought of so grand a gala.

How the girl handled herself this evening could very well influence her reception for the rest of the season. Lucy was determined to make her, if not the belle of the ball, then at least the center of her own court of acceptable beaus.

And Lucy would be right there to cull through them and steer Valerie toward the best of the lot.

Six

It was not yet midnight and already the McClendon ball was being termed the first true crush of the season. Lady McClendon was ecstatic; Lord McClendon was justifiably proud, if a trifle deep into his cups. Their two unmarried daughters, once relieved of their duties in the receiving line, had not paused a moment in their mad series of dances.

At first Valerie had clung to Lucy like a child, just staring about at the fabulous gowns, glittering jewels, and constantly shifting sea of humanity. However, as she'd been introduced around by Lady Westcott, and complimented and fussed over, she'd begun to warm to the hectic social scene.

Then Valerie had made two unfortunate blunders, calling the Duchess of Wickham my lady, and the Viscountess Talbert, your grace. It hadn't helped that Lady Westcott had rebuked the child with a sharp pinch. Once again the poor girl had become too frightened to say more than a word or two.

Fortunately that had not deterred any of her numerous admirers. She'd been introduced to so many eager young lords, honorables, and misters that even Lucy was having a hard time recalling who was who.

At the moment Valerie was dancing an invigorating galop with the Honorable Chester Davies. With a less intimidating partner than Ivan Thornton, the girl had no trouble mastering the steps. They made a rather fetching couple, Lucy decided from her vantage point among the other chaperones. But then, Valerie was so lovely that any fellow would be cast in a better light while in her company.

Lucy was humming along with the music when a murmur shimmied through the room, faint but unmistakable, like the current of a stream.

"You see? I told you he was coming," a voice to her left whispered.

"My lady gave me strict instructions: my girl may dance with him, but not with any others of his crowd."

"Not even the one they say is the king's bastard?"

Lucy didn't listen to the rest. She didn't need to. Only one man could remain unnamed and yet be recognizable to everyone, from doting mamas to dancing misses to disapproving chaperones. Ivan had arrived along with his friends from Hyde Park. The three R's.

Nervously she smoothed her neat chignon, then took a deliberate breath and instructed herself to calm down. With any luck Valerie's dance card was already filled. If not . . . If not, well, she would suffer no real harm for dancing with Ivan's friends. Her popularity had been fairly well established with the eligible young men of the ton. If a few of the more extreme snobs disapproved of some of her dance partners, she could easily weather the storm.

The galop progressed anon, with silks, sateens, and muslin skirts whirling and belling out before her. But Lucy no longer concentrated on the dancers. Instead she peered about, striving not to crane her neck too obviously. Where were they?

No, where was *he*?

Though she should not be interested in the whereabouts of the Earl of Westcott, except insofar as it affected her innocent young charge, the truth was, every part of her was vitally interested in Ivan Thornton's whereabouts. It was idiotic, of course, and if she could have convinced herself it was purely due to her interest in the minds and motivations of people in general, she would have given it her best effort.

But it was not because of that at all. It was because his thigh had warmed not just her thigh but her entire being. Because when he had whispered to her through the door to her bedchamber, she'd fancied his breath had touched her ear, and she'd trembled. Because he was smart and driven, and he held the ton in even more contempt than she did.

"This is how young women are ruined," she muttered. By inappropriate fascinations of just this sort.

"What is that you say?" the lace-capped chaperone to her left asked. "One of them's ruined a young lady?"

"No, no," Lucy hastily corrected her. "I said the . . . the May Day celebrations were ruined. When it rained," she added when the woman cocked her head and stared at her, a skeptical expression on her face.

Lucy gave her a taut smile, then turned away and searched out Valerie's fair head. Across the crowded dance floor she spied Lady Westcott, flanked by her friends Laurence Caldridge, Lord Dunleith, and Viscountess Talbert. Lord Dunleith was whispering in Lady Westcott's ear, while the elegant old woman stared at someone off to Lucy's right.

Ivan, of course. If she could have, Lucy would have shrunk back into the milling crowds to avoid him spotting her. But the music was ending and in a moment Mr. Davies would be returning Valerie to her side.

Ivan and his notorious friends spied Valerie first and followed her to where Lucy waited. He gave Lucy a quick appraising glance. But his first words were directed to Valerie, which was only proper.

"Good evening, cousin." He greeted her with a sweeping bow, kissing her hand and holding it longer than he rightly should.

Valerie pressed her lips together nervously. Lucy cleared her throat. Was this little display for his grandmother's benefit, or did he seek to rattle Valerie on purpose? For she was most assuredly rattled. The self-possession she'd earned basking in the glow of so much masculine admiration promptly disappeared under Ivan's disturbing attention.

The diamond stud glinting in his left earlobe didn't help either. Had ever a man surpassed him for sheer gall?

"Good evening, Lord Westcott," Lucy said when it appeared he would stare at Valerie until she dissolved into pudding on the floor. At once those vivid eyes turned on her.

"Good evening, Miss Drysdale. Tell me, is Lady Valerie living up to your expectations?"

Lucy frowned at the rudeness of such a remark made in the girl's presence. Then she spied the arrogant gleam in his eyes. He was baiting her. Again.

She smiled as serenely as she could, considering that her heart raced at a pace considerably beyond serene. "Lady Valerie far surpasses my expectations, not that I ever doubted she would."

"Did you mark down a dance for me?" Giles Dameron interrupted. He bowed his greeting to Valerie and to Lucy, then repeated his question.

Valerie, thankfully, regained some portion of her aplomb when the rustic Mr. Dameron addressed her so directly. "Why, yes, Mr. Dameron, I did." She smiled up at him, then averted her eyes, opened her mother-of-pearl fan, and began modestly to flutter it.

They went off together: Mr. Dameron without even seeking the chaperone's approval; Valerie plainly anxious to escape the earl's overpowering presence.

"They make a handsome couple," Alexander Blackburn drawled. As before, he was dressed in the height of fashion and displayed a practiced ennui that would be the envy of any rake in society.

Elliot Pierce's boredom, however, was of a different nature entirely. "Have they opened the gaming tables yet? My apologies, Miss Drysdale, but aside from my duties to Lady Valerie, you will not see me often on the dance floor."

"That's quite all right," Lucy murmured.

"No it's not," Ivan countered. "I apologize for my friends' lack of manners, Miss Drysdale. Since they have not invited you to dance, then I will."

So saying, Ivan reached for her hand. But Lucy snatched it away, burying her fist in her skirts. She did not *dare* chance dancing with this man, not the way he affected her! "If you would think about it, Lord Westcott, your offer to dance with me out of duty is much more the insult than any your friends have given me. At least theirs was not deliberate," she added.

"Careful, Miss Drysdale, else you shall ruin my reputation as a gentleman," he whispered, bending too near to her.

Lucy could hear the laughter in his voice, but she also saw, to her chagrin, that they had become the focus of an inordinate amount of interest. Some discreet, some not, more than a dozen pairs of eyes watched their little foursome. And in the chaperone's area, no less!

But Lucy had never liked bowing to public pressure, whether that pressure was exerted by a crowd or by a single individual. Her chin went up a notch and she stared straight into Ivan Thornton's unnerving blue eyes. "Why do you hate your grandmother so?"

Mr. Blackburn coughed; Mr. Pierce laughed out loud. "I think we'll be going now," he said, taking Mr. Blackburn by the arm. "Come, Alex, I want to *have* a smoke, not go *up* in smoke when this fire flares out of control."

They quit the ballroom together, drawing stares as they went. Lucy watched them go, feeling somewhat disconcerted by their absence. No, not by their absence, but by Ivan's solitary presence. Though surrounded by dancers and music and a hundred other guests, she was nonetheless completely alone with Lord Westcott. Would no one come to her aid?

Apparently not. Again her chin went up and again she went on the offensive. "Why do you hate your grandmother?"

His face had gone rigid and the emotion that burned in

that disturbing stare looked more like fury than the teasing light from before. "That is none of your business, Miss Drysdale. Come, dance with me." Without warning he took her hand and led—no, pulled—her toward the area marked out for dancing.

"I don't want to dance," she hissed, but quietly, for she did not wish to draw undue attention to herself. Not that he hadn't already done that.

"I do," he replied. Then suddenly she was in his arms and it was her dark skirts belling out as he spun her around and into the stream of dancers.

Why must it be another galop? Lucy fretted as she reluctantly placed her left hand on his arm. With his right hand at the small of her back, he seemed to be pressing her nearer with each half-revolution.

"Not so close," she muttered. Deliberately she trod on his foot.

"Step on my foot again and I will pull you flat up against me," he warned. Then he grinned down at her. " 'Flat' is probably not the correct word, is it?" he asked, letting his gaze drop to her bosom.

Though she was far more decorously dressed than most of the women in attendance, embarrassing color rushed into her cheeks. "You are too rude to believe!"

"That's because I wasn't brought up any better."

"That's not true."

"Isn't it?" He was no longer smiling. For a full circuit of the capacious ballroom neither of them spoke—at least not with words. What his strong, masculine body was saying to her, however, she was certain she did not want to hear. Valerie danced by on Mr. Dameron's arm. He seemed a pleasant enough fellow, albeit a little thin on the social graces. Not at all like Ivan, who knew precisely how to behave. If *he* behaved badly, it was most definitely by design. She decided to goad him as he'd previously goaded her.

"Since you refuse to answer my question, I will have to rely on what I have heard of you, as well as on my own impressions, and then draw my own conclusions regarding the ill will between you and Lady Westcott.''

"This should be entertaining."

His handsome features had settled into the patient expression of a wise elder resigned to tolerate a foolish young woman. Lucy vowed to wipe that half-smirk from his face.

"I gather we are of a similar age—"

"You are that old? I had no idea."

"—but that we had a very different upbringing," she continued unperturbed. "I grew up in the bosom of my family, loved and cosseted. Well, perhaps not precisely cosseted, especially in recent years. Meanwhile, you grew up in a Gypsy tribe without benefit of a father."

"I had a father there."

Lucy gnawed her inner lip. That was something Lady Westcott had not revealed. "I see. You had a father there. That means that when Lady Westcott brought you to Westcott House—"

"She never brought me to Westcott House." His grasp on her waist had turned to iron but his step never faltered. Lucy had the distinct impression that were she to lift both her feet up, he would continue the dance without misstep, whirling her in his unyielding grip.

"You went straight from your mother's arms to Burford Hall?"

"I spent several hellish days confined to an upper room at the family estate in Dorset. Then I was sent to Bastard Hall—excuse me if its truer name offends you. I remained there ten years without a break. Without a visit from my sire," he added in a voice devoid of inflection.

Any lingering trace of malice she might have felt toward him dissipated in the face of that answer. He must have felt the softening in her stance, for he bent nearer and whispered in her ear. "That is your cue to clasp me to your breast and offer me whatever comfort you possibly can."

Lucy jerked back as if stung. He'd seduced her with his sad tale, and she, who prided herself on her understanding of human nature, had gone along more than willingly. Her eyes narrowed. "How disappointing to find that you are, after all, of a common type. You know the sort. They believe their upbringing grants them the right to behave in any manner they wish. It is most especially typical of eldest sons. My nephew Stanley is the same," she continued in an offhand manner that she knew would irritate him. "He knows he will inherit everything—title, property, and all the rest—and he behaves accordingly. No one punishes him too severely, not his parents, his tutor, or any of the senior servants. After all, in the near future he will be the one wielding power over them."

"If you think to rouse my temper by lumping me in with those soft, pampered boys who grow up believing the world exists only to please them, you are wasting your time, Miss Drysdale. My younger years could not have been more different."

"Perhaps," she conceded. "But the result is, nevertheless, the same: a spoiled and arrogant young lord who lives only to satisfy his own whims."

She'd struck home with that sally. He did not reveal it by so much as a twitch or frown or anything else. Still, she was certain she'd nicked his pride. When he again whispered in her ear, she knew it.

"Would you like to know what my *latest* whim is?"

To her dismay her aplomb promptly fled. Fortunately the music ended and she was saved having to answer him.

Unfortunately, he did not let her go.

She stepped back from him but he kept hold of her right hand. "Let's have our promenade," he said. "As I'm sure you instructed Lady Valerie, that's the proper way to end a dance with a gentleman."

"Proper for younger ladies," Lucy retorted. "And assuming her dance partner *is* a gentleman." But he would not let her go and in the end she had no choice but to yield to him. He tucked her hand in the crook of his elbow, then covered it with his free hand.

"You needn't hang on to me as if at any moment I might

bolt,'' she muttered as they strolled the edge of the dance floor.

''You mean you won't?'' he mocked her. ''Dare I hope that you enjoy my company?''

''I know my duty to my dance partner includes a brief promenade between sets.''

''And you always do your duty.''

It was a statement, not a question. She chose not to respond but instead smiled at the people they passed, greeting the few she knew and generally trying to behave as if nothing at all out of the ordinary was happening.

Everyone stared at them. And why shouldn't they? What an incongruous pairing they made. The spinster chaperone and the notorious Gypsy earl.

A few of the men ogled her, as if seeing her in a whole new light. The women studied her more critically, as if wondering why the fabulously wealthy bastard earl had chosen her as a dance partner when there were so many more eligible partners.

They were fascinated by him, and frightened too, Lucy realized. And he liked it that way. Well, she refused to let him know he frightened her too.

''So you hate your grandmother because she had you taken from your family, then abandoned you in that school. Do I have it right?''

His hand came back to cover hers. ''That's old gossip, Miss Drysdale.''

''Old gossip? Why? Because it all happened some twenty years ago? It's my observation that childhood experiences haunt a person and influence their adult behavior. Both good experiences and bad ones.''

Their eyes met in a silent battle of wills. Then he smiled, a slow, confident smile. ''Now that you remark on it, I seem to recall as a boy being beaten with unwelcome regularity. Assuming your theory is sound, that must account for my heretofore inexplicable aversion to anyone raising a fist to me. Even now, as I approach my thirtieth year, I tend to defend myself stoutly against any and all attackers," he finished in a mocking tone.

"Scoff if you wish," Lucy responded with unruffled calm. "But your animosity toward the dowager countess is due to the dramatic upheavals in your childhood." She stared curiously at him. "Your mother was a good mother, wasn't she? It's the contrast between your life *with* her and your life *after* her that is the deepest source of your discontent. If your earlier life had been awful, I doubt your anger now would be so great."

She'd spoken impulsively. It was more thinking out loud than anything else. But once again it was plain she'd struck home. Without warning he steered her past an open arch and into a less-crowded hallway. Another turn and they were suddenly alone in a marginally lighted library.

Lucy felt the beginnings of alarm. "I don't believe I wish to carry on this conversation in here where—"

He shut the door with a decisive click.

The alarm changed to out-and-out fear. A bead of perspiration rolled hot and telling down between her breasts. She knew, however, that to show him her fear would be a fatal mistake. She crossed her arms across her chest with a nonchalance that was pure affectation.

"You know very well, my lord, that closeting the two us alone together will do far worse damage to my reputation than to yours. If your purpose is to intimidate me, then rest assured, you have done so. Now, you shall please allow me to return to the ball and to my duties to your cousin."

"And here I was prepared to expound upon my anger to you. Does this mean you are no longer interested in that particular subject, Miss Drysdale?"

What she was interested in was getting out of this dangerous situation she'd somehow placed herself in. Or at least that was what she should be interested in. Unfortunately curiosity seemed to have taken over where caution should have reigned. The more she knew of him the better she would understand this perverse attraction she felt for him. She'd always considered herself too intelligent for such silliness as crushes and infatuations. That was for other women, not for her. But here she was, behaving as foolishly as a girl fresh from the schoolroom. Even Valerie was not fool enough to become enamored of Ivan Thornton.

"I'm always interested in the workings of the human mind," she finally managed to answer. "But I'm also mindful of society's rules. Go ahead, my lord. Expound upon your anger. But do so quickly," she added, "so that I may return to my role as Valerie's chaperone."

His fine lips turned up in a mocking grin. "Quickly," he echoed. "Very well, I will try to be brief. But before I begin, I wonder if you will be equally forthcoming with me."

Lucy studied him warily. "What do you mean?"

"Well, for one thing," he began, pushing away from the door and approaching her with a lazy, graceful stride. "What is it in your own childhood that has made you so avid an observer of other people's lives? Is your own existence so boring and unremarkable that you are forced to live vicariously through the lives of others?"

"Is this a new tack, to annoy me by insulting me?"

"I meant no insult, Miss Drysdale. May I call you Lucy?" he added in a low rumble that managed to rattle her right down to her toes.

"I . . . I don't think . . . No. It would not be proper," she at last got out.

"Then Lucy it is. The last thing I want is to be considered proper." As if his words weren't outrageous enough, he had the brass to smile deeply into her eyes.

Was he trying to seduce her? It was ludicrous, of course, and yet there was no mistaking the slumberous look in his impossibly blue eyes. No. Sulfurous would be a better description, for he looked at her as if he would burn her to cinders!

She slid a little to the side, putting more distance between them, and deliberately broke the hold of his forceful gaze. She searched her mind for a way to change the subject and douse the fire he'd brought to life somewhere deep in the pit of her stomach. "I find it very interesting—though you may find it less so—but once again you put me in mind of . . . of my nephew. He is forever trying to goad his brother, to irritate him and tease him until he explodes in anger. He tries the same ploy with me as well, but not too often any more, for he knows I am onto him. As I am onto you, my lord."

She had moved behind a broad oak library table, and so felt a trifle more sure of herself, even though she knew she was babbling just like Hortense did. But then, perhaps that was why Hortense babbled, to cover her nervousness. Hortense was not, however, her concern right now. Ivan Thornton was.

Perhaps if she were very careful she could divert his attention and at the same time exercise her responsibilities toward Valerie. Summoning every bit of her nerve, she smiled at him. "I propose a pact between us, Lord Westcott. An agreement that might benefit us equally."

"An agreement that might benefit us equally?" He surveyed her with an insolent thoroughness. She'd never realized eyes that blue could appear so warm. Could *feel* so warm upon her. "My dear Lucy, are you propositioning me?"

"What?" That jerked her attention away from the color of his eyes. "Propositioning you? What do you mean— Oh!" Her eyes narrowed and she planted her fists on her hips. Her cheeks were hot with color so there was no hiding her embarrassment. But that only increased her anger. "If you are going to insist on behaving like a troublesome little boy, then I doubt we have anything further to discuss."

He spread his arms, affecting an innocent expression. "A little boy? You wound me deeply. Do I look like a little boy?"

Her rattled nerves caused her to be more blunt than usual. "Oh, no. You look like a man, a man who is more than sure of his own appeal to women. But there's a scared little boy inside you, nevertheless. An angry, howling little boy who has not yet recovered from his lonely, terrifying child-hood.''

As if her words were shards of ice, the atmosphere in the library chilled instantly to December.

The humor fled his face. ''I suspect your experience is more with boys than with men, Miss Drysdale, and that must account for your misjudgment. I have not been a boy since the day I was stolen from my mother. I have not been a boy since I was abandoned at Bastard Hall. I have not been a boy,'' he continued in a low, awful tone, ''since learning of my connection to this amoral family, this amoral society that *dares* call itself the quality. Whatever there was of the boy in me was driven out too many years ago to remember.''

He was magnificent in his anger, magnificent and threatening and oh, so dangerous. But he was vulnerable too, and it was that tiny crack of vulnerability that touched Lucy's heart and would not let her back down from him.

''You have every right to be angry with your grand-mother,'' she murmured, wanting somehow to comfort him. ''You have every right to want to hurt her as she has hurt you.''

But he did not want her comfort. In three strides he was around the table. He grabbed her shoulders with hands that would not relent. ''Any anger I feel for her I will reserve to vent upon her. At this moment, however, my anger is reserved solely for you, Miss Drysdale. Lucy,'' he amended in a huskier voice.

''What are you doing?'' she cried in a voice pitched far too high to be her own.

''I'm venting my anger on you. A man, not a boy, vent-ing his anger on a woman, not on some little schoolroom chit.''

Lucy's heart had begun to hammer so hard she could barely breathe. Yet somehow she found words. ''If you think you're going to kiss me, you could not be more wrong.''

His face lowered to hers. ''My dear Miss Drysdale, I'm going to do much more than merely kiss you.''

Seven

*L*ucy had been kissed before. Several times. So many times, in fact, that though she remembered the number—eleven—she couldn't remember the particulars of each and every occasion when it had happened.

But she would never forget this kiss.

That was the very first thought that broke free of the fog that had taken over her brain. She would never forget this kiss, for it was soft and fierce, tentative and demanding, generous and greedy, all at the same time. He flooded her with sweetness and singed her with passion. She could swear she smelled smoke.

Then he drew back, just enough that he could look down into her face, and she knew she would never forget him either. He was not sincere about his affections toward her, nor was she toward him. So there was no real harm done. But he was the first man—the one and only man—who'd ever made her want to kiss him back. And to kiss him again.

Without weighing the consequences, she rose up on her tiptoes and pressed her lips once more to his.

Those consequences were swift in coming. One of his arms circled her back; his hand splayed open at her waist and pressed her fully against him. His other hand caught the back of her head, holding her steady for the wicked onslaught of his mouth. This time there was less softness, and more fierceness and greedy demand. There was no tentativeness whatsoever. But there was still generosity.

He slanted his mouth over hers, fitting them closer than before. She could feel the connection between them, all the places their bodies touched: belly, breasts, mouth. Where his hands held her steady.

Then his tongue moved along the seam of her mouth, teasing her lips apart. She gasped at the startling feel of it and he immediately pressed his advantage, caressing her incredibly sensitive inner lips, then plunging in fully.

She'd heard about such kissing, of course. Whispered gossip. Fragments of conversation. She'd even found a brief reference to it in a book in a friend's library, a French tome on health and hygiene, which had discussed in limited detail the physical relationship between a man and his wife.

But this kiss was nothing like what she'd imagined from that dry and awkward description. And anyway, they were not husband and wife—nor would they ever be.

That thought alone should have revived some portion of her good sense. Unfortunately he'd moved his very clever kisses around to her ear and neck, and she was tilted off balance, both physically and mentally. Or was her reaction emotional?

When the hand at her waist slid farther down to cup her derriere she knew it was none of those, however. These feelings he created in her were something else altogether, something that melded her emotional and rational and physical selves into something much bigger than the sum of its parts. Something unimaginable. Something she'd never known she'd been missing.

No, she would never forget this kiss or this man, though she lived to be one hundred.

"You kiss like a courtesan." He murmured the words between sensuous nibbles at her earlobe.

Lucy swallowed hard. He was teasing her, of course. Mocking her considerable inexperience in this sort of kissing.

"I'm sorry you're disappointed," she muttered. "Had I

known your intentions, I would have practiced my technique. Now please, let me go!'' she demanded, twisting her face away when he sought her mouth once more.

"I'm hardly disappointed," he murmured, nuzzling her ear again. "What you lack in technique you make up for in enthusiasm. I know you like kissing. So come, don't fight me, Lucy. All I want is another taste of your sweet, provocative mouth."

Sweet. Provocative. The words were too seductive for Lucy to resist. She'd been called handsome and witty. One suitor had described her cheeks as downy soft; another had called her hair silk. But none of them had ever described her as provocative. They would not have had the nerve, even had they wanted to.

But this Gypsy earl, Ivan Thornton, had more nerve than ten men. Than eleven.

Just one more kiss, her fevered body begged. Just one more, her foggy mind rationalized. Just one more, her foolish heart pleaded.

She turned to meet his seeking lips, his clever, scorching lips that ignited every part of her, from neatly coiffed head to stylishly clad toes, and everything in between. Of their own account her arms circled his wide shoulders and she threaded her fingers through the longish waves of his Gypsy-dark hair.

Their lips met and the kiss went on forever. Or maybe it was several kisses, kisses beyond number. He kissed her. She kissed him. Once more his tongue delved deep. Then without her knowing how, he drew her tongue into his mouth. She explored and tasted, and as she did, she discovered the unparalleled feeling of wanting to possess him.

When the necessity for air finally drew them apart, Lucy was too shaken to be embarrassed or ashamed. What had passed between them had been too astounding to believe, as if all the most extreme emotions, like terror, panic, and joy, had been united into one intense moment, one exquisite act.

His embrace loosened and his hands slid back to hold

her upper arms. But they remained mere inches apart, his brilliant blue gaze burning into hers. "So, my dear Miss Drysdale, my lusty Lucy. Will you teach your young charge how to kiss a man as thoroughly as you do?"

Like ice-cold rain his mocking tone chilled Lucy's euphoria. She pulled out of his grasp, and he let her go.

She could hardly breathe. Her heart raced so violently she feared it would expire from the effort. But somehow she managed to answer him. "If you have been sufficiently amused, I believe I shall go."

"Your hair is mussed." He leaned back against the library table, crossing his arms and his ankles in a position of remarkable poise.

With painful clarity she noticed that he was not breathing nearly so hard as she. Was she the only one rattled apart by the power of that kiss?

She smoothed back her hair with a hand that shook. There was more than her hair askew, she realized. What she had just done with this man was foolish beyond belief.

And unforgivable too, should her employer, Lady Westcott, ever find out.

She willed herself to look unaffected by either their kiss or his casual reaction to it. "Is this how you end every dance, my lord? You whisk your partner off to a private room and proceed to kiss her silly? Or try to?" she added, wanting to wipe the smug expression off his face.

But her attempt to denigrate his talent for kissing only caused his grin to deepen. "I have my reputation as a rake to maintain."

"You will not long remain a rake, footloose and fancy free, if you continue such incautious behavior. It would take only a watchful chaperone and an irate parent to force you into an unwelcome union."

He pushed off the table, then casually adjusted his neckcloth. "It will take far more than a nosy chaperone and an enraged father to force me into anything, Lucy. Just remember that before you thrust Valerie at me."

"Thrust Valerie at you?" she exclaimed. "Surely you

jest. I couldn't possibly imagine a worse husband for her than an unfeeling rake. And it's Miss Drysdale to you!''

She was nearer the door than he, so when he crossed the room to her, she had to suppress the panic that made her want to beat an ignominious retreat. When he stopped just before her she reminded herself to keep breathing.

His eyes glittered like sapphires. ''If I decide I want Lady Valerie, I assure you, I can make her want me too.''

Just like I made you want me.

He didn't have to say the words out loud for them to reverberate in the silence of the library. And like oil thrown on a banked fire, they ignited her temper beyond its exploding point.

''Lady Valerie is not for the likes of you and she never will be. I'll see to that!''

That only drew a mocking laugh from him. ''Are you challenging me, Lucy? Do you really think you can protect a girl like Valerie, one of three daughters, from the ardent pursuit of a man with my means? With my titles? Even were I a crude, slobbering pig, her family would never turn down an offer, should I make one. It's the way of the ton. It's what the marriage mart is all about. Surely you know that.''

Unfortunately she did know it. But she would never admit as much to him. ''You are a bully,'' she bit out. ''Just like my nephew. You act as if you disdain the ton and your place within it, but you rely on your title and fortune to get exactly what you want.''

His expression hardened and his jaw tensed. He lifted his hand and she flinched. But he only ran his knuckles lightly down her left cheek. ''Was it my title or my fortune you were after when you came in here with me? Or was it both you had designs upon when you pressed yourself so passionately against me? When you opened your mouth to me?''

Lucy sucked in a painful breath. In that moment she despised him. She truly did! She swallowed hard. ''I was merely curious, my lord. I wanted to know whether you would live up to the gossip circulating about you.''

He smiled. ''And do I?''

Her eyes spat daggers at him. ''Oh, yes. You are in every sense the *bastard* earl.'' Then not waiting for his response, she whirled and fairly ran from the room, for the safety of the ballroom and the security of other people around her.

But she was neither safe nor secure, she feared as she searched out Valerie, who was dancing a schottische now with a Mr. Clarence Hopkins. For the moment she might have had the last word, but she was not done with Ivan Thornton. Nor he with her, she fretted.

The rest of the evening proved to be exhausting. She was asked repeatedly to dance—an unheard-of occurrence for a woman who was supposed to be chaperoning one of the season's young ladies. She was hard-pressed to turn the offers down—as Ivan must have known. It was he who'd engineered the offers, she quickly realized. For whenever she was occupied, he made it a point to pay court to Lady Valerie. He and his friends kept a constant circle around her, monopolizing her attention and discouraging any others from approaching her. And every time Lucy tried to get to her young charge, she was intercepted by one or the other of Ivan's cohorts.

First the rake claimed a dance, Alexander Blackburn, who was rumored to be one of Prinny's bastards. He was charming and a very good dancer, but she could not enjoy his company when Ivan was across the way, working his wiles on poor Valerie.

Giles Dameron whirled her around the floor next. He was not so easy a conversationalist, and a trifle less graceful at the waltz, but oh, he was a handsome man. But not handsome enough to erase her worries. As she watched, Valerie actually smiled at something Ivan said, and her heart sank.

She glanced desperately around for Lady Westcott, hoping she would intercede. She spied the older woman sitting with Lord Dunleith and Lady McClendon, watching the gaiety, and that caused her heart to sink even further. She'd been correct in her suspicions about Lady Westcott, to her bitter disappointment. The countess was observing the little circle that included Ivan and Valerie, and she did not look in the least displeased.

So why had she told Lucy to protect Valerie from Ivan? The answer was so obvius Lucy groaned. To provoke his interest, of course. To create a challenge he could not resist. Obviously it had worked.

But why had he bothered to kiss a chaperone?

Because he saw every woman as a challenge, she decided. Because he'd had a miserable childhood and was taking it out on everyone.

Or perhaps it was because he'd had so little love all those years that he sought it now in the arms of every woman he met. That was not really love, however. Only how could he know that?

She frowned, unsettled by this new possibility. She refused to feel a moment's sympathy for him. He certainly felt no sympathy for anyone else. Still, she could not shake the image of a frightened dark-haired little boy from her mind. How would Stanley or Derek withstand the fear and sorrow of being so unceremoniously thrust into a strange place and left there for over ten years? How would anyone be expected to react?

She was grateful when the dance ended, but when she looked around, Valerie was nowhere to be seen. Then the music started up again and the final third of Ivan's dubious friends showed up, requesting a turn about the floor with her.

"Thank you, Mr. Pierce. I'm flattered. But I fear I'm sadly out of practice with such exercise. I'm quite out of breath after my dance with Mr. Dameron."

"I assure you, Miss Drysdale, that you will not have to work nearly so hard at dancing with me as you did with Dameron."

"He is a more-than-competent dancer."

"I am better," he stated with a roguish grin. "Though perhaps not so talented as is Thornton."

Just then Lucy spied Valerie—with her head bent close to Ivan's—and she gritted her teeth.

Following the angle of her gaze, Mr. Pierce laughed. "You worry overmuch about your young charge, at least insofar as Thornton is concerned."

Lucy slanted him a look. Next to Ivan, he was the one of the four bastards, as they were beginning to be called, who most unsettled her. Mr. Dameron was unnervingly handsome; Mr. Blackburn was unnervingly wry. Neither of them, however, frightened her. Not that Mr. Pierce frightened her precisely. It was more that there was an aura of danger about him, as if dark undercurrents churned beneath his suave, smiling exterior. At least she knew something of the past that had molded Ivan. Of Elliot Pierce she knew nothing.

"Why shouldn't I be worried?" she asked, forcing herself back to the subject of Valerie.

He shrugged. "He will pursue her. Catch her. Then throw her back, as he has all the others."

"Yes. And she will have a broken heart by then. I prefer to protect her from such unnecessary pain. He does it only to feed his monstrous ego," she added, though she suspected it was more likely a monstrous vulnerability he was protecting. No matter which it was, however, Valerie would be the one hurt. Her duty was to see that didn't happen.

"He is a good man," Mr. Pierce said, surprising her with the simplicity of his words.

"I'm sure he treats his friends well," she conceded. "It's his behavior toward women which concerns me. In particular his behavior toward Lady Valerie. If you'll excuse me, Mr. Pierce, I must go to her before he deliberately ruins her reputation."

But he caught her arm before she could leave. His face was intent when he spoke. "What if his intentions were sincere? Would you object to him then?"

Lucy paused. "If he were sincere, not only in his intentions but also in his affections for her, then no, I would not object. But that is all conjecture, for we both know he's *not* sincere. Nor does he feel a jot of true affection for her.''

She thought that would anger him, but his expression revealed nothing. ''What if I or one of the others of our group paid suit to her—untitled bastards all. How would you react if one of us felt true affection for her?''

His eyes fairly burned into hers, and again she hesitated. Was he declaring his own intentions toward Valerie? Somehow she didn't see the two of them together.

She cleared her throat and picked her words carefully. ''I could not in all fairness encourage the suit of a man—even a man I personally approved of—knowing that her family would turn him away. I am only her chaperone. It falls to her godmother and her parents to give their consent.''

''And they would never agree to an alliance with me or Alex or Giles.''

She gave him an apologetic look. ''I rather doubt it.''

''But they wouldn't mind Thornton for a son-in-law.''

''I suspect that they would be ecstatic,'' she answered honestly.

''And yet you would discourage his intentions, even though they would approve.'' He shook his head. ''Let me be sure I understand. You will go along with them when they disapprove a suitor, but you countermand them with a suitor they *do* approve of. It appears you attend to only one half of your responsibilities, Miss Drysdale.''

Lucy shifted on her feet, uncomfortable with the truth of his words. She tried to explain. ''I take my duties very seriously, Mr. Pierce. I am well aware that while two people may appear eminently suitable, they may, in truth, be terribly mismatched. I am also well aware of the limits to my sphere of influence. Though I am reasonably certain I can sway Valerie should she venture in an unwise direction, I am hardly optimistic about my abilities to do the same with her family.'' She frowned at him, frustrated by the situation she was in, and frustrated, as well, at having to explain herself to him. She squared her shoulders and met his amused gaze. ''To put it plainly, I do my duty to Valerie first, then to her family. Now if you will excuse me, I must find my charge.''

Ivan sauntered into the ballroom at the same moment Lucy tore away from Elliot. She was in high dudgeon, he noted, if her color was any indication. She and Elliot hadn't been dancing, for the music yet continued and anyway they hadn't been on the dance floor. So why had they been together? And what had he said to her to put that hot stain on her cheeks?

Ivan's fists tightened. Had he embarassed her with his attentions, or even insulted her? The fact that Elliot's eyes followed her troubled Ivan even further. Elliot Pierce was not the right man for a woman like Lucy Drysdale. Elliot Pierce was not the right man for any woman, if his past history was any indication.

He tore his eyes away from his friend, and watched Lucy make a circuit of the room, obviously searching for Valerie. Perhaps he should go and put her mind at ease. Why he would want to do that he did not want to examine too closely. Not five minutes ago he'd stolen a very chaste kiss from his pretty cousin. If there had been even the least chance he was interested in her, that brief kiss had killed it. For he'd contrasted that kiss to the ones he'd shared with her spinster chaperone and Valerie had lost out sorely in the comparison.

He caught up with Lucy near the punch table. ''She is closeted in an upstairs bedroom,'' he whispered in her ear. ''You'd better get there before she comes to any serious harm.''

She whirled about so fast he had to catch her by the shoulders lest she be completely overset. Her green eyes blazed, shooting sparks of absolute fury at him.

''What have you done to her?'' she hissed, pulling him away from the table, to a more private spot in the hall. Her grip on his wrist was strong and determined, and warm. Very warm. ''If you have hurt her in any way—''

''She is not hurt—though I would not put it past the old witch to threaten her with bodily harm.''

He grinned when his words began to sink in. Her expressive features lost their fury and turned wary instead.

"Lady Westcott has her? But why?"

He shrugged, but he was vitally aware her hand still circled his wrist. "She has a nasty habit of manipulating other people's lives. Unfortunately, it seems it's Valerie's turn."

"Blast," she muttered. Then, as if just then realizing she still had a hold on him, she yanked her hand away.

"Burns, doesn't it?"

He had his answer when her cheeks turned bright pink. "Where are they?" she demanded to know.

"Are you asking me to escort you upstairs, Miss Drysdale? Perhaps you don't understand the seriousness of such an action, for I would most certainly be pressured to marry you were we to be discovered slipping away from the party to go abovestairs together."

If possible her cheeks burned even more scarlet. The fact that she wore her emotions so near the surface pleased him to no end. But despite those emotions she was like a determined dog with a bone she refused to let go. "Just tell me where she is."

He grinned. "Take these stairs and try either of the two wings. I expect the old bag's voice will guide you to them."

She turned and hurried up the steps, not bothering even to thank him. Ivan stood at the base of the stairs, watching her anxious departure, especially the way her hips swayed with each step.

He wanted to follow her up those stairs and into one of those rooms, then lock the door and lose himself in her. "Bloody hell," he swore when he felt the unseemly rise of his manhood. It had been a good while since he'd reacted so strongly to any female—and never to one who disliked him so much.

But it wasn't really dislike, he told himself. They'd just started off on the wrong foot. He'd gone a long way today toward correcting the poor first impression she'd had of him, if her reaction to their kiss was any gauge. Perhaps later tonight he would find out if he could go all the way and reverse her opinion of him entirely.

Why he would want to do that gave him pause. He didn't need her to approve of him. He didn't care whether she liked him or not. The fact that she desired him should be enough, for of all the emotions women were said to possess, lust was the only one he trusted. Lust could not be long hidden, nor could a woman pretend to desire a man when she did not. She might moan and groan and wriggle about in a show of enthusiasm, as prostitutes were wont to do. But a discerning man could tell the difference. And he was a discerning man.

Miss Lucy Drysdale had experienced lust for him tonight, and that was enough for him. Love, honor, honesty. Those emotions existed rarely in the human soul—and never in a female's. A mother's love was easily traded for gold coin. A grandmother's caring was no more than despicable self-interest.

His face darkened in a frown as he watched Lucy disappear into the second-floor hall. No, he didn't care at all what the tart Miss Drysdale felt for him, save for lust. And he meant to explore the depths of that lust during the coming weeks. He meant to explore it in great detail.

Lucy felt the weight of Ivan's stare as she hurried up the stairs. Impossible man! What was he up to now? Then, as he'd said she would, she heard their voices—or rather, Lady Westcott's voice. It was clear, when Lucy burst into a green and burgundy sitting room, that Valerie had not uttered even a word during her godmother's tirade.

". . . they are bastards, and worse than that, they are penniless!" the old woman ranted. Then she spied Lucy and her invective turned from cowering girl to errant chaperone. "What are you thinking, Miss Drysdale, to allow her to be surrounded by that swarm of unsuitable young men?"

Lucy had been besieged all evening. First by Ivan. Then by his friends, one by one. Lady Westcott's unfair criticism snapped the fragile limits of her control.

"Those unsuitable young men, as you describe them, are

your grandson's friends. And while they are indeed bastards, they are not without prospects. One could very well be recognized as a prince someday. Another, though of the merchant class, was raised a gentleman and, I am told, has amassed a considerable fortune of his own.'' She'd learned those facts about Mr. Blackburn and Mr. Dameron through the grapevine. Of Mr. Pierce she knew nothing, save that he spared no expense on his clothing and horses. But there was Ivan too, and she decided it was time to end this game of cat and mouse her employer had been playing.

"The fact is, Lady Westcott, if you wish to pair Valerie with Ivan, she will have to be pleasant to his friends."

Lady Westcott straightened to her full height and glared at Lucy. "Perhaps you heard my instructions incorrectly, Miss Drysdale. I told you to *prevent* a match between Ivan and Valerie."

Lucy crossed her arms over her chest. "Yes, I am quite clear on what you *said.* I'm referring, however, to what you *meant.*"

Across the span of the overdone room their eyes held as they each took the other's measure. Lady Westcott, ever the shrewd manipulator, grasped the head of her cane and sniffed. "I would have an audience with you tomorrow, Miss Drysdale. Ten o'clock in my private quarters. Meanwhile I encourage you to decline vigorously any further offers to dance and keep a closer watch on Valerie." Then she turned and stalked from the room, regal even though Lucy had just trounced her.

Of course, this had been merely a skirmish. As anger fled and more rational emotions returned, Lucy realized that Lady Westcott could very well dismiss her in the morning—and probably would. Then who would have trounced whom?

Feeling suddenly quite defeated, Lucy looked over at Valerie. Tears streamed down the girl's face, but instead of sympathy, Lucy felt only annoyance. If Valerie was to survive in society—both the duration of this season, and the rest of her life as some lord or another's wife—she had better stiffen her backbone.

"Dry your tears," she instructed, though more charitably than she actually felt. "You will find weeping a poor defense in life. Strong will and a determined direction will serve you far better. Come," she added. "Sit down a moment and compose yourself."

"But I don't understand," Valerie wailed. "I was having a rather nice time. I know they are not the sort of fellows my parents want for me, but this is my very first dance. I didn't know—" She broke off and dabbed at her eyes with her handkerchief. "And what of Lord Westcott? *Does* she wish to pair us? You know I cannot, not with him, Miss Drysdale. You *must* help me!"

She began to cry again, this time in great hiccuping sobs that tore at Lucy's heartstrings and made her feel horribly guilty. Valerie was a middle child, she reminded herself. She'd been shaped into the timid creature she was by her demanding siblings and overwhelmed parents. It did no good to berate her for being the way she was. Better for Lucy to put her energy toward helping the girl develop her own strengths.

But as she comforted Valerie, reassuring her and helping her to repair her ravaged face, Lucy was mindful of her own plight. Tomorrow's interview with Lady Westcott could very well signal the end of her sojourn in London. She had better think fast or she would be back in Somerset before the week was out.

Then what would happen?

Valerie would very likely be browbeaten by Lady Westcott into a miserable match.

As for herself, she would miss attending Sir James's lectures. She would lose her chance to meet the one man whose intellectual nature seemed suited to her own. She would never know if they might have formed an attachment, for she would be confined to Houghton Manor, playing governess to Graham's rowdy brood for the rest of her life while her brain rotted from boredom.

Meanwhile, Ivan Thornton would go on his merry way, the only one unaffected by this whole mess. A spurt of righteous anger fired her blood. It always came back to Ivan Thornton.

Tomorrow morning she would have to remind Lady Westcott about that. Her grandson's disdain of his grandmother was at the root of the old woman's scheming. If the dowager countess wanted to obtain her goals, whatever they might be, she would have to begin thinking of Lucy, not as a tool to be manipulated, but as an ally.

Lucy didn't have a clue, however, of how she was to convince the old woman of that.

Eight

*L*ucy awoke before dawn. This was becoming an unfortunate habit, she fretted as she tossed about, fluffing up her pillow in an attempt to get comfortable. She wanted to go back to sleep, for she'd gone to bed very late, mere hours ago.

She turned to her other side, then winced when her plait caught beneath her shoulder. That didn't help the nagging headache that had plagued her last evening and had not dissipated at all while she'd slept.

She let out a frustrated sigh and stared up at the pleated satin lining of the tall canopied bed. Why was she awake? There had been no ring of carriage wheels on the pavement outside. Ivan Thornton was not bidding some tart farewell at the front door.

She grimaced. *Be fair, Lucy.* Even he would not bring a common tart into his home. Still, the sort of loose woman he'd had here that other night was not much better than a common tart, only better dressed.

"Blast," she swore, punching the innocent down-filled pillow. The troublesome Ivan Thornton might not have awakened her with his nighttime escapades, but he was, nevertheless, the cause of her sleeplessness.

Why had he kissed her?

Why had she become so undone by that kiss?

And why, *why* had she returned his kiss so passionately?

As if that disaster were not enough for one evening, she'd then careened right into another one. Whatever had she been thinking, to challenge Lady Westcott that way? And in front of Valerie, no less?

She groaned and pulled the pillow over her head. For someone anxious to remain in London, she certainly was going out of her way to ensure she would be sent packing, right back to the boring environs of Houghton Manor.

Somewhere she heard a cock crow—not a sound she would have expected in London. Flinging the pillow aside, she stared again at the precisely gathered fabric that lined the bed overhang above her head. She might as well rise. Perhaps a turn in the garden would ease her aching head and calm her rattled nerves. Besides, she needed to be at her sharpest when she met with Lady Westcott this morning. If she were to undo the damage she'd done last night, she would have to engage the wily old woman's imagination.

She dressed quickly, in an everyday dress, plain slippers, and a knitted shawl wound around her shoulders. Then, sans gloves and with her hair still in its untidy nighttime coiffure, she slipped into the silent hall, made her way down the back stairs, and let herself out the service entrance.

The breeze carried a light chill, with the faint fragrance of coal smoke in the air. My, but Londoners were extravagant, she decided. Heating their houses on so mild a night. At home Graham would turn out the servant who dared to light a fire on such a night.

She strolled across the gravel drive toward the box garden that extended between the two back wings of the house. On one side the library flanked it. On the other the morning room. A pair of silvered garden benches sat opposite one another with a sundial positioned between them. The benches were too damp to sit on, however. So instead of sitting, Lucy meandered through the shadowy garden, fingering an unfurling fern frond, gathering dew from the cupped petals of a rose.

She breathed deeply, and exhaled, then loosened her hair from its confining plait. Massaging the back of her neck, she tried to banish the nagging ache buried deep in her head. She luxuriated in the dim quiet of the garden, the moist feel of the spring dawn against her skin and the fragrant peace of its stillness surrounding her. But she could not entirely control her churning thoughts.

What was she to do about Lady Westcott? How was she to dissuade the dowager countess from packing her off to Somerset?

Then a hinge creaked, Lucy looked up, and the morning peace was shattered.

"You're up early. Or is it late?"

Lucy wasn't certain whether her heart sank at the sight of Ivan or soared. There was no arguing, however, that its pace increased tenfold.

Why was he here? And why now?

"I woke early," she answered at last, watching his tall, broad-shouldered silhouette approach. "Why are you up and about at such an hour?"

He stopped on the opposite side of the sundial, near enough that she could begin to make out his features. He had a half-smile on his face. "I was having dreams. Erotic dreams. What's your excuse?"

"Certainly not that!" she answered without thinking. But an unpleasantly honest voice in her head said otherwise. Perhaps her thoughts had not been erotic in the fullest sense of the word, but that was only because she was not experienced enough to imagine anything completely erotic. But she *had* been thinking of Ivan, and of their kiss and the way it had made her feel.

"You wound me terribly, Lucy, for I was certain our—"

"Don't call me Lucy! I haven't given you leave to be so familiar."

"Your enthusiastic participation in our kiss seemed rather familiar to me. Or were you simply toying with my affections?" he added, giving her that charming half grin of his.

Lucy's heart pounded so violently that her chest began to hurt. "You are deliberately misconstruing everything and you know it."

He moved to his left, following the path around toward her. At once Lucy moved left too, trying to keep the ornate sundial between them. "If you have come here to irritate me, then I shall be forced to leave," she warned.

"Does that mean you will stay if my goal is *not* to irritate you? For I assure you, Lucy, that irritating you is the very *last* thing on my mind."

"You see? You see? You're doing it again! You're saying these . . . these suggestive things. You're calling me Lucy when I've told you not to. And you're stalking me like some great beast of prey!"

He let out a noisy sigh and shook his head as if dismayed. But at least he stopped the stalking. Only then did she notice how casually he was dressed, with neither coat nor vest to cover his shirt. Nor did he wear a neckcloth. His collarless shirt was open at the throat and even in the first light of the shadowy dawn she could see the dark curls revealed by the deeply cut neckline.

With his long hair in as much disarray as his clothing, and that damnable diamond in his left ear, he looked every bit the Gypsy he'd been born, a dark and dangerous man who set every one of her senses aflame.

But she must take charge of those wayward senses of hers, she reminded herself. And the best way to do that was not to let him control the situation.

"Did you find the McClendons' soiree enjoyable?" she asked, deciding to keep the conversation strictly superficial. *You should go inside and end this conversation entirely,* a voice in her head scolded. But the rebellious part of her soul chose to ignore that voice.

"Enjoyable? 'Entertaining' might be a more accurate word."

"Well, at least you took some pleasure of the evening."

"Pleasure indeed," he replied. His eyes moved over her,

taking in the wild abundance of her loosened hair, her bare arms, and her casually clad form.

Was he remembering their kiss? Had he taken as much pleasure from it, after all, as had she?

Lucy pulled her shawl tighter. But that did nothing to counter the riot of emotions his murmured words and vivid gaze roused within her. It was not working, these feeble efforts to control her reaction to him. Her very skin seemed to tighten in his presence and become incredibly sensitive when he turned his attention on her.

"I believe I shall return to my chambers," she murmured, hugging her arms close about her as she backed away from him.

"Are you cold?" Before she could react he came around the sundial and its encircling bed of moss roses.

Lucy wanted to turn tail and run. She wanted to rush into his arms and have him take her in a bruising embrace. Thankfully the one sane part left of her brain prevented her from reacting in either of those disastrous fashions.

But simply standing there, waiting for his approach, seemed equally disastrous.

He stopped just before her, then reached out to her.

Lucy caught her breath. She swayed toward him and very nearly closed her eyes in anticipation of his kiss.

But he didn't kiss her. He pulled the folds of her shawl up closer to her neck and tugged it up to better cover her chest. Then his hands fell away from her. He remained standing in the same place though, closer than was proper, but not so close as to be entirely improper either.

But propriety was more than a matter of proximity, as his next words so rudely proved. "I know a much better way to keep warm than with an uninspiring shawl."

She was already warm, but she would never reveal that to him. "I'm sure you do, my lord. However . . . However, I find this shawl perfectly adequate to my needs."

"And what needs are those, Lucy? You are approaching thirty, an age which will brand you forever a spinster, the dried-up maiden aunt to your brother's children. Are you telling me you have no needs as yet unmet?''

''I really do not wish to continue this conversation. If you will excuse me?'' She pushed past him on the path and marched for the servants' entrance she'd used before. Only ten more steps, she told herself. Nine more. Eight. Seven.

He caught her just three paces from the door. He snatched up the end of her shawl and gave it a sharp tug, and she, most unwisely, turned and tried to pull it out of his hold.

''Let go,'' she demanded, refusing to cower before him.

''And if I don't?'' He grinned the devil's own grin.

''I am not about to be drawn into this silly game you play, Lord Westcott.''

''Call me Ivan.''

''Perhaps I should call you John,'' she said, suddenly remembering how the English version of his name had angered him when his grandmother had used it. But if it angered him now, he hid it well.

''Ivan, John. My love,'' he suggested in a mocking tone. ''So long as you breathe the word warmly in my ear, I don't care which name you use.'' He leaned nearer as he spoke, slowly gathering her poor shawl in his hands.

Lucy couldn't help it; she panicked. She didn't mean to. Indeed, showing him how he so thoroughly unnerved her was the very *last* thing she wished to do. But she couldn't stop herself.

With a cry of dismay, she let go of the shawl—the thin wool triangle she'd crocheted when she was fourteen—and did what she should have done when she'd first seen him in the garden. What she should have done the very first time she'd laid eyes on him and his Gypsy's power of seduction. She turned and she ran.

Antonia watched Miss Drysdale's hasty exit from the garden with considerable interest. Ivan didn't follow her, to Antonia's vast disappointment. But that disappointment faded as she continued to observe him. For he stared a long while at the door the girl had disappeared through. Then he drew the shawl up to his face and held it there.

Breathing in the scent of her, Antonia would wager. A satisfied grin broke across her face. He wanted the outspoken chit. Her plan was working.

She let the heavy drape fall back in place and crossed to the door. Ivan wanted Lucy Drysdale. But did Miss Drysdale want him?

Time to find out.

When she heard the muffled sound of hasty footsteps in the hall she pushed open her door.

"Why, Miss Drysdale," she said, feigning surprise. "What are you doing up so early? I thought it was only the aged who rose at this ungodly hour." Then she let her gaze run over the startled girl, and she forced herself to frown. "Have you been out somewhere? Is something afoot? Something I would not approve of?"

"No. No, it's . . . it's nothing like that. I . . . I couldn't sleep and so I thought . . . I thought a turn in the garden might help."

"It's chilly outside. You ought to have brought a shawl to keep you warm."

"Yes. Yes, I . . . I ought to have," the girl stammered. "I'm sorry if I disturbed you, my lady. If you'll excuse me?"

Antonia waved her hand in dismissal. "Don't forget. My sitting room. Ten o'clock."

Miss Drysdale nodded then without further word slipped into her room and softly shut the door.

Well, well, and very well, Antonia thought as she let herself back into her own room. She crossed to the window and looked down at the garden again, but Ivan was gone. So was the shawl, however, and that brought a chuckle to her lips.

Really, but she hadn't enjoyed a season in town this much since her own season, when she'd fallen so desperately in love with Gerald Thornton. It had been wonderful and terrible and exhilarating, as she recalled. Wonderful to discover such intense feelings inside her. Terrible to think they might not be reciprocated. Exhilarating to learn they were.

Which phase of those feelings was Miss Drysdale experiencing now? The terrible part, she suspected. And Ivan? Her satisfaction faded just a bit. Was Ivan in the wonderful phase, for surely he recognized the effect he had on Miss Drysdale? Or was he merely stalled in the lustful stage? She would have to be very careful lest he suspect her plan.

As for Miss Drysdale, they would have their little talk later this morning. But no matter which way their discussion turned, one thing was certain: Lucy Drysdale would be placed squarely between Ivan and Valerie, a position which would afford him plenty of opportunity to discover the wonderful feelings of love. For it was love which would catch him most securely, she'd decided.

Still, if love didn't quite do it, she was certain lust would. It had only to push him far enough for it to result in marriage. And result in a child.

Lucy knocked at Lady Westcott's door promptly at the tenth chime of the long clock down the hall. Had ever a day started so badly? Then again, had ever an evening gone so badly as last evening? This morning was no more than an extension of last night, both of which fiascoes were directly attributable to none other than his lordship, the Earl of Westcott. Even her sleeplessness could be charged directly to his account.

And now she must try somehow to appease his difficult grandmother, her difficult employer. For two people so at odds with one another, grandmother and grandson were certainly cut from the same cloth: intelligent, devious, and arrogant in the extreme. They deserved one another, she decided, tugging in irritation at the embroidered trim of her waist.

"Come in." Lady Westcott's autocratic voice carried clearly through the heavy door.

Lucy let herself in and found her employer seated in a

sunny corner of her sitting room, a silver tray of hot chocolate and muffins perched on a painted folding table before
her. The older woman waved Lucy to a seat opposite her,
then gestured to the tray. "Have you had breakfast, Miss
Drysdale?"

"Yes," Lucy lied. Her stomach had been far too knotted
to eat anything. It still was. "Perhaps we should just get
on with it," she said, deciding that forthrightness served
her best. "I gather you are displeased with my performance
as Lady Valerie's chaperone. On my own behalf I must tell
you that I am equally displeased with your performance as
my employer."

Lady Westcott halted in the act of lifting a cup of hot
chocolate to her lips. She stared at Lucy over the rim of
the Sevres china. "My performance as your employer?"
Her thin brows rose so high her forehead creased in a mul-
titude of parallel furrows. "Tell me, Miss Drysdale, are you
deliberately attempting to have yourself dismissed?"

Lucy could have groaned out loud. She had a wretched
habit of going on the offensive whenever she was put on
the defensive. It worked with snarling dogs, unpleasant
children, and tipsy boors. But it was the wrong tack to take
with autocratic dowager countesses.

"No, milady. I most heartily do not wish to lose my
position in your household. You must admit, however, that
you have not been entirely honest with me."

Now *there* was a huge improvement in attitude, she immediately castigated herself. Accuse the woman of lying.

Lady Westcott's reaction, however, was to shrug, then
take a long sip of her chocolate. "I withheld some aspects
of my intentions from you," she admitted. "I thought it
would lend your performance more authenticity if you truly
believed I did not wish a union between my grandson and
my godchild."

"They are not at all suited to one another."

The old woman studied Lucy a long moment before an-
swering. "Had I known you were a secret romantic I would
not have hired you, Miss Drysdale, though I see now that

all the signs were there. You are not a spinster because no one would have *you* but because *you* would have no one. Were you waiting for love to strike you, silly girl? It seldom works that way, you know. Not in society, anyway.''

A week ago Lucy would have laughed off such a suggestion. Now the woman's words made her wince. Once again her defense was to go on the offensive. ''Did you hate being married so much that you would inflict such an unhappy existence on all the young people of your family?''

That roused the woman, Lucy plainly saw. Lady Westcott's placid blue eyes swiftly turned a snapping ice-blue.

''I was one of the lucky ones, miss. In ten generations of the Westcott family there has not been so fortuitous a match as my own.''

It was Lucy's turn to stare at the older woman. ''Then why would you mismatch Ivan and Valerie? Why would you employ me to keep her from him, knowing it would cause him to pursue her all the harder?''

''Because he does not know his own mind.'' Lady Westcott set down her cup. ''If he were but to single out an acceptable young woman—*any* acceptable young woman—and focus on her long enough to actually come to know her, he might finally find what he needs.''

''And what is it you think he needs?''

Antonia met Miss Drysdale's skeptical gaze with a sincere expression firmly in place. Inside, however, she was congratulating herself. Really, but she could have made a glorious career on the stage. While Miss Drysdale did not agree with what she'd said, she did believe her motives. Time for the *coup de grâce.*

''What my grandson needs is someone to love him. Someone he can love in return.'' Though she said the words to move the girl's emotions, Antonia realized, even as she spoke them, that they were true. ''He does not believe that, of course. I doubt he believes in love at all. But it's what he needs.''

Miss Drysdale's skepticism had faded. She leaned for-

ward with an earnest expression. "Don't you think he's
better able to find the right person for himself than you
are?"

"But he's not looking for her," Antonia scoffed. "Don't
you see? It's only by denying him access to Valerie that
he will ever take the time to do more than dance with her,
flatter her, and steal a kiss or two from her. That's his
pattern with women. If I can just slow him down a bit,
make him work harder to charm her, I believe she can sink
her hooks in him."

"But she doesn't want to sink her hooks in him."

Antonia waved one hand dismissively. "She is a pliable
child. I told you that before. In time she will come to love
him. For now it is sufficient that she be terrified of him."

They stared at one another over the silver tray with its
pitcher of hot milk and melted chocolate, its twin bowls of
strawberry preserves and creamy butter, and its delicate
plate of muffins. Then Miss Drysdale stood up and Lady
Westcott's heart nearly stopped.

"Under the circumstances I do not believe I can continue
to act as Lady Valerie's chaperone. As soon as you can find
a suitable replacement for me, I will depart the premises."

"You cannot!" Antonia surprised both herself and the
stubborn Miss Drysdale with the vehemence of her response. She had lurched to her feet. She forced herself now
to sit down.

"I cannot believe you would prefer to rot in Somerset
the whole summer through, and all because we do not agree
on the right woman for my grandson."

"You have it quite wrong, Lady Westcott. I have no
opinion or interest in the right woman for your grandson.
You hired me to help Lady Valerie secure a good marriage.
'Tis her well-being I care for. If you wanted me to find a
suitable mate for your grandson, you should have informed
me of that fact long ago."

"Perhaps I should have," Antonia snapped, impatient
with the direction this conversation was taking. Damn the
girl for being too smart, too forward, and too cheeky by

half. "Is there anyone you *would* recommend for the position of his wife?"

It was a facetious question, of course. But the fact that the troublesome young woman across from her hesitated, as if giving it serious thought, heartened Antonia. Miss Drysdale wanted that role, she silently gloated. Oh, the chit might not be ready to admit it, even to herself. But Antonia knew it was so.

"All right. All right, Miss Drysdale," she said, waving one hand as if in defeat. "Have it your way. Keep Ivan away from her, if you must. Find my godchild a more suitable fellow—suitable to her temperament. But allow me this much. Should Ivan come around a bit, and should Valerie display any interest in him, you will not discourage her. Agreed?"

"I don't believe she will," Miss Drysdale warned.

"Perhaps not. But I'll want your word that you will not try to unduly influence her should she warm up to him."

For a long, nerve-wracking moment the girl did not respond and Antonia fought back the urge to give her a good shake. Finally the chit nodded. "Very well. I'll try to keep an open mind."

"One other thing," Antonia said, hiding her relief. "Since you have ruined my plans for Ivan, you must make up for it."

"Make up for it?" The younger woman's eyes narrowed in suspicion. "And how, precisely, am I to do that?"

Antonia shrugged. "Keep your eyes open. Tell me if he shows any particular interest in one of this year's crop of young misses."

"You want me to find a wife for him?" Miss Drysdale stared at her in disbelief.

"I wouldn't put it that way. You needn't *find* him a wife. As you said, he will probably find one far better than I can. I only wish to speed up the process a bit. Are we agreed?"

The hardheaded creature wanted to say no. Antonia could see that plain enough. Though the chit tried to hide the struggle going on inside her, she was not entirely successful. Thank heaven she was so loath to return to the country. In the end, however, Miss Drysdale sighed.

"We are agreed," she answered in a tight voice.

They were agreed also on who that future wife was to be, Antonia thought. Miss Drysdale just didn't know it yet.

Nine

The modiste and her several assistants came at eleven. Lucy made a brief appearance in the morning room to exclaim appropriately over the vast array of fabric bolts. Silks, muslins, sateens. Feathers and netting; buttons and braids. After narrowing the colors for Valerie's wardrobe to blues, whites, pinks, and a stunning silvery-gray, Lucy made her excuses, then made her escape.

Lady Westcott was footing the bill for Valerie's extravagant wardrobe; Lucy thought it only appropriate that she select the patterns and decide on the dresses themselves. She was just thankful the dowager countess had allowed her this reprieve.

She'd just narrowly missed being sent back to the drowning tedium of Somerset, and though she still didn't entirely trust her erstwhile employer, she'd been reminded rather pointedly just how precarious her position here was. She needed to take every advantage of her time in town—including searching for another position once this one ended in the fall.

At the moment, however, she needed to think about this evening's lecture, about how she should approach Sir James after his talk was finished, and what she should say to him. She prayed she would be less addlepated in his presence than she'd been in Ivan Thornton's.

Now why was she thinking about *him*? The last thing

she needed was to think about Ivan Thornton and everything that had happened last night—and this morning.

Hurrying up the stairs, she slipped into her bedchamber to fetch her bonnet and don her spencer before she went out. She meant to take a walk in Berkeley Square to compose her thoughts. When she spied the neatly wrapped box lying on her bed, however, she came to a quick halt.

A box. On her bed.

Her heart began to race. Ivan. She was sure of it.

It made no sense, this certainty she felt. It was completely illogical. But logical and Ivan didn't belong in the same sentence, she feared. Not where she was concerned, anyway.

She approached the box slowly. *He's not going to pop out of it,* she chastised herself when she reached a trembling hand toward it. It was no doubt her shawl, returned to her, albeit in a rather grandiose manner.

But it was not the shawl, at least not the old one she'd worn for more than ten years. This shawl was an exquisite piece of work, heavy silk with the luster of sunlight in its luxuriant depths.

She ran her hand over it, over the cool sleek fabric and the rich silken fringe that edged it. It was absolutely beautiful—and it must have come very dear. Even the color, a deep teal-green shot through with threads of gold and silver, was perfect.

Unable to prevent herself, Lucy drew it out of the box and held it before her. There was no note, but it was from Ivan. Who else could it be from?

Lucy sighed and rubbed the incredibly soft fabric against her cheek. Why had he done this? He must know an unmarried woman could not accept such a personal gift from a man. Yet how was she to return it? To send it back to him through one of the servants would be to alert everyone in the household about what he'd done. But for her to return it privately would be too dangerous. The last thing she wished to do was go anywhere near his suite of rooms.

So what was she to do?

Against her better judgment Lucy swirled the exquisite garment around her shoulders, then arranged it just so and stared at herself in the dressing mirror in the corner. It brought out the gold highlights in her dark hair, and intensified her eyes to the same teal color. How could he have selected so perfect an item for her? When had he found the time to do so?

No, the better question was, why had he done it? Why hadn't he simply returned her old shawl? Why had he taken it in the first place?

Because he was perverse.

She whipped the gorgeous shawl off and flung it onto the bed. She would have to return it to him. He had to see that he could not continue to toy with her, as he did with all the other women of the ton. He could not manipulate her as if she were some impressionable young miss.

Indeed, she should intimate to him that he was being manipulated by his grandmother. Wouldn't that infuriate him! Unfortunately, it would also infuriate Lady Westcott, and Lucy was not willing to risk her stay in town merely for the satisfaction of enraging Ivan Thornton.

Gnawing the inside of one cheek, she stared at the shawl. She'd have to hide it somewhere, just until she could return it. If one of the maids saw the box, there would be talk.

Picking up a corner of the shawl between her thumb and forefinger, she laid it back in its box, replaced the top, and shoved the whole thing under the bed. She was not going to think about Ivan Thornton today. Absolutely not, she vowed as she shoved her arms into her hunter-green spencer, snatched up a bonnet of Dunstable straw, and tied the strings beneath her chin. She'd waited a long time to meet Sir James. She refused to let an arrogant Gypsy earl ruin this day for her.

Rummaging in one of her hatboxes, she retrieved the thin packet of letters she'd received from Sir James. She would go out into Berkeley Square Park, find a quiet bench, and reread all her idol's letters. She would reflect on her true purpose for being in London, and she would relegate the

Earl of Westcott to his rightful place in her life. He was a charming rake, a practiced seducer, and it behooved every young woman to learn how to deal with that sort. But to put any stock in his attentions was to play the utter fool—no matter how much one might sympathize with his awful childhood.

Ivan watched Miss Lucy Drysdale stride across the smoothly paved street and into the park that took up the center of the square. She wasn't wearing the shawl he'd sent her, not that he'd expected her to. Any other unattached female of his acquaintance would have worn it. Any other unattached female would have flaunted it before all of society and made sure everyone knew who'd given it to her.

But not Miss Lucy Drysdale.

Not Miss Lucy Drysdale who never minced but rather strode purposefully down the street. Who dressed like a spinster but kissed like a courtesan. Who could be the belle of any ball, but who would rather attend a musty old lecture.

He let the curtain fall then stared down at his nearly naked body. He was hard. Just watching the stubborn wench walk across the road and disappear into the shrubbery across the way had made him as hard as a green lad in the throes of his first love.

Only it wasn't love. Not for the green lad nor for himself. It was lust he felt for the bluestocking Miss Drysdale. Plain, uncomplicated lust.

"Your bath is ready," the manservant behind him intoned.

"Thank you. You may go," Ivan added. The last thing he needed was to remove the robe wrapped loosely around him and reveal his uncomfortable condition to the man acting as his valet. Not that the man would suspect the source of his arousal. Nonetheless, he preferred to keep his feelings private.

Too bad Lucy wasn't here to see what she had wrought.

The door clicked behind the servant and Ivan let out a harsh breath. Damn the wench!

He threw off the robe and stepped into the tub, then sank down into the steaming water. It was so hot it burned, but that didn't distract his wayward male member from its focus.

He should have called for a cold bath; maybe that would have diverted him from the prurient thoughts circulating in his head. But he doubted it. In the several days he'd spent whoring with Elliot, he'd not once been nearly so aroused as he was right now—and all on account of a woman not even in the same room with him; a woman most of society would think not a very good match for so wealthy a young lord as himself; a woman who was on the shelf, reduced to chaperoning more eligible young women.

Of all the women he'd met in town, she was by far the most interesting. Were he serious about marrying, she would head his list.

But he wasn't looking for marriage, not to her or anyone else. What he wanted—what he *needed*—was a more satisfying bed partner than his most recent company.

He closed his eyes, resting his head on the rolled edge of the tub. What he wouldn't give to have Lucy's slender hands soaping him down right now.

Of its own accord his right hand found his engorged member. The hot soapy water let his fingers slide erotically up and down. His fevered thoughts let him pretend the hand was smaller, and the stroke less urgent. He pictured her in the shawl he'd sent to her—and not a stitch on beneath the heavy silk. Her hair would be wild and loose about her shoulders, as it was this morning. Her legs would be long and bare below the rich silk fringe.

He let out a low groan and his hand moved faster. This was insanity, to lust after a damned bluestocking spinster when he could have any woman he wanted!

But lust he did, and as the water sloshed over the edges of the tub he succumbed to the frustration he felt.

Afterward he sat in the cooling water, sated and yet not

truly satisfied. It had been a poor second to what he truly wanted. But perhaps it would take the edge off his need for a while. The last thing he wanted to do was alert her to his desperate feelings.

But he would have to do something about this, he knew. Flirting with her was only making it worse. He needed to seduce the stubborn woman and be done with it. Once he'd had her he'd get over her. It had always been that way for him.

He took a slow breath then let it out. Time to be up and about. Time to get on with the day.

Time to take a brisk turn in Berkeley Square Park.

. . . their minds are like sponges, soaking up both the intentional and unintentional lessons we would teach them. They learn their alphabet and also how long they must scream in order to attract their parents' attention. They learn to count and do complicated mathematical computations, and how to compliment or threaten or otherwise manipulate the people around them. In short, there is far more to the whole education of the child than what is presented to him in the schoolroom.

Lucy stared at the words in the letter. What was that about mathematical computations? She reread the passage, concentrating this time. She'd had the same problem all morning. No matter how she tried to focus on Sir James's letters, her thoughts kept slipping away in other directions.

No, not directions, plural. Direction, singular. One direction only: to Ivan Thornton. Ivan the terrible. Ivan the troublesome. Ivan who tortured her thoughts and tortured her body.

With a frustrated sigh Lucy shifted on the hard park bench. Rhododendrons bloomed directly across the path from her, a brilliant mix of pink and white. The tall linden trees that marched single file around the edges of the park were in full leaf, green and vibrantly alive this brisk spring day. Cheeky sparrows and tiny finches quarreled in the oak tree just to her left, and a gray squirrel scampered by, pausing to stare hopefully in her direction.

But Lucy's mind was not on squirrels or birds, nor on flowers and trees. Ivan Thornton had placed a claim on every thought in her head, and he simply would not let her go.

Why was she allowing him to affect her so? She, who was usually so logical and in control, seemed ever to behave like a fool where he was concerned.

Logic. That was the key, she decided. Straightening up, she folded Sir James's letter and set the whole bundle of them aside. Instead of succumbing to emotion, she needed to remind herself of all the perfectly sound reasons Ivan was so unsuitable, as much for herself as for Valerie.

He was insincere. That was the main reason.

He was outrageous. From his outrageous earring to the outrageous gift he'd sent her.

He was far too rich for the likes of her, and far too good-looking as well. And he was eaten up with anger from his unhappy past.

She'd been doing very well with her logical assessments of his drawbacks, up until that last one. He was eaten up with anger, and justifiably so, for he'd apparently endured the most wretched and lonely childhood.

But then, had his earlier life in one of England's nomadic Gypsy bands been any better?

Lucy stared at the rhododendrons across the way without really seeing them. She'd never considered what sort of life Gypsies lived, especially Gypsy children. She suspected, however, that Gypsy parents must love their children every bit as much as did regular British citizens. Assuming that was so, it followed that no matter the circumstances of a child's upbringing, growing up loved was the most essential factor of all. Language, clothing, culture—even religion— were of lesser moment than the security of a family's love.

It was a bitter revelation to admit how much she took for granted her own family, and how critical and impatient she could be toward them. She vowed never to be so un-appreciative again.

But that did not alter by a jot her confusing feelings for Ivan. If he had been loved those first few years in his mother's care, how much crueler must the ensuing years have been for him.

"What I wouldn't give to decipher that frown between your eyes."

Lucy gasped. Her gaze shot to the tall man standing just before her. Ivan! Her face went immediately scarlet.

Why must she blush so readily? She did it in no one's presence but his. And why was he here?

"What were you thinking about?" he continued when she did not answer, but only stared stupidly at him. "Dare I hope your thoughts were of me?"

"No. No, I wasn't thinking of you. Anything but," she lied. Then thankfully, her muddled brains managed to right themselves and she drew herself up. "Are you following me?"

He smiled down at her, looking impossibly handsome in a dark blue coat with striped vest and casually tied stock. "As you know, I'm not one to sleep in. Like you, I find a turn in the park a good way to begin the day."

"I came here to be alone with my thoughts."

"And to reread old letters, it seems." He pointed to the packet she'd laid aside. "Love letters?"

"That's really none of your business," Lucy retorted. She reached for the letters and tucked them as casually as she could into her reticule. Unfortunately he chose to interpret her action as an invitation to sit beside her on the now vacant bench. Far too close beside her for her peace of mind.

She started to rise, but his gloved hand clamped down on her arm. Not a harsh or painful hold, but an unyielding one, just the same.

She stared down at his gloved hand and struggled to control the quick thundering of her heart. Slowly she raised her gaze to meet his. "You cannot continue this high-handed treatment of me. It is not proper and I will not allow it.''

He grinned. ''How will you prevent it?''

''For one, I plan to return that shawl you left in my room.''

''Someone left a shawl in your room?'' he replied with an innocent expression she could almost believe. Almost.

''Don't tease me. I shall return the shawl and expect you to give back my old shawl.'' She tried to pull her wrist out of his grasp with no success. ''Let me go, Lord Westcott,'' she demanded, determined not to let her sudden breathlessness show.

''Call me Ivan.''

''No.'' She tried to pull her arm away without success.

''In case I didn't mention it last night, you dance very well.''

''You did not come here to discuss dancing.''

''You kiss very well too. After our dance, I expected as much.''

Lucy drew as far away from him as she could manage. Could he hear the frantic tattoo of her heart as distinctly as she did? He'd remarked about the relationship between dancing and other, more passionate activities that night in the parlor when Valerie had played and they'd danced. There was no mistaking his meaning now.

She should slap him for his impertinence, just as she'd slapped him once before. Only he'd rattled her so completely she could not seem to react.

''Will you please release me?'' she demanded once more.

''Call me Ivan,'' he insisted.

Lucy looked away, clenching her teeth and fighting for control. Some battles were better conceded. Though she would rather it be cool-headed logic that ruled her decision, she knew it was actually rising panic. ''Let go of my arm. Ivan,'' she muttered, staring straight ahead.

''Say 'please,' '' he murmured from far too near her ear.

Her startled gaze swung around and collided with his

mocking one. ''Please,'' she breathed, without even knowing she'd spoken.

For a moment he did not comply and she had the fanciful thought that he meant to kiss her. Here. In broad daylight. In the middle of Berkeley Square Park.

When his hand slid away from her wrist, she was almost disappointed. Fortunately, when he broke his physical hold on her, it seemed to free her temper as well. Jumping to her feet, she gathered her fury around her like a protective shield.

''I'll thank you not to bully me again. I wish to have no discourse with you, Lord Westcott. Most certainly no private discourse.''

He lolled back on the bench, relaxed and yet dangerous, all at the same time. ''Discourse. What an interesting word. What if I wish to have private discourse with you, Lucy?''

Her eyes narrowed in outrage. How she wanted to bat him over the head with her reticule. ''Have you ever really considered the ramifications of that sort of behavior, Lord Westcott? I suspect you have not. Let's imagine for a moment that I allowed you to call me by my given name. That I called you by yours.''

''You can't say it even now, can you, Lucy?'' He grinned at her and her fury fairly trebled.

''Let's imagine I called you Ivan,'' she continued, but in a decidedly more husky tone. ''Ivan,'' she repeated, huskier still when she saw the undisguised hunger that sprang into his eyes.

''I might allow you to hold my hand as we sat on a park bench. I might even instigate a kiss instead of waiting for you to do so.''

He straightened up on the bench. She had his attention now.

''Of course, since you are the type to abandon a woman the moment you suspect you've caught her, it would behoove me not to give in too easily, wouldn't it? No, I should give in only a little, then pull away and wait for you to chase me once more.''

"Your game sounds delicious, my sweet Lucy. I wonder if you would plan to ever let me catch you."

"Oh, yes, my lord. Indeed I would. But only if I were sure others would catch us at the game as well. What is the point of the game for a woman, if not to snag a wealthy husband?" she finished with an arch smile.

He did not like that, if the glitter of his gaze was any indication. To his credit, however, his smile did not falter. "When I choose to seduce you, Lucy, I assure you, it will not be where we will be interrupted."

"When I choose to seduce you," she countered, "it will be where it will gain me the most good."

His lazy gaze swept over her, pausing briefly at her breasts and again at her lips. "You're seducing me now," he drawled in a voice meant to unnerve her. It very nearly did.

"Not enough witnesses," she quipped. Then she drew herself up. "Good day, Lord Westcott. You need not see me back to the house. I am quite able to find my way there unaided." Then she quit his presence and marched swiftly away.

She felt his eyes on her back, as if his fingers trailed boldly along her bare, prickling flesh. Even worse, that prickle managed somehow to arrow in on the most embarrassing portions of her body. Her nipples tautened to peaks, rubbing most distressingly against the fabric of her chemise. Her lower belly tightened too, and seemed to heat inside with a wicked little flame.

A flame of desire, she now knew, though no other man had ever lit it in her.

Curse your Gypsy soul for tormenting me so! If he were sincere in his pursuit of her it would be one thing. But he was not, and that nicked her pride sorely.

But two could play at this game of seduction, she vowed as she exited the park and headed straight for the house. He did not want to be caught any more than she did. So long as she reminded him of that fact, she would be safe.

At least she prayed that she would be safe.

Ivan knew he was grinning. Anyone who looked his way would no doubt be able to read his every thought. But for once he didn't care.

As unlikely as it seemed, Lucy Drysdale was the most intriguing woman he'd ever met. Had any other woman spoken to him of giving in, then pulling away, of instigating a kiss—of *her* seducing *him*—he would have been entertained and probably aroused. But he would have known that the game was won, save for the predictable capitulation.

With Lucy, however, the outcome was not nearly so foregone.

No, he amended, the outcome was certain. They would end up taking their complete pleasure of one another. He had absolutely no doubt of that. But when it would happen, and the delicious, unexpected twists and turns he would have to make to get her to that point, he could not begin to predict.

"Bloody hell!" Just thinking about the contrary Miss Drysdale had made him hard all over again. She was fighting her attraction to him and that was a more potent lure than all the unsubtle stares and silly attempts at fan language he'd witnessed in the past few months in town.

He shifted on the park bench, trying to find a more comfortable position, lest he embarrass himself. Taking a slow, deliberate breath, he forced himself to think of other things. He stared at several strollers who shared the square with him this morning. Two matrons meandered by, caught up in their gossip. A governess escorted a little boy and his dog. A gardener pruned an already perfectly shaped hedge.

Then Ivan's gaze returned to the boy. He was of indeterminate age, small with a shock of thick blond hair and wearing a lace collar and sleeves. He carried a stick which the little dog tried valiantly to snatch from him. But the governess interrupted their play with her fussing.

"You'll dirty your gloves," she warned him.

"You mustn't let him jump on you!" she scolded.

"If you don't behave we'll have to go home," she threatened.

The boy paused at that, allowing the disagreeable woman to catch up with him. At once she yanked the stick from his hand, snapped it in two, and threw the pieces in the rhododendrons just in front of Ivan. The dog, of course, plunged headlong into the shrubs, set on fetching the stick. Meanwhile the governess caught the boy by the arm and gave him a shake.

"If you're going to misbehave we shall return home."

"But I want to stay," the lad complained.

"Then behave. I mean it, John. If you cannot behave like a proper young gentleman—"

Ivan did not hear the rest, for just that quickly did his good mood turn sour. He'd been that lad, he thought as he watched the boy follow reluctantly in his governess's wake. Denied the freedoms he sought, the freedoms he needed.

A muscle in his cheek began to tic. If he had children he'd let them run free and wild in the fields and woods. He'd refuse to let them wear gloves, and have them learn the names of the trees in the forests before expecting them to learn the order of the rulers of England.

But he did not intend to have children, he reminded himself harshly.

Shoving himself up, he turned his back on the boy, John, and his governess and dog. If the boy had any backbone, eventually he would rebel. If not, then he would in turn raise a batch of spineless images of himself and continue the cycle ad nauseum.

As for himself, however, he had no intentions of sinking into that miserable pit. He had an afternoon to kill and an excess of energy to dispose of. If he couldn't vent that energy upon the lovely, tart-tongued Miss Lucy Drysdale, he'd head over to Pall Mall and find himself some other willing woman.

But he'd already tried that, he reminded himself, and it had not been particularly satisfying. Better to head to the Mayfair Athletic Club, he decided. Someone was sure to be in the boxing ring. Someone willing to go three rounds with him.

If he was to pursue the wary Miss Drysdale with any amount of success it behooved him for now to vent his excess energies elsewhere and in some other way.

Some hapless young lord in the boxing ring would be just the ticket.

Ten

*L*ucy was ecstatic. They'd escaped the house without running into Ivan. They'd made their way to the lecture hall without incident, and now, in a few minutes she would finally see Sir James Mawbey and hear for herself the erudite expressions of his brilliant mind.

Beside her Valerie peered about. "There are more people in attendance than I would have expected."

"And of a considerably different sort than we've been surrounded with of late," Lucy quipped. As they bought their subscriptions and entered Fatuielle Hall, they joined a unique company indeed. For the most part the audience for Sir James's lecture were middle-aged and older: dark-coated graybeards, neatly attired matrons. But there were others. Serious-faced scholars in their cheap coats and shiny trousers. Shopkeepers in their serviceable duds. Tradesmen in heavy boots. A few ladies were sprinkled about, distinguished by the quality of their garments.

All in all, a rather thrilling cross section of the British citizenry, Lucy decided. She could hardly contain her excitement.

"Will it be very long?" Valerie inquired.

"It should start very soon," Lucy replied as they found two seats in the very first row.

"No. I mean, will the lecture last very long?"

Lucy glanced at Valerie. "I gather you were not overly fond of your lessons."

Valerie gave her an apologetic smile. "History and ciphering were boring. I enjoy reading though. Especially novels."

"I suspect you have never studied anything similar to Sir James Mawbey. I know I most certainly had never read anything quite so enlightening until I discovered his articles."

Then the man himself came onto the stage and Lucy forgot all about Valerie. He was here. She was in the very same room with him.

He was precisely as she'd envisioned him: of medium height, though he appeared taller due to his gauntness. He had dark, unkempt hair and long side whiskers—to make him look older, she suspected, for he was younger than she would have guessed. But was he married?

Sir James surveyed the audience for a long moment. "Primogeniture is the greatest cause of familial discord in our beloved land. Across all of Europe," he pronounced. With that inflammatory statement he launched an hour-long discourse, punctuated by the occasional grumble of dissent or clap of applause by those assembled. But whether they agreed with him or not on this particular subject, there was no mistaking the man's deep and abiding concern for children.

"From the first moment they enter this hard world we live in they are learning. Whose arms are warm and welcoming; whose are not. Who provides food and shelter; who will not. Who they may trust—and here is my point." He paused and stared intently at the waiting audience. "They learn who they may *not* trust. Too often they learn they may not trust anyone. Not their parents who betray them on behalf of the oldest son. Not their other siblings who are out to get as much as their grasping hands can take. So what becomes of them?"

Sir James leaned out over the podium, his dark eyes lit with the fervor of a zealot. Lucy shivered when that fiery gaze swept over her and Valerie, then paused on them as it had numerous times during his lecture. "What happens is that this unloved child becomes an adult with no sense of what it is to love or be loved. This adult raises more children of the same ilk: the eldest petted and cosseted until he becomes a self-centered monster; the next in line ignored and trained, therefore, to become a jealous conniver; the younger siblings ignored except, when due to their truly horrible behavior, their parents have no recourse but to pay attention at last."

Abruptly he pulled back from the lectern. "Next time I will address in more detail how a parent might avoid the pitfalls that are too common to children within our modern society."

He left the stage before the applause was fully done. At once he was surrounded by admirers and besieged by questions. Lucy wanted to join that circle too, but she was so filled with awe she could not at first move.

"Wasn't he wonderful?" Valerie sighed just next to her.

Lucy nodded, her eyes fixed upon her idol's barely visible head. "Yes, he was. Didn't I tell you that you would think so?"

Valerie stood up, shaking out her skirts, but staring all the time at the jostling crowd around Sir James. "Let's go speak with him, Miss Drysdale. What do you say? Can we? I think we should."

"And shall we also attend his subsequent lectures?" Lucy asked, smiling. Her answer was a view of Valerie's backside as she hurried to join the others clustered around the charismatic young scholar.

Valerie's haste, however amusing, was nevertheless a relief to Lucy. She needed to compose herself before meeting the man she'd corresponded with this past year and a half.

She stood, smoothing out the wrinkles and folds of her skirt. She reached for her reticule and felt the slender packet of letters. *He would not have wasted his time writing you if he were not approachable,* she reminded herself. He would be pleased to see her, and flattered too. They would strike up a conversation and it would be as easy and natural as their letter-writing had been.

Where things might lead from there, she did not know. But now, for once, she let herself imagine.

Few marriages were founded on love, that is, not on the love the poets wrote of. Property and bloodlines were considered far more important to modern society when it came to making a good match. But property and bloodlines had never mattered to Lucy, nor did they matter to Sir James. Respect, admiration, and mutual interests were far more likely to ensure a felicitous match between a man and a woman, and she and Sir James possessed those qualitities in abundance.

But he did not excite her sensibilities in the same way Ivan Thornton did.

Lucy swallowed a frustrated oath at such a perverse thought, especially here and now. The sensibilities Ivan Thornton excited in her would lead her to nowhere but disaster. But what she felt for Sir James Mawbey . . . That could sustain her for a lifetime.

She pictured the two of them together in his library— their library—sitting quetly reading. Thinking deep thoughts. Having deep conversations over tea.

Yes. That was the future she wanted. That was why she'd come to London. She would not let foolish maunderings about the distracting Lord Westcott deter her from her goal.

When the crowd around Sir James began to thin a bit, Lucy sucked in a breath and started forward. Valerie had already maneuvered to a position facing Sir James. The girl would be introducing herself to the man if Lucy didn't hurry, and that would never do. Bad enough that Lucy would have to introduce the two of them. At least she was older and it would not be considered too forward, given the fact that they were correspondents. A child like Valerie, however, might appear in her enthusiasm to have an unseemly interest in the man.

She moved up beside Valerie and caught the girl's arm so as to prevent her from behaving in an unladylike manner.

For his part, Sir James seemed intensely aware of both Valerie and Lucy, and as soon as he was able, he ended his conversation with a wiry-haired older woman.

"May I ask whom I have the honor of addressing?" he asked, giving them a slight bow.

"It is our honor," Lucy replied. "May I introduce Lady Valerie Stanwich. I am Miss Lucy Drysdale."

For a long moment he stared at Valerie. Then, as if Lucy's name had belatedly registered, he tore his gaze away from Valerie's admiring expression. "Miss Drysdale. I am flattered that you made the effort to attend tonight. You are up from . . ."

"Somerset," Lucy supplied.

"And you, Miss Stanwich. Are you from Somerset as well?"

"No, my lord. I am from Arundel in Sussex," she answered, blushing just enough to make her complexion glow and her eyes sparkle.

Lucy could have groaned. Sir James should not be addressed as "my lord." Any ninny should know that. Especially a ninny whose father was an earl. Would he be offended, given his general antipathy toward the entire British class system? Would he correct poor Valerie and humiliate her in front of all these people?

"Arundel," he said, focusing his unblinking interest on Valerie. "I've often considered lecturing in Arundel. Are there any appropriate lecture houses there?"

Lucy's relief that he was not offended swiftly deteriorated into another sort of dismay when Valerie proceeded to monopolize the conversation with Sir James. No, that was not an entirely accurate assessment of the situation. Sir James actually did most of the talking. Valerie only supplied brief responses as needed, as well as many admiring glances at the scholarly fellow. And he sent as many admiring looks back at the lovely young girl.

Lucy had never before experienced the unpleasant emotion of jealousy. But she experienced it now. In spades.

"Will you discuss your theory on discipline during one

of the coming lectures?'' Lucy inserted when Sir James paused to take a breath.

''That is the subject of my third lecture in the series,'' he answered, finally looking over at her. Then he turned back to Valerie. ''Will you be in attendance, Miss Stanwich?''

''*Lady* Valerie,'' Lucy muttered. She was immediately ashamed of her petty response. Sir James, however, appeared not to have even heard her. Neither did Valerie as she answered him in the affirmative.

At once Lucy's jealousy was joined by alarm. Surely Valerie was not forming an attachment to Sir James Mawbey. Surely he was not smitten with a girl of such limited intellectual interests.

Surely, Lucy prayed, surely she was mistaken!

''Appears to be a match made in heaven.''

Lucy flinched at the words—at the voice. So unmistakable. So mocking. What was Ivan Thornton doing here?

She turned her head, just enough to see him standing right behind her. ''Go away,'' she muttered.

''What? And allow you to circumvent my grandmother's plans by pairing my esteemed cousin with a radical scholar? I'm afraid I would be doing my family a grave disservice should I abandon her now. Don't you?''

Lucy turned fully to face him. He was teasing her, of course. If she doubted it, the gleam of humor in his dark eyes gave it away. She suspected he would find it uproariously funny should the eminently marriageable Valerie make a match with so unsuitable a fellow as Sir James. Though Lucy was aware of the conversation continuing behind her, Ivan was now the focus of her attention. ''What are you doing here?'' she hissed. ''Are you following us?''

''I'm following *you,* Miss Drysdale. Just you.''

Lucy's heart lurched, then lodged stubbornly in her throat where it proceeded to pound with painful force. ''Me?'' she squeaked, then immediately gritted her teeth. She sounded like a fourteen-year-old in the grips of her first crush.

She cleared her throat. "You have no business following me."

He arched one brow in a maddening display of male arrogance. "I'm an earl. I can do anything I bloody well please."

"Including curse in polite company?" she snapped, regaining her senses at last.

"That's my poor upbringing again."

Lucy sent him what she hoped was a withering glare. "That's no excuse. Now, if you don't mind?"

She turned away from him, determined to break up the conversation between Valerie and Sir James. But she was excruciatingly aware of Ivan's presence behind her. Then he whispered in her ear. "Aren't you going to introduce me?"

Not if she could help it.

Unfortunately Valerie noticed Ivan just then and the choice was no longer Lucy's to make.

"Why, Lord Westcott," the girl exclaimed, no trace of her previous nervousness apparent. "Have you attended Sir James's lecture as well?"

"I regret I arrived a little late and did not hear all of Sir James's comments on the negative effect of primogeniture." He extended a hand to the silent scholar. "Ivan Thornton. Lady Valerie's cousin."

Sir James returned the greeting. Then he added, "Lord Westcott? You are the Earl of Westcott?"

"The same."

"A first son, I take it," he said, a hint of disapproval in his voice.

"An only son, and an unacknowledged one at that," Ivan retorted in a tone Lucy feared was deceptively pleasant.

The two men took one another's measure for a long, chilly moment. Then Sir James nodded. "Yes, of course. Of course. I wonder, would you and Lady Valerie and Miss Dinsdale—"

"It's Drysdale," Lucy corrected him.

"My pardon," he absently replied. "Would the three of

you join me for supper? I never eat before I lecture. Now I find myself famished,'' he added, shifting his gaze back to Valerie.

"Thank you, Sir James. But I'm afraid that will not be possible," Lucy replied before either of the others could. "We are expected at Westcott House," she added, when Valerie turned a pleading gaze on her. "Lady Antonia would be quite put out should we be late."

If Valerie appeared crestfallen, Sir James seemed doubly so. "Perhaps on Thursday, then. You will be at my Thursday lecture, won't you, Lady Valerie?"

"I'll see to it personally," Ivan answered for her. "Meanwhile, we'd best be on our way."

Without warning he tucked Lucy's hand under his arm. "I'll see the ladies home, Mawbey. See you on Thursday."

"Very good, Lord Westcott. Ladies." He bowed to Lucy first, then to Valerie. When Valerie extended her hand, an infatuated expression on her young face, Sir James took it and pressed a fervent kiss to her fingers.

Lucy could only stare at the scene being played out before her, her emotions in a shambles. He was supposed to be captivated by *her,* not by Valerie. He was supposed to be impressed by *her* knowledge of his work, by *her* empathy with his ideas. He was supposed to invite her to dinner so they could continue their conversation.

He was most certainly *not* supposed to become infatuated by a girl fresh from the schoolroom, one without an original thought in her head.

"Don't they make a lovely couple?" Ivan whispered.

Lucy would have roundly denied it except that his breath tickled her ear, and her heart made another lurch.

No, no, no! She was not supposed to respond this way to Ivan Thornton. It was Sir James she was interested in.

But it appeared Sir James was not interested in a spinsterish bluestocking. Like every other living man in England, he was interested in a fresh-faced innocent with a title and an inheritance to go with it.

Stifling a very unladylike oath, she disengaged her hand

from Ivan's hold, then took firm grasp of Valerie's arm.
"Good evening, Sir James." Then without allowing Valerie room to protest, she practically hauled her out of the lecture hall.

As they exited into the gaslit street, Valerie was silent, caught up in her thoughts. Ivan, however, was not.

"How fortunate I am to happen upon you two lovely ladies tonight."

"Happen upon?" Lucy snapped. Though she knew he was not the source of her anger and disappointment, he was an awfully convenient focus for it. Besides, he'd followed them. Her, that is. She felt a silly thrill run though her but brutally suppressed it. Her emotions were too raw right now to be trusted. "If you wanted to accompany us, you could simply have asked to do so."

"And you would happily have agreed, right, Lucy?"

"Don't call me that!" she hissed. When Valerie looked up at her short tone, Lucy had to force herself to calm down. "If you wish to make yourself useful, my lord, you will hail our carriage."

"By all means," he said, giving her a wink. A wink, blast the man!

But at least he did as she asked. In the few moments she and Valerie waited on the front landing of the lecture hall, Lucy contemplated how best to deal with Valerie's new infatuation. She wanted to tell the girl in no uncertain terms to stay away from Sir James. That he was not the right man for her and that, furthermore, her family would never allow her to marry a poor scholar.

But that would probably only serve to entrench Valerie's fledgling feelings more firmly. No, Lucy decided. It would be better to treat Valerie's quick infatuation for the intense young scholar as exactly that: an infatuation. A passing fancy. Men had them all the time. There was no reason why a woman couldn't.

Just to be sure, though, Lucy would have to keep the girl far away from Fatuielle Hall on Thursday, and every other night of Sir James's lecture series.

As if she divined the direction of Lucy's thoughts, Valerie sighed. "I can hardly wait until Thursday night."

"I'm not sure we'll be able to attend every one of the lectures," Lucy cautioned, adopting a calmer tone. "We'll have to see what Lady Westcott has planned for you."

"Oh, but you must convince her," Valerie pleaded.

Whatever else she said Lucy did not hear, for the carriage pulled up, and to her vast dismay, Ivan had hitched his handsome steed to the back. Did he mean to ride home with them?

Despite the evening cool, Lucy felt a bead of perspiration trickle down between her breasts.

She could not deal with him tonight. She simply could not! Her feelings were too unsettled. First her disappointment over Sir James. Then her worry about Valerie's attachment to the man. Added to that was the perverse reaction she had to Ivan's presence. She detested him and yet he managed to arouse the most primitive feelings inside her.

And now he seemed set on promoting Valerie and Sir James as the ideal couple. Like a homing pigeon Ivan Thornton had the uncanny ability to pinpoint the areas of her greatest vulnerability. Without a doubt the possibility of Valerie capturing Sir James's affections was precisely that.

But whether or not Lucy could deal with Ivan, it was clear that Ivan meant to share the carriage with them.

He helped Valerie in first and the girl gave him a rather absent smile. She was no longer intimidated by him, it seemed. That was because he'd turned the force of his iron will away from her and onto Lucy instead. But why? Did he think to thwart his grandmother by paying more attention to the chaperone than to his pretty young cousin?

Oh, but she was so weary of both the grandmother's and the grandson's endless plotting!

Lucy was already frowning when she approached the carriage doors; the frown turned into a downright scowl when Ivan caught her lightly around the wrist.

"You look displeased with this evening's turn of events. I hope you did not find Sir James's lecture disappointing."

"Quite the opposite," she stated, raising her chin to a belligerent angle. "I was fascinated by his denigration of our national preoccupation with class differences."

"You are a part of the very system he vilifies."

"As are you."

"Only by default."

"That can be said of anyone who inherits a title, or estate, or even a decent amount of money. Everyone who inherits does so only because no one else has as strong a claim."

"Yes. But you refer to people who fight and claw to claim what they see as their rightful inheritance. My situation could not be more different."

"But the outcome is the same, isn't it? I must say, my lord, that you wear the mantle of your office as well as anyone I've ever seen."

He raised his brows at that. "What is this? A compliment? I can scarcely believe my ears."

"It's only a compliment if you consider arrogance a virtue," she replied, hiding her confused feelings for him behind a mask of irritation. "If you'll excuse me, Lord Westcott?" She turned to mount the carriage step.

But he would not release her wrist, and when she tried to yank it free, his fingers manacled her all the tighter. "It's Ivan," he reminded her in a low, husky tone.

He bent to kiss her hand before allowing her to enter the vehicle. Only it was not her gloved knuckles he kissed. Somehow he found the exposed skin of her wrist, where her sleeve and the stylishly short glove did not quite overlap. He kissed the tender skin where her pulse raced so alarmingly. He kissed her with both lips and tongue—as he'd kissed her mouth in the McClendons' library.

At once bubbles of effervescent emotion surged through Lucy, zinging out from that tiny location on her wrist to every other portion of her body. She nearly swooned from the impact of it.

Any thoughts of Sir James flew right out of her head, usurped by a total awareness of Ivan. Only Ivan. The feel of his lips; the warmth of his touch. The scent of soap and tobacco and some other unidentifiable something that was uniquely him.

She was falling under his spell, even though she knew all the reasons why she should not. He was all good looks and insincere charm. Yet even knowing that, she was succumbing to him like some green country miss newly introduced in town.

"Please. Don't," she whispered, unaware she'd spoken.

When he raised his head and stared at her, she knew her feelings were transparent. Unwisely so. But she could no more tear her eyes away from his than she could remove her hand from his grasp.

It took Valerie to break the unbearable moment. "Miss Drysdale? Aren't we returning home?"

This time when Lucy pulled away he let her go. Furious with herself, she climbed into the carriage, avoiding his proffered hand. She perched stiffly beside Valerie.

Blast it all. Why did she always have this perverse reaction to him?

Ivan came in right behind her, pulled the door closed, and settled himself opposite the two women. With a sharp rap on the front panel he signaled the driver to start up and at once the carriage lurched forward. Then Ivan stretched his arm across the seat back and studied both women through the inky darkness of the carriage interior.

The small lantern had not been lit, and Lucy thanked her lucky stars. She did not want him reading anything further into her expression, neither the anger nor the creeping terror. She'd forgotten, however, the effect of his low, silky voice in the dark.

"I take it you both enjoyed the lecture."

"Oh, very much so!" Valerie exclaimed. "Wasn't Sir James simply marvelous? He was ever so enlightening. I'd never before considered why my brother Claude has always criticized Harry so. But Sir James made it perfectly clear.

Wasn't he simply marvelous?'' she repeated.

Ivan chuckled. Lucy heard the amusement in his voice. ''And what of you, Miss Drysdale? Did you also find him marvelous?''

''I did,'' she answered in a cool tone. ''And you?''

''Quite interesting. More so than I expected. I believe I understand now why you were so adamant about attending his lecture.'' He paused, just long enough to make Lucy question the meaning in his words.

''What I cannot understand,'' he continued, ''is why you brought Lady Valerie along. Sir James's incendiary ideas will not help her make a good match.''

''Making a good match is not everything,'' Lucy retorted. But inside her heart was sinking. He knew. He'd deduced her interest in Sir James and witnessed her awful jealousy of naïve Valerie. She wanted to die!

But she could not allow him to get the upper hand. So she went on. ''Making a match is not everything. I, myself, am far more content in my solitary state than I would be were I trapped in an unhappy marriage.''

''As am I,'' he said. ''Take heed, Lady Valerie. Marriage is not an admirable goal.''

''That's not what I said,'' Lucy snapped. She clutched the window post as the carriage made a left turn. ''For some people marriage is the right choice, for others it is not. In any event, you are hardly the one to be advising her on such matters.''

''Nor are you, it would seem. Not if you are as content in your current state as you profess to be.''

Ivan knew he was irritating Lucy. She had a sharp tongue and a ready temper that took little enough goading. Why he should take such pleasure in goading that temper was a mystery to him. But take pleasure in it he did.

''Be honest, Miss Drysdale. Sir James was not at all what you expected, was he?''

He heard the sharp intake of her breath and it confirmed what he already knew. She had deeper feelings for the gaunt Sir James than she let on. The man's immediate interest in Lady Valerie had caught his hot-blooded little bluestocking entirely by surprise, and she was having a hard time dealing with her jealousy.

Ivan had to stifle a laugh. Any man who would select a silly twit, no matter how lovely, over a woman as smart and stimulating as Lucy Drysdale had dust for brains.

"Sir James was every bit as enlightening as I anticipated," Lucy vowed in a voice he could only describe as pinched.

Was he now? Ivan turned to Valerie, who had been silent the whole time. Probably thinking of Sir James. "He certainly seemed smitten with you, Lady Valerie."

The girl started to giggle, then abruptly stopped when Lucy laid a stern hand on her arm.

"I'll thank you not to tease her," Lucy said in the censorious tones of a chaperone hard at work. "Sir James was polite, but I'm certain he knows, as does Valerie, that she and he move in vastly different circles."

"So they do. So they do," Ivan agreed. But not for long, he decided. Sir James Mawbey was sadly in need of a little excitement in his life, and Ivan was just the man to provide it.

Eleven

*L*ucy did not sleep well. She kept waking, thinking she
heard a knock at the door.

Ivan?

But no one was there, and as she struggled with sleep,
restless despite the comfort of the luxurious bed, her stubborn thoughts refused to focus on anything but him.

He was not at her door—and she was mighty glad of it,
she told herself. But was she? In the quiet of the night her
mind wrestled with a new sort of demon. A part of her had
been thrilled when Ivan whispered to her through the
door—right into her ear, it had seemed at the time. She'd
become dizzy and filled with violent and frightening emotions when he'd kissed her at the McClendons' party.

Now even his lips upon her wrist made her faint with
the most improper sort of desire.

What on earth was she going to do? Nothing was working out as she'd intended. Even Sir James, whom she'd so
longed to meet, was a disappointment. Though she'd enjoyed his lecture well enough, his unexpected attention to
Valerie had taken Lucy aback. And he was too pompous
by half.

In all honesty, however, she knew that her disappointment over Sir James was not the primary source of her
discontent. Ivan Thornton held solitary claim to that honor.

Feeling too warm for comfort, she kicked the covers

down then rolled over, punching her pillow, trying to find a position that would allow her to relax.

The fact that her first meeting with Sir James hadn't gone precisely as she'd imagined, didn't mean anything. They hadn't really had the chance to get to know one another. But once they did . . . Once they did, he would come to appreciate her much more than Valerie. And before long he would drive all thoughts of Ivan Thornton right out of her head.

The problem was, she was dwelling on Ivan too much. But not any more. She would make herself think of Sir James instead of Ivan. She would imagine him kissing her wrist, instead of Ivan. She would imagine him dancing with her and sweeping her away into an empty library, then kissing her like a starving man.

His hold would be possessive. His lips would be firm, but tender, and incredibly exciting.

Lucy sighed and gave her imagination free rein. She could almost feel his hands hauling her up against him, then circling her body and pressing her even closer. She pictured his mouth on hers, and the exquisite slide of his tongue.

What if she let him go further? What if his hands slid other places—places that only a husband's hands were free to touch?

Of their own volition one of her hands pressed against her heart, the other against her belly. She knew about husbands and wives, about what went on between men and women. She'd always thought it sounded extremely awkward and more than a little unpleasant. But now to imagine herself and Ivan like that raised the most wonderful wicked feelings—

No! She let out a groan. Not Ivan. She hadn't meant Ivan at all!

With a guilty start she snatched her hands away then pushed herself upright on the big bed. She was not going to think such thoughts! She simply refused to.

If her feelings for Sir James—and his for her—were not what she had hoped, then so be it. But she was not about to let herself be seduced by a handsome scoundrel, who was as little concerned for the hearts he broke as he might be for a pair of boots he had ruined. He cast the former off as easily as he did the latter.

If only he were sincere.

But that was wishful thinking and Lucy ruthlessly squelched it. Though it was not yet dawn, she abandoned her bed and instead set about preparing for the day. A hundred strokes of the brush through her hair and a chilly wash, to be followed by an hour in the library.

No, she did not dare venture out into the still sleeping house lest she come upon Ivan again.

She let the hairbrush fall idle as she racked her mind. She would write a letter home. She had paper and pen, and soon enough it would be dawn. The house would come alive and then it would be safe for her to leave the sanctuary of her chamber. At least she hoped so.

Two hours later Lucy started down to breakfast. As it happened, Lady Westcott was departing her chamber at the same time.

"This is convenient, Miss Drysdale. I had hoped to quiz you this morning about the lecture you and Valerie attended. Was it a worthwhile use of your time and hers?"

Lucy fell into step beside the aristocratic old woman. "I enjoyed it very well," she began. Then an idea occurred to her, a rather devious idea. "I enjoyed it, but I'm afraid Valerie enjoyed it perhaps too well."

"Too well?" Lady Westcott paused at the head of the grand stairs. "Pray tell, what do you mean by 'too well'?"

Valerie would be furious with her, but Lucy consoled herself that what she was doing was in the girl's best interest. "I'm concerned that Valerie may have formed an unwise attachment to the lecturer."

"An unwise attachment? Precisely what do you mean by 'an unwise attachment'? She was only in his presence for an hour or two. And who is this person, anyway?"

"He is Sir James Mawbey, and Valerie was very favorably impressed by him, both by his intellect and his person.

He was equally impressed by her," Lucy added, feeling like the worst sort of sneak.

"If I am to interpret your concern rightly, he must not be the right sort of person for her. He is not already married, is he?"

"Oh, no. No, not married. But he is not favorably disposed toward the British system of primogeniture."

Lady Westcott let out a short laugh, then started down the steps. "No doubt a younger son. If you find him unacceptable, then discourage her from seeing him. You are, after all, her chaperone."

"I plan to do just that. However, I myself would still like to attend his lectures, as we agreed I might on the day I consented to become Valerie's chaperone."

They had reached the bottom of the stairs and once again Lady Westcott paused. She turned to study Lucy. This time she was frowning. "Why would you wish to do that? He sounds unhinged to me. Could it be you are interested in this man for yourself?"

Lucy vehemently shook her head. "No. Of course not. It's just that I have read his articles and wish to attend his lecture. They're not all about inheritance. Mostly they're concerned with children and the effects of upbringing."

"His lectures. Harrumph. I hope I have not introduced a radical into my own household."

"I suspect your grandson is far more radical than I am," Lucy answered with some asperity.

That brought a faint smile to the older woman's face. "Well said, Miss Drysdale. But tell me, what is it you wish me to do concerning this matter with Valerie?"

"If you would make plans for Valerie on Thursday afternoon that do not require my presence, I believe we shall all be content."

"All of us except Valerie," Lady Westcott pointed out.

"I do not believe she shall long mourn him," Lucy said. "They spoke but a few words. She will forget him."

Lady Westcott considered that, all the while still studying Lucy. "Your diligence in the discharge of your duties is to be commended. First you would protect her from an earl, her own cousin whom you perceive as a poor choice for her. Now you guard her from some radical lecturer, penniless, no doubt. You certainly cannot be faulted in your sincerity, Miss Drysdale. I must say, I look forward with great anticipation to meeting the paragon you think worthy of our dear Valerie.''

Put that way, Lucy supposed she did seem an exceedingly conscientious chaperone. But as the two of them made their way to the dining room, Lucy feared it was less diligence and more selfishness that motivated her. For of Valerie's two so-called suitors, the one she desired for his intellect; the other . . . the other she simply desired.

She had filled the plate at the sideboard. Now she sat down at the table, staring at the eggs and ham and scones on her plate. In the face of this new self-knowledge, she had lost her appetite.

Could a woman be in love with two men? One man's mind and the other man's physical person?

A knot of self-disgust formed in her stomach. She should never have come to London. She should have stayed in Somerset and tried harder to find contentment in her life there. How many times had her brother exhorted her to be satisfied with her situation, to be less particular of the men who courted her, to find satisfaction as other women found satisfaction; in a pleasant husband, a household to manage, and a nursery full of children?

But no, she'd always been too high-minded for that. And look where it had gotten her: reduced to lust and petty jealousy.

Then a footstep sounded in the hall and her self-disgust trebled. It was Ivan. She recognized his step, though why that should be so, she did not understand.

She wanted to run and hide. But of course, she could not do that. So she awaited his entrance in terrible anticipation, eager and dreading and more confused than she'd been in her entire life.

"Good morning." Ivan addressed them both, but his gaze lingered on Lucy.

Lady Westcott had already settled herself at one end of the table with Lucy beside her. After filling his plate, Ivan took a seat opposite Lucy. "Isn't this cozy," he remarked as a servant poured coffee for him.

"My, but you're in a jovial mood this morning," Lady Westcott said.

"So I am."

"Dare I hope it is on account of a woman?"

Ivan's gaze locked with Lucy's a moment before he turned to his grandmother. "You would be overjoyed if I answer yes. So I'll say instead that I had an enjoyable evening, a good night's sleep, and the most interesting dreams. Now I am awakened to what I hope will be a pleasant day. Unless, of course, you decide to make it unpleasant."

Lady Westcott's mouth pursed in a tight circle of lines. "Up to now it has taken no more than my presence to make your day unpleasant—or so you have led me to believe. Could it be we are making progress, you and I?"

Ivan gave the old woman a cool look. "Your presence here, or more rightly, the presence of your entourage, specifically Valerie and Miss Drysdale, has provided a greater distraction than I anticipated." His gaze returned to Lucy.

A distraction. How kind of him to remind her. Here she'd been berating herself for being too interested in the man— in love with his physical person, she'd even termed it. But she was only a distraction to him. How had she allowed herself to forget? It was, after all, that very insincerity of his which made him unacceptable for Valerie as well as for any other good and sensible young woman. Including herself.

As quickly as that her self-remorse was obliterated by a righteous anger. "I'm sure I speak for Lady Valerie as well as myself when I say we both live for a chance to be a distraction to a man of such discriminating tastes as yourself, my lord."

He grinned at her and his gaze fell to her lips before

rising again to her eyes. "Dare I hope this sarcasm of yours reveals a wish to be more than simply a distraction?"

Lucy shoved her chair back from the table and lurched to her feet. "Don't hold your breath," she snapped. "If you'll excuse me?" she said to Lady Westcott. Then not waiting for a response she stormed out of the room.

In Lucy's wake a resounding silence fell. Ivan was so caught up in visions of that magnificent anger released in another, more passionate fashion, that he did not consider his grandmother's reaction to this little scene.

"Is something going on here that I have not been informed of?"

When he only stared at her, she continued. "Are you trifling with the hired help, Ivan?"

His good humor soured. "Would it matter to you if I was? I'd only be following the example of my esteemed father."

"Miss Drysdale is a lady and deserving of your respect."

"Whereas my mother was a Gypsy and deserving of nothing. Right?"

She patted her mouth then laid the monogrammed napkin aside. "Do not put words in my mouth. I never said that."

"But you believe it. You believed it when you found out your son had impregnated a Gypsy. You believed it when you learned she'd borne you your first grandson. You believed it when you resigned yourself to the fact that I would be your *only* grandson. Your *only* heir. You stole me from my mother—"

"She *sold* you to me!"

She'd made that accusation before. Then, as now, it caused Ivan to see red. "What in hell choice did she have! She probably believed I'd have a better life as the son of an earl. Little did she know." He jerked to his feet, sending his chair toppling backward. "You tried so hard to keep your precious Westcott name from being tainted by Gypsy blood. But you failed. I am half Gypsy, and when I take a wife, it'll be a Gypsy wife. They're a damn sight more appealing than any cold-blooded English bitch!"

He left while she was still in shock, slamming out of the dining room then out of the house. He stormed out to the stables, called for a horse, and impatiently saddled it himself. Then he was off, flying out the service gate and down the alley to Berkeley Street. Unmindful of traffic or pedestrians, he urged the horse down Picadilly, giving the animal its head as they approached the park. But he stayed away from Rotten Row and any other place where he would encounter other riders.

As he raced the eager steed flat-out over the uncut meadows and through the dappled shade, he and the horse were like one—just as his Gypsy forebears were said to be. He whispered to the gallant animal, urging him on. The horse's ear flicked back to listen, and as if it understood, its efforts increased.

Over a hedge. Through a creek. Then up a rise into the deep shade of a pollarded stand of hornbeams.

Only then did he slow the animal. Only then did he allow himself to think past his anger and pain.

Though he'd used the words as a weapon, the idea of a Gypsy wife held a certain appeal. He'd long thought it more than appropriate. But he'd been with enough Gypsies during the years he'd been gone to know that was not the answer. He didn't fit in with them any longer. He was no more at ease in the company of Gypsies than he was in the company of the ton. He was neither fish nor fowl, but a man caught between two families. Two cultures. He'd been at war with himself as long as he could remember. But now, when he was poised at last to wreak vengeance on the woman and the society that had made his life an unending hell, he found that the one thing he most craved was peace.

It was the one thing that most eluded him. Worse, he had the sinking suspicion that nothing he did to shock or humiliate his grandmother would bring him that peace.

For a moment he thought of Lucy, of how earnestly she fought his attentions, first toward Valerie and now toward herself. Was it his Gypsy blood she objected to, or was it the person he'd become, the disenchanted, insincere rake who cared for nothing and no one but his own selfish pleasure?

Weary and covered with sweat, he flung himself off the blowing horse and began to walk it beneath the canopy of interlaced branches.

Maybe Lucy was right. He did behave like her young nephew, like a spoiled, resentful child. But only when it came to his grandmother. His feelings regarding Lucy were those of a man for a woman. And though she fought them, her feelings for him were those of a woman for a man.

Except that she thought she wanted Sir James.

He patted the horse's damp neck and continued to walk. The branches of the ancient hornbeams formed a dense roof above him, alive with the chatter of sparrows, jays, and scolding squirrels. Thick trunks surrounded him like a living wall. He could almost believe he wasn't in London, in the midst of over a million people, each beset by his own troubles.

How he would like to get away from town, from the ton, the marriage mart, and most of all, his grandmother. And how he'd like to have Miss Lucy Drysdale accompany him.

He halted and considered that idea. If her purpose for being in London were removed, she would be left at loose ends. First he needed to rid her of any hopes regarding a certain scholar. It galled him to even think of her attachment to the man. He would also have to end her association with Valerie, and therefore his grandmother.

Then he grinned, for the solution was obvious. An added bonus was that it would enrage the dowager countess.

With his good humor restored, Ivan mounted the rested animal and turned it back toward town. Precisely what his long-term intentions were for Lucy he could not yet say. For now it was enough that he had a plan of action. The rest he would deal with as necessary.

"A dinner party? Why was I not informed?" Lady Westcott demanded to know.

"I . . . I am informing you, my lady. That's exactly what

I'm doing right now—'' The housekeeper fell silent under
Lady Westcott's withering glance. She buried her hands in
her skirt.

In the ensuing silence Lucy looked up. The dowager
countess met her gaze.

"Well. Did you hear that, Miss Drysdale? After all that
unpleasantness yesterday at breakfast, it appears that my
grandson has decided to host a dinner party. What do you
make of such a turn of events?"

"I'm sure I cannot fathom what goes on in Lord Westcott's head,'' Lucy answered. In truth, the man was a total
enigma to her—as were her convoluted reactions to him.
She hadn't seen him after breakfast yesterday. Nor had he
been around at all today. She should be glad, she told herself. But the truth was, she was annoyed and unhappy and
exceedingly confused.

She threaded a hat pin through her bonnet, catching a
knot in her hair and securing the pin well. As she pulled
on her gloves she turned to face Lady Westcott. "Thank
you for providing the carriage to take me to the lecture."

Lady Westcott waved off her thanks. "Where is Valerie?"

Lucy grimaced. "Taken to bed with a sick headache. I'm
sorry your plans with the Pintners are ruined."

"Hettie Pintner is a blowhard. Even more so than her
husband. A quiet evening may be just the ticket." She
paused and for a long moment just gazed at Lucy. "Enjoy
the lecture, Miss Drysdale. At least one of us is benefitting
from our time in town."

Benefitting? As Lucy made the solitary drive to Fatuielle
Hall she didn't feel like she was benefitting at all from
being in town. London was not turning out as she'd hoped.
She was not supposed to be infatuated with an amoral
rogue, but with a high-minded scholar. As for the scholar,
he was supposed to become interested in her, not a pretty
heiress fresh from the schoolroom.

No, London was not turning out at all as she'd hoped.
She was in as grim a mood as she'd ever known by the

time she arrived at the lecture hall. Once inside she recognized several of the same people in attendance from the previous night. She chose a seat in the back, not certain whether or not she should approach Sir James this time. If he were to look disappointed at Valerie's absence, Lucy didn't think she would be able to bear it.

The house lights went dim when the lamps at the podium were lit. Just before Sir James took the stage, however, a group of latecomers made their noisy entrance.

Lucy hoped the group would not sit in front of her, for she wanted an unobstructed view of Sir James. She meant to convince herself that he was just as attractive to her senses as was another man—a man she refused to think about. But sit in front of her they did. Three men and one woman, judging from their silhouettes.

Then a fifth member of their party took a seat right beside her and she looked over, irritated by his boldness. "If you don't mind, sir."

"Is this seat reserved?" asked a familiar voice.

Lucy's heart flipped over. Ivan! Blast the man for torturing her so unmercifully.

"You're following me again!" she accused, struggling mightily to hide her emotional reaction to him.

"As a matter of fact, I am. Bad enough that I spirited your innocent charge out of the house without anyone the wiser. But her reputation would be ruined beyond even my ability to repair it were she to be seen alone in the company of not one, but four notorious rakes."

Lucy gaped at him, unable to believe what he'd just told her. The woman one row up and three seats over was Valerie?

"The only chance of salvaging her reputation," he continued, "was to find you, her erstwhile chaperone."

Lucy continued to stare at him, still unable to speak. In the next row Valerie turned a fearful gaze toward her. But there was no apology in the girl's expression, Lucy noted. None at all.

So much for the malleable child Lady Westcott thought

her to be. When it came to what the girl truly wanted—Sir James, it seemed—Valerie obviously possessed a will of iron.

Embarrassment, disappointment, and absolute fury hit Lucy all at one time. She glared at Ivan, the author of this latest outrage. "You are truly despicable," she hissed. "Even worse than I imagined. You care for nothing at all, only the amusement you might have at the expense of others."

She jerked to her feet, set on leaving and taking Valerie with her. But with a grip like steel he caught her arm and forced her down into her seat. "We're staying for the lecture. All of us," he stated in no uncertain terms.

"Cheer up, Miss Drysdale," said Alexander Blackburn, turning to face her from the seat directly in front of hers. "We'll do our very best to be entertaining company."

"It's not your company I object to, Mr. Blackburn. It's his," she said, glaring again at Ivan. "No doubt he duped you into this hateful scheme just as he has duped Valerie."

She tried to pull her arm free of Ivan's hold, but to no avail. Indeed, it only caused him to lean nearer her.

"Are you angry because I am here, or because Valerie is?"

"That's an idiotic question."

"I don't think so. It's a question that cuts right to the heart of the matter. The fact is, you don't want Valerie here because you have your own designs on the good scholar." He gestured toward the stage just as a polite applause rippled through the audience. Sir James crossed the stage and took his place behind the podium. He was the same gaunt young man he'd been two days before when she'd first laid eyes on him. But the impact on Lucy wasn't the same this time.

From Sir James, Lucy's gaze shot over to Valerie. Even in profile the girl's fascination for Sir James was evident. Lucy's spirits sank even further. Still, she was not about to admit anything to Ivan Thornton. With jaw set she stared straight ahead at Sir James, though not a word he said registered with her.

"Would you please let go of my arm," she muttered from the corner of her mouth.

"Promise you won't bolt?" he whispered, very near her ear. Too near. She felt his warm breath upon her neck and swallowed hard.

"I came here to listen to Sir James. I have no intention of leaving on your account."

When she glanced at him she saw he was smiling. That wicked, satisfied, one-sided smile of his. What little light there was in the lecture hall seemed to glitter in his eyes. He released her wrist then, and she looked away. But though he gave her no further cause for distraction during the balance of Sir James's lecture, not a word of the earnest scholar's pronouncements registered in her head.

In the row in front of her Alexander Blackburn fell asleep. Giles Dameron stared about, up at the water-stained ceiling, and around at the peeling walls. Elliot Pierce was not even that polite. After only ten minutes or so, he stood up, made his excuses, and left for the lobby.

Valerie's attention, however, remained riveted to the man on the stage. By the time the ushers relit the wall lanterns, Lucy was ready to accept the fact that the girl was serious about her affection for the man. It was totally illogical, of course, but there it was. And when Sir James anxiously scanned the room, then broke into a foolish grin when he spied Valerie sitting in the rear, Lucy unhappily resigned herself to the inevitable.

One adoring look from an ingenuous young woman had carried far more weight with Sir James Mawbey than had months of correspondence from someone who admired his mind and shared all his interests. When Valerie hurried up the aisle to greet Sir James, Lucy rolled her eyes in disgust.

"True love. Revolting, isn't it?"

Lucy glared at Ivan. "You're encouraging her when you know it is sure to lead to heartbreak."

"Heartbreak for her, or heartbreak for you?"

Lucy gritted her teeth and stood. She refused to be drawn into this cat and mouse game of his. "You know Lady Westcott will not approve, nor will her family. But then, that's precisely why you're doing it. You wish to wreak havoc on everyone's life, especially your grandmother's. It doesn't matter at all to you if you crush a few innocent people along the way. So long as you make your grandmother miserable."

His face remained remarkably calm. "Jealous, are we?"

"I am not!" Lucy was too angry to be rational. She shoved past him and stormed down the aisle to Valerie, who stood in a knot of admirers gathered around Sir James.

". . . and I am a middle child," Valerie was saying.

"As am I," Sir James replied. They smiled at one another.

An elderly matron tittered and nudged her companion. Lucy glared at the woman, then turned her attention back to her young charge.

"Excuse me, Valerie. But we must be going."

At Sir James's crestfallen look she felt a twinge of guilt. But resolutely she pressed on. "Lady Westcott will be worried. After all, you have been ill." She gave Valerie a pointed look.

Valerie had the good grace to look guilty. Before she could respond, however, Ivan spoke. "I assure you, Miss Drysdale, that my cousin is in safe hands with me."

"Nonetheless, Lady Westcott will not be content until she is returned home."

He studied her with an impassive gaze. He no longer looked amused; neither did he seem angry. But by that very dearth of emotions he seemed especially threatening. Behind him his gallery of rogues was gathered, and Lucy's heart sank.

How had she become embroiled in this terrible mess? She'd but wanted to come to London to hear Sir James and meet him. She'd never wanted to become the hapless mediator in a war between Ivan Thornton and his grandmother. No. More like Ivan Thornton and the world. And now she'd lost her hopes for Sir James as well.

Valerie turned an imploring expression on Ivan and an alarm bell sounded in Lucy's head. What was going on here? Since when had Ivan become Valerie's source of support?

As if on cue, Ivan stepped nearer the hopeless couple. "If you would like the chance to meet Valerie's estimable godmother, the Dowager Countess of Westcott, I urge you to join us at dinner, Mawbey." He handed Sir James a card. "Wednesday evening. Should we expect you?"

The play of emotions that ran across Sir James's face was almost comical. Surprise. Suspicion. Disbelief. Then finally, delight. "I am most flattered, Lord Westcott. I shall mark it on my calendar." He turned the card over, studying it, then looked up at Valerie. "I especially look forward to seeing you there, Lady Valerie." He gave her a shy smile.

It was going to be a fiasco, was all Lucy could think. Ivan was engineering a fiasco and everyone in attendance would come out the worse for it. Everyone except for him, of course.

They said their good-byes to Sir James. But when Lucy would have taken Valerie's arm, she was usurped by Mr. Dameron and Mr. Blackburn. Mr. Pierce offered Lucy his arm, but she only glared at him.

Ivan, however, did not offer her a choice. He took her hand and tucked it under her arm. "My dear Miss Drysdale, if you will take advice from one who wishes you only the best, you should try harder to curb that temper of yours."

"Really? The same might be said for you, though not of your temper. It's your unreasonable need for vengeance that does you so little credit." Then she dropped all pretense of civility. "Exactly what is it you hope to accomplish at this dinner party you plan?"

"What makes you think I hope to accomplish anything?"

"Because I know you. You would not do this merely out of the goodness of your heart."

"You wound me, Miss Drysdale." He laughed. "Then

again, perhaps all I want to do is goad you, to prod that prickly temper of yours.''

They had reached the foyer of the lecture hall and through the open doors Lucy spied the Westcott carriage. Behind it was Ivan's curricle. She pulled her hand from Ivan's hold, trying hard to ignore the feel of his muscular arm beneath her palm. ''If you and your friends prefer the larger carriage, Lady Valerie and I can take the curricle.''

''I wouldn't think of sending you ladies home without a proper escort.''

''I'm her chaperone. I *am* the proper escort,'' Lucy reminded him.

''Nevertheless, I insist on seeing you both safely home.''

''You mean you insist on making certain your grandmother knows how you have tricked her.''

''If anything, she will be pleased that I take so avid an interest in my very marriageable cousin.''

Lucy glared at him. ''Aren't you worried your grandmother and Valerie might trick you? That they might trap you in a compromising position—say, you sneaking Valerie out of the house for a secret rendezvous?''

''What a devious mind you have,'' he scolded. ''That's why I brought my friends along. Come now, Miss Drysdale. Lucy,'' he added more softly. ''Let's not debate this matter any further.''

Lucy searched his face. He was the most baffling man she'd ever met. ''I thought you wanted to goad me. To prod my prickly temper, to quote you.''

Their eyes met and held, and in the brief silence the tenor of their conversation changed. He was the first to speak. ''Your temper is volatile. You dance with sensuous grace. It makes a man curious to know what other passions lie hidden beneath that carefully restrained façade of yours. I happen to be a very curious man.''

There was no mistaking his meaning. While Lucy knew such boldness deserved a sharp setdown, she was not up to it. Shock had turned her mind to mush.

Fortunately, it did not deprive her completely of her

senses. She turned awkwardly away from Ivan. Spying Valerie, she made directly for the girl, like a pigeon homing in on its roost.

How she endured the ride to Westcott House, with Ivan's gaze constantly on her, as vivid as a caress, she did not know. Once home, however, she did not linger belowstairs. She sent Valerie to bed, then escaped at last to the solitude of her own bedchamber.

Solitude, however, was no bosom friend. Not this night. For without the distraction of her responsibility for Valerie, she could not hide from her thoughts.

Ivan was curious about her hidden passions? If he only knew!

For most of the night she dreamed of her passions being well met by his own.

And for the rest of the night she lay awake imagining the bitter aftermath should she ever be so unwise as to let that happen.

Twelve

L ady Westcott handed the guest list to Lucy. "Look at this," she snapped. "How am I to work with a list that includes nothing but bachelors? And such bachelors!"

Lucy took the list. It was written in a bold, slashing script. She'd never seen a secretary with such an aggressive writing style. That meant it must be Ivan's.

An unwelcome knot began to coil in her stomach, a twisty, turny knot of heat. She hastily thrust the sheet of parchment back at Lady Westcott. Was everything the man did bold and forceful? Must even the paper and ink he touched churn her emotions until she became a blithering idiot?

"Well? Who is this Sir James Mawbey? Another of Ivan's natural-born companions?"

Lucy focused on the letter she was writing to her brother and his family. *Trying* to write. "Sir James is the scholar whose lectures I have been attending."

There was a short silence, but Lucy could fairly hear the wheels turning in the older woman's brain. "The one Valerie has formed an unwise attachment to?"

Lucy put down her pen and looked over at the dowager countess. "The very same."

. To her surprise, however, Lady Westcott did not seem terribly upset by that bit of news, only a little thoughtful—and perhaps marginally amused.

"Could it be that Ivan is playing the matchmaker? Knowing, of course, that I must disapprove of a poor scholar for Valerie?"

"Something like that," Lucy muttered. He also didn't mind rubbing Lucy's nose in the fact that Sir James was not interested in her. Lady Westcott did not need to know that, however.

Unfortunately the old woman seemed to have a sixth sense for affairs of the heart, for she studied Lucy shrewdly. "I still believe you have a *tendre* for this man, this penniless lecturer. You know," she continued, forestalling Lucy's denial with a raised hand. "You know, you haven't the wherewithal to marry a man with no income to speak of."

"I am well aware of the limitations of my situation," Lucy retorted. "However, you are quite mistaken in your assessment of my interest in Sir James." *Once I might have had such a silly idea, but no more.*

Other than one arched eyebrow, Lady Westcott did not comment on Lucy's sharp words. Instead she shook Ivan's note in front of her. "Well, what are we to do about this ill-advised guest list?"

Without comment Lucy reached for the paper again, and despite the butterflies in her stomach, reread Ivan's list. Four bachelors, a couple of younger married couples, and Laurence Caldridge, Lord Dunleith. "Are there any other young ladies and their parents we might include?"

"Not any from the higher levels of society. They would be scandalized to think I meant to pair their darling daughters with the penniless bastards of the ton. Even a royal one."

"They're not all penniless," Lucy said, unaccountably angered by the dowager countess's haughty attitude. "In fact, Mr. Dameron and Mr. Pierce are wealthy in their own right. It's only Mr. Blackburn who is without a reliable income, and he, presumably, the son of the king."

"Wealth is nothing without family connections, and you well know it."

"Unless, of course, you have a title and are drowning in debt."

"Drowning in debt." Lady Westcott considered a moment. Then her blue eyes narrowed. "Perhaps we should invite that Riddingham girl and her parents. He has gambled away everything but the family seat in Essex. Viscountess Latner is likewise without two pence to rub together, and three daughters to wed. Well done, Miss Drysdale. We may yet make a success of this dinner party."

That was highly debatable, but Lucy wisely kept such thoughts to herself. Still, there was the matter of Sir James. "I don't think we can leave Sir James off the list. Ivan has already issued him a personal invitation."

Lady Westcott shrugged. "He cannot do much harm at one dinner party, especially if you attach yourself to his side. We shall be very careful in our seating arrangement. Now, if you would be good enough to call for my secretary?"

The night of the dinner party Lucy dressed with special care.

She had not gone to Sir James's third lecture. She and Valerie had accompanied Lady Westcott to the theater that night. Lucy had not been sorry to miss the lecture, though. Nor did she particularly look forward to the long evening she must spend at Sir James's side tonight. But at least she had some basis for conversation with him. A few questions about the lecture she'd missed, and he would be off on his favorite topic. She would have only to nod now and again in order to get through the long, tense hours to come.

So why had she spent the better part of the afternoon washing and drying her hair, brushing it while sitting in a sunny spot in the garden?

She'd always been a little vain of her hair and how it gleamed like the polished mahogany of her mother's pianoforte. But what was the point tonight? Her hair was twisted up in a simple fashion, as befitted her role as a chaperone. Except for several soft, curling wisps along her neck, the style was strictly severe.

But even were her hair loose and streaming about her shoulders, it would not matter. There was no one attending tonight's dinner whom she wished to impress. Sir James would never notice—not that she cared any more whether he did or not.

Of course, Ivan could always be counted on to make some leading remark. But she was too wise to credit anything he said.

Still, for all her mental self-flagellation, once dressed she gave herself a critical examination. Her shoes gleamed with a fresh polish. Her teal-green dress of India muslin had been brushed, then ironed with rose-scented water. She wore her favorite gold and aquamarine ear bobs, and a very feminine pair of lace mitts with cutaway fingers. Her outfit wanted only the addition of that magnificent silk shawl to complete it—

She groaned out loud. Where had that idiotic thought come from? The last thing she ever meant to do was wear that shawl. It was lovely, of course, but it had been given to her under decidedly improper conditions. She had to get it back to him, and soon.

Still, the shawl was not her most pressing problem. Her appearance was, for even her face, though devoid of any powder or other contrivance, nonetheless held a heightened color, as if she'd rouged her cheeks with carmine and tinted her lips as well.

Lucy sighed. She looked like a blushing girl—not a particularly desirable effect in a woman of her age and station in life. With a last frown at her image she left the room and headed for the stairs.

Half the way down them she stopped.

Ivan was already in the foyer. Lady Westcott had decreed they must have a receiving line, and though Lucy had doubted that Ivan would participate, it appeared she'd been wrong.

With her heart lodged high in her throat, she forced herself to resume her descent, step by slow step, and all under the disturbingly dark gaze of Ivan Thornton, Lord Westcott.

He approached the stairs, forcing her to halt one step up, and bringing them eye to eye. It had a most disconcerting effect on her, for instead of making her feel more his equal, it somehow made her feel small and fragile. Vulnerable.

But only to him.

"You're looking lovely tonight, Lucy."

As if a hot wind had blown suddenly over her, Lucy began to perspire. "Thank you. You look quite . . . quite handsome yourself." *Quite disturbingly, heartbreakingly, unbelievably handsome.*

The moment stretched out. He didn't move. She seemed unable to sidestep him.

Not until Lady Westcott's cane made sharp contact with the marble threshold between the parlor and the foyer did either of them look away.

"Harrumph." The old woman gave an inelegant snort. Her sharp bird's gaze flitted from Lucy to Ivan, then back. "Where's Valerie? Why are you down here without her?"

Grateful for a reason to leave, Lucy picked up her skirts and made a hasty return to the upper story.

Downstairs Ivan watched her disappear into the brightly lit upper hall before turning to face his grandmother. She was watching him closely.

"If you would seduce the hired help, I recommend you confine yourself to those of lower birth."

Ivan didn't smile. "Be content that I am here, madam. Do not presume to tell me what to do or how to behave."

The old woman's mouth pursed in outrage. "Miss Drysdale is under my care, and if you had an ounce of honor in you, you would respect that. I will send her home before I'll allow you to ruin her."

"You throw Valerie at me, and yet would protect Miss Drysdale from my dishonorable intentions. It would seem that you are rather disorganized in your thinking. Regardless, I intend to make my own decisions without regard to your wishes. Or your threats."

But that was not entirely true, he admitted as Lucy and Valerie made their appearance together. He had resolved neither to pursue or abandon any woman because of his grandmother's wishes or interferences. That didn't alter the fact, however, that her efforts to control him invariably left him in a vile mood. Though he meant to diminish her negative effect on him, it would not always be easy. Like now.

He turned to the two young women. Valerie was a vision in a white gown trimmed with pale blue rosettes and streaming ribbons. With her blond hair in a soft style of upswept curls, here and there cascading loosely down, she was the picture of ethereal beauty. An angel come down to earth to charm a hapless male populace.

By contrast Lucy was darkly garbed with her rich hair restrained—much as her emotions were restrained.

But those emotions were as primed for release as was her glorious hair, and Ivan felt the profoundest need to be the one to release both her hair and her emotions. To let those dark locks down and tangle his fingers in the silky thickness. To kiss her until her defenses crumbled and her natural passions flared out of control. And his with them.

He stifled an oath as his own passions began to rouse. Damned if the woman wasn't turning him into a randy young lad, newly introduced to the tortures of the heart.

No. Not of the heart. This emotion was rooted much lower in his anatomy.

Knowing that, unfortunately, didn't lessen the power of it.

"Good evening, Lord Westcott," Lady Valerie said, giving him a shy smile.

"Lady Valerie." He bowed. "You're looking more beautiful than ever. I fear you shall start a riot among the male guests tonight."

She rewarded him with a grateful smile as dazzling as it was unaffecting. Ever since he'd come to her aid in the matter of Sir James, she'd cast him in the role of beneficent older brother—an odd role for him, but not entirely unpleasant. Besides, it confounded his grandmother, judging by her watchfulness.

He shifted his gaze to Lucy. "Your charge does you credit, Miss Drysdale. Might I add that you look particularly fetching in that shade of green. It lends a sparkle to your eyes."

He let the rest of what he wanted to say trail off. That he'd like to peel that green fabric away. That he'd like to put a different sort of sparkle in her eyes—

The heavy door knocker put a merciful end to his inappropriate reverie. Lucy murmured a brief acknowledgment of his compliment. Then they formed their receiving line, him at the beginning, to greet the first of their guests.

It came as no real surprise to Ivan that the first to arrive was Sir James.

"Lord Westcott. Lady Westcott." He made a creditable bow when he was introduced to the dowager countess. "I am honored to be a guest in your home."

"You are quite welcome," the old woman said. "I believe you have previously met my godchild, Lady Valerie Stanwich."

Ivan was not in the least interested in Sir James's besotted greeting to Valerie. But Lucy's reaction to it—*that* concerned him. As he watched, her expression went from pleasant, to determinedly pleasant, to grimly pleasant.

Like a temperature rising, he felt the hot burn of resentment, something akin to the sick jealousy he'd felt when other boys' parents had sent for them to come home from Burford Hall.

Damnation! How could she prefer this bumbling scholar over him!

For her part, Lucy watched and worried as Sir James greeted Valerie. He had eyes only for the blushing young girl, and she eyes only for him. What a disaster! This would only lead to heartbreak, she feared. How could Ivan use his blameless cousin so cruelly?

She shifted her gaze past the still conversing couple to

Ivan. To her dismay, he was watching her with that dark shuttered gaze of his. He was not smiling.

Only when Sir James finally turned to her was she able to break the hold of Ivan's eyes.

"Miss Drysdale. How nice to see you again."

"It's my pleasure, Sir James. I'm sorry I was not able to attend your last lecture. How is the series going?"

Fortunately she did not have to suffer his lengthy answer for long. Lord Dunleith arrived next, followed by Mr. and Mrs. Hartford Bass and the elder Mr. Bass, Ivan's two men of business. Soon after them came Sir Francis Riddingham, his wife, Maryanne, and their daughter Miss Violet Riddingham, then Viscountess Latner with her two eldest daughters, Ernestine and Edna.

The foyer was filled with people and the butler had begun to usher some of them into the drawing room when the final guests arrived. Ivan's friends came together and Lucy had to admit they made quite an entrance. Three men, each of them handsome in his own striking way. And each of them both attractive and dangerous to every young woman there. Money and the potential for a royal connection weighed in against their lack of normal family connections.

It was enough to make a poor girl's heart flutter. Unfortunately, it was none of them who affected Lucy's heart. That role was reserved for Ivan who, though equally dangerous, came with society's belated approval.

Mr. Blackburn greeted her first. "You are looking very well, Miss Drysdale. I hope you do not intend to hold my association with Ivan against me," he drawled, giving her a friendly grin.

"I would never do that, Mr. Blackburn. But you will forgive me, I hope, if I worry for you for that same reason. Lord Westcott will lead you into trouble if you are not careful," she added in a teasing voice.

"I'll keep him safe," Giles Dameron put in. "Hello, Miss Drysdale. It's nice to see you again."

"Indeed," she answered. "It's a pleasure to see you here. And you too, Mr. Pierce."

"The pleasure is all mine," Elliot Pierce replied. As he was the last of their guests, Lady Westcott and Valerie joined the others moving toward the drawing room. Lucy would have gone too, but Mr. Pierce did not release her hand.

When she looked at him questioningly, he gave her a mocking smile. "You do know you are playing with fire," he murmured in a tone reserved for her ears only.

"Fire?" But Lucy knew exactly what he meant. She pulled her hand from his. "You're his friend. Why would you want to warn *me* away from *him*? Shouldn't it be the other way around?"

He gave an idle shrug, but his black eyes did not waver from hers. "Let's just say that I don't believe his plans for you will make him very happy."

"His plans for me? He has no right to make any plans for me," she exclaimed. Then she frowned. "Exactly what *are* his plans for me? And why should he be discussing me with you and his other friends?"

He smiled, but Lucy could no longer tell if he was mocking or sincere. "Ivan keeps his own counsel. But I've known him a very long time. I know what he needs—and what he doesn't need."

For some absurd reason his words hurt. She drew her wounded pride around her like a shield. "Contrary to what you seem to think, Mr. Pierce, I have no designs on your friend Lord Westcott. Most certainly I have not set my cap for him. I'm not pursuing him," she reiterated. "Now, if you don't mind?"

She turned and headed for the drawing room, fuming all the way. The nerve of the man to imply that she was the wrong woman for Ivan Thornton. She'd never once indicated that she thought she was the *right* one.

Of course, she'd danced with him at the McClendons' party. And she'd kissed him too. Had he revealed that to his friends? Or that she'd never returned the shawl he'd left in her room?

By the time she joined Valerie in the drawing room, she was in quite a state. When she should have been directing her young charge to mingle more, she instead just stood alongside while Valerie and Sir James conversed about brothers and sisters and the role of parents.

Ivan watched her; she felt the weight of his stare. But she refused to look anywhere even close to him.

So there, Elliot Pierce. See how wrong you are?

But although she kept her gaze away from Ivan, she nonetheless managed at any given moment to know precisely where he was and with whom he conversed. By the time Simms the butler rang the small silver dinner bell, Lucy was ready to slap Miss Violet Riddingham, and scratch the eyes out of the younger Miss Latner.

Dinner was no improvement either, for she was partnered with Sir James on one side and Viscount Latner on the other. Ivan, meanwhile, was paired with Valerie and the elder Miss Latner.

There were several courses. By the time Lucy had mutilated the stuffed game hen, stabbed disinterestedly at the baked oysters, and had her third glass of wine—on the heels of two glasses of champagne—she was sick to death of Sir James's theories on child rearing and bored to tears by Lord Latner's opinion about the king's position regarding the American colonies.

"They're no longer colonies," she reminded him with barely restrained impatience. "They haven't been in over fifty years."

"And we've the king's father to blame for that," Lord Latner pointed out. "I say he was already mad, even in the seventies."

Lady Westcott rose to her feet before Lucy could say anything truly insulting to the witless fellow. "Ladies, let us adjourn to the parlor, shall we?"

As the ladies rose, so did the gentlemen. Sir James's eyes followed Valerie. Lucy felt as if all the others' eyes—at least Ivan's and his friends'—rested heavily on her.

One and all they disapproved of his interest in her, that was clear. Why they should care, she did not know. She was not looking for a husband, and he most certainly did not appear to be in the market for a wife. So what did they fear, that she would corrupt him somehow?

"We'll have coffee now, Simms. Would any of you ladies like to freshen up?" Lady Westcott asked once they had gained the parlor.

It was Lucy's chance to escape. While the other ladies alternated visits to the necessary in the back hall, Lucy excused herself and made her way up the stairs. She desperately needed a few minutes to compose herself, otherwise she would not survive this ghastly evening.

Once in her bedchamber, however, Lucy was confronted by the unwelcome truth. Only one solution to this perverse dilemma existed. Returning home to Somerset would take her out of harm's way once and for all. It would remove her from the temptation of Ivan Thornton. At the same time it would relieve his friends who worried unnecessarily over his temporary interest in her.

Lucy felt the sting of tears but fiercely beat them back. She was not the weepy sort. She never had been. Why she should want to succumb to them now she couldn't begin to fathom. Just because she ought to leave London? The fact was, she no longer had any reason to stay in town. The peace and tranquillity of the countryside were beginning to seem very appealing. Besides, any fascination she'd felt for Sir James had disappeared once she'd met him.

Or had it begun to fade only when she'd met Ivan?

"Blast!" She poured a little water into her wash bowl, bent down to refresh her face, then rinsed her mouth. Her head began to spin, however, and she quickly straightened up.

She'd drunk too much at dinner. Another reason to return to Houghton Manor. She'd been behaving like a silly girl of late, drinking too much, dancing until all hours. Mooning over a man who didn't have it in him to return a woman's honest affections.

It simply would not do, she told the pale reflection that peered back from her dressing mirror.

Telling herself that, however, would not do a jot of good. No, she must get away from here. From Ivan.

She patted her face dry, and avoiding her reflection, she took a deep breath. She would go downstairs now, but first thing in the morning she would request an interview with Lady Westcott. Then as soon as possible she would take the Exeter coach home.

But all the resolve in the world was not adequate defense when Lucy left her room. The door clicked closed, she turned toward the stairs, and Ivan was there.

She stopped, then made herself start forward again. "My lord." She nodded politely as she approached him. If he thought she had any intention of lingering abovestairs with him, just the two of them alone, then he must have had far more to drink than she.

He stopped when he saw her. Now he sidestepped, forcing her to halt as well. Given Mr. Pierce's oblique warning, the Riddingham girl's ill-disguised interest in Ivan, and his notorious insincerity, this arrogant display pushed Lucy's control past its limits.

"What do you think you're doing?"

He smiled, but she could tell he was far from happy. "I might ask the same of you."

She drew herself up and belligerently thrust out her chin. "If you must know, I needed to refresh myself. And you?"

He locked his hands behind him and rocked back on his heels. "Just making sure nothing untoward is going on in my house."

Lucy's jaw dropped open. "I hope you are not implying that I might engage in such behavior."

"You've done it before."

"Me! Me?" Lucy was so incensed she sputtered. "If you're referring to what I think you're referring to—"

"You kissed me more than willingly. It makes a man wonder who else you've been kissing."

Lucy glared at him. "Just what are you implying? That I'm meeting someone up here? You must be blind if you think that. Sir James is so besotted with Valerie—"

"What of Elliot Pierce?"

That brought her up short. "Elliot Pierce? You can't be serious!" It was too ludicrous to believe. Ludicrous or not, however, Lucy was not amused. She planted her fists on her hips. "I have no assignation with any man, my lord. I suspect it's your own guilt which gives you such shabby ideas. Who did you come up here to meet? The elder Miss Latner or the younger? Or could it be Miss Riddingham—"

"You."

Lucy broke off in mid-sentence. In the middle of her accusation. In the middle of her anger. She stared at him dumbfounded, silenced by that one word.

"Me?"

"You."

He reached out and brushed his thumb over her lower lip, a light, sensuous caress that made mincemeat of her resolve.

"You . . . You are toying with me. You shouldn't . . ."

"No? Then turn the tables on me. *You* toy with *me,* Lucy."

Her lips tingled from his touch. They burned. Then his knuckles stroked her cheek, tracing its shape right down to her neck.

When his palm opened against the side of her neck she began to shake.

He was so good at this, the one functioning bit of her mind made note. So very good. It was as if he turned on some power, unleashed some force, and like a willing victim, she succumbed.

Someone please help me, for I cannot help myself!

"Toy with me, Lucy. I want you to."

One of her hands came up to grab his wrist. But instead

of pushing him away, she only gripped him tighter. "Why are you doing this?"

"It seems I cannot help myself."

"But . . . But you must. You must stop this . . . this very bad habit of seducing hapless young women."

"Then help me," he murmured. "Make me stop."

"How?" she whispered as his face bent nearer to hers. "How?"

"Kiss me."

It was a request. It was a command. It was as inevitable as the tides and the seasons. As life and death themselves.

Ivan's mouth descended on hers and she was lost. Like the strike of lightning igniting a tree and setting an entire forest to flame, so did the hot press of his lips start a conflagration that set all of her afire. Her logic burned to cinders, her caution turned to ash. Propriety should have doused the flame, but it was no match for the fuel of her emotions.

Oh, how she wanted this man!

And how Ivan wanted her.

He'd endured too many restless nights and too many frustrating days of late. This evening had been the worst. She'd been seated beside Sir James, and though he'd known the man was infatuated with Valerie, it hadn't helped. Lucy harbored a not-so-secret admiration for the man, and the very idea drove Ivan mad.

On top of that, Elliot displayed more interest in Lucy than any other woman of his dubious acquaintance, inquiring on several occasions about her. When Elliot had held her back in the foyer for private conversation, Ivan had naturally become suspicious. When Elliot had excused himself from the gentlemen's company after dinner, Ivan had been overcome by an insane fit of jealousy. Elliot Pierce was a rakehell of the worst sort.

But Elliot Pierce was not up here kissing Lucy; he was. And he meant to burn the thought of any other man right out of her mind.

So he kissed her without restraint, letting her feel every

bit of his desire for her. If he frightened her he didn't care. He would take her past fear to the exquisite pleasures of the flesh.

To his immense satisfaction, she did not act as if she were afraid. She arched up to him, opening to the hungry assault of his lips and tongue. When he slanted his mouth over hers, searching for the deepest, the closest, the most intimate connection possible between them, she welcomed him completely. His tongue took possession of her mouth, thrusting and claiming. And she let him.

She was sweet and delicious, and he wanted to devour every piece of her. He drew her harshly to him, pressing her hard against his arousal. God, but he needed her! He had to have her!

The kiss ended and they broke apart, both of them gasping for breath. That was not the end, however, but only the beginning. Ivan ran one hand down her back, roaming past her slender waist to the enticing curve of her derriere. When he heard her involuntary groan, he pressed his advantage.

He'd known from the first that she had a mighty capacity for passion. It had been too long hidden, too long tamped down. But he would release it, as she likewise released his.

"I want to eat you up, Lucy. To taste you. To lick you. Here," he said, nibbling at her earlobe while his hand encircled her right breast.

"Here," he murmured, trailing kisses down her neck, while his other hand pressed between the back of her thighs. He pushed one of his knees between hers, forcing her to straddle his leg.

"Here," he whispered, thumbing her taut nipple while his thigh rubbed urgently between hers.

"Ivan," she whimpered, caught in the throes of her tumultuous desires.

To hear her moan his name that way raised him to new heights of arousal. "Lucy," he murmured, returning his mouth to hers. "I burn for you."

When she thrust convulsively against his thigh and into his hand, he added, "Do you burn for me?"

"Yes."

He barely heard her answer, for she wound her arms around his neck and kissed him with wild abandon. It was the culmination of his every fantasy since the night she'd danced with him in the downstairs parlor. He wanted her and he would have her.

He swept her up in his arms and, without breaking the kiss, somehow found her room. With one kick the door flew open. With another it slammed shut.

Then still holding her, he fell back on her bed, rolled over, and trapped her beneath him.

She was probably a virgin, and he tried to remember that fact. But it was hard. While he raised her skirt with one hand, he freed her hair with the other.

She was no less occupied, for she managed to loosen his cravat while threading her fingers through his hair and kissing him everywhere else she could reach. His mouth. His ear. His throat. Her tongue made tentative forays, then bolder ones. Her fingers did the same.

When she slid one hand inside his coat, he helped her tear it off him. When she freed two of the buttons of his waistcoat, he ripped the garment off, sending the other buttons flying.

Then he bent over her again, his eyes devouring every inch of her delectable body. Flushed cheeks, pale thighs. Her dark hair in tangled disarray on the cream-colored counterpane. She was the ultimate picture of what a woman should be. Soft and yet strong; sweet and yet spicy. Smart and beautiful, and his.

He kissed the edge of her bodice, then moved the kiss lower, until he felt the aroused bud of her nipple through the fabric.

He circled it with his tongue, and when her breaths came faster, drew it between his teeth. One of his hands roamed lower, sliding along the bare skin of her thighs, and slipped between them to where she was hot—and wet.

He wanted to kiss her there too. He wanted to kiss her everywhere, and bring her to shuddering climax.

Then the door crashed open and, like ice water, the flame was doused.

"Dear God in heaven!" his damned, interfering grandmother exclaimed. "What is going on here?"

Thirteen

"What is going on here?"

If the situation had not been so utterly dreadful, Lucy would have laughed at such a ridiculous question. What was going on? Lady Westcott had been married. Surely she knew the answer to that.

But the situation was dreadful. It was humiliating. Unbelievable. Disastrous.

Ivan jerked upright and spun around, trying to shelter her from prying eyes. Lucy scrambled to sit up, though she feared that did nothing but draw attention to her bared legs and tangled petticoats. Worse, when she sent a guilty look at the door, she discovered more than merely one set of shocked eyes upon her. Lady Westcott led the way, but behind her stood Sir Laurence and Elliot Pierce.

Blood rushed, hot and telling, to her face. Dear God in heaven! What madness had possessed her that she would abandon all good sense in this way?

The answer was obvious. Ivan Thornton. He was the madness that possessed her. He seemed able to convince her to do anything. She'd nearly given in to him. The truth was, she *had* given in to him. It was only by chance they'd been interrupted.

"I'll thank you to give us a little privacy," Ivan growled.

"You've had too much privacy already," Lady Westcott

snapped. "I'll thank *you* to get out of Miss Drysdale's bed-chamber."

Lucy was behind Ivan, and though mortified beyond belief, she gave him a nudge. "Go. Just . . . go," she whispered.

He turned to face her and for a few seconds their eyes held. He wanted her still. The truth of that burned in his eyes. But it was over, she realized with an awful certainty. She would be dispatched back to Somerset in disgrace.

Then his gaze fell to her bosom and she realized in horror that he'd left a damning wet spot in a prominent location on her bodice.

Dear God in heaven!

Her hand flew to her breast, while her heart plummeted to her feet. "Just go. Please," she mouthed to him. Then she turned away, walked to the window, and stared blindly out into the night.

She heard Ivan leave. He snatched up his coat and waist-coat and stalked to the door.

For those awful, endless seconds, Lady Westcott remained silent. But Sir Laurence muttered continuously under his breath. "In his own house . . . Innocent girl . . . Outrageous . . ."

Then Elliot spoke, something low that Lucy couldn't make out.

"I'll have your hide for this!" Ivan growled an immediate response to his friend.

Lucy spun around to see the two men glaring at one another. They stood in the hall just outside the door, Elliot the picture of arrogant nonchalance, Ivan rigid, with fists knotted at his side.

"Just name the place and time, Thornton. I'll be there."

"No!" Lucy cried. She stared at them both. Though she did not understand the cause of their animosity, she knew it was somehow on account of her. "He has nothing to do with this, Ivan. Nothing. I will not have you fighting one another like hooligans when you are as close as brothers."

"Thank you, Miss Drysdale," Elliot said, smiling and inclining his head.

"Enough of this!" Lady Westcott snapped. "Ivan, I will see you in the library directly after I speak with Miss Drysdale."

The men left and the door closed with an awful, accusing thud. Lady Westcott stared at Lucy across the silence. "Well." She moved across the room, carrying her crystal-headed cane. "I blame myself for this."

"You blame yourself?" That was the last thing Lucy expected from her. She'd practically ruined the woman's plans to pair Ivan and Valerie. She expected the woman to rant and rave and throw her out. Certainly she had every right to.

"I should have kept a closer watch on him. And on you," the dowager countess added, shooting Lucy a sharp look.

"It's hardly your fault," Lucy muttered. "You hired me to chaperone Valerie. I certainly should have known better. I *do* know better. The fault is entirely mine."

Lady Westcott tapped her foot. "By teatime tomorrow everyone will know. We will have to act fast."

Lucy nodded. "I'll pack immediately. Should I . . . Will you . . . Can Simms have someone deliver me to the coaching inn?"

"The coaching inn? If you expect to ever circulate in polite society again—even polite country society—there is only one solution, Miss Drysdale. And retreat is not it."

Lucy stared at the older woman blankly. "Surely you're not saying I should stay on as Valerie's chaperone. To brazen it out for my own self is one thing. To do so as Valerie's chaperone would attach scandal to her name. You can't mean to do that."

"I mean to make this matter right in the only way possible. I mean for you to wed my grandson, and as soon as possible. There will be talk, of course. But once you are wed, this peccadillo will be charged to the grand passion you share. Now," she went on without pause. "I suggest you write a letter to your brother and mother directly. I'll send a messenger tonight to Somerset to inform them of the upcoming nuptials. They may stay here if they do not have a city house available to them on such short notice.''

She broke off and stared expectantly at Lucy. ''You *do* want your family here for the wedding, don't you?''

Lucy had been staring at her, mouth agape, unable to quite comprehend the enormity of what the woman was saying.

Upcoming nuptials? Hers and Ivan's?

She shook her head, trying to make sense of it. ''Lady Westcott, I fear that is not possible—''

''It most certainly is. You have ruined all my plans, young woman. Seducing Ivan when you knew I had other intentions for him. The least you can do now is make things right. There's more than *your* reputation at stake here, you know. You've been selfish long enough. I'll not allow you to behave so one minute longer.''

So saying, she turned and stalked out of the room, much as Ivan had done just minutes before, shutting the door sharply behind her.

Lucy was so stunned by the massive upheaval of her entire life that she could think of no response but one.

''Ivan will never agree to this,'' she shouted at the closed door. ''He won't agree! And neither will I.'' This last was muttered in frustration, punctuated by the stamp of her foot. But the tall door muffled her voice and the carpet muffled her angry gesture.

Still, Antonia heard the girl's brave vow. She just did not believe it.

A smile lit the old woman's face and her eyes gleamed with triumph as she made her way to the library. She was very close to getting what she wanted. Very, very close. Against all odds, this last-ditch plan of hers had worked. She had only to land Ivan now, and if his level of frustration were any indication, he was ready to leap by his own accord right into the boat.

But not if she appeared too eager.

Antonia paused outside the library. She smelled tobacco smoke, but heard not a thing. They were all there, probably glaring at one another. She drew a slow breath. She had to pick her way carefully and choose her words well. But she was up to the task.

Ivan would not thwart her. Not this time. She'd baited her hook too well.

Ivan sprawled in a massive leather chair and watched the smoke from the cigar he held. He'd lit it to annoy Lord Dunleith—and also to occupy his hands so that he didn't strangle Elliot. He'd see the man in hell before he let him get anywhere near Lucy again. And he knew just how to do it.

The old witch made her entrance, stiff and erect. Determined. Ivan watched her with a detached eye, something he'd never been able to do before.

She was a cold-hearted bitch with nerves of steel. She tried to control the lives of her family the same way she controlled the vast properties her son had refused to manage. For that Ivan grudgingly gave her credit. She'd done a commendable job with the family estates and investments, better than most men could have done. But she failed miserably when it came to manipulating people.

For a moment he wondered what his father's life had been like with her for a mother. Had his complete inadequacy as a man been due to her, a son's only way of rebelling?

He frowned. He didn't give a damn why his father had been a spineless ass. It was enough that *he* would never fall into that role.

She paused just inside the door and glared at him. "Had I known you planned a debauchery tonight I would have devised a completely different guest list."

"I trust I would still have appeared on it," Elliot remarked.

"Now see here, young man!" Lord Dunleith sputtered. "We'll have no insolence—"

"You would be at the top of the list," Lady Westcott snapped. "Second only to my amoral grandson, of course."

"I congratulate you, madam," Ivan interjected. "You have the sensibilities of a first-rate procurer. If I ever plan an orgy, I'll consult with you firsthand."

"Now see here!" Lord Dunleith repeated. He pushed himself to his feet. "You will not insult Antonia this way. Nor shall you get off scot-free from tonight's embarrassment."

He faced Ivan, shaking his knotted fist. "Since Miss Drysdale has no one here to defend her honor, I will take that responsibility for myself. Make an offer for her, Westcott. Make an offer for her now, else I will be forced to issue you a challenge!"

Ivan took a slow drag of the cigar, then blew out a perfect circle of bluish-gray smoke. "You will challenge me?" He grinned at the angry old fellow. "Swords, I presume?"

"Don't think I can't skewer you," the old man swore.

"And if by chance you don't succeed, I will," Elliot drawled.

In an instant Ivan's fury returned. If Elliot thought he could play the role of savior to Lucy and thereby win her affections for himself, Ivan was more than ready to disavow him of that notion. He put the cigar down and stared coldly at the man he'd so long considered his friend. "I believe it falls to the challenger to name the time and place?"

"There will be no dueling!" Lady Westcott interrupted. "I will not have it."

"Your wishes are immaterial, madam. They always have been," Ivan bit out.

She stared at him in utter contempt. "My God, but you are even worse than I imagined. You've toyed with the affections of every heiress you've met, yet refuse to offer for any of them. Now you embroil yourself in a tawdry affair with one of the chaperones."

"If she's respectable enough to be your godchild's chaperone, you'd think she is respectable enough for me."

"I'm not saying she isn't respectable. Quite the opposite.

She might not possess a title nor have much of a dowry. But at least she had one thing of value: a sterling reputation. But now you've stolen even that from her. You've ruined a perfectly respectable young woman. And why? Just to spite me. If you were even—''

"I have no intention of ruining Miss Drysdale."

"You already have!" she cried. "Do you think this can be kept quiet?''

"I certainly hope not,'' Ivan replied. He shifted his gaze to Elliot and glared a warning at him. "I want to make certain everyone knows that I am marrying Lucy Drysdale. That she is *my* wife and therefore off limits to anyone else.''

Their individual reactions to that surprising announcement were interesting to watch. Elliot gave him a considering look then grinned. Whether he mocked Ivan or concurred with him, though, was impossible to tell.

His grandmother's eyes narrowed, as if she didn't believe him. Then slowly a look of relief crept into her lined face. Could it be that her concern for Lucy was even greater than her wish to settle him with young Valerie?

Only Lord Dunleith frowned. "What did you say? What did he say, Toni? I couldn't make it out.''

"He said he'd marry her,'' she answered the man. But she watched Ivan. "You, married to Lucy Drysdale.'' She shook her head. "I suppose I should be relieved that at least one of you is being sensible about this.''

Ivan resisted the urge to frown. "Am I to assume from that obtuse remark that one of us, namely Lucy, is not being sensible?''

She shrugged. "The last thing she said to me was that marriage to you was not possible.''

Of all the replies she might have made to him, that one was the worst. Though outwardly Ivan maintained the appearance of calm, inside he cringed as if from a blow to the gut. He flicked off the ashy end of the cigar. "Not possible? Unless she is already wed—in which case I am off the hook—anything is possible.''

"Perhaps she isn't pleased by the prospect of marriage to you," Elliot mused. "Maybe her affections are otherwise engaged."

Ivan fought the urge to wipe the smirk from Pierce's face with his fists. "I believe I know better than any of you where Lucy's affections lie. Her affections are the reason we are even having this discussion." He stood up. "I believe Lucy and I need a few moments alone."

"Alone? Harrumph," Lady Westcott snorted. "I'll send for her. You can have five minutes here, in the library. That's all."

She stared at him a long moment, then sighed. "Despite the less-than-ideal circumstances of your impending marriage, Ivan, I hope . . . I wish you the best." Then she herded the other two men out of the library and Ivan was left alone with that unexpected remark echoing in his ears.

She wished him the best?

He stared blankly at the tip of the cigar. She'd wanted him to marry all along. The fact that she had not hand-picked the bride must grate on her pride. But she obviously approved of Lucy Drysdale—albeit grudgingly—else she would not already be wishing him well.

It was enough to make him withdraw his offer.

He stubbed out the cigar and pushed himself out of the chair. Damn the woman! He was handing her just what she wanted.

But it wasn't just what she wanted. She'd wanted an heiress for him, a silly, brainless twit with more extensive lands than she already held—than *he* already held. What he was getting, however, was a prickly bluestocking with at best a piddling settlement from her brother.

The fact remained, however, that he hadn't intended to marry at all. He crossed the room to the bar tray and poured himself a healthy glass of whisky. Bloody hell! It was not supposed to have happened this way. He was not supposed to take total leave of his senses, then be caught in the act by his grandmother!

With a nearly silent creak the door opened. With a meta-

llic click it closed. He drank from the whisky tumbler, lowered it and waited a moment, then lifted it once more and
quaffed the contents. Only then did he turn to face her.

She stood just inside the doorway, as if she meant to
bolt. She'd repaired her hair and her clothes were back in
order. But she nonetheless looked changed.

Her lips were red and swollen. The color in her cheeks
was high. He suspected that if he stared at her breasts, her
nipples would tighten until he could see their hardened silhouettes right through the fabric of her bodice.

God, he wanted her!

But if the look in her eyes was any indication, she did
not want him. At least not at the moment. She stared at
him with a wary expression.

It would be a challenge to change her mind.

"Why is marriage to me not possible?"

Her chin came up. "We are not well matched. Surely
you don't believe that we are."

"I have money, land, a title. Isn't that every woman's
dream?"

"If that was all I wanted, I would be ten years wed by
now, with four or five children already of my own."

"I see. So, what do you want?"

"I might ask as much of you, my lord."

"My lord? After what very nearly happened between
us—and what is about to happen—you would call me my
lord?"

She swallowed and he was entranced by the smooth
workings of her throat. He wanted to kiss her there.

"Nothing is about to happen between us. For I plan to
return to Somerset—"

"Not bloody likely!"

She swallowed again. "I plan to return to Somerset and
you . . . You can continue this unhappy war you wage with
your grandmother."

She looked so brave and so fragile that despite his volatile temper Ivan had to suppress a grin. Life with Lucy

would never be dull. "You haven't answered my question. What is it you want in a husband?"

"I don't want a husband at all. And you don't want a wife," she added. "So why are we doing this?"

"Actually, the more I think about it, the better a wife sounds. At least no one would interrupt me when I wanted to make love to her."

She blushed, as he'd expected she would. He crossed the room and halted less than an arm's length from her. "And no one would interrupt you, Lucy. Were we wed, I could lay you down right here on this silk carpet. I could remove every stitch of your clothing," he said, in a voice gone hoarse from his own erotic thoughts. "And I'd have you remove mine too. Then . . . Then we'd both be very happy to be married to one another."

He was hard, fully aroused by the mental picture he'd painted. She was aroused too, for her breathing had grown shallow and her eyes were dark with desire. Her gaze fell away from his and he felt them touch upon his bulging erection.

"You do that to me," he whispered. She jerked her eyes back up to his. "Don't be embarrassed. I'm not. And I do this to you," he continued, reaching out to rub one knuckle across the hard pebble of her nipple.

With a small cry of anguish she slid away from him. Ivan faced the door, then leaned stiff-armed against it, struggling to regain his composure. He should have better control than this. But he didn't. At the moment he felt as if he'd explode from his pent-up desire for this woman.

"Lust is insufficient reason to get married," she said in a strangled voice.

"Fine. Then you can be my mistress."

"I will not!"

He turned to face her. "I was being sarcastic, Lucy. And if you think putting that table between us changes anything, you're wrong."

"I won't marry you."

He stalked toward her. "Why the hell not?"

"Because . . . Because we would make one another supremely unhappy."

"Whereas being ruined and a social outcast will make you supremely happy." He leaned forward on the table and for a long moment their eyes met and held. He could see he'd scored a direct hit with that.

But she rallied gamely. "Eventually the talk will die down."

"Only if you bury yourself in the country."

She shook her head. "I will not agree to so unwise a union, no matter what you say."

Ivan's patience began to unravel. She meant it. She was refusing to marry him, rejecting an offer she ought to have been ecstatic to get. He drew back and glared at her. She was just like his father—more than ready to fuck a Gypsy. But God forbid she should link her name with his!

Except that he was no powerless Gypsy like his mother had been. He was Ivan Thornton, Earl of Westcott, Viscount Seaforth, and Baron Turner. He could have anything he wanted. And what he wanted now was to show her the full extent of the power he wielded.

"We will be wed within the week. I'll send a formal request to your brother. I'm sure he'll be more sensible about this than you."

"You can't make me do this, Ivan. We'll both regret it if you do."

"I regret it already," he bit out. He reached across the table and caught her by the arms, then jerked her against the unyielding table between them. "Give in, Lucy. You have no other choice." Then he kissed her, a hard and brutal kiss, to prove to her that she could deny him nothing. He wanted to punish her for rejecting him.

When she fought him, he held her still. When she tried to twist her face away, he pressed her all the harder. And when her closed lips finally opened to his assault, when his tongue possessed her until she was soft and pliant, he wanted to devour the very essence of her.

How could she prefer that pitiful scholar to him? How could she look at Pierce?

He was as hard as the table between them, and he ground himself against the unfeeling oak. He could not wait a week. He would not!

Then he tasted her tears, warm and salty, and reason raised its unwelcome head.

He pulled back. Her face was flush with desire, and wet with despair. The fact that he could make her body want him, but not her heart, drove him to madness.

"I'll have you, Lucy. It's a foregone conclusion. It would be easier if you just resign yourself to that fact." Then he let go of her, spun around, and stalked out of the room.

The last thing he'd let her see was the pathetic proof of how much he wanted her.

The last thing he'd ever let her know was how close he'd come to confusing the lust she roused in him with love.

Fourteen

*I*t was the worst week of her life.

Ivan had moved out of the house. She hadn't seen him once since their dreadful scene in the library. Lady Westcott said it was improper for a bridegroom to live in the same house with his fiancée and apparently Ivan had agreed.

No matter how Lucy protested that she was not his fiancée, she was ignored. No matter how often she insisted that she be allowed to speak to Ivan herself, he was not summoned.

A special license had already been obtained, waiving the usual posting of the marriage banns. Hasty arrangements had been made for a private wedding at the Chapel of St. Mary of the Archangels.

When the modiste was summoned for her dress, Lucy refused to coöperate. But even that did not deter Lady Westcott. "Take the measurements from one of her other dresses. Make the gown a pale aqua silk, trimmed with teal and cream. Something elegant and not too frivolous, as befits a woman of her age."

"I won't wear it," Lucy swore. "And I won't marry a man who hates me."

"He doesn't hate you."

"He hates everyone. You. Me. Even his closest friends."

But Lucy got nowhere with the dowager countess. Then

three days after that awful dinner party, her family arrived. Not just Graham, which would have been bad enough, but also Hortense, all the children, her mother, and four servants.

It was enough to rival Bedlam itself.

"You'll bring ruination upon us all!" Graham ranted.

"I can't believe, my only daughter . . ." Lucy's mother wailed.

"Poor Prudence," Hortense sobbed. "Poor Charity and Grace. After this none of them will be able to raise their heads in good society. And they'll never be able to make good matches of their own!"

"I'll cut off your allowance," Graham swore. "You'll be out on the streets, for you shan't be allowed near my children."

"Oh, Graham," their mother had cried. "Not that!"

Lucy wanted to scream. She wanted to escape them all, just run away somewhere—anywhere—and have a good cry. Yet even with a good cry she would still be in the same predicament: trapped like a rat in a hole.

If only Ivan were not so insistent on this foolish marriage. Graham would not be threatening her so if Ivan were not an earl with a fortune to go with his title. As for Ivan's motivations . . .

She'd handled things badly with Ivan. She could see that now. He'd obviously taken her rejection far more personally than he should. His feelings had been too hurt to see the practical reality of her decision. If only she could talk to him under calmer, less emotionally charged circumstances.

"I'll think about what you said," she told Graham, cutting him off in mid-sentence. Hortense looked up. Lucy's mother paused with her handkerchief halfway to her eyes.

"And well you should think about it," he snapped, tugging indignantly on his waistcoat.

"I believe I shall lie down a while," Lucy said, biting back a much sharper retort. "I'll take my supper in my room," she added to Lady Westcott, as she made her hasty retreat.

But once in her room, with only her own unhappy company, Lucy was more miserable than ever. In two days she and Ivan were to wed. The household had been turned upside down with preparations; announcements had begun to appear in all the appropriate newspapers.

She sat in the window, staring out at the streetscape. Why was she fighting the inevitable? Any other unmarried woman of her advanced years would be giddy with joy to entrap a handsome and wealthy man like the Earl of Westcott. No doubt several young ladies had tried just such a method to obtain an offer from him. He was not fighting it, so why was she?

Because she loved him and he didn't love her back.

She let out an unhappy sigh. There was no use denying it any longer, at least not to herself. It wasn't simply lust she felt for him, the physical desire natural to a woman of her age for a man who attracted women wherever he went. No, somehow along the way it had become something much greater than that. He was not as harsh and forbidding as he would pretend, nor as impervious to slights. He was a man who had never known love, nor did he think he needed it. But it was just that fact that made her love him so desperately. She wanted to surround him with her love, to protect him with it. To make him happy with it.

Only it was not her love he wanted. And it was not love he meant to give her in return. A title, beautiful homes, and a generous allowance would be hers. And all he demanded in return was the use of her body. He would never have any deeper feelings for her than that.

The bitter and uncompromising truth brought tears to her eyes.

The inequality in their relationship terrified her. To love him and not be loved in return . . . She did not believe she could bear it. It was too awful a fate to endure.

She wiped her eyes, then stared out into the twilight. Across the street a carriage pulled off, leaving a man standing there, gazing after it. It reminded her of the night she'd

watched Ivan bid farewell to that woman, and it caused her
heart to sink even further.

What if after they wed he continued to carry on with
women of that sort?

Surely he wouldn't do such a thing! But then, why
should she expect him to change? He might even keep a
mistress. Perhaps he already did!

She jumped up and began to pace as her stomach twisted
into a sick knot. She was working herself into a lather over
mere conjecture, she told herself. She was letting her imagination run away with her. But she couldn't help it. She
had to see Ivan, she decided. She had to try one more time
to talk him out of this marriage. Otherwise, she feared they
would both live to regret it.

It proved almost too easy to find him. After worrying
over getting caught, she had only to bribe one of the stable
boys. Ivan was probably staying with Mr. Pierce and Mr.
Dameron in Tyne Street, the lad told her. He would take
her there himself.

"With Mr. Pierce? Are you certain?"

"He often stays there. So does Mr. Blackburn. It's a
well-known bachelors' quarters." The boy hesitated. "Are
you certain you want to go there, miss?"

"Yes." She slipped him another shilling. "Let's be off."

The house was quiet with few lights burning. "No one's
to home," the boy reported. "The butler says they're often
out till late."

Till late. No telling how long that would be. Lucy de-
bated what to do: wait or return to Berkeley Square. "I
should like to leave a note for Lord Westcott. Ask the man
if he will show me into the parlor," she said, climbing
down from the curricle unassisted. "Tell him I shall require
pen and ink and paper."

It took Lucy several false starts to get the letter going.
Though she prided herself on both her writing and her pen-
manship, this particular document suffered from numerous
scratched-out areas.

She was despairing of ever getting it right when steps in

the hall drew her attention. Ivan? She leaped up in a dither of emotions, hope and dread being the most persistent.

But it was Mr. Pierce, not Ivan, and at her deflated expression he gave her a wry smile. "Apparently I am not the person you were hoping for."

He advanced into the room, removing his gloves and loosening the buttons of his coat. "If you wished to speak to him you had only to send word and he would have come to you."

"No one would summon him for me. So I decided to come myself."

"He'll be very pleased to see you. Shall I show you to his private chambers so you can . . . prepare yourself for his return?"

Lucy pursed her lips disapprovingly. "I have not come here for *that*."

He considered her for a moment. "If not *that*, then what?"

"Not that it's any of your affair, but . . . but I wanted to speak to him about . . . about our impending wedding."

"I see. And since he's not here you've written him a note instead?"

Lucy gripped the three sheets of scribbled parchment tighter. "Yes."

He held out his hand. "You'd better give it to me, then. He may be out all—For a good while," he finished. "But I can deliver it to him, if you like. I have an idea or two about where he might be."

Lucy bit the inside of her cheek. She had an idea or two herself, and it made her heart ache to even think on it. She nodded. "All right. Let me just sign it and seal it up."

"A wax seal is not likely to prevent me reading it, should I be so inclined." He chuckled.

Lucy bristled. "I thought you were his friend."

"I am, though he's not been too kindly disposed toward me of late. Still, we've patched things up the past few days."

"This is private correspondence."

"You'll simply have to take your chances, Miss Drysdale. If you wish Ivan to get your note it will have to go through me." He drew off his neckcloth and lowered himself into a chair. "I suggest you get on with it."

Though Lucy glared at him, it did no good. Furious at him, and at all men in general, she plopped down into the chair and once more snatched up the pen.

> . . . *And so, as you can see, this marriage will do neither of us any good, especially you. The embarrassment of our predicament will fade much faster than will the results of an ill-advised union between us.*
>
> *I wish you the very best in the future and hope sincerely that you will find a woman whom you can love and honor, and who will return the same feelings to you.*
>
> *I remain your friend,*

She paused at that. His friend? She would remain always the woman who loved him and wanted nothing from him save his love in return. Sadly, that was the one thing he didn't have in him to give her.

> *I remain your friend,*
> *Lucy Drysdale*
> P.S. *Mr. Elliot Pierce may have read this note. I hope that fact will not cause you any additional embarrassment.*
>
> > > > > > > > > > > > > > > *-L-*

Then she folded the three sheets, placed them in an envelope, and sealed them with the wax of a burning candle and the crisscross marks of the letter opener.

"Here. Break the seal if you must. But promise me that you will deliver it to him. Tonight," she added.

"I swear on the blood of my unlamented father."

Lucy handed Mr. Pierce the lengthy message then stood

there, staring at him. "Well. Aren't you going to look for him?"

He smiled up at her, playing with her missive. "You are not his usual sort, you know."

Lucy was depressed enough. That unpleasant observation only brought her lower. "I know."

"Then again, he only toyed with all those other women. Or used them for sex," he added bluntly. "Maybe they were the ones not his sort, and in fact, you are."

How Lucy wished that were so. "He thinks there is something between us. You and I," she clarified with a nervous flutter of one hand.

He smiled. "So he does. But no doubt your letter here will disavow him of that notion." He stood and showed her to the door. "Unless you wish to heap coals on the fires of gossip already burning about you, you'd better be going, Miss Drysdale. We wouldn't want to give anyone reason to believe that something *is* going on between us."

But with every step Lucy took toward the carriage, she became more and more alarmed. What if Mr. Pierce didn't give the letter to Ivan? Or what if for reasons unbeknownst to her, he wished to fuel Ivan's misconception about his interest in her?

"You *will* give my letter to him."

"Of course."

"Do you swear it?"

"Now what good will that do? If I am devious enough not to give it to him, I'm certainly devious enough to tell you any lie you need to hear."

Lucy frowned. "I think I'd like my letter back."

They stood on the front steps now, and he stared down at her through the darkness. "Go home, Miss Drysdale. Believe me when I say I have Ivan's best interests at heart." Then without warning he caught her chin in one hand and pressed a swift kiss to her forehead.

Lucy stumbled back, completely shocked though not by any perception of impropriety. Neither the kiss nor his wry expression indicated anything more than a brotherly sort of affection. But even that seemed unlikely coming from Mr. Pierce. She didn't know what to say.

"Good night, Lucy. Sweet dreams."

She got into the curricle, then looked out at him. "Good night," she answered, confused and yet, for some reason, reassured.

The mounted figure in the shadows across the street was not so reassured. Enraged by what he'd seen. Crushed. But reassured? Never.

Ivan stared after the departing carriage, hardly able to breathe. Like a vicious sucker punch to his gut, she'd caught him unawares. Damn the conniving little bitch!

Then his bleak gaze swung back to the house and his pain hardened into a rage so violent the horse began to dance in a nervous circle. He kicked it forward, and before the door had even closed behind Elliot, he was off the horse and bounding up the steps. He burst in to find Elliot sitting on the stairs, his elbows propped on his knees and a letter dangling between his thumb and forefinger.

"Looking for me?"

Ivan checked his urge to plant his fist in Elliot's grinning face. After twenty years he should know that Elliot never did anything without a purpose. Those purposes were most often perverse, for the man feared nothing and would try anything. But in his own twisted way he'd always remained loyal to his friends. They'd never fought over a woman before, Ivan reminded himself. But then, neither of them had ever known a woman like Lucy.

He advanced on the seated Elliot until he towered over him. "What the hell is going on here?"

Elliot gave him a taunting grin. He offered Ivan the letter in his hand. "I believe this may explain things. It's for you. From the delightful Miss Drysdale," he added knowingly.

Ivan glared at him, then snatched the letter out of his hands. He turned away, broke the rough seal, then stood beneath one of the wall lamps to read.

. . . We should not wed . . . a terrible mistake . . .

Three pages of weak excuses that avoided the truth. His rage increased with every one.

> . . . *I will make a terrible countess. You deserve some-one who would do the title honor, and give credit to the role of your wife. You should marry someone you can care for.*

Ivan crushed the parchment in his fist. Someone he could care for? What drivel. She was speaking of herself, not him. She wished to marry someone she cared for. Someone she could love. And he was not that person.

The fact that this foolish particularity of hers was prob-ably the source of her spinster status gave him no satisfac-tion. The fact that he probably joined a long line of dismissed suitors gave him no comfort.

The indisputable fact was, she would rather be a pariah in society than the wife of the Earl of Westcott, wealthy, respected, and fussed over. She would rather be ruined than be forced to marry him.

"So. Is the wedding off?" Elliot drawled. "Has she turned you down or prevailed upon you to withdraw your offer? Faced with such a desperately reluctant bride, I won-der what a true gentleman is supposed to do?" He paused a moment. "If you were to withdraw your offer, she would appear the wronged party, while you, of course, would ap-pear the scoundrel. Public sentiment would rest with her and perhaps help assuage the damage to her reputation. Then again, she would still be publically humiliated. You, of course, would be no worse off than you already are: the bastard earl who doesn't give a damn about anyone or any-thing. That is the reputation you court, isn't it?"

Ivan lifted his head slowly and gave him an icy stare. Initially jealousy had gotten the best of him, but he had it under control now. "What's your interest in this, Pierce?"

Elliot shrugged, then leaned back on the stairs, propping himself up on his elbows. "I'm bored. Business is good—no challenge there. Playing entourage for you and shocking

all the well-bred young ladies of the ton has lost its value
for entertainment. But this new twist, you lusting after a
bluestocking spinster and she turning you down.'' Again
he shrugged. ''This is by far the best entertainment I've
found since we've been back in town.''

''Are you giving odds yet on who will win, me or
Lucy?''

Elliot grinned. ''Giles is naïve enough to believe the chit
cannot be forced into doing anything she does not want.
Alex says a title and money will always win. Naturally. His
advice is that you make a nice marriage settlement upon
her, enough to make her reconsider her position. Money
will bring her around, so long as you let the independent
Miss Drysdale know that she can support whatever little
causes she likes.'' His grin grew crafty. ''Perhaps she'll
wish to come to the aid of misunderstood scholars.''

Ivan's fingers tightened around Lucy's letter. He'd be
damned if his wife chased after idiot scholars like Sir James
Mawbey. ''How do you bet?''

Elliot pushed to his feet. ''My money is on Miss Drysdale. I have great faith in her, for she is sensible in her
behavior and passionate in her convictions.''

Ivan bristled to hear that word applied to Lucy by anyone
but himself. He knew Elliot was baiting him, but it was
hard not to bite.

''It's those very passions of hers that ultimately will
drive her to the altar,'' Ivan stated.

''With you?''

''With me.''

''Would you like to lay a friendly wager on that?''

Ivan considered the man a moment. Elliot had an odd
interest in Lucy, and while Ivan meant to marry the woman
and thus lay his claim to her, it wouldn't hurt to get Elliot
away from her. ''Immediately after I marry her on Thursday, you shall leave town—leave the country, in fact. For
at least a year,'' he added.

Elliot rubbed his chin. ''And if you do not marry her on

Thursday, you shall step aside and let someone else court her.''

Ivan's fists knotted and his jaw clenched. "You?"

"Would you rather she remain a spinster forever?"

Lucy Drysdale would not remain a spinster for long, Ivan vowed minutes later as he rode through the midnight streets of London. The moon was a dim and distant company through the lamplit lanes and avenues that led him to Berkeley Square. A dog howled and was answered from afar. The shadow of a cat darted across the street. But otherwise he was alone with his thoughts.

He'd taken the bet with Elliot, and he meant to answer Lucy's letter tonight, in person, and resolve once and for all the matter of her reluctance. No matter what her letter said, she could not possibly prefer ruination over becoming a countess.

Could she?

Lucy sat in the window brushing her hair. It was late and the lights in the various bedchambers had all been turned down by the time she'd sneaked up the servants' stairwell and crept down the hall to her own room. She'd changed swiftly into her bed clothes, but her nerves were far too overwrought for her to sleep.

Would Elliot deliver her letter to Ivan? Would Ivan read it—*really* read it—and understand what a dreadful mistake it would be for them to wed?

She stared out at the street, mindlessly forcing the brush through her long hair. She looked, but did not really see a carriage go by. A hunting cat crept along the fence and leapt silently down into the shadows of a bush.

Then a rider turned into the square and her focus sharpened.

It was the deliberateness of his approach that struck her. As he made straightaway toward Westcott House her hand paused with the brush in midair. Her breathing ceased and her heart began to pound.

Was it Ivan? Could it be?

It was.

He pulled up at the front door, vaulted from the saddle, then stared straight up at her.

Lucy fell away from the window. The brush clattered forgotten to the floor as she scurried for her bed, then stared aghast at the window. He was coming up here. She knew it. He'd read her letter and he was furious that she would choose ruin over marriage to him.

She should have anticipated this, she realized. As a child he'd been rejected by his own family. As a man he refused to let anyone reject him and to his mind she had just rejected him. It wasn't rejection, though. She would love to be his wife, if she thought he'd let her truly play that role.

But how was she to explain? I love you but you don't love me, and I can't marry you unless you do?

No. She couldn't tell him that. But she would have to tell him something.

Lucy shifted her panicked eyes from the window to the door. He wouldn't come up here, would he?

Of course he would.

She started for the door, intent on locking it against him. Then she sat down on the bed again. *Get a hold on yourself.* She'd wanted to talk this thing out with him. Now was her chance. Only not in here, with her in her nightgown.

She snatched her wrapper from the chair, and again started for the door. But a knock halted her. Not an angry pounding, nor a sharp, demanding one. Just three soft, restrained raps. There was danger in that softness, however, and warning in that restraint.

"I'm coming," she said as she fought the twisted arm of her wrapper.

"No. I'm coming in." In a moment Ivan was inside the room.

Lucy froze, one arm in the wrapper, the other caught halfway down the inverted sleeve. She stared at him in a state of total shock. He should not be in her bedroom. They should not be here together. He must leave or else she must.

But when the door closed with a decisive thud—when

he turned the key and locked them in together—she knew
that neither of them was going anywhere.

You wanted to talk to him. So talk.

"Now see here, my lord—"

"Ivan." He advanced on her without the least indication
of embarrassment. "Let me help you with that." He
reached for the bunched fabric of the uncooperative wrapper.

"Thank you—No! I want it *on*!" she exclaimed, when
he deftly peeled it off her. She grabbed for it, but he flung
it in a corner.

"Now, Ivan," she began in a warning tone. "You cannot
come storming in here—"

"Too late, Lucy. I've already done it." He stared at her
with those burning blue eyes of his.

Lucy gulped and folded her arms nervously across her
chest. "If you wish to speak to me we can go down to the
library."

"The library." He smiled and let that hot gaze run over
her. "What I have in mind is better suited to the bedroom
than the library. Then again, I'm nothing if not flexible."

"Stop that! You're being deliberately obtuse and . . . and
you're not in the least bit flexible," she added. She was
treading in deep water here. The only way not to drown
was to provoke a fight with him.

But Ivan was not in a fighting mood, and she feared he
had only one purpose in mind. She decided to be direct.
"If you think you're going to seduce me and thereby put
an end to my opposition to our marriage, you are quite
mistaken. Not unless your intentions lean toward . . . toward rape," she finished, throwing the ugly word out between them.

For a moment his eyes narrowed. Then he smiled, a slow,
confident smile that made her heart do a quick flip-flop that
she was certain could not be healthy.

"I would never force you to do something you did not
wish, Lucy. I think you know that. But I am not averse to
reminding you how much you like it when I kiss you. And

touch you,'' he added in a voice that vibrated inside her very bones.

Lucy began to back up. ''Don't do this, Ivan. Please. We need . . . We need to talk, not to . . . to . . .''

''Not to make love?'' He shook his head as he followed her, devouring her with his eyes, melting her with their fiery touch. ''I need to make love to you right now. More than I need to breathe. And you need to make love to me. Don't you?''

Lucy had come up against the bed. Now he stopped just inches from her. *You need to make love to me.* The words reverberated in the air between them. *You need to make love to me.*

Oh, God, but she did!

She stared helplessly up at him, trapped as much by the power of her unwise feelings for him as by his superior physical strength.

''Kiss me,'' he commanded her, even as his eyes traced the contours of her mouth.

Lucy struggled to control her breathing, to control the awful impulse to throw herself into his arms. He wanted her to. She wanted to. So why not just do it?

Because he did not love her. She was merely a challenge to overcome.

''Kiss me,'' he repeated.

Without thinking, she curled her fingers in the fabric of his opened coat. She bowed her head against his chest, still resisting. ''Go away. Please, go away,'' she begged him, even as her hands tightened on his lapels.

''I can't.'' With his thumb and one finger beneath her chin, he tilted her face up to his. ''I can't.''

Then his face descended until they were so close their breath mingled. ''Kiss me, Lucy.''

And this time she did. She rose up on her toes and pressed her lips to his, and felt an immeasurable joy in the doing of it. She was so tired of fighting him. Of fighting her need for him.

That it was unwise, she would not argue. That she would

be sorry on the morrow, she did not dispute. But she needed this—this wonderful, terrifying rush of emotions that went through her every time they touched.

So she clutched the wool lapels of his coat even tighter, and kissed him as if there were no tomorrow.

It was not how she'd imagined coming together with the man she loved would be. There was none of the wooing she'd imagined, the pretty compliments and tentative touches. She was not dressed and perfumed, with hair piled high and pins to undo.

No, she was naked underneath a thin night rail, with her hair streaming down to her waist. His hands roamed her greedily, finding no barriers at all. Indeed, the soft linen only served to heighten the feel of his hard palms and strong fingers as they slid down her back, circled her waist, and curved around her derriere.

His other hand tangled in her hair, tilting her back to accept the onslaught of his mouth.

Not that she meant to fight him. Not that she ever could.

When he pulled her against him, drawing her up into the kiss, it became more than merely a kiss. His lips teased and seduced hers; his tongue deepened the contact. His arms enveloped her and his body swamped hers with his heat.

And his need.

But it was a need that went beyond physical desire, and that need proved to be the most potent of his many allures. For Lucy wanted to assuage that neediness in him. She wanted to satisfy more than the physical hungers that drove him. She wanted to love him and make love to him, until he was sated and at peace. Completely at peace.

The bed was behind her, and with a bold tug, she tumbled them backward onto it. Their lower bodies pressed together in the intimate way they had before, the fateful night of the dinner party. He braced himself on his arms and with her help shed both coat and waistcoat. But Lucy could go no further than that, for she was now in new and foreign territory.

"Pull my shirt up," he told her, kissing her ear, then

moving the kiss in hot nibbles down the side of her neck and around to the hollow of her throat. "Now over my head," he added, when she complied.

Somehow they managed, for Lucy soon found herself staring at his broad, naked chest, at the dark mat of hair and the flat male nipples nestled within. Her own nipples tightened at the sight.

As if he knew the direction of her thoughts, one of Ivan's hands moved down to curve around her breast, and his thumb moved languidly over the aching crest.

When she let out a little moan, he replaced the thumb with his mouth. He scraped the peak with his teeth, then drew it fully into his mouth.

A groan of fear and ecstasy escaped her, and unwittingly she thrust her body up against his. He thrust back, pressing her deep into the feather bed, and let out a groan of his own.

"I cannot wait any more," he muttered.

He rolled away from her and for a moment disappointment overwhelmed her. But only for a moment. For he kicked off his boots and stripped off his breeches. Then he turned back to her and, with an impatient gesture, pushed her maidenly gown up, past her thighs and belly. He paused and stared down at her naked form.

Had it not been for her fascination with his naked body, Lucy would have tried to cover herself. But he was so magnificent, so arrogantly masculine, that she could do nothing but stare. He put the classical statues to shame. She had held onto his wide shoulders and felt the press of his muscular chest before. But naked they were so much more impressive. Smooth olive skin accented with dark, curling hair. Well-defined muscles, that rippled down to a hard, flat stomach. A huge jutting—

She jerked her eyes back up to him, suddenly terrified. What was she doing? This was not possible. There was no way *that* could fit where . . . where she knew it was supposed to fit.

"Are you a virgin?" he asked.

Lucy nodded, unable to speak.

Ivan smiled, drinking her in with his eyes. He bent down to kiss her again. "Good." Then with one hand he slid the gown even higher, exposing her breasts, while he moved his mouth in a hungry trail of kisses. He devoured her neck, nuzzled past the bunched linen, then began to lick and taste the bare flesh of her breasts.

"Ivan . . . Ivan, I don't think . . ." She trailed off, lost in the wonderful turmoil of sensations he roused in her.

"Don't think," he murmured, as he began to tease one aching, straining nipple. He pulled the gown over her head, leaving her to struggle with her trapped arms. "Don't think. Just feel."

When he drew the nipple between his lips, Lucy could do nothing else but feel. His erotic attention to her nipples caused the most incredible, terrifying feelings to erupt in her belly. She felt as if she were melting from the inside out, getting hotter and hotter, until she turned to liquid and began to boil.

She clutched at his shoulders, trying to make him stop. Urging him never to stop.

In the midst of this panic of emotions, he slid further down her body, pressing his clever, wicked lips in the depression beneath her breast bone, counting each rib with his tongue. Then he pressed the side of his face against the soft flesh of her belly.

She felt the rasp of his stubbled cheek on her sensitized skin. One of his hands circled her derriere and pressed her all the harder to him as he rubbed his face against her tender flesh. Then he moved his mouth, as if to kiss her lower still.

"Ivan," she gasped, afraid of what he meant to do. "Please, I . . ." She trailed off when he looked up, forgetting what she'd meant to say. There was such hunger in his eyes, such a fiery passion.

"Please," she begged as she cupped his face with her hands. "Please. Kiss me again."

Slowly he slid up her, letting every portion of his incredibly masculine body rub against hers, forcing her legs apart to accept the full weight of his body. He caught her mouth in a kiss, pinning her to the bed with the crushing force of his desire.

Then, as he filled her mouth with his probing tongue, his hard male member probed the entrance to her femininity. Urging her on with the rhythmic thrust of his tongue, he thrust his hips against hers, going deeper each time.

It was an excruciating pleasure, an exquisite stretching, an indescribable friction that made Lucy want to jump out of her skin. She circled his shoulders with her arms and ran her hands restlessly up and down his back. He possessed her wholly and she let him, circling her legs around his straining hips.

She felt him tense and start to lift his head. But she drew him back into the kiss and she heard his groan of capitulation.

Then without warning he thrust deeper than he had before, and she felt a quick, tearing pain. But he did not allow her time to savor the pain or understand it. For he began a new rhythm, hot and fast, with an unholy urgency. Like a mighty wave it sucked her in until she was meeting him stroke for stroke, crying out her anguish and need, and finally erupting from the inside out.

He'd set her on fire. He'd burned her up. He'd consumed her and now she was his, mere ashes, burned in the fire of his passion.

Their passion.

Fifteen

*H*is hand was shaking.

Ivan pulled his boot on with an angry jerk, then reached for the other one. He dressed quietly. Swiftly. But his eyes kept stealing back to the slumbering woman on the rumpled bed.

Lucy Drysdale, damn her bluestocking little soul, was more passionate than any self-professed wanton, at least any of the ones he'd had the pleasure of knowing. What those other women provided had been nothing more than sex, a midnight snack to ease his hunger. But Lucy had given him a twenty-course feast, every delicacy imaginable to man.

And several beyond imagination.

He stood, then paused, just staring at her. He wanted to stay. He wanted to slip back under the covers, now scented with their joining, and curl around her. He wanted to make love to her again, to sleep a while with her, then wake her up and make love to her all over again.

He felt the demanding rise of his desire and grimly beat back an oath. He would have time enough to spend with his bride after the wedding. He'd accomplished what he'd wanted tonight by laying final claim to her body. She would not dare oppose their marriage now.

His anger at her revived as he recalled her steadfast opposition to their impending nuptials. He pulled the crushed letter she'd written out of his pocket. She'd rather be ruined than marry him. Though she'd not said as much, that was the effect of her message. But she'd not been completely ruined when she wrote it. Now she was.

He frowned and looked back at her, at the feminine sprawl beneath the rumpled covers, of slender arms and shapely legs, of innocent maiden and passionate lover.

Only an idiot would consider her ruined by what had just occurred between them. But it was the opinion of idiots that would force her into this marriage. Lucy could not deny his offer any longer.

He ripped the letter in half, and at the sound she stirred then opened her eyes. It took her a moment to remember. In the amber light of the sputtering candles he saw her blink and stare at him. Then her eyes widened and she sat up like a shot.

The sight of her bare shoulders and wildly tangled hair sent blood surging to his loins. But he curbed his baser needs and focused instead on the matter at hand.

"I'm returning your letter." He flung the shredded pages at her. They settled across the bed. "I assume you'll give up this pointless opposition to our wedding now, considering the events of the past hours."

He saw her swallow and was unable not to stare at the smooth undulations of her throat. The throat he wanted to lick and taste and devour.

With an effort he ignored that and forced himself to remain focused. "Agree to my offer of marriage, otherwise I'll have no choice but to inform your brother about what has passed between us."

She gasped and clutched the wrinkled bed linens to her chest. "You wouldn't!"

Ivan's eyes ran over her. She was naked under those few layers of sheeting. He could have her again, right now, if he wanted to.

"Oh, but I would," he said. "If you don't agree to my proposal now, you leave me no option but to admit what we've done. He'll have no choice but to defend your honor.

Is that what you want, for him to challenge me over your honor?''

Slowly she shook her head. Again she swallowed, only this time it was jerky, as if she fought down a knot of tears. But she didn't cry.

He nodded. "Tomorrow you will tell your brother that you agree. And on Thursday we will wed."

They stared at one another a long moment. Ivan realized he was holding his breath.

Finally she said, "On Thursday we shall wed. Only . . ."

Ivan frowned. "Only what?"

She looked down at her lap. Her hair fell around her face and in the shadowy room he could not make out her expression. She continued in little more than a whisper. "I was only wondering . . . well . . . If you plan to come . . . you know . . . here. Tomorrow night."

Like a tidal wave, pride and possession and a fierce need for her rushed over Ivan. She wanted him to come to her bed again. She couldn't bear to wait even another night to be with him. Desire struck him once more, like a ravenous clawing beast that would not be satisfied.

He took a step toward the bed, then stopped, wrestling with the beast inside him. He would not give her that power over him. She didn't need to know how violent was his need to possess her—and not just her body. He wanted her to want him. He'd never needed that of any woman before. He clenched his jaw.

"If I didn't already have proof of your innocence, I would wonder at such a bold request."

She lifted her face and he could see in its heightened color what her words had cost her—and how his callous reply had hurt. Before he could find a way to take them back she spoke.

"If you expect me to be a sweet and malleable wife, then I am afraid you shall be disappointed, my lord. There is a reason I have remained so long unwed."

"The same can be said for myself. I will see you on Thursday, Lucy. Until then." He gave a curt bow, then afraid to linger a minute longer in her presence, he turned and left.

Outside the room he paused, heart hammering and body fully aroused. Damnation, but the sassy wench tied him in knots!

Inside the room Lucy sat as he left her, staring at the door with a sinking heart. How could he love her body so well and yet seem to hate *her*?

Across the hall Antonia kept her ear pressed to the drinking glass she held against the door. She strained to hear anything further. Ivan had been two hours in the girl's room, then left with a frustrated oath on his lips. He was bedeviled, all right. Miss Drysdale might be wise to fear a marriage to him, but that was not Lady Antonia's concern. He wanted the chit and tonight the girl had sealed her fate. She would see to that.

Antonia put the glass down and hobbled back to her bed. Lord, but she was tired. Her feet ached all the time. The social obligations of town life were wearing in the extreme. Once Ivan was safely wed and the marriage legally consummated, perhaps she would return to Dorset and the peace of the Westcott family seat—and there await the news that her great-grandchild was on the way.

Lucy would much rather slap Ivan than kiss him. Fortunately her sense of fairness—and her sense of the ludicrous—kicked in and she had to admit, at least to herself, that she was not being totally honest. She did want to slap him. But she wanted to kiss him more.

It had been a day and a half since she'd last seen him—one day, one night, and the awful remains of another night since he'd left her sitting naked in her own bed. Thirty-five and a half hours of utter misery. Frustration, longing, panic, and confusion had been just the least portion of her maelstrom of emotions. Utter fury had been there too.

For Ivan had not been content merely to hold her wanton behavior over *her* head. Oh, no. He'd let her brother know, and she'd had to suffer Graham's sanctimonious preaching ever since. It wasn't enough for Graham that she'd agreed to marry the wretch. He had taken advantage of her fall from grace—not just a partial fall, but a full-fledged tumble into shameful debauchery, to hear him tell it—and relieved himself of every frustration he'd ever suffered on her account. If she'd married Winston Fletcher, this would never have happened. If she'd accepted Carlton Claverie's suit, the family would not be humiliated by so rushed a wedding. If she'd consented to be courted by George Anderson, their good family name would not be shamed, as she'd shamed it.

The only thing that had shut him up was her sharp reminder that Ivan was an earl, while Carlton and Winston had merely been honorables, and George Anderson second in line to be a viscount. She hadn't liked using that argument, but at least it had worked.

Now, however, as Graham led her down the aisle of the nearly empty Chapel of St. Mary of the Archangels, it was not Ivan's title she was thinking about. It was him, the man who stood waiting beside the minister, his gaze shuttered, his face expressionless.

In a matter of minutes they would be wed. Then he would kiss her in front of her family and his and the few friends who'd attended the hasty wedding.

For some reason she was terrified by the thought of that kiss. She had visions of herself melting into a puddle in front of everyone, for he could do that to her if he chose. He knew it and so did she. And there was no reason to think he would not choose to humiliate her like that. After all, she'd humiliated him by trying to turn down his very honorable proposal.

She swallowed hard when Graham halted just before Ivan. The silence in the chapel was deafening.

"We gather in the sight of God and man," the minister began.

It was an endless blur; it was over in a moment. The only portions of the ceremony Lucy was later to recall were the two times when Ivan touched her, for her heart kicked

into a gallop each time. First when he took her left hand
and placed a ring on it. It was exactly the right size, she'd
vaguely noted, and it was heavier than any ring she'd ever
worn. The second time he touched her it was to kiss her,
after the minister pronounced them man and wife. But none
of Lucy's fears came to pass—at least none of her fears
about making a fool of herself. For his kiss was as devoid
of feeling as hers was fraught with it. He didn't even touch
her shoulders, but only bent stiffly forward and gave her a
dry, impersonal peck on the lips.

It didn't prevent her heart from racing, though. It raced
directly to the depths of despair.

"Congratulations," said the minister, shaking Ivan's
hand.

Graham hugged Lucy. So did Valerie, Hortense, and her
weeping mother. Even Lady Westcott gave her a sort of
hug. But all the good wishes in the world could not disguise
what everyone had seen. Ivan Thornton's so-called passion
for his bride had either burnt out or it had never truly existed at all.

Lucy wanted to weep.

Instead she pasted a fixed expression on her face and
allowed herself to be carried along when the dowager
countess directed the small group toward the church vestibule. Ivan walked a little apart from Lucy, receiving her
brother's enthusiastic good wishes.

As much as Graham had harangued her about the humiliating circumstances of her marriage, he was obviously
ecstatic to have an earl for a brother-in-law. Lucy sighed.
If only Ivan showed one tenth the enthusiasm that Graham
did.

As if he sensed her perusal, Ivan looked up. Their eyes
met and held, but Lucy found no solace in his hooded gaze.

Oh, but the man was wearing! He blew hot one day and
cold the next!

Then again, perhaps he thought the same of her. That
put an altogether different slant on things.

Lucy took a deep breath. Did she dare? She smiled down

at Prudence and gave her a squeeze. "Mind your sisters," she told her. "I fear I am neglecting my husband." Then fighting down a fear that had her knees trembling and her mouth dry, she made her way to Ivan's side.

"Could we have a private word?" she asked, placing a hand on his arm. The surprised look on his face, though brief, lent her courage. "Please?" she added in a whisper.

He gave a curt nod. Everyone stared as Lucy drew him away from the vestibule and out into the small churchyard. "Go on. We'll be there soon enough," she told them.

"My word, now what?" Lucy's mother exclaimed.

Alexander Blackburn laughed. "You're supposed to wait until—"

He broke off when Hortense clapped her hands over Prudence's ears. Giles barely muffled a guffaw.

Elliot was not there. Lucy had noted that earlier. She would have to do something to mend this silly rift between Ivan and him. But first she had to mend the huge one between Ivan and herself.

She kept a tight hold on his arm until they reached the small garden that separated the church from the rectory. Once out of sight of their well-wishers, however, she was beset once more by nerves. She let go of his arm and wove her fingers nervously together and tried to find the right words. His silence was no help at all, especially when he folded his arms across his chest and stared belligerently at her.

"It's too late to back out, Lucy. The deed is done. Both deeds," he added sarcastically.

"I'm not trying to back out," she snapped. "Though I shall never forgive you for telling my brother about . . . about the other night."

"I didn't tell him a thing."

"Well, I certainly didn't, so who could have but you?"

"Perhaps one of the servants saw me enter your room."

"Or your grandmother might have overheard us." Lucy's face flamed at the very thought. "Well, I . . . I suppose that doesn't matter any more," she said with a nervous wave of one hand. "The thing is . . ." She faltered, then grimaced at her cowardliness. "The thing is, it occurs to me that although we have taken our vows, you have no idea what my feelings about our marriage truly are."

"Your feelings about our marriage," he echoed. "I have reason to believe you think us supremely ill-suited to one another."

Lucy swallowed and bit the inside of her cheek. "I know I said that. The thing is . . . I want this marriage between us to work. I know I tried to avoid it, but . . . But I want you to know that . . . that I am not sorry we are wed."

One of Ivan's dark brows arched. "I'm overwhelmed with your enthusiasm."

"That didn't come out right." She wrung her hands. Words weren't going to do the trick, she realized. She would have to take things into her own hands. Literally.

With a confidence that was pure sham, Lucy crossed the short grassy space between them. She loosened his folded arms, stepped between them, and looped her arms around his neck. Then she looked straight into his wary blue eyes. "I'm going to give you a proper wedding kiss, Ivan. I hope you want to receive it. I hope you'll kiss me back."

Then, afraid she would talk herself right out of it, Lucy kissed him.

It was like kissing one of the marble statues at the Egyptian Hall in Piccadilly—at first. When she did not relent, however, when she slanted her mouth against his and used her tongue to stroke the rigid seam of his lips, coaxing him as he'd coaxed her in the past, she felt him begin to soften. She teased his lips apart and deepened the kiss, and his arms tightened around her. Without thinking she arched against him, bringing them fully together.

He was not so immune to her as he seemed! By the time they came apart, both gasping for breath, his heart was hammering just as hard as hers.

"In some ways we are very well suited," she admitted, ducking her head against his chest.

Ivan cupped her cheek and tilted her head up so that they

were face to face. "For a bluestocking you have a shock-ingly passionate nature. For that matter, you're probably far too passionate to be a countess either."

Lucy's heart sank. "I will try not to embarrass you, my lord."

"Don't you have that backward? It's more likely I'll embarrass you. And call me Ivan," he added. "Never again are you to call me my lord."

She smiled up at him, encouraged by his easing tension. "Yes, Ivan. Unless I am very angry with you."

"Anger is just another passionate emotion. Like lust," he said, moving one hand down to cup her bottom and lift her against his arousal.

Lucy sucked in a breath, unable to control her response to him. But as much as she returned his lust, she was also deflated by it. She wanted there to be more between them than that.

He lowered his head, capturing her mouth in a stinging kiss that was filled with lust but also, perhaps, with need. It was that need she must focus upon, she decided with the fleeting portion of her mind still able to think. She would make him need her. She would make herself necessary to him.

"I expect you to be faithful to me," she said, when she could again speak.

"Keep me satisfied and I will be," he said. He bunched her skirts up in one hand, baring the lower portion of her legs to the fresh air.

"Keep me satisfied and I'll be faithful too," she replied, half fainting now with desire.

Abruptly he pulled away, just enough to stare down at her. "You'll be satisfied. I'll see to that. But I'll have no talk of you being anything but faithful to me. You took your vows and you will abide by them."

"As shall you. My lord."

Though locked in an embrace, they glared at one another. Hot and cold. Would things always be so volatile between them? Lucy wondered.

Then Ivan grinned, that wicked one-sided grin that melted her bones every time. "I can hardly wait to get you back to the house, my dear, for I plan to wear you out. In fact, I can't wait at all. Come." He grabbed her wrist and began to pull her toward the rear court where the carriages waited.

"But . . . But what of the reception? Wait, Ivan. We can't—"

"We can," he vowed. "I am too hot for you to dither over champagne and finger sandwiches, and toasts from people I don't give a damn about."

"No!" Lucy caught an iron fence post with her free hand and dug in her heels. "Please, Ivan."

He stopped and faced her, a gleam in his eyes. "If I agree, what will you agree to in return?"

Lucy was too befuddled to think. How had he turned matters upside down so fast? "What do you mean?"

"If I must linger amidst our families—neither of which do I much care for—then you must make it up to me. For instance, you can agree to make love to me in the carriage on the way home."

"In the carriage?"

"In the carriage."

"But how? I mean—" Lucy stared at him. "You can't be serious."

"It's either in the carriage later, or in the carriage now." He gave a sudden tug and she lost hold of the fence.

"All right! All right!"

His eyes moved over her like a stroke of fire, burning her with their intensity. Her insides began to tremble with the most delicious sort of anticipation. "I'll need some token from you," he said. "Something to guarantee you mean what you say."

"Really, but this is getting ridiculous."

"I'll have your pantalets."

"No!" she gasped.

Ivan laughed, and despite her panic, Lucy saw a side of him she'd not seen before. He was having fun with her, teasing her like a little boy might tease a little girl. Except that the stakes here were grown-up stakes. If there was any doubt in her mind that she loved him, it disappeared in a flash.

"Your pantalets or else we leave now," he threatened, letting his eyes run over her once more.

Lucy shivered with erotic delight. Two could play at this game. She let out an exaggerated sigh. "Oh, all right." She glanced around them, then lifted her skirts and untied the front strings of the undergarment. With just a few wriggles it fell to her ankles. She stepped out of them and backed away, her cheeks crimson with embarrassment.

"There. Take them. But I ought to tell you, Ivan, that though I know we must attend our own wedding reception, I'd much rather make love to you."

Then without allowing him time to reply, she turned and fled to the dubious safety of the rectory.

The reception was an agony. Ivan's every look tortured her with wicked promises and delicious threats. There were sixteen toasts in all. Lucy counted them in mounting frustration. She couldn't eat a bite, and between her nerves, her empty stomach, and the sixteen gulps of champagne, she felt as if she were afloat in bubbles. It was a form of torture and yet she knew the building anticipation would only increase the pleasure they would find together.

Stanley and Derek had long ago slipped outside to play in the churchyard. Prudence and the younger girls had followed them. Now Graham pushed back his chair and started to stand, then plopped down when his balance deserted him.

Ivan stood instead. "I thank you all for your good wishes, but now I would like to be alone with my bride."

The men laughed. The women gasped. Or at least Hortense and her mother did. Lady Westcott only smiled, a faint smug smile. She was vastly relieved to have Ivan wed to anyone, Lucy realized. Even her.

Lucy glanced up at Ivan, hoping he hadn't seen that sat-

isfied smile on his grandmother's face. Unfortunately he
was staring right at the woman. Though his expression was
noncommittal, Lucy saw his hand tighten into a fist. On
impulse she grabbed his fist and worked her fingers between his.

When he looked down at her she squeezed his hand and
smiled. Their eyes held and after a moment the pad of his
thumb rubbed across her knuckles.

"Come, Lucy," he said. Then hand in hand, they made
their escape.

Dusk was hours away. But when Ivan lashed down the
shades of the carriage, its interior took on the shadowy
warmth of a summer twilight. The driver started forward
and in the quiet cab Lucy and Ivan faced one another.

"We are taking the long route home," he said. He took
off his coat and threw it aside.

"Really, Ivan. Can't . . . Can't we simply wait until we
get to the house? I mean, it's but a few minutes away."

"No." He untied his stock and flung it on the coat.

Lucy's insides began to twist into all sorts of interesting
knots. "But . . . But the driver—"

"Is otherwise occupied." He shrugged out of his waistcoat.

"Yes, but he'll hear—"

"Nothing. Unless, of course, you are unable to suppress
your moans of pleasure." He unfastened his cuffs and
pulled his shirttails out of his breeches. "How many slips
are you wearing?"

Excitement skittered across the surface of her skin, raising goose bumps and making her perspire. "I . . . I don't
know—Ivan!" she cried when his feet spread hers apart.

"We're married now. You can't deny me my husbandly
rights."

"I'm not denying you. I'm just . . . just . . ."

"Delaying me?"

She nodded. Then she abruptly shook her head. The truth
was, she didn't want to deny him *or* delay him. "Three,"
she said.

"Three?"

"Three slips."

Their eyes held and the atmosphere of the leather-upholstered interior turned positively sultry. He leaned forward, placed a hand on each of her knees, and began to slide his warm palms up and down her thighs. Slowly.

Lucy could feel herself melting from the inside out. How had she ever thought herself alive before now, before she'd discovered these heretofore hidden emotions he managed to rouse in her?

"Give me the first slip."

She gave him all three, one at a time, wriggling free as he guided her. He left her without stockings, garters, or shoes, with her aqua silk skirt bunched up around her hips.

The carriage rocked along its way, sometimes over cobbled streets, other times macadam paving, and eventually onto smooth gravel. Outside the sounds of street traffic gave way to the trill of birds and the steady thud of the horses' hooves. Inside the carriage, however, there was only the sound of rapid breathing, of her faint whispers and his hot kisses moving along the tender skin of her inner thighs.

Lucy clutched Ivan's shoulders, but did not protest. Oh, no. She did not have it in her to protest the incredible things he was doing to her. He kissed her where he should not, where she should not want him to kiss her. But he wanted to, and she wanted him to, and so she let him.

It took all her concentration not to cry out at the exquisite joy of it. Every time he flicked his tongue back and forth over the secret spot he'd discovered there, she felt herself giving in to the urge. Her hands tangled in his hair as he pressed his face between her thighs. One of his fingers slipped inside her and he began the rhythm she'd learned too quickly to crave. He kissed her; he stroked her; and suddenly it was all too much.

With a cry of utter capitulation she let go, shuddering with the onslaught of violent release.

"Ivan! Ivan . . ."

She would have remained there, collapsed against the

plush seat, a boneless puddle of female flesh. But with a low growl of satisfaction Ivan pulled her across the short space to straddle him on the opposite seat.

At the first touch of his fully aroused maleness against her thigh, Lucy opened her eyes. He'd satisfied her. Now he needed as much from her. Despite her exhaustion, his desire for her roused her at once.

She braced herself on his shoulders as he positioned her over him. "Do you think he heard me?" she asked. "You know, the driver?"

Ivan's hands tightened around her waist and he slowly pressed her down over him. "Does it really matter?"

"Yes . . . No . . . I don't know," she moaned when he thrust up into her, first a little way, then farther, then all the way. "I don't know," she repeated as they began to move together. Up and down. In and out. Faster and faster, until she didn't care if the entire world heard.

He laid claim to her, husband to wife—man to woman— just as she made her own claim on him. She would make him need her or die trying. And perhaps somehow, someway, if she were lucky, she might eventually turn that need into love.

Then he clutched her and let out a mighty groan, and once again she cried out her own release. And if in the flood of sticky warmth and mutual exhaustion it was not love he felt, she took comfort in the thought that it felt very much like love to her.

Sixteen

*I*van swept her up the front stairs, taking two steps at a time. He did not give a thought to her dishabille, but Lucy did. She buried her face in his shoulder and prayed that the servants did not see—and if they did, that they would not gossip too widely about it.

But how could they not? It was clear what he was about, for he made no efforts to be quiet or discreet. He strode boldly down the wide upstairs hall, carrying her in his arms, like a prize he'd just won.

The irony was, Lucy felt as if *she'd* just won the prize. This man—this lusty Gypsy—was hers now. Her husband. As he turned toward the master's wing of the enormous Westcott town house, she pressed a kiss against his neck, in the place where his neckcloth should be, but was not. He hefted her higher and increased his pace.

He paused before a mahogany six-paneled door and kicked it open. In that first glimpse of his apartment, Lucy's impression was of dark woods, luxurious fabrics, and the most enormous bed she'd ever seen.

Then she was flat on her back in that bed with Ivan covering her body with his.

This time they removed all their clothes. But their joining was just as urgent, just as demanding as it had been in the carriage. And just as overwhelming.

Afterward they must have dozed a while, for when Lucy

next became aware, Ivan was kissing a trail along her spine, from the nape of her neck, down her back, and past her waist. When he nipped her derriere, she squirmed breath-lessly beneath him. How could she want him again so in-tensely?

This time they made love more slowly, experimenting with different positions. In the end, however, when she straddled him while he tortured her breasts so sweetly with his mouth and hands, it was just as frantic as the first time. She rocked back and forth over him, drawing him in then out, at a pace she feared would kill them both.

And in that moment of the little death, the *petite mort* she'd read about but not understood until now, she wanted no more in life than this. To lie with Ivan, and die with Ivan, and forever rest in Ivan's arms.

But the sweetness of their entwined collapse did not last. Lucy awoke to Ivan's muffled curse and a determined knocking on the door.

"Wake up. Wake up, I say!" came Lady Westcott's shrill voice.

"Get the hell away from that door," Ivan growled. "Get the hell out of my house and out of my life!" he added viciously.

"I will do no such thing." Then the latch clicked, the door swung open, and the dowager countess advanced into the room.

"Son of a bitch!" Ivan leaped out of the bed. Horrified that the woman would discover them naked in their bed, Lucy yanked the covers over her head. "Isn't it enough that I am wed?" he roared. "Do you wish to witness the consummation as well?"

"Something terrible has happened."

"I don't give a damn what has happened. Get out of here!"

Lucy peeked out from beneath the silk damask. Despite her embarrassment and the uncertain light cast by the gut-tering candles, she could see Lady Westcott's distress. "What is it?" she asked. She pushed herself to a sitting position, clutching the sheets up to her chin. "What's wrong?"

"Nothing I can't remedy," Ivan answered. Naked though he was, he advanced on his grandmother. "Get out or I'll put you out."

"Ivan, please," Lucy cried. "Let her speak."

"Why should I?"

"Valerie is gone!" Lady Westcott cried.

Lucy's heart began to hammer. "What do you mean, gone?"

"Good for her," Ivan muttered.

"She has absconded with that scholar. The one *you* introduced her to," the old woman added, shaking a crumpled sheet of parchment at Lucy.

Ivan snatched up a robe and donned it, then took the note from his grandmother. He scanned it, gave a short laugh, then handed it to Lucy. While she read it, he sat back on the bed, leaning against the headboard. He crossed his ankles and folded his hands over his stomach as his anger turned to amusement.

"So she's gone to Gretna Green with the man she loves," he said. "Let's hope she consummates the marriage before she's caught and forced to have it annulled. That's what you've come here for, isn't it? To have me find her and stop the wedding?"

Lady Westcott stared at him, looking every bit her age and more. Lucy caught Ivan's arm. "Please, Ivan. Don't make light of what is a very serious situation. Your grandmother is rightly concerned about her goddaughter's future."

"You mean she's concerned that this will make *her* look bad. Everyone knows Valerie was in town under *her* protection."

"*You're* the one who brought Valerie to hear that man speak. *You're* the one who introduced them!" Lady Westcott accused, shaking her fist at Lucy. "This is the thanks I get?"

"The thanks you get for what?" Ivan bit out.

He was enjoying this far too much, Lucy realized. "What's important here is Valerie," she reminded them both.

"Valerie is apparently marrying the man she loves—unlike most proper ladies," Ivan added, staring pointedly at Lucy. When she had no response for that, he turned back to his grandmother. "So tell me, just what is it Lucy should be thanking you for? Surely you do not intend to take credit for her newly elevated status as Countess of Westcott?"

Lady Westcott's face turned from pale with distress to mottled red with rage. She advanced on them, stomping her cane on the floor with every step. She stopped at Lucy's side of the bed. "It was I who brought her to London. You would never have met her had I not found her first."

Lucy wanted to groan. That was the last thing Ivan would want to be reminded of. She glanced nervously at him and, sure enough, he was glaring at his grandmother through narrowed eyes.

"What do you want from me, my thanks?"

Lady Westcott smiled, a cold, thin grimace that sent an uneasy shiver up Lucy's spine. Lucy laid a hand on Ivan's arm, hoping desperately that she could keep him calm. "This is all pointless. While you two argue, Valerie could be anywhere."

"He doesn't care about his cousin," Lady Westcott snarled. "He cares nothing about any of his family, nor about our position in society. He doesn't worry at all about the scandal that could be attached to the Westcott name. He would have let our line end, just to thwart me. Only I outwitted him, didn't I?"

"Outwitted me?" Ivan echoed in a dangerously mild voice. Beneath her hand Lucy felt his arm stiffen.

Lady Westcott gave a smug croak of laughter. "You are wed, aren't you? And it's due entirely to my careful planning."

Lucy could not believe her ears. Careful planning? Then she had an abysmal thought. Could it be that the dowager's scheming had been even more devious than she'd suspected?

Unfortunately, Ivan had leapt from the bed and now glared at the old woman. "What careful planning?"

Lady Westcott gestured toward Lucy. "I hired a pretty woman with a sharp intellect, as unlike the silly girls you dallied with as I could find. I hired her to keep you away from Valerie, and in the process flung her directly in your path. And you stumbled right over her, didn't you? Stumbled over her, fell into bed with her, and now are married to her."

Lucy wanted to stop her. "It was not that way at all!"

Lady Westcott swung around to face Lucy, and though Lucy knew that she was not the focus of the old woman's rage, it was clear she would nonetheless be equally burned by it. "No? You were bored and wanted to escape the country and come to town. Every woman wants a wealthy husband, especially penniless spinsters like you." She stared triumphantly at Ivan. "I have given both of you what you wanted."

Lucy had never seen Ivan so angry, and she could hardly blame him. A vein throbbed in his neck and for a moment she feared he would strike the defiant old woman down. She felt like doing the deed herself. But instead, he grabbed his grandmother by the arm and grimly ushered her from the room.

"You wanted her! You cannot deny that!" the woman shrieked, brandishing her cane as she tried to strike him with it. "The least you can do in return is to find Valerie and save her from the idiot scholar! Don't you have any loyalty to your own flesh and blood?"

He pushed her out of the room, then stood tall and menacing in the doorway. "My flesh and blood? Surely you jest. When have any of you ever treated me as your flesh and blood? All my life I've been an embarrassment to you, not good enough to be a Westcott—until it was clear there would be no other Westcotts *but* me. And now you think you can flay me with guilt regarding my own flesh and blood?''

He let loose an ugly laugh. ''Valerie has a father; go to him. She has brothers and uncles and other cousins. Let them see to her welfare. As for me, I applaud Mawbey's boldness. Frankly, I did not think him up to it.''

Then he swung the door closed and with a crash of wood on wood, the conversation ended.

Lucy had remained in the middle of the bed, frozen by Ivan's awful words. How wretched his childhood had been. How lonely. How forsaken and unloved he'd been all those years.

Oh, how she wanted to make up for that unhappiness of his, to shower him with love and drive all those terrible memories out of his head.

But a person was formed by the experiences of his childhood. She'd always believed that, and when he turned to look at her, his face a mask of bitterness and suspicion, she knew more than ever that it was so. His childhood had been bitter indeed. He had reason to suspect the motives of everyone of her class, including her.

Especially her, it now seemed.

He stopped beside the bed. His eyes pinned her with an awful intensity and chilled her with their complete lack of warmth. ''Now. Where were we?''

Lucy shook her head. Her hands tightened on the sheets. ''Ivan. We need to talk about this. I—''

''No. We don't.'' He reached out and caught a wayward lock of her hair and wound it around one finger. ''Nothing has changed. In this, at least, the old bitch is right. You married what every woman of your class wants: a man above you in station with enough money not to care whether you have any of your own. But I too have married what every man wants: a lusty wench who does my bidding in bed. So it seems we are perfectly matched.''

A muscle ticked in his cheek. ''Remove those sheets. I want to see what I have bought and paid for.''

Lucy gritted her teeth and lifted her chin. "That's not how it is between us."

She felt the pressure on her scalp when he wound the lock tighter still.

"No? Then tell me, how is it between us? No one would ever call us a love match. The last thing you wanted was to marry me—as you made so painfully clear. As for myself . . ." His eyes ran over her, and though she remained shrouded in the silk sheets, every square inch of her skin grew taut. "As for myself, I have wanted you naked in my bed since the first moment I saw you. And now I have you there. It's that simple. Remove the sheet," he repeated in an emotionless voice.

Lucy could no more have complied with that order than she could take back the vows they'd made just hours ago. But her hesitation did not matter to him. With a sharp jerk he bared her to the cool night air and the colder sweep of his darkened eyes.

She wanted to cry. She wanted to cover herself and hide from that cool, assessing look. How could he treat her with so little feeling? She knew he felt betrayed. She knew he felt duped. But how could he come to her as if their joining owed nothing to emotion but were purely a physical act, as casual as scratching an itch—and equally memorable?

But perhaps that *was* how he saw it, she realized sadly. After all, it was she who'd fallen in love with him, not the other way around. So she sat there, frozen awkwardly against the pillows, half sitting, half reclining, as he raked her with his awful gaze. That his unforgiving eyes burned her with their touch only increased her misery.

It was not supposed to be like this between them.

"Spread your legs for me."

Lucy swallowed hard. "Why are you doing this?"

"Spread your legs."

"I was never a part of your grandmother's plotting, Ivan. You know that! I fought you at every turn."

If anything, his expression grew grimmer. "So you did. But none of that matters. My grandmother's untimely interruption has reminded me of something I had momentarily forgotten: that our marriage is like all other English marriages, a convenient arrangement for both parties. You accused me once of using my title and wealth to get me whatever I wanted, and it seems you were right. In return for my Westcott name and money, I have purchased a wife. You. And now all I want in return is my money's worth. So come. Spread your legs. Show me what my Westcott name and money have purchased for me.''

With a cry of pain and rage, Lucy rolled away. She could not bear another moment of this!

But Ivan was faster and stronger and possessed of not one ounce of sympathy for her plight.

In a moment he had her trapped beneath him. With one hand he imprisoned her wrists above her head. With the other he unfastened his robe. Then he used his legs to force hers apart so that she lay helpless and exposed beneath him.

"You have what you and every other English miss wants, *Lady Westcott*," he hissed in her ear. "Now give me what every husband wants in return."

He shifted over her, letting her feel the full weight and strength of his virile male body. The muscular chest that pressed against her soft breasts. The lean stomach and hard loins that ground into her belly. The powerful thighs that kept her helpless against the invasion of his arousal.

Lucy was terrified and furious—and sad beyond all telling. Her eyes swam with tears. "I would gladly *give* you what you want. But I cannot—" She broke off, swallowing a sob. "I cannot bear it if you *take* it."

Ivan did not want to hear her words. He did not want to see her tears. What he wanted was to take his selfish pleasure of her body—then drink himself into oblivion.

He should have known better than to let his guard down with her. He should have known his grandmother's poison was somehow involved!

But even in his rage and pain, Lucy's words rang in his ears, an echo and an accusation that would not go away. I cannot bear it if you *take* it.

Damnation! What was he doing?

With a groan he rolled off her and lay there, one hand flung across his face while he fought back the demons that had him in their grip. But hiding his eyes could not blind him to the ugliness of what he'd almost done. Beside him she lay as before. He could feel, however, the soft shaking of the mattress.

She was weeping. He'd done that to her. And why? Because once again that old bitch had set off his temper?

For a short while he'd believed there could be something good between Lucy and him. He hadn't wanted to call it love, but now he knew that was what he'd hoped for. He'd hoped that she had married him for himself. For Ivan Thornton, born of uncertain parentage and uncertain future.

What a fool's dream that was! And though he knew she had not set out to marry him for his title, at the moment that didn't really help. He'd wanted more from her. Unfortunately he'd overlooked the fact that she was a woman—not so weak as his mother, nor as vicious as his grandmother, but a woman nonetheless. He'd vowed long ago never to allow a woman to have control over him again.

And now, by trying to take control of her, by forcing himself on her, he'd killed what little affection she did have for him.

He pushed himself upright and glanced warily at her. On the luxurious silk her long legs appeared paler than ever. Her skin was the alabaster of moonlight, her hair held the luster of mink. Her silent sobs had eased, but she looked cold and vulnerable now.

More than anything he wanted to warm her and protect her. But he couldn't bear the thought of her flinching away from him in fear.

His gaze traveled up the sweetly curved length of her until their eyes met. When he saw her fear, he turned away, disgusted with himself.

"I'm sorry," he muttered. "I'll leave now."

But when he tried to rise, she caught him by the arm. "Ivan . . ."

He set his jaw and shook his head. "I have to go."

But she would not release him. Instead she knelt on the bed, face to face with him when he stood. "I don't want you to go." Then she wound her arms around his neck and pressed herself against him.

His body responded at once. She was not cold at all but warm as melted wax, and just as pliable. But still he fought the pull of her. He tried to remove her arms. "You don't have to do this."

"I know." She kissed his jaw, his chin, the place where his neck curved into his shoulder.

Ivan shivered. He wanted to make her stop, but he could not. Though her caresses were carnal, and meant to fire his passions, there was something in them that was more than merely physical. She soothed him even as she aroused him. She surrounded him with the sweetness of her heart even as she surrounded him with the sweetness of her body.

But that was an illusion, he reminded himself. The so-called sweetness of a woman's heart was a myth. A fairy tale. Once again he tried to put her from him.

She would not relent though, and when she pulled his head down and captured his mouth with hers, Ivan could fight no longer. With a groan of anguish and of longing, of denial and of need, he wrapped her in his arms and carried them both down onto the bed.

This joining was not as fierce as before. It was tender and silent and almost reverent. But when they were done, when he poured himself into her welcoming body and collapsed into her welcoming embrace, he knew he'd never been so connected to another human being. She'd pierced his armor and burrowed under his skin and found her way unerringly into his heart.

In the aftermath she slept while Ivan lay beside her on his huge bed, staring up into the darkness—and sweating.

This wasn't what he'd bargained for. He'd wanted her to need him. He'd wanted to be the one to control their relationship. He hadn't considered the consequences should *he* need her—should he actually go so far as to love *her*.

Seventeen

*I*van drained the whiskey bottle, watching as the last amber drop wobbled, stretched, then fell into the glass he held in his other hand. His right hand did not shake as he lowered the bottle to the table. Nor did his left when he raised the glass and took a gulp of its fiery contents.

But inside he was shaking.

He glanced around restlessly. Giles and Alex were hunched over a backgammon board. They'd wagered ten sovereigns on the outcome of the game. Alex was intent on his moves—he needed the money. Chances were he didn't have the wherewithal to settle his debt should Giles win. But Giles was intent too; he always played to win, whether anything of value rested on the outcome or not.

Although Alex and Giles were occupied, however, Elliot was not. When Elliot met his eye, Ivan raised his glass and the two of them drank in silence. But it was an uneasy silence, at least for Ivan.

He swore at himself. Why in hell had he abandoned his bride and made his way here, to the Piss Pot? He set down his glass with a sharp thud.

"Did Mawbey say anything to any of you that might have indicated his plans?"

Giles shrugged. Alex said, "Not to me. You have to applaud the man's boldness, though. He has more balls than I would have given him credit for."

''My money's on the chit.''

Everyone's gaze turned to Elliot. ''You think Lady Valerie put him up to it? She's so innocent I doubt she's even heard of Gretna Green,'' Giles said.

Ivan tilted his head, stretching out the kinks in his neck. ''Elliot is probably right. My dear, innocent cousin seemed determined to have him. It wouldn't surprise me at all if she pressured him into it.''

''So. What are you going to do about it?'' Elliot asked.

''Why should I *have* to do anything about it?''

Elliot smiled and Ivan was reminded of a day more than twenty years ago when a younger Elliot had bullied him unmercifully. He was no longer that terrified little boy; but Elliot still had a treacherous streak.

''If you're not going after your sweet soon-to-be-deflowered cousin, then why have you abandoned your delicious little wife?''

Ivan's hands tightened into fists. ''It seems to me that you display an unnatural amount of interest in my wife.''

''Unnatural?'' Elliot's grin increased. ''It would be unnatural for a man *not* to be interested in such a—'' He broke off, laughing, when Ivan lurched to his feet.

Though Ivan knew he was being baited, he was unable to control his temper when it came to Elliot and his perverse interest in Lucy. ''I've had enough of your interference, Pierce.''

Elliot threw his hands up in the air, the perfect picture of innocence. ''Interference? You show up here while we're having a quiet night still celebrating your nuptials—your unexpectedly sudden nuptials—and *I'm* interfering?''

Ivan swore. He was acting like a fool—a besotted fool. Unfortunately that was precisely what she'd turned him into. But not any more. Not any more.

He gritted his teeth. ''What goes on between me and my wife is not your concern. As I recall, we made a wager a few days ago, a wager I have won. I'll expect you to make good on it by the time I return from the North. I'll expect you to be gone for an extended trip to the Continent.''

His eyes met with Elliot's and held until the other man grinned and nodded. Only then did he snatch up his coat. "If none of you has any information to offer, I believe it's time for me to be on my way."

Elliot wisely kept quiet. So did Giles. Alex studied him. "If you think the girl plotted her escape with Mawbey, why are you interfering?"

"Who says I mean to interfere?"

Lucy stared at the bed. She sat curled sideways in a chair across the room from the huge mahogany four-poster.

It was probably a hundred years old. Maybe two hundred. Innumerable generations of Westcotts had slept in it. Made love in it.

But had any other Westcott wives awakened alone in it after only one night of marriage? Had any other of the Westcott women been abandoned by her husband only hours after being wedded to him?

She stifled a rising sob and ruthlessly squashed any hint of tears. He hadn't abandoned her and she was a ninny to think he had. He was gone, yes, but he was off to see about Valerie, and that was good.

Still, there were others who could have tended to that. A father and other male relatives, as he'd pointed out last night. But Lucy knew better. Valerie's elopement with Sir James had just provided Ivan with an excuse to get away from her. The fact was, he'd never wanted to marry her. Not really. And now he felt duped—and trapped. She feared he now lumped her in with the other women who'd used him so poorly. But she hadn't! She hadn't.

Oh, why had Lady Westcott, after achieving her aim to see him securely wed, burst in on their privacy and ruined everything?

Lucy buried her face in the curve of her arm along the stiff padded chair back. Outside a dog began to bark. A woman's voice called out and a man's answered. Lucy looked up, hope leaping in her chest. But it wasn't Ivan. The man outside laughed and it wasn't Ivan's laugh.

Unbidden, a tear leaked out and, though she swiped it away with the back of her hand, another one followed. Then another.

"Don't be a goose," she ordered herself. She pushed up from the chair and stared around her. She'd never been the weepy sort, she reminded herself. She refused to become so now, simply because her husband was inconveniently gone. After all, it was family business. He would be back.

As the days passed, however, she grew less and less sure of that, for the longer Ivan was gone, the less likely it became that he had found Valerie and Sir James, and the more likely that the two of them were already wed. Had he gone to look for them at all?

Her emotions during that time were volatile in the extreme. One moment anger ruled; the next, despair. He had never wanted to marry her. So why had he? Just to make the point that he could? Then again, even though their marriage had not been born of the best circumstances, she believed they could rise above it—if he wanted them to.

On the fourth day of Ivan's absence, Lucy was roused when they received a post from him. He had business to attend to and wished for her to go to Dorset, since he meant to close up the house in town. No mention at all about the escaped lovers, which had infuriated the dowager countess. No mention of his own plans, which had crushed Lucy.

They had also received two posts from Valerie. The first one had apologized for any inconvenience and embarrassment she might have caused her godmother. The second had been a note from Sir James and Lady Mawbey, announcing their recent marriage and requesting permission to call on them in Dorset.

That particular correspondence had set Lucy all aflutter. Valerie could only know they were going to the Westcott family estate in Dorset if she'd been in contact with Ivan, Lucy had reasoned. Which meant that at some point he'd intercepted them.

Did it also mean he would join them in Dorset?

Lucy had been unable either to sleep or eat, so consumed was she by that unanswerable question.

Now Lucy and Lady Westcott sat opposite one another in the Westcott traveling coach. "You'll need your own maid," Lady Antonia said as the cumbersome vehicle rocked along the macadam road. They'd left Guilford and were en route to Winchester where they would change horses, then cross the river Test at Stockbridge. "I have two girls among the staff who may do."

"Can either of them read or write?" Lucy asked, staring unappreciatively at the passing scenery.

"I do not employ idiots, Miss Drysdale—"

She broke off when Lucy turned a pointed stare on her. Lucy was no longer a miss, but rather the Countess of Westcott. And though that was what the old woman had thought she wanted, it was clear that fact didn't sit too well with her at the moment.

They would probably never get on well, Lucy suspected. That awful scene in the bedroom had ensured that. The dowager countess was not one to relinquish power to anyone. Likewise Lucy had no intention of kowtowing to the difficult old woman. Their eyes met now in frosty acknowledgment.

"I employ only the best," Lady Westcott continued sullenly. "Whether it be maid, milliner, or modiste."

"I shall endeavor to remember that. However, it may take a while for me to adjust from spinster governess to abandoned countess."

Lucy turned away to stare out the window. Now why had she said that? It made her sound so pathetic. But then, she was pathetic, at least in the eyes of the rest of the world.

Across from her Lady Westcott's heavy skirts rustled as she shifted in her seat. "You are not abandoned. Not unless you allow yourself to be perceived so."

The words were brisk, but the old woman's tone was, for wont of a better word, conciliatory. Lucy peered sideways at her. "I go to my new home without my new husband at my side, and no indication of when, if ever, he will join me. Who will not perceive me as abandoned?"

"He went off to find his cousin, as well he should have. Besides, I thought you had more backbone than to wither and die at the least sign of adversity."

"Is that why you picked me for Ivan? Because of my backbone?"

The old woman stared at her belligerently. "It was. I hope I was not mistaken in my judgment."

Lucy looked away. Backbone was something she'd always possessed in abundance. The problem was, falling in love seemed to have sapped it right out of her. That was something, however, that Lady Antonia did not need to know.

She stiffened, gritted her teeth, and tilted her chin up. "Rest assured that I plan to assume my responsibilities as Countess of Westcott with a purpose no one will doubt. Neither my absent husband, nor you," she added. Then Lucy closed her eyes and settled back for the rest of the long, unhappy journey to the Dorset countryside.

They arrived at the Westcott family seat at dusk, when the waning summer sun bathed the house's west-facing façade with gold. It was a handsome residence, built of Portland stone, and it boasted five stately gables on the façade and enough windows to keep a team of window washers occupied the year round. Ivy clambered up its rusticated walls, giving a comfortable appearance to a house that would otherwise have appeared austere. It sat low to the ground and, as a result, its two and a half stories did not seem so imposing as they might have in a basement house.

All in all, not nearly as ostentatious as she would have expected.

Inside was another matter entirely. The ceilings throughout were high, coffered, and elaborately painted. Whether plastered or paneled, the rooms boasted gold leaf or faux painting or both, and then were heavily covered with works of art. The floors were works of art themselves, inlaid with every type of wood imaginable, then warmed with carpets from every Eastern country she'd ever heard of.

Furnishings ranged from the antique to the most modern, and two bathrooms offered running water—an almost unheard-of luxury by anyone's standards. But for all its luxury, the place lacked something.

Human warmth, Lucy decided as her footsteps echoed hollowly on the ornate stairs that curved up to the second floor.

The dowager coutness had her personal possessions moved to the guest room nearest the east bathroom. Lucy claimed the master's chambers and the western bathroom.

In a moment of anger she ordered Ivan's few belongings moved into a storeroom in the attic. If Lady Westcott did not appreciate Lucy's high-handedness, either then or in the weeks that followed, she kept any dissatisfaction she felt well hidden.

Without actually discussing it, the two of them fell into a comfortable sort of routine. Lucy walked the grounds in the mornings, brooding. Thinking was how she referred to it, but it was really brooding. When she returned around ten they breakfasted together.

Lucy took over the decisions related to the running of the household, but she made those decisions within Lady Westcott's hearing. The dowager countess occasionally offered advice—usually good—which Lucy considered—and usually took. In the early afternoon Lucy learned her way around the well-provided library while Antonia read the several newspapers she subscribed to, then napped.

They kept country hours, eating an early supper. Sometimes Lucy rode in the long summer twilight. The grounds of the estate were extensive, and the stables, though not enormous, did boast several fine hunters.

All in all, theirs was an idyllic existence, save for the huge uncertainty they labored under. When would Ivan return?

Valerie wrote twice more. First, that they were delayed in York, visiting Sir James's family, but still intended to come to Dorset. Then, that they would arrive in Dorset the last week in July, after visiting first with Valerie's family in Arundel.

Ivan wrote as well, but his posts were little better than curt notes.

Business keeps me in York for another week, the first one said. Then two weeks later, *I travel to Wales regarding a new business venture.*

He did not indicate when they might expect him in Dorset.

Lucy tried not to become morose, but it was impossible. Reading could not distract her. She lost her appetite. Even the smell of food began to turn her stomach. On the afternoon Valerie and Sir James arrived, Fenton, the ancient butler, had to rouse her from an impromptu nap on the Chesterfield couch in the library. Antonia awaited her in the foyer, and together they went outside to greet their guests.

Valerie was nervous. Lucy saw that plainly. But the girl approached her godmother without hesitation, holding tightly to her husband's arm. "May I present my husband, Sir James Mawbey," she began, deferring to her godmother's greater age and rank.

"I know who he is," Antonia retorted. She eyed the unsmiling young man and the faintly frowning Valerie. "Don't give me that look, girl. I am entitled to my ill humor, for you have embarrassed me to no end. Answer me this. Is there no chance for an annulment?"

Sir James bristled. "Madam! You have no right—"

"No chance at all," Valerie interrupted her outraged husband. "We are legally wed, and even if we were not, there is no turning back. We love one another."

The dowager countess gripped her cane with her bony fingers, kneading its crystal head. "Very well, then. You are wed. Come, give me a kiss and let us go inside. This heat is enough to make a person faint."

As quickly as that did the tensions disappear—at least the ones emanating from the old woman. Valerie too was relieved and hooked her arm gratefully in the dowager countess's. Sir James, however, was less accepting, and he stared suspiciously at the old woman.

It fell to her, Lucy realized, to soothe his ruffled feathers. "Come, Sir James. You are family now and all will be well."

His arm was stiff beneath hers, and his manner even more so. "She is not likely to forgive me my lesser standing in society."

"I believe she already has," Lucy pointed out. She gave him a long, steady look. "I wonder what it was in your childhood that caused you to dislike the peerage so—and yet at the same time continue to use your courtesy title."

She expected he would take exception to her rather sharp words. To her surprise, his brow furrowed in thought. "It is a curiosity, I know. And one I have considered more and more of late. The truth is, I should have married you, with your quick mind and unexceptional background," he said quite bluntly. "Instead I fell in love with Valerie. Who is also quite intelligent," he added hastily. "But she does not share our particular interests, yours and mine."

Lucy gave him a wry smile. "Perhaps your brilliant mind is better complemented by her social standing. I am known to be every bit as annoying as you."

He grinned at that and she grinned back.

They had come into the front parlor and there was no further opportunity for so frank a conversation. But Lucy knew she'd found a friend in Sir James. If she'd had any doubts about his suitability for Valerie, the last of them disappeared. While they seemed unsuited on the surface, the truth was, they complemented one another very well.

In Valerie, James had found the perfect unspoiled girl who was, nonetheless, a woman. A personality he could mold, with a face and figure he could love. As for Valerie, she'd always been the middle child, lost and ignored in the hubbub of family life. But in James she had found an austere fatherly sort of man who showered all his attention on her.

Their curious marriage was going to work. Lucy was sure of it.

If only she could feel as sure about her own.

Eighteen

"*I*'m not ill. Truly," Lucy protested.

Valerie studied her, doubt written plainly on her face. "Your appetite is nonexistent. Your color is off." She tried to press her hand to Lucy's brow, but Lucy ducked her head.

"I'm perfectly fine," she vowed. "It's just all the changes in my life. Marriage. A new home."

"A husband missing?" Valerie softly added.

Lucy grimaced. They were sitting on a garden bench just off the front drive, watching the sunset. Today marked seven weeks she'd been at Westcott Manor. Seven weeks and six days since she and Ivan had wed.

Seven weeks and five days since last she'd seen her husband.

Thank heaven Valerie and Sir James were here, else she would long ago have gone mad. So much for backbone.

Grief. Anger. A crushing despair. She'd been tortured by all those emotions, separately and together, and in dizzying sequence. She wanted to strangle Ivan. She wanted to hold him and never let him go. She wanted this awful waiting to end.

But most of all, she didn't want anyone to guess what she'd already guessed: that she might be with child. Her heart clutched every time she thought of it. Her child. And Ivan's. As joyful an event as it was to her, however, it was equally sorrowful. For Ivan seemed to have abandoned her to the country and, in the process, their child as well. When he found out about her condition, she feared it would drive them even farther apart.

"How is James's article coming?" she asked, determined to steer the conversation in another direction.

As she'd anticipated, Valerie gave her a brilliant smile. "He's working on it now. We shall be leaving for London day after tomorrow to get it to the publisher's in time for the September issue of 'Hasting's Journal for Research on the Human Brain.'"

Like all her other emotions, Lucy's feelings toward Valerie and James's imminent departure were twisted and confused. They were the quintessential newlyweds, so utterly in love that she could scarcely bear to be around them when they were together. They made her own poor excuse for a marriage seem even more pathetic than it was.

But if they left she would have no distractions at all. Misery would be her only companion. That and Antonia, and Ivan's infrequent posts. His travelogues, she called them in her bitterest moments, for they were always sent from different locations. York for a week. Three days in Scarborough, then back to London before leaving for Portsmouth. It did no use for her to write back to him, for he seemed to be constantly on the move.

With an effort she suppressed her unhappiness and smiled wanly at Valerie. "You will come back to us after that, won't you? We shall be so lonely here without you."

Valerie patted her hand. "I would love to, of course. You and Lady Westcott have been so kind to have us these last few weeks. But James has his lecture series to reschedule. And the fall term at the Driscoll School will begin soon. Then there are his quarters, which I have not seen, but which I expect to be no better than any other bachelor's abode. I fear I will have my hands quite full making it livable, let alone comfortable." She cocked her head. "Perhaps you would like to stay with me a while in September and help me with my redecorating. Oh, yes," she added with rising excitement. "It would be so wonderful if you came to London with us."

Lucy pushed back a stray curl the evening breeze had loosened at her temple. Perhaps she should return to London. Though she was not certain if Ivan was there, his friends were bound to be, and they might shed some light on his whereabouts, if not his behavior. Besides, she was tired of hiding out in the countryside as the pathetic, abandoned little wife. Better to return and face society as the new, razor-witted Countess of Westcott, she decided as the idea took root. Better to make a big splash in town before the season ended. And maybe, just maybe it would bring Ivan out of his hiding.

"I believe I *shall* come to London with you," she stated with new confidence. "I'll have the town house reopened and we can stay there while your apartments are made ready."

A worried expression replaced Valerie's excited one. "What if . . . That is, do you think—"

"Do I think Ivan will be in residence there? We shall soon see," was Lucy's grim reply. "We shall soon see."

Three days later she had her answer. He was not in residence there. But the butler had it from the cook whose sister was in service at the Varneys' that the Earl had made an appearance at a dinner dance there, not a week earlier.

He'd been in a foul mood. He'd danced with every woman there, nearly come to blows with Lord Haverling over his sister, then quarreled as well with one of his friends and parted early—already well into his cups.

Lucy listened to the news from the reticent butler with arms crossed and one foot tapping an agitated rhythm. She didn't know what hurt her more, his attentions to those other women, his determined avoidance of her, or his obvious unhappiness. But no matter what, he had no right to treat her so poorly. And no reason.

"Have someone determine where he is residing, for I wish to send him a message."

The butler nodded. When she did not continue, he bowed

and turned to leave. But Lucy was seized by a demon, it seemed, for she stopped him before he reached the door. "Also, Simms, I would like to meet with you and Cook and the housekeeper. The sooner the better. I mean to plan a reception—a grand reception, actually—to introduce my cousin and her husband to society before the hunting season begins and everyone repairs back to the country."

That she'd only just decided to do so—and that she knew nothing whatever about planning a society fete—was immaterial. Valerie deserved it, and as the new Countess of Westcott, Lucy would be expected to entertain. Soon enough, when her pregnancy became obvious, she would have to retire from society. Between now and then, however, she refused to let anyone feel sorry for her.

Besides, it would kill two birds with one stone. She would launch Valerie and establish Sir James in the society he professed to dislike. And she hoped, she would flush Ivan from whatever hole he'd gone to ground in.

Valerie was ecstatic when she heard the news, Sir James less so. But he would do anything for his precious wife, and so he reluctantly agreed to attend. To plan the grand evening Lucy contracted with Madame Leonardo, a French widow who hired herself out to plan and oversee only the poshest of society parties.

It was Lucy's intention to make this the crush of the season. The fact that it had apparently been a very dull season, save for the shenanigans within the Westcott family, worked to her advantage. Lucy knew the ton was inordinately curious about her recent marriage. A chaperone and the bastard earl—a Gypsy bastard, no less. Then there was Valerie, arguably the prettiest young lady to come out this year, who had chosen a penniless scholar when she might have had almost anyone.

Oh, yes. There would be few people, if any, sending their regrets for the Westcott reception.

But whether or not Ivan planned to attend Lucy could not predict. One person she did not intend to invite, however, was the dowager countess.

She soon learned that Ivan was staying with Giles. Every time she went out she half expected to run into him. She hoped to. She dreaded the very possibility.

She didn't go out much. Mornings she took to staying abed—to hide the awful nausea that overcame her upon rising. Afternoons she spent recovering from the morning. That left only the evenings and she did her best to play the role of the high-spirited countess out in society. She laughed; she flirted; she danced with anyone and everyone. Unfortunately, she was usually too tired to stay out very late, and that spoiled the image she was trying to create. She would fall into bed exhausted. Then, with the new dawn the cycle would begin anew.

It was at the opera one night that she ran across Alexander Blackburn. She and Valerie were returning from the ladies' powder room during the intermission and he was standing on the stairs, his arm around the waist of a stunning brunette. Though he saw her at once, he did not acknowledge her except to nod. She, likewise, did not stop to chat. No doubt the woman, who made no secret of her amorous interest in Alex, was not the sort of woman a man introduced to a countess, Lucy told herself. He was behaving in her best interests.

Still, she couldn't help being crushed. He was Ivan's long-time friend, and he would not even do her the courtesy of addressing her. Then it occurred to her that Ivan could very well be in attendance tonight. What if he too had such a woman on his arm? The very thought made her stomach turn.

She spent the remainder of the opera using her glasses to scan the other boxes, and then the floor also. But she found neither Ivan nor Alex. She was as low as she'd ever been by the time they arrived home and she made her way to her lonely bed.

As the days passed with no reply from Ivan, however, she became angrier and angrier. No matter his provocation, he was behaving like a spoiled five-year-old. Notwithstanding the demands of managing the extensive holdings he'd inherited, he had no reason to avoid her this way. *He'd* forced *her* into this marriage, yet now he played the role of the injured party.

In her calmer moments she recognized that in his eyes she'd rejected him, just as his mother and grandmother had done. Unlike those cases, however, he'd been able to prevail over her and force her into the marriage. Unfortunately, he had no sooner achieved that objective than he'd abruptly learned that once again he'd been manipulated by his grandmother. And so he stayed away.

When her emotions were less controlled, however, that sort of reasonableness did not hold up. He had never recovered from his terrible childhood and now punished her for the sins of mother and grandmother. He could not punish them so he punished her. It wasn't at all fair, for she was the only one among them who truly loved him.

Whether her mood was controlled by reason or emotions, that one truth remained constant. She loved him. She was furious at him; she ached for him. She loved him.

Ivan was no happier than Lucy, and just as unable to rectify the situation. His initial anger at her—an anger he knew was better directed at his grandmother—had long burnt out. Valerie's utter happiness with her most inappropriate husband had completely doused it.

He'd caught up with them before they'd said their marriage vows, and he'd had a long, stern talk with Sir James. Did he love her? Where would they live? Had he the wherewithal to support her?

Once assured of Valerie's future happiness, he had stood up as a witness for the ceremony that joined them as man and wife.

If he'd had an ounce of sense he would have returned then to London and have had an equally candid discussion with his new bride. But the thought of that conversation scared the hell out of him.

What would it accomplish—to make her admit her true feelings toward him? He already knew she had not wished to wed him. They were well suited physically, but that did not erase the gaping chasm that lay between them. He'd been duped into marrying her. She'd been forced to marry him. If he could not forget the former, could she be expected to forget the latter?

So he'd lingered in York to check on the Westcott holdings there, then traveled to Wales regarding a tin mine. He'd justified it as necessary, for he'd neglected business, and anyway, he needed time to think. But the weeks had passed, and the longer he was gone, the easier it became to stay away. On to Scarborough regarding a shipbuilding venture. Then down to London. Anywhere but Somerset.

He was miserable, though. The night Alex reported to him that he'd seen Lucy at the opera, however, had been the worst. How Ivan had wanted to go to her, to take her in his arms and forget all the mistrust between them. But how could he? After all this time and his inexcusable absence, she was bound to hate him.

So he drank and quarreled, and offended even his closest friends. But he did not go to her for fear that she would reject his apology. That she would reject him.

When he received her note regarding the reception for Valerie and Sir James, however, he knew he could avoid her no longer. She'd thrown down the gauntlet, and in doing so, thrust their personal differences into a very public arena. If she thought she could make him look the fool, she was sorely mistaken.

She had made a grave miscalculation, Lucy feared, and she would most certainly look the fool for it. For Ivan had not responded to her post and the reception was this very evening. Around noon Sir James sought her out.

"Would you have me call on him, Lucy? To demand he appear with you in the receiving line?"

Painful color crept into Lucy's face. "No. No, that is not necessary." Unwilling to elaborate, she hurried away. A man could not be forced to behave as a good husband, she told herself. Especially a man like Ivan. He was bent on flaunting all of society's rules—and on punishing the women in his life through her, it seemed.

But oh, how she wished she could force him. Or convince him. Or even just coax him.

She sighed. There was no use wishing for what would never be. She'd learned that lesson long ago, or so she'd thought. It seemed, unfortunately, that she needed to learn it all over again, to accept that fact and get on with her life, such as it was. And first on her list of things she must do was to get through this wretched party she'd planned.

She donned a high-waisted gown with long, close-fitting sleeves. It was teal-blue silk, with an overlay of matching chiffon, shot through with silver and gold threads. The colors of the shawl Ivan had given her. The result was stunning, for she literally shimmered with every step she made.

The bodice was cut square, low, and wide, so as to display a handsome amount of bosom. And what a bosom it was, she thought as she examined herself in her dressing-room mirror. There was no denying to herself that she was pregnant, for if the morning nausea did not confirm it, her enlarged breasts most certainly did. Her figure had become amazingly lush in the last month.

Would Ivan approve?

She turned away from the mirror frowning. It didn't matter if he approved or not, she told herself as she stepped into the embroidered mules she'd had made. She pulled on her sheer mitts, then took a slow, steadying breath. Time to go downstairs and check everything. The guests would soon begin to arrive and she wanted to be ready, and completely composed, when they did.

The foyer gleamed with golden light. The finest beeswax candles burned in every wall sconce and in the countless silver candle braces that adorned the commodes and tables scattered about. She moved into the drawing room where two huge candelabras holding sixty candles each added to the sweet honey smell. Crystal candle lamps and cut-glass votives contributed to the glow, and spread among the creamy candles were roses. Everywhere red roses.

Red roses for love, she thought bitterly. Valerie and James's love, not hers.

She stared at the grandest arrangement of all, a special design Madame Leonardo had called for. Red roses, white baby's breath, and heart-shaped ivy leaves formed an arch over the pier mirror that filled one huge bay in the paneled end wall.

In the silvered glass she looked rather striking. The roses framed her stark teal image. She actually looked like a countess, she thought as she stared at her unfamiliar reflection. Regal. Confident.

How ironic, she thought, when the truth was, she'd never felt less confident.

She lowered her gaze, unable to bear the sight of this new her, this Countess of Westcott. How could she ever have thought she could pull this off? How would she ever endure this evening? Her stomach clenched and she feared she would be ill.

"Red roses. For love?"

Lucy gasped at that low, mocking voice.

Ivan.

Her startled eyes lifted to see him in the mirror, standing just behind her, slightly to her right. In his hand he held one long-stemmed red rose. He wore exquisitely tailored evening attire. The stark black of his coat and the snowy linen of his shirt showed his dark complexion to advantage. In his ear the diamond stud glittered, and Lucy thought she'd never seen so effective an adornment on a man. Rather than lessen his masculinity, it seemed somehow to emphasize his raw, untamed virility.

He was here, her glad heart cried out. He was here.

Then her joy turned abruptly to outrage. He was here, damn his hard Gypsy heart. And to add insult to injury he did not look pleased to be here.

Their gazes met and held in the watery depths of the silvered glass, his eyes dark and shuttered, hers shooting angry sparks. He advanced and she watched as he extended the rose to the bare spot where her shoulder curved into her neck.

"Tell me about these roses," he commanded, as he slid the half-furled velvet petals slowly along her skin.

She vowed to remain unmoved. If he wasn't going to apologize for his lengthy absence, she certainly wasn't going to act the pathetic little wife by begging for an explanation. She gritted her teeth. "They're for Valerie and Sir James."

A thin smile curved his lips. "You celebrate *their* love? What of *your* fascination with the good scholar?"

"He no longer fascinates me. He hasn't in an age." She stared at him. Surely he was not still jealous about Sir James. First that little scene with Elliot Pierce. Now Sir James Mawbey?

Ivan did not reply. Instead he stroked the rose along her collarbone, then down, slowly tracing the edge of her revealing neckline.

Lucy's skin prickled all over with an aching awareness of him. He was touching her and yet he was not. He wanted her but he didn't want her. He was so perverse!

But she was just as perverse, for as much as she wanted to rage at him—she also wanted to beg his forgiveness. To slap the rose away, and clasp him to her.

Unable to do any of those, she simply stood there, watching him use the rose on her like a wonderful, wicked weapon.

"You play the role of countess very well," he murmured, reading her mind a second time. "These," he added, stroking the rose across the upper swells of her breasts, "will gain you many admirers tonight. Male admirers. The females will all despise you."

She batted the rose away. "I'm not seeking any admirers, most especially not any male admirers."

He moved closer to her, and where the rose had moved over her skin, one neatly manicured square nail now stroked. "Nevertheless, you shall have them. They shall all desire you."

"As you desire me?" she scoffed. But her heart had begun to race.

"I've never made any secret of my desire for you."

That simple statement managed somehow to sap her resistance. When his other arm circled her, Lucy leaned back against his solid chest. Their eyes held in the mirror. Then his gaze moved lower, to the reflection of her breasts. Hers did too, and she watched as his thumbs edged beneath the lush teal fabric to stroke over her taut nipples.

A small cry of aching pleasure tore from her lips. He stroked again, using the hard edge of his thumbnails to excite her. Her head fell back against his shoulder, but still she watched the erotic image they made.

Then his hands moved down to her stomach and he pressed her hard against his rigid arousal.

Lucy could scarcely breathe. In the mirror their desire was visible to anyone who cared to look: she with heightened color, parted lips, and ruby-red nipples, and Ivan, a sultry Gypsy, able to seduce the most upright of women with his easy touch and potent allure.

She wanted him. She should not, considering all the pain and anger he'd put her through during the past weeks. But want him she did.

He smiled as if he read her thoughts. "I'll have you on a bed of roses, Lucy. Sweet and white, splayed open on a bed of red velvet petals." He lowered his lips to the tender skin of her neck and though the caress was as light as the stroking of the rose had been, it seared like the lick of fire. It lit her from the inside out; it filled her with unbearable heat. Unbearable need.

"Ivan." His name escaped on a sigh.

Again he thumbed her nipple and she arched into his touch, wanting more. He moved his other hand over her stomach in a hot circle, pressing against her belly, and she ground her derriere against his arousal.

"I've thought of nothing but this." The words were a rough whisper, a hoarse admission in her ear, and they roused her further still. Yet they also managed to bring her back to reality. She pushed his hand away from her breast. "If that is true, then why did you stay away?"

She tried to twist out of his grasp but he wouldn't let her. Their eyes held in the mirror.

"Business," he answered after a short hesitation.

"Surely you received my posts."

"I received them. But you've been in town a week."

"So I have. Perhaps I should have come to you then. But . . ." She felt his shrug. "I did not. For that I apologize. Now, where were we?"

He raised up her skirts, baring her legs to their view, and despite Lucy's anger at his unsatisfactory reply, she could not help staring at the erotic picture they made. Her legs were pale against the black of his trousers, naked and vulnerable against the strength of his still garbed form. She shivered with desire at the sight, then immediately cursed her weakness for him.

"You have no right—"

"We are wed. I have every right."

One of his hands slid down and his rough palm caressed the sensitive skin of her inner thighs. At the same time he thrust his hips against her, letting her feel the power of his desire for her.

Lucy groaned low in her throat. She was succumbing. She knew it and feared that he knew it too.

Then a voice sounded in the foyer beyond them. A tray rattled, silver on silver, and reality slapped her rudely in the face.

In the mirror before her a rosy wanton leaned into a dark man. In her drawing room, with servants outside and guests arriving momentarily, the mistress of the house was making love with the master.

The mistress of the house wanted to continue making love to the master.

But while much would be forgiven an earl and a countess, fornication in front of the servants was not one of them.

The war between physical need and rational behavior must have shown on her face, for Ivan began to chuckle.

"I believe the first of your guests have arrived."

She jerked away from him in a flash. Her skirts fell in luxurious folds to cover her legs. She tugged her bodice back into place and tried to smooth her coiffure where it had become frayed. But there was no disguising the bloom in her cheeks nor the glitter of full-fledged arousal in her eyes.

Behind her Ivan let out a heavy sigh. "I suppose we will have to wait until afterward," he said, letting his eyes run over her.

Lucy swallowed hard. The wretch! He had no right returning like this. His explanation for his absence was inadequate. His apology was lacking in sincerity.

But his skills at seduction were as good as ever. Better. She didn't know who to be angrier at. Him for trying to seduce her, or herself for succumbing so easily. For there was no denying that a part of her could hardly wait until after the party and the heavenly delights he promised with his dark, glittering eyes.

Before she could think of a cutting response, however, she heard Valerie call for her. Then the tall doors to the foyer swung on their heavy hinges and the young woman burst into the room.

"Lucy! Oh, there you are—Ivan! When did you arrive?"

"Just a few minutes ago," he answered. He took Lucy's arm and they turned as one to face his smiling cousin.

"I'm so glad you've come," Valerie exclaimed. She turned back to the foyer. "James. James! Ivan is here after all."

Ivan whispered to Lucy. "I am most certainly here, and I want you to keep me in your thoughts all evening." He handed her the rose he'd teased her with before. "Think about what we've done here. Think about what we'll do later."

He drew her toward the foyer then, and Lucy followed, her hand on his arm, the perfect image of a countess entertaining with her husband the earl. But inside her emotions careened out of control.

She wanted to slap him in front of everyone for the pain he'd put her through. But more, she wanted to drag him up the stairs to their private bedchamber and explore the sensual promise in his voice, the erotic threat that had turned her legs to rubber and her will to mush.

Think about what we will do later.

At that moment she could not have said if she loved him or hated him.

She clutched the rose as if it were a lifeline. She had to put his deliberately provocative words out of her head, else she knew she'd never get through the evening. Besides, she wanted to hang on to her anger. She wanted to skewer him with it. But she could not.

What we will do later.

Yes, the truth was, they would very likely do any number of wicked, wonderful things during the night to come, for she seemed unable to resist him for long.

But if he thought he could simply waltz in here at the eleventh hour and have everything as he wanted it to be, he severely underestimated her. Two could play at this game.

Two could play very well indeed.

Nineteen

They smiled. They drank. They toasted Valerie and
James, and received toasts on their recent nuptials in
return. They entertained everyone who was anyone, and if
the number of guests still at Westcott House at three in the
morning was any indication, the fete was an unqualified
success.

Lucy danced with a dizzying number of men. Sir James
was not among that number, however. On the few occasions she was anywhere near him, Ivan materialized like
magic to monopolize her attentions.

For all those attentions, though, Ivan did not dance with
her either. He danced with Valerie. He danced with every
unmarried young woman there, and many of their mamas
as well. But he did not dance with his own wife.

If she hadn't felt the touch of his eyes on her whenever
she danced with another, Lucy might have been slighted by
his perceived inattention. But she knew why he did not
dance with her. For the same reason she feared dancing
with him. Her physical response to him was too strong. It
would be too apparent to anyone looking their way. If he
took her in his arms and pulled her body close to his—

She missed a step with her current partner, Alexander
Blackburn.

''A penny for your thoughts,'' he said, adjusting their

step so smoothly her mistake caused no disruption to the group dance.

"My thoughts?" She looked away from his insightful gaze. "I'm sorry if I appear distracted. I was only . . . only contemplating which of these lovely young ladies is most deserving of your charming company next."

He laughed, and she knew he was not in the least fooled by her bright chatter. "My dear Lucy—or should I say, my dear Lady Westcott. I assure you that I am your friend, as are Giles and Elliot."

"My friends? If that's true, kindly explain to me why I have been nearly two months without my husband. Explain why he now plays the anxious and attentive spouse. Explain why he blows hot and then cold, why he leaves me befuddled and—"

She broke off, appalled at her unexpected outburst. She'd had too much to drink. That must be it. She looked up at Mr. Blackburn. "I should not have said any of that."

"I don't see why not."

"I'm your hostess. You are my guest—and Ivan's friend."

"Nonetheless, I am not ignorant of his shortcomings."

They separated to circle the adjacent couple of dancers. When they came back together Lucy was better composed. "Then can you explain his behavior to me?"

Alex shrugged. "It makes no sense to me. Except . . ." He studied her. "Except that you scare the hell out of him."

"I scare *him*?" Lucy shook her head. "That's ridiculous."

"So it would seem if you confine yourself merely to logic. But tell me, are your feelings for him based on logic?"

Lucy stared at him, and when once again he grinned, she knew he'd heard her silent answer. No, her feelings for him were not based on logic. But before she could question him further about Ivan's feelings for her, she was whirled around, straight into Ivan's arms.

Alex gave her a mocking grin, and Ivan a nod. Then he backed away and she was dancing with Ivan at last. A few of their guests laughed. Someone joked about the jealous new husband. But Lucy ignored them all. She stared up into Ivan's midnight-blue eyes and his impassive features, and she had the profoundest urge to wipe that controlled expression off his face.

Jealous? A jealous man did not abandon his wife for almost two months. Scared? Of what? He'd lived through a hellish childhood and survived. Now he had more than most men dared dream of: good looks, fabulous wealth, a title. And any woman he wanted.

And yet none of that counted for anything if you were lonely, Lucy reminded herself. If you were not loved.

The dance drew them apart and in the few moments she had out of his embrace, Lucy's resolve deepened. She would not let anger divert her from her goal. Nor passion. Indeed, now that she thought about it, it seemed that Ivan deliberately provoked those emotions in her as a way to protect himself from deeper emotions.

Like love.

But not any more.

Lucy vowed to break through the barriers he kept between them. This time she would provoke him, and she would use every weapon at her command, to force him to reveal his feelings to her. One way or another, she would make him admit his intentions, and there was no time like the present.

They came together again and she deliberately pressed closer to him than necessary. Her breasts, even more sensitive than usual, pushed against his chest, and with just the slightest shifting of her weight she rubbed them from side to side.

His fingers tightened on her hand. "Are you trying to seduce me here, in the ballroom?"

"You did as much to me earlier," she answered, though breathlessly. She had not expected to excite herself so well.

"Perhaps I should encourage our guests to leave."

"*Our* guests?" She stared straight into his eyes.

A muscle ticked in his cheek. "Your guest list. My house. *Our* guests."

"Is that all you expect to bring to our marriage? This house? The Westcott title and all the accouterments that come with it?"

"Is there something else you want?" he asked with a maddening insolence.

"To bring you to your knees," she snapped, without pausing to think. "To strip away this arrogant façade you've perfected."

She pulled out of his arms just as the music ended. For a moment they faced one another, she hot with quick fury, he ice cold with it. Instead of provoking him to passion, she'd provoked him to rage.

Then she remembered the rose.

She'd carried it all night, the stem tucked in her bodice, the half-furled bud resting between her breasts. She drew it out now and tucked it between two of the studs of his formal shirt.

"I've kept it warm for you, Ivan. Now you keep it warm for me." Then she turned away, and on shaky legs made a beeline for Valerie and Sir James.

She kept strictly away from Ivan after that. As soon as the breakfast buffet was ready she began steering the guests toward it. They ate and they drank more still. They lingered for another hour and more, and all the while she played her role as the gracious hostess, until finally, she sent them off with smiles and warm wishes and a promise to call on them soon.

But during all that hubbub, she also kept an eye on Ivan and the rose he left in place on his chest. She knew he watched her as well. She could feel that brooding gaze of his on her, that threatening, enticing look he did so well.

But she played her part too. She promised him many things with the gazes she returned to him. She played the courtesan as best she could, staring at him too long. Letting her eyes run over his strong, lean body. Licking her lips as if she hungered for him. Which she did.

When the last knot of guests took their leave, however, occupying Ivan, Valerie, and Sir James, Lucy beat a hasty retreat. Her teasing gazes had brought about one unfortunate side effect: she was far too excited to be rational. She needed a few minutes to compose herself. If she were to break down the barriers between Ivan and her, it would take more than physical desire. They already had that in abundance.

But she wanted more from him, and she would need all her wits to get it.

Ivan was well aware of Lucy's quiet departure up the stairs, and he wanted desperately to toss his lingering guests out the front door. Instead, he suffered their lengthy good-byes with barely repressed impatience.

Giles stood in conversation with the recently widowed Lady Rowe. As his friend handed her up into her carriage Ivan would have wagered a hundred pounds they planned to meet again, probably within the hour.

Alex had set his sights on younger game this night. He'd been in rare form, charming every unmarried young lady in sight. Now Sir Henry Smythe had an arm around Alex's shoulder. Smythe was newly come to his title, but he had pots of money—and a mousy little daughter that Alex had danced with several times. If she'd decided she wanted Alex, her father would no doubt try to buy him for her. Whether or not Alex would sell himself to such a dull creature was another matter altogether.

At the moment, however, Ivan didn't give a damn. He clapped Alex on the back. "Glad you could come. You too, Smythe." He gave Alex a not-so-subtle nudge toward the door.

Alex grinned, then looked around him in mock surprise. "Dear me. Are we the last to leave? And where is your lovely wife, Thornton?"

Smythe, who'd drunk far more than he could hold, guffawed, then belched. "She's . . . She's pro'bly naked in bed awaitin' his pleasure. You know, milord, that wife of yours has got an abs'lutely magnif'cent pair of—Ow!"

"Oh, dear. Excuse me, Sir Henry," Alex said, shoving the man toward the door. "I believe your lovely daughter is calling for you."

Ivan slammed the door so hard the sidelights rattled. It was either that or smash the man's nose in. The old goat! He had no business looking at Lucy's breasts—even if they were magnificent. Ivan had hardly been able to keep his eyes off them himself. Was it his imagination or was she even more voluptuous than she'd been before?

No, it was only that he was randy as hell. He had been for weeks. Their earlier escapade in the ballroom had taken a slight edge off it. But it had also whetted his appetite for more.

He locked the door and, with a slight nod to Simms, turned for the stairs. He stopped when he found Valerie and Sir James standing there arm in arm, staring at him. He was not amused.

"I sincerely hope you don't mean to deny me access to my own wife, and in my own home."

"You haven't treated her as if she is your wife," Sir James stated.

Ivan strode across the foyer. "Step aside," he ordered, glaring at Mawbey. When the man swallowed hard but did not budge, Ivan stifled a curse. He didn't want to fight the man, but if that's what it took . . .

Valerie placed herself between them. "Ivan. Please. We don't want to interfere—"

"Then don't."

"You don't realize how unhappy she has been!"

Ivan gritted his teeth. "Actually, I believe I do. I plan to make it up to her tonight."

She took one of his hands in hers. "You were gone nearly two months. That's not something that can be made up for in only one night."

Nearly two months. It had felt like two years to him. How much longer had it seemed to Lucy? Ivan took a slow breath then released it. He stared down at Valerie's earnest face. "When did you become so wise?"

She smiled, the guileless smile of a child, the knowing smile of a woman. "Falling in love opens your eyes."

"Falling in love," Ivan repeated.

"I caution you not to confuse love with lust," Sir James put in. "While the two may happily coexist, they are not at all the same thing."

The muscle in Ivan's jaw began to tic. "I assure you, that's not a matter I've ever been confused about. Now, if you'll excuse me."

Valerie looked hopeful; Mawbey less so. They let him pass without incident, though, and that was all that mattered to Ivan. He made his way up the stairs, no less eager than before. But where he'd been sure of his goals, now he felt a niggling unease. A confusion.

He and Lucy were married, and despite their differences, his rights as her husband were clear. In return she had the right to entertain as she had tonight, to play the role of countess, and to spend the very generous allowance he meant to settle on her. Happiness, whether his or hers, did not enter into it.

She'd had her fun this evening. Now he meant to have his.

She was waiting in the master bedroom. But she was not in the bed. She sat curled up in a heavy upholstered chair in the corner, still wearing her shimmering blue gown. Her shoes and stockings lay abandoned on the rug beside the chair. Although she'd removed a handful of hairpins, her glorious hair was still confined in a coil that lay heavy across her shoulder.

When she met his gaze she was not smiling.

Ivan shrugged out of his coat. "Do you need help with your gown?"

She shook her head. He removed his cummerbund.

"I see you've made yourself comfortable in the master bedroom. Where are my things?" he added when he noticed his toiletries were missing from beside the wash bowl.

"In the attic."

Ivan paused in the act of removing his pleated shirtfront. "The attic. An act of retaliation, I take it?"

"So you admit I have cause for retaliation?"

He resumed his methodical disrobing. "It doesn't really matter. What's past is past."

"Is it?"

Ivan stared at her. He'd caught her off guard earlier today and she'd reacted to him instinctively. She'd been angry, but he'd made short shrift of that anger. Now, though, she'd had time to think—and time to restoke her anger. There was no disguising the fact that once more she was furious with him.

He'd just have to catch her off guard again, he decided. She thought she was going to control this confrontation, but she was wrong.

He tossed the studs onto a side table then, without responding to her challenging words, strode up to her. He leaned down, bracing a hand on each arm of the chair and trapping her in it.

"If you need to rage at me, then go ahead and do so. It won't change the fact that you want me. Or that I want you."

Something flashed in her eyes. Something that could have been pain—but was more likely fury, he told himself.

"You have no idea what I want." She spoke softly, without inflection.

"You think so?" Still holding her gaze captive, he moved his fingers up her arm, sliding over the silky fabric until he reached her shoulder and the place where the wispy cloth ended and her creamy flesh began. Then, even slower, he began to trace the deep neckline of her gown, down to where it revealed her breasts to an almost scandalous degree.

Every portion of his body responded to the feel of her— to the warm scent of her. To the very proximity of her. But he forced himself to concentrate on her reaction, not his. He forced himself to rouse her and repress his own growing excitement. She had to learn that he would be lord and master of his wife, not the other way around.

"I think you want this," he murmured, watching her eyes darken with pleasure until only a green rim showed around their luminous black centers. "I think you want my lips to run along here," he whispered as his fingertip slid just above her nipple.

"I think you want my tongue here." This time he let his finger slide over one peaked nipple, caressing it through the sleek fabric.

She was fighting not to respond. That was clear. But her sharp gasp at his erotic caress, and her breathy exhalation when he ended it, told him she was failing.

"If I'm wrong about what you want, Lucy, why don't you tell me what it is you *do* want."

She was breathing hard, and her eyes were bright, as if with a sheen of tears. But she didn't cry and Ivan pushed back any hint of alarm. She was excited, that was all. And that was all he wanted her to be. She needed this from him. It was the one thing he could give her that she really wanted. It was the one thing that would bind her to him forever.

Or for as long as he *wanted* to bind her to him, he told himself.

He moved his finger over her sweet, quivering flesh and heard the satisfying intake of her breath again. Then, to his surprise, she took his face between her hands, holding him still before her. Their faces were but inches apart. Their eyes remained locked together. But there was an intimacy between them now, a clarity of vision that made his heart hammer from more than just physical arousal.

He wanted to look away but she wouldn't let him. "I want you to make love to me, Ivan. That's what I 'want, for you to make love to me."

It was easy to do. It was nearly impossible.

Make love to me.

Ivan knew she meant more than touching her. Caressing her. Filling her body with his own. Those things he could do—he *needed* to do. Those things he must do or die if he did not.

But it was the other love, the emotional need she wanted him to fill, that came close to deflating him.

There was only one way to break the excruciating connection of their eyes. With a half-curse, half-groan, Ivan kissed her.

It was like being sucked into a whirlpool, a dizzy, terrifying spiral, dark with emotion and rife with danger. But he was a man inured to danger, impervious to fear. At least that's what he told himself as he sank into the warm welcome of Lucy's arms. She could not hurt him, only provide him with the pleasures of the flesh. She was only a woman, albeit one he liked better than any other. But she was no more to be trusted than the rest of them, and no more to be relied on. If he needed her, it was only for this, this ability she had to rouse his body and excite his mind. If she thought this was love, she was wrong. And if she thought she could touch his emotions and make him believe love even existed, she was worse than wrong. She was a fool.

But what a delicious little fool. A sweet fool. A ferocious, hungry, passionate fool . . .

They never made it to the bed. She sat in the chair, her bodice pulled down, her skirts raised up while he made up for leaving her unfulfilled earlier in the evening. He made her grip the decorative carving at the top of the chair back while he teased her breasts and tortured her nipples. He made her stay in the same position when he moved his attentions to the sweet place between her legs. She was wet and hot for him, and it took very little to push her over the edge.

When she cried out and gave herself over to the passion, he was hard as a rock, as aroused as he'd ever been in his life. He wanted to possess her and fill her up, to explode inside her and mark her as his. Only his.

But some perverse demon had him in its grip, and he needed more from her than merely that. As he knelt between her legs, watching the shuddering aftereffects of her climax, he wanted to make her admit that she belonged to him. He wanted her total capitulation. He wanted everything she had to give with nothing held back.

So he started it again, only this time using his fingers and hands. He wanted to watch it happen this time. He wanted to see her face, look into her eyes as she gave herself up to him.

He thumbed one perfectly formed breast, one rosy-crested nipple. Meanwhile he slid a finger inside her. Immediately she tightened around him. When he rubbed his thumb over the taut bud protected by her dark curls, she jerked in reaction.

"Look at me, Lucy."

She opened her eyes, eyes glazed still with the power of her climax, and met his gaze. She was his, Ivan knew, and his overengorged manhood actually hurt from the knowledge. Still, he forced himself to concentrate on her, on arousing her further still. He stroked in and out of her and used her own dewiness to moisten the place his thumb still teased.

She was panting and flushed. Her bare breasts were rosy and her cheeks stained with color. Little cries of helpless pleasure accompanied her every breath. Her eyes began to close but he wouldn't allow it. "Look at me," he commanded, in a voice hoarse with desire. "Look at me, Lucy. You're mine now, aren't you? Mine."

When she nodded, he could barely suppress a cry of triumph. When she cried out, however, then erupted beneath his hand, never once turning away from his hot eyes—he could not hold back his emotions any longer. She was open to him, body, heart. Everything. And he meant to take everything she offered.

He loosened his breeches, releasing his demanding arousal, and with a groan, entered her. At once she seemed to melt around him. To conform to him. To meld herself to him.

Or maybe it was the other way around.

But for the blessed moments of their union, it didn't matter. Ivan didn't care. As he poured himself into her and collapsed onto her, he cared only that they were together. That he'd found her, that he'd married her.

That he'd never let her go.

Twenty

*L*ucy awoke to the feel of her husband's hand exploring her body. It was still night. Their room was completely dark. She had no memory of them coming to bed. Nor of undressing. But she was naked and so was he, and he was wide awake.

"I'm going to corrupt you," he murmured.

His husky voice sent a quiver of desire racing through her. He was curved around her and his hand roamed her body at will, touching her, exploring her. The soft skin behind her knee. The depression of her navel. The crease between her buttocks and her thighs. He kissed the nape of her neck, then moved his mouth down her spine.

When she shivered and started to turn to face him he said, "Don't move. I'll do everything."

Lucy sighed. Let him do everything? That would be easy. That would be heaven.

It was heaven, and more. But it turned out to be far from easy. For as he roused her with warm, damp kisses and ever bolder caresses, she found it impossible to simply lie there. She wanted to kiss him back. She needed to touch him too. But Ivan was adamant.

Only when he was in her and moving over her was she able to give back to him. She welcomed him into her arms and wrapped her legs around him as the full weight of his body crushed hers into the bed. Then he began to move, slowly at first, and it was so erotic, Lucy almost fainted. His chest and its coarse patch of hair rubbed against her sensitive breasts. The fine linen sheets slid against her back. She was helpless beneath him, and yet powerful too.

His breathing was hot and hard against her neck, his lips lost in her hair as he brought them nearer and nearer to that final, exploding madness he invoked in her.

"Ivan," she gasped, clutching the sheets as it began. "Ivan!"

"I'm here." The words were a steamy torture in her ear. "I'm here, love."

Love. Though melting in passion, Lucy heard that one word and her heart soared. Love.

"I love you," she whispered as the explosion began. "I love you, Ivan."

They erupted together. They exploded into one another and around one another. The fire sucked them in and it burned them up.

But in the scorching aftermath, as they collapsed into the sweaty, twisted bed linens, something even better was formed. Something better than them apart, Lucy imagined. It was them together. Together and in love.

Ivan was already awake when Lucy first stirred. He'd been lying there as the dawn began to fill the room with light, lying there as still as death. Petrified with fear.

She loved him.

He'd heard her breathy words, but he didn't believe them. She believed them, though, and that was a problem.

But why should it be? The truth was, he should be well pleased with her admission. After all, that's what he'd wanted, to own her, to possess her. But as for love . . .

A woman's love was fleeting. His mother's had been. His grandmother's had never been love at all. He gritted his teeth. The fact that Lucy had professed her love meant nothing. Even if she had meant it—which she might have at the time—it didn't mean it would last.

Still, as angry as that knowledge made him, it wasn't

what had his heart pounding and his palms damp with sweat. The reason for that was far, far worse. For he could no longer deny the truth, at least to himself. And the bitter truth was that *he* had fallen in love with *her*.

To even think it made sweat bead on his forehead.

She moved, stretching her legs, arching like a cat. Her foot grazed his leg and his panic increased.

Then she stiffened and he knew she was fully awake—and that she was uncomfortable to find him in the bed with her. Was she already regretting what she'd said to him in that moment of complete surrender?

They lay there quietly. He pretending to sleep, she obviously debating what to do. Finally, with carefully controlled movements, she began to edge away from him.

Ivan wanted her to go. He wasn't ready to face her just yet. But it galled him that she wanted to slip away from him. As she reached the edge of the bed and began to rise, he could restrain himself no longer. He caught her by the arm.

"Where are you going?"

The startled face she turned toward him was white as chalk. Her eyes were huge and frightened. Frightened. But of what? "I . . . I . . . I'll be right back. I need to visit the . . . the water closet," she stammered.

She was lying. He could tell, and it devastated something deep inside of him. Last night she'd loved him. This morning she couldn't get away fast enough.

His eyes ran over her, over the naked perfection of her soft, white skin, her full breasts, and her glorious, disheveled hair. Desire reared its head once more, but ruthlessly he tamped it down.

"The water closet?"

"Yes. Please, Ivan. I must go. I have to."

His eyes narrowed. There was no color in her cheeks this morning. In fact she was more than pale. Her face held a pallor that was closer to green.

"What's wrong?"

"Please. Let me go. Oh!" She gave a desperate yank

and stumbled back when he released her. She ran for the door, but stopped when she realized she was completely naked. Wild-eyed, she stared about and Ivan felt the first inkling of alarm.

"Lucy? What's wrong?"

She didn't answer. Instead she lurched toward the commode, grabbed the porcelain bowl that sat there, and vomited violently into it.

Ivan shot off the bed, then stopped. What should he do? She was obviously sick and he had no experience with sickness save for that due to overimbibing. Had she drunk too much last night? He didn't think so. Was she ill?

She heaved again and he felt like a cad for his initial anger at her. He had to do something, but what? He yanked his breeches on then moved nearer to her, frustrated by an unaccustomed feeling of helplessness.

"Are you all right, Lucy? Can I do something to help you?"

She shook her head. "Just go away. Go away—" Again her body spasmed as her stomach rebelled. Ivan's heart began to pound. She looked so vulnerable and pale, so weak and frail. Had he used her too harshly?

Panic overwhelmed him. He tore across the room and jerked the heavy door open. "Help! Somebody help her!"

By the time the two maids and the butler burst into the room he had covered Lucy with a thin robe. But she still hung over the bowl.

"Please, Ivan, just . . . just go . . . I'll be fine. Fine . . ."

"My lord. Can we be of service?" Simms asked.

"My lady, are you all right?" one of the maids asked in a concerned voice.

"Oh, my," the second maid gasped. "Could it be milady is expecting?" she whispered to the other two servants.

Though she hadn't meant her voice to carry, Ivan heard her. So did Lucy, for she stiffened. One of Ivan's hands rested on her back and he felt it, and he went cold.

Expecting? As in, expecting a baby?

Ivan pulled his hand away from her as if he'd suddenly

been burned. He felt as if someone had punched him in the gut. Hard. She couldn't be expecting a baby, could she? Not so soon.

But when she looked up at him, her eyes huge and watery, and filled with dread, he knew. She *was* expecting a child. His child.

He drew away from her, too stunned to think straight. The two maids hurried up to Lucy. The older one pushed him gently away. "We'll see to her, milord. She'll be feelin' better soon enough. You just take yourself off now. We'll take good care of her. You needn't worry over that."

Ivan was only too happy to comply. Lucy sick was bad enough. Lucy in the family way was inconceivable. He grabbed his shirt and boots and strode from the room, but not before hearing Simms exclaim, "Won't the dowager countess be pleased?"

The dowager countess. The vicious old harridan who'd manipulated his life from the beginning. Yes, she would be pleased, damn her miserable witch's soul. This was what she'd wanted all along. This was why she'd introduced Lucy into his life in the first place.

Between the house and the stable Ivan jerked on his boots. While the surprised groom saddled a horse, he shrugged into his shirt, shoving the tails into his pants. She'd gotten everything she wanted. He'd become the Earl of Westcott, he'd married a suitable woman, and he'd planted the seed for his heir in his wife's very fertile body.

"Son of a bitch!" He swung up into the saddle, unmindful of the groom's startled expression. Then, unable to stay another minute within the stifling confines of the Westcott family's grand mansion—a place that was his and yet would never truly feel like his—he kicked the horse into a gallop, turned it away from town, and let it run.

Lucy sat in the window of her bedchamber, staring out at nothing. She should have told him sooner, she berated herself. She should have known this would happen. After all, it had happened every morning for the past two weeks.

Why she'd thought she could hide it, she didn't know. Why she'd tried to was even harder to understand.

If he hadn't been absent these past two months she would have told him right away. The fact still remained, however, that she could have told him last night. She'd planned to. But somehow when he came upstairs after the ball, she'd been too distracted to tell him about the baby she carried. His baby and hers.

But he knew now, and considering that he'd been gone nearly four hours, Lucy could only assume that he was not thrilled with the idea.

The selfish wretch! Had he ever considered that she wasn't precisely overjoyed with the idea either?

She turned away from the window, immediately ashamed of her thoughts. She twisted the scrap that had been her handkerchief into knots. She did love the idea of having a baby—Ivan's baby. But the thought of raising it alone was too terrible to contemplate. Every child needed a father. Ivan should know that better than anyone. And every wife wanted to share both the joys and the sorrows of being a parent with her husband.

She wanted to share them with Ivan.

But he didn't want to share them with her. He'd left as fast as he possibly could. Did he plan to go off for another two months, pretending it was on account of business when it was really on account of her?

Lucy stifled a sob. She'd never been so lonely in her entire life. She pressed her hands to her abdomen. "Poor baby," she whispered. "No father to love you and a hateful great-grandmother—"

But there was a grandmother who was not so hateful, her own mother. And an uncle and aunt, and cousins too.

Though her heart was heavy, Lucy tried to take comfort from the fact that her child would be loved, if not by its father, then by its mother and the rest of her family. Unlike Ivan, this child would be surrounded by love every day— every minute—of its life. And once grown, he or she would know how to love in return, something she feared Ivan would never know how to do.

A knock sounded at the door—too soft to be Ivan, she knew. Besides, he wasn't likely to knock at the master bedroom door. She wiped her cheeks, lifted her chin, and tried to compose herself. "Come in," she called, pasting a pleasant expression on her face.

Valerie peered past the door. Her worried face swiftly turned to delight. "Lucy! I'm so happy for you!" She sped across the room and enveloped Lucy in a hug. "A baby! I'm so jealous."

Lucy tried to smile as Valerie sat down on the footstool at her feet. "Yes. Well, I would rather not have announced it in so . . . so unflattering a manner."

Valerie laughed. "I don't think anyone minds that. All the servants are abuzz with the news." She stopped abruptly and her expression altered. Lucy knew what she was thinking.

"Are they also abuzz with the news that my husband has once again run off?"

Valerie took Lucy's hands in her own. "He is only experiencing a bit of shock. I don't believe he'll be gone so long this time."

Lucy could no longer maintain her false smile. She stood and began to pace. "You don't know Ivan as I do. He cannot bear being forced into doing anything. Especially by a woman. He doesn't trust women at all, and I can't say that I blame him. In his eyes his mother betrayed him. His grandmother ignored him and used him. And now I've trapped him into marriage—"

"But you didn't want to marry him—" Valerie broke off, and a frown marred her forehead. "That's part of the problem, isn't it?"

Lucy sighed. "I wouldn't doubt it. In his eyes I rejected him. Or tried to."

"Then why did he marry you? Just for spite?"

Lucy had never felt so sad. "I suppose so. I don't know." She shook her head. "All I know is he never meant to marry, but now he's married to me. I suspect he never intended to have children either, and now I've sprung that on him as well. He's so angry with me,'' she finished in a voice that wavered despite her best efforts to control it.

"Does he know that you love him?"

Lucy had halted at the window. Outside it was drizzling. She looked over at Valerie, making no attempt to hide the stricken expression on her face. "Is it so obvious?"

Valerie smiled. "To me. To James. And probably to anyone else who cares to look."

"But not to Ivan."

"It sounds as if he's not too familiar with love. He may very well not be able to recognize it. He might have to be told. Have you tried telling him?"

Lucy remembered last night. She remembered in the midst of their passion that he had called her love. She remembered telling him she loved him. She knew he'd heard her, but it obviously hadn't mattered. "I told him last night."

Valerie had no reply to that.

Lucy sighed. "I think I'll lie down for a while. And . . . And if you would be so good as to alert Simms that I will want the carriage prepared for a trip to Somerset. As soon as I'm feeling up to travel," she added, as a latent wave of nausea swept through her.

"You're not going back to Dorset?"

Lucy could hardly speak for the lump that lodged in her throat. "The Westcott family seat is not my home. I'm going back to Houghton Manor. I want to be with my family. I want to be with my mother."

Valerie studied her with sad eyes. "You want to be with the people who love you. I understand that. If you think about it, though, that's all that most of us want. Even Ivan."

She closed the door when she left. But for Lucy, Valerie's words lingered in the air. *Even Ivan.*

He was no different than everyone else. He wanted to be loved. But just as he did not know how to love, he did not know how to *be* loved either. He wouldn't let her love him. And unlike many other traits, such as good manners and proper diction, love was not something a person could be taught to do. A child could, she knew. But not a man who'd been taught so well not to love.

A hot tear trickled onto her cheek, but she dashed it away. Instead of lamenting what could never be, she should take joy in all she had.

She curved one hand around her still flat stomach. "I will love you, Ivan. I will love your child and give him—or her—the sort of childhood you should have had, a happy, loving one."

But though she could be a good mother, she nevertheless knew she could not fill the role of loving father. Only Ivan could do that for his child.

And maybe he would, she thought, still hoping for the best. Though Ivan did not love her, maybe, once his child was born and he saw the innocent babe, he would have a change of heart. Maybe this child of theirs was the only way Ivan *could* be taught to love.

A small sense of renewal lifted Lucy's heart, restoring at least a portion of her spirits. Ivan might not love her, nor want her love. He might reject her, now that he'd had the one thing he seemed most to want from her. But reject this innocent child of theirs? Not if she had anything to do with it.

Twenty-one

*I*van arrived home just after four in the morning. Lucy knew that because the tall case clock in the upstairs hall had tolled its somber message just minutes before.

Her sleep had been fitful at best. She'd alternately worried about him, then raged at him. Now, as his steps sounded slow and uneven on the stairs, that worry and rage were replaced by uncertainty. He was so unpredictable. She never knew the right thing to say to him.

If he were a child she would shower him with love—with stern discipline too, but always tempered with love—until he gave up his rebellion and loved her right back.

But he was not a child. He was a man with scars upon his heart, a man so deeply wounded that he refused to accept her love. And unlike a child, he had the power to hurt her back. As her husband—as the man she loved—he had the ability to break her heart.

She lay completely still, straining to hear him. The drapes rustled as the cool evening air surged against them. Some night bird called out in the garden. Then a muffled voice sounded in the hall. ". . . assistance, my lord?"

"I know where my chambers are."

"Yes, sir. But—"

"Go back to bed, Simms."

That last was clearer, from just outside the door. Then the handle turned, a faint streak of candlelight cut across the room, and he was there. The door closed and the room once again went dark. But Lucy was attuned to Ivan's presence as clearly as if he carried a bright lamp with him.

She also smelled whisky. Had he gone off somewhere drinking with his friends? Was he drunk?

She jumped at the sudden sound of a thud, followed by a crash and a string of oaths. "Son of a bitch! What the bloody hell?"

Her trunk. He'd run into her half-packed trunk, and tumbled over it, from the sound of things. Though it was difficult, she resisted the urge to get up and check on him. He deserved a little pain. Maybe it would knock some sense into him.

Still, she couldn't help pushing up onto her elbows and peering through the darkness. The trunk was a nearly invisible shadow. So was Ivan. Only when he cursed again then rolled over and pushed to a sitting position on the floor could she locate him.

He stared toward the bed. "Don't pretend you're asleep, Lucy. I know you're not. What the hell was that, some sort of booby trap or alarm to warn you I was coming?"

His irritated tone chased away any sympathy she might have felt for him. "It's my trunk," she snapped. "I'm packing to go home."

"Home?" He snorted. "Already you call that place home? How swiftly you have adapted to your new role as Countess of Westcott."

Lucy gritted her teeth. "I *hate* being a countess. And the last place—the very *last* place—I'll ever call home is your family seat in Dorset. Or this place either. I'm going home to my family. I'm going home to Somerset."

His shadow unfurled as he stood. When he approached the bed she drew the coverlet up to her chin. Still, those thin layers of silk and linen did nothing to slow the frantic pounding of her heart. He'd gone from irritated to angry; that was clear. And when he stopped, less than an arm's length from her, she had to fight the urge to flee—as well as the urge to draw him into her arms and comfort him.

But he didn't want her comfort, she reminded herself. Or her love. Those were the last things he wanted.

When he spoke, his tone was cold and mocking. "Home? To Somerset? Not bloody likely."

"Are you saying I may not visit my own family?"

"I'm your family now."

"You? Hah! We've been wed almost two months, and this marks only the third night we've spent beneath the same roof. At this rate I shall see you less than two weeks out of the year."

"So you've missed me?" He reached out and fingered the trailing ends of her plaited hair.

"You flatter yourself," she snapped, scooting to the other side of the bed. "What I miss is having a husband."

"What am I to make of that? That any husband will do, just so long as you have one handy?"

"Had just any husband been adequate, I would have wed ten years ago. I was holding out for a *good* husband." She glared at him. "Instead I ended up with you."

His jaw tensed. She'd nicked his pride with her angry words, and she was immediately sorry. She sighed and shook her head. "I'm sorry. It's just that I'm tired, and confused. I didn't really expect you back tonight."

He stood there a long silent moment. Then he shoved his knotted fists into his pockets. "I suppose you had no reason to expect me. It's not my intention to abandon you, Lucy, nor the child you carry. I intend to do my duty to you. If you truly wish to visit your family, I'll accompany you there, though I cannot stay. I've ignored too many business matters of late and will have to return to London to attend them," he added without further explanation. "But once I'm finished in London, I will carry you back to Dorset. This child will be born at Westcott Manor. Unlike its father," he finished bitterly.

He wasn't going to abandon her! Lucy's heart leapt with joy. He meant to order her life around—or try to—and that was sure to cause trouble between them. But she could deal with that. The fact that he referred to their child as an "it," however, was what commanded her immediate attention.

She placed one hand over her stomach. "I think of this baby as a she. Ivana. Or a he. Little Ivan," she said with a smile. "She's a she or a he. But never an it."

Ivan drew himself up. Lucy could practically see him pull in his bitterness and any other emotions he might be feeling. He pulled them in, hiding them behind a mask of indifference that stabbed at her heart.

"He. She." He shrugged. "Whatever you wish."

"What I wish has no bearing on whether our baby will be male or female." When he stiffened at her use of the word "our," she felt a spurt of protective anger for her child. *Their* child. She resolved to confront him head-on.

"I know you did not want a child, Ivan. But you seem to enjoy your husbandly rights. Well, those rights carry with them some husbandly responsibilities, one of which is to care for your children."

He frowned. "I told you I would not abandon you. What more do you want of me?"

Lucy's hands knotted in the sheets. "I want you to be a better father than your father was—and a better husband too."

"Don't compare me to him!"

"Then don't behave like him."

He glared at her, but she refused to back down. Then he swore and shook his head. "I must have been mad when I married you."

He turned on his heel to leave, but before he could stalk from the room, Lucy leapt from the bed and caught his sleeve.

"Your father and his mother thought they'd done right by you when they stuck you at Burford Hall. They didn't see what they did as neglect, but rather as a rare privilege for a Gypsy bastard such as you. But you didn't think so."

He threw her hand off. "I have no intention of emulating their behavior. I don't want this child. I admit that. I never wanted children. But I won't shirk my responsibility to it."

Lucy stood before him in her white embroidered nightgown and bare feet. She knew he didn't want to think of the tiny life inside her as the beginnings of a living, breathing child that would be half his. He didn't want this baby and yet she could not give up. "Part of your responsibility is to love your child. Your children," she added in a soft voice. "I know this is hard for you, Ivan. I know I have ruined all the plans you have nurtured so long for revenge against your grandmother. But the fact remains that in a few months you are going to be a father. And if we continue to share a bed, we will probably continue to have more children."

She paused, wondering what he would say to that. A muscle began to tic in his jaw, but other than that he did not respond. That rigidity fired her temper as nothing else could. "I hope I am not wrong in thinking you man enough to rise to your responsibilities," she finished in a sharper tone.

Ivan looked as if he wanted to strangle her. His hands tightened to fists and his arms trembled with the force of his tension. But he didn't strangle her. He didn't touch her in any way. Instead he stepped back as if he needed to keep as much distance between them as possible.

"The difference in our outlooks—and our upbringings— has never been more obvious than now," he began. "You think a person can be commanded to love. To love because it is their responsibility. Believe me when I say it cannot be done. If it could, I would have commanded my mother to love me—and not sell me to another. I would have demanded that my father love me—or at least acknowledge me. I would have forced my grandmother to love me—or if nothing else, visit me once in a while. But I could not do any of those things as a scared and powerless little boy, any more than I can do them now as a wealthy peer of the realm. Nor can you do it. So don't even try."

His words were angry; his tone furious. But Ivan's sarcastic little speech did not enrage Lucy. Rather, it made her want to cry.

"I cannot believe she really sold you," she said, appalled at the very idea.

His lips twisted in a bitter smile. "Don't worry. I'm sure she received more from the deal than my grandmother wanted to spend. I console myself that at least I cost a pretty penny."

Lucy was not fooled by his sarcastic reply. His own mother had sold him. Even if the woman had thought she was doing the best thing for him, how excruciatingly painful that knowledge must be for him to bear.

Without thinking, she crossed to him. But the instant she touched his hand he jerked away.

"We can leave for Somerset tomorrow," he said, turning for the door.

"Ivan, don't go. Don't leave. Please. We need to talk."

"You need your rest," he countered. "Especially now."

"I don't need to rest. I'm not sick."

"That's not how it appeared this morning."

"That's a temporary malady. It will soon go away."

He paused at the door and looked across the dim room at her. "You want this child, don't you?"

"Of course I do."

"Why?"

"Why?" Lucy studied his face, and even in the shadows she recognized the wariness in his eyes. His mother hadn't wanted him, so naturally he doubted Lucy's sincerity about the child growing inside her now. She knew it was imperative that she say the right thing. "I want this child because I love children. Because like most women, I could never be totally fulfilled unless I raised a child of my own. But not just any man's child," she added. "I want *this* child. I love *this* child already because it is *your* child. Our child," she finished in a hushed voice.

His face revealed nothing. That was disheartening enough. The edge of sarcasm in his voice, however, was devastating. "Two months ago you refused to marry me at all. You expect me to believe now that you treasure this child because it is mine?" He let out a humorless chuckle.

"I think, Lucy, that we will get along better if we leave emotion out of our relationship in the future."

Lucy hid her heartbreak in indignation. What else could she do? "And how, pray tell, shall we accomplish that? Are you saying you will not be returning to our bed?"

He scowled. "And are you saying that now that you're pregnant you no longer want me there?"

"No! Of course not." Her face turned pink at that revealing response. "But how can I leave emotion out when you ... When we ... When we consummate our union? You don't seem unemotional then. Are you saying that in the future you will be?"

She thought she had him there, for he clenched his jaw. Twice. She saw the muscle jump in his cheek. Then his eyes narrowed. "I believe you are confusing passion with other, more enduring emotions. Lust is not love. Desire is a fleeting thing. Like hunger. I suggest you not make more of it than it is."

Like a harsh slap, the words found their mark. Lucy gasped and fought the urge to step back, to scurry away from him and his cruel words. He knew how those words hurt her, how they affected her. He'd heard her say she loved him. Now he was using that knowledge as a weapon to torture her.

He was succeeding very well.

She gathered her hurt up and shoved it deep inside her heart, to a place he could not see. "I bow to your greater knowledge of *love*," she said, adopting the same sarcastic tone he'd used. "Regarding my journey to Somerset, you need not bother to accompany me. I'm sure your business in town is far more pressing."

"It's not a bother. I've been a neglectful husband and I mean to rectify that," he said in a clipped, perfunctory voice.

Lucy turned away. He was so calm, so unaffected by all of this. Meanwhile, her heart was bleeding as if from a mortal wound. "Good night, then," she murmured as she crawled back into the high bed. She pulled the coverlet up

to her chin, fighting back the sting of rising tears. If he
didn't leave soon she was afraid she would embarrass herself completely. *Just leave,* she prayed. *Dear God, make
him leave!*

Ivan stood next to the door, one hand on the knob as he
looked back at his wife.

Why had he returned here? What had he been thinking?

He'd panicked when she'd become ill. He'd never felt
so completely helpless as he had those few desperate moments when he'd not been able to help her. When he'd
discovered the source of her illness, however, that panic
had turned to fury. He'd felt as if she'd betrayed him.

It had taken the whole day and half the night—and most
of a bottle of whisky—for him to recognize that this pregnancy was more his fault than hers. He could have taken
precautions as he'd always done in the past. But he
hadn't—never mind why—and now she carried the heir
he'd never wanted to have.

So he'd come back, only to run away now once more.

But he didn't have to leave, he told himself. He could
close this door, strip off his clothes, and get into bed with
his wife. Angry as she was with him, it would still take
very little to turn her anger to passion. That was the one
thing he was sure of—the only thing he was sure of when
it came to Lucy—that her passion for him was very nearly
as powerful as was his all-consuming desire for her.

He looked over at her, at the curvaceous form beneath
the thin sheets, and felt her eyes on him. It would be a
challenge to seduce her tonight, but he knew he could. She
would protest. She might even fight him. He would understand if she did. But in the end she would capitulate and
he would make her very glad she did.

But what if she again professed her love?

Sweat beaded on his forehead at the thought. He didn't
want her love. He didn't want anyone's love.

He didn't believe there was such a thing anyway. At best
it was a combination of lust and affection. At worst it was
a manipulative trick, one he was not fool enough ever to

fall for. That some women loved their children, he supposed might be true, and he sorely hoped Lucy would love this child she bore. The last thing he wanted was to have his child—any child—grow up in the care of women like his mother and grandmother.

But love between a man and woman? No. He liked her, that was all. And he desired her. He didn't love her, though, any more than she loved him.

Regardless, however, he had to do something. He had to either go to her or leave. But he was frozen by indecision. Then she blinked and shifted restlessly, and panic made the decision for him. He jerked the door open, charged through it, and in his haste, slammed it harder than he meant.

That only deepened his despair, for he knew how women were. Though she was not the weepy sort, he'd seen the sheen of tears in her eyes. She'd held them back, though. But not now. Not after he'd slammed the door on her.

He made himself wait, to listen for the telling sound of her sobs. When they didn't come, he turned down the hall, still sweating, just as panicked as he'd been when she'd become so violently ill. He couldn't handle it. Not her sickness, nor her tears, nor her lack of them. He couldn't deal with her and that fed his panic all the more. No other woman had this effect on him. He'd vowed none ever would.

But Lucy did.

And now that he was married to her—was having a child with her—he was at a complete loss as to how he was to deal with her. He couldn't keep running away. But what other choice did he have?

At the awful crash of the door against its frame Lucy turned her face into the pillow and burst into tears, hard, cruel sobs that shook her body, they were so strong. But they were silent. She saw to that. She buried herself beneath the sheets and silken coverlet and poured all her pain and sorrow into the muffling solace of the uncritical pillows.

That the bed linens smelled of him—of their lovemaking of the previous night—only wrenched her all the worse.

How could he love her—*make* love to her, she amended—and hate her at the same time?

Intellectually she suspected he hated all women. Or perhaps he feared them. It was no wonder, given his dreadful childhood experiences with them.

But it was not her intellect he'd torn to shreds. It was her heart. As she sobbed out her pain and loneliness in her cold, solitary bed, she curled around her baby.

"You shall always be loved," she vowed between hiccuping sobs. "Always."

And so shall you, Ivan, though you may never believe it. You shall always be loved by me.

Twenty-two

T he long day's ride to Somerset was wretched. Lucy was nauseous the entire journey, and they had to make frequent stops. She'd never suffered from the traveler's malady in the past. Her pregnancy, however, seemed to have turned her into a foreign creature, totally unlike the strong-willed, healthy person she'd always been. Or was it her unhappy marriage to Ivan that had her so weepy and ill?

Ivan accompanied them, but astride a high-spirited gelding that he said he'd recently purchased and needed to ride. He left Lucy to the company of the maid he'd insisted that she bring along.

It was just as well, she told herself. Although she ached with sorrow over his remoteness, his proximity while she was so sick would have been infinitely harder to bear.

They reached their destination after the late summer dusk. Houghton Manor was lit as if for a ball, with lamps burning in almost every window. Lucy knew neither her mother nor Hortense would instigate such an extravagance. Graham must be even more pleased to have an earl for a brother-in-law than she'd suspected.

They were met by everyone, even young Charity and Grace. Lucy had never been so happy to see her family. Since meeting Ivan she'd begun to value them in a way she'd never done before. She hugged each of them in turn, even holding tightly to Graham. For all his priggishness, he was a good brother who had always cared deeply for her welfare.

When her mother opened her arms to her, Lucy was close to tears.

"Oh, my darling. My darling," Lady Irene crooned, holding her with unusual strength. "I have missed you so much." She cupped Lucy's face with both hands and kissed her, then stared at her with bright, hopeful eyes.

Lucy knew what that look meant. But she was not ready to reveal her condition. Not here in the foyer with everyone standing around—with her own emotions so raw and Ivan so near.

"You look exhausted," her mother said, eyeing her shrewdly.

"It has been an extremely tiring day. If you don't mind, I should like nothing better than to collapse into my bed."

"I've had your old bedroom freshened up," Hortense said, slipping her arm in Lucy's. She glanced at Ivan then leaned nearer Lucy, whispering, "I had another feather mattress added to the bed."

Somehow Lucy managed a meager smile. But inside she began to shake. They would have to share a room. Not once during the horrendous journey here had that thought occurred to her.

"Now, Hortense," Lucy's mother interrupted. "You have your children to attend to. Let me attend to mine. Come, Lucy. I'll help you unpack while Ivan and Graham have a drink in the library."

Lucy glanced at Ivan. He stood with his hat and gloves still in hand. He looked no worse for wear, considering he'd spent the entire day astride. If anything, his windblown appearance made him more unbearably handsome than ever. He met her gaze, then looked away, greeting Graham with every appearance of ease.

"A glass of Irish whisky would sit very well."

"Then come along, come along," Graham urged.

So they dispersed, Ivan to indulge in the drinking he

seemed to enjoy more and more, Hortense to tend to her boisterous brood, and Lucy to face the determined grilling of her mother.

"Well?" Lady Irene began before the bedroom door had scarcely clicked closed. "Have you any particular news you wish to share with your mother?"

Lucy sank onto the chaise longue that angled away from the window. She'd imagined many sorts of futures for herself while curled up in this very spot, but never that she'd marry a man who didn't love her and who didn't want to have children.

"May I at least remove my traveling coat before you begin this inquisition?" She broke off when she realized how tart her words sounded. This was her mother who loved her, who wanted only good things for her. She did not deserve any part of Lucy's ill-temper.

She stared at her mother, whose face hid no emotion, not her consternation nor her continuing curiosity. Here was one person, at least, who would be deliriously happy to hear that Lucy was expecting, and for no more reason than that she adored babies. Especially her own grandchildren.

"I'm sorry, Mama. It's been a long, grueling day and . . . and I've been in the most horrid mood of late."

"Of late?" The woman moved closer to Lucy. Her eyes sparkled with anticipation. "Do you notice any other changes?"

Lucy smiled. She couldn't help it. "You mean like nausea or weepiness or—"

"You're in the family way!"

"I am."

Lucy was immediately smothered in a glad embrace. "Oh, my darling, darling girl! I've waited so long for this day. So long! Have you told your husband yet?"

The beginnings of Lucy's pleasure in her mother's enthusiasm faded at once. "Yes. He knows."

Lady Irene frowned at Lucy's obvious lack of animation. "He is not pleased?"

The urge to tell her mother everything was nearly overwhelming. But Lucy held back. It would only make things worse if Ivan were subjected to his mother-in-law's scrutiny.

"He was . . . shocked," Lucy finally answered. "But he's getting used to the idea. You must remember, Mama, that we married rather suddenly. Now, to immediately have a family, well, it's rather daunting to both of us."

"There, now," Lady Irene said, patting Lucy's hand. "What is there to find daunting in starting a family? If you'd waited any longer, well, it would very likely have been too late. It's not as if you're fresh from the schoolroom. But you didn't wait, and now, come the spring, I shall have another grandchild to hold. You won't be going back to town, will you? No, of course not," she said before Lucy could respond. "It would be far better for you to remain here for the duration of your confinement—although the dowager countess will, no doubt, want you at Westcott Manor. Have you informed her yet about the baby?"

Lucy wrote to Lady Westcott the next morning. She didn't tell Ivan what she was doing, for she suspected he would object, and that would lead to a scene, and then her entire family would want to know about the unpleasantness going on between Ivan and his grandmother—and perhaps deduce what was going on between Lucy and Ivan as well. She rationalized that she hadn't had a chance to tell him anyway. He'd come to bed late, slept on the chaise longue, then been gone before she rose. According to Prudence, he and Graham, along with Stanley and Derek, were now out fishing on the Exe.

So even though she knew he would not approve, Lucy wrote the letter anyway. She refused to let herself become caught up in the Westcott family feud. She meant to treat them both as good manners dictated they be treated. Lady Westcott deserved to know about the new life that bloomed inside her, the new Westcott heir. But Lucy knew Ivan would be furious.

She told him as they descended together for dinner. It

was the first time she'd been alone with him.

"You wrote her about your condition?" Ivan paused at the stair landing. "This child is not something I plan to share with her. She will never be a part of its life. Do you understand?"

Lucy looked up at him. He'd dressed for dinner, leaving off the earring for once. But that did not diminish one whit the wild, Gypsy look of him. If anything, the more restrained his clothing, the more flamboyantly did his heritage shine forth. And just as his proper dress and aristocratic blue eyes set off his Gypsy darkness, so did his quiet tone and impeccable manners toward her now only emphasize his anger—and also the vengeance he still meant to wreak upon his grandmother. The pain he still needed to inflict on her.

It made Lucy want to cry. But then, lately, everything made her want to cry. She buried the urge and met his steady glare. "I plan to correspond with whomsoever I please. Just as I always have."

His eyes were cold. "Why do you persist in contradicting me?"

"I thought that was what attracted you to me, that I disagreed with you and tried to thwart you." Though her answer was tart, inside Lucy was aching.

He smiled, just a faint curve of one side of his mouth, but it made her heart beat faster. "What attracted me to you was the passionate nature you keep tamped so tenuously beneath the proper façade you wear."

Lucy knew he was trying to unsettle her and she hated that he was succeeding. She tilted her chin up. "You have a rather curious way of showing your interest in my so-called passionate nature."

A light began to glitter in his eyes. "Feeling neglected, are you?"

"Hardly," she snapped. "I just find it awkward to pretend for my family's sake that we are content."

"Then don't pretend," he said. His hand came up and his knuckles grazed the side of her neck.

Lucy swallowed hard. "Don't pretend we're content? Shall I air my unhappiness to everyone, then? Is that what you want? Or will you air your unhappiness for them?"

He leaned nearer to her. "What I want is for you *not* to have to pretend. I can make you content, and we both know it."

He was going to kiss her. She could tell by the slumberous look in the depths of his azure eyes. She wanted that kiss, as he no doubt could tell by the melting expression in her own mesmerized gaze. He was going to use that powerful masculine appeal to cast his spell on her—his potent sexual spell.

If she had an ounce of sense she would fight that spell. This was not the way to peace between them.

But that was an intellectual response, and at the moment she was feeling anything but intellectual. Their mutual attraction was the one place they met as equals, with the same goals and desires.

Desires.

She leaned forward, eager for the kiss. Desperate for it.

"Lucy! Aunt Loo-cee!"

Five-year-old Grace skidded to a halt at the foot of the stairs, her seven-year-old sister fast on her heels. "Mama says hurry."

"No," Charity corrected her with all the self-importance of an older sister. "Mama says what are they doing up there? It's still daytime and they better not be . . . be . . ." She shrugged. "I don't remember the rest."

Lucy had jerked away from Ivan at Grace's first call. Now she hurried down the steps, painfully aware that her cheeks had heated with color. Was that what Hortense thought was delaying them? She frowned at the two girls. "How many times have I told you children not to run—"

She broke off as the pair turned guilty faces up to her. Grace had blond hair, blue eyes, and plump baby cheeks. Charity had serious gray eyes, darker hair, and a face that already hinted at the lovely young woman she eventually would become. They both regarded Lucy warily.

On impulse Lucy crouched down and gathered them in her arms. "I don't suppose a little running indoors will hurt anything. Just watch out for vases." She stared at their innocent little faces. "You both look very nice. Who did your hair?"

"I did Gracie's hair," Charity said. "And Prudence did mine."

"My, but you're all getting so big. You're not my little babies any more."

"Papa says there's to be another baby in the family soon," Charity confided in a lisp.

"He told you that?" Lucy was surprised that Graham would discuss such things in front of his children.

"We were playing hide-and-seek in the library and we heard him say there's a baby in the oven. But we can't find it," Grace said. "Will you help us look for it?"

Lucy laughed and hugged them tighter. Why hadn't she let herself enjoy them more in the past? She'd studied them and analyzed them and tried to develop the right system for instructing them and disciplining them. But she hadn't let herself just enjoy them. Or love them.

She meant to enjoy them and love them now.

She tickled Gracie, then tickled Charity too. They giggled and wriggled in her arms, but they didn't try to escape. Instead they tickled her back. Lucy laughed, then overbalanced and tipped backward so that they all landed on the floor, laughing hilariously.

Ivan had remained on the landing above them. But when Lucy and her nieces ended up on the floor, he hurried down the stairs. "Be careful," he ordered Lucy, taking her arm and pulling her upright. "You have to be more careful now and not allow yourself to be overrun by these children."

"But I want to be overrun by them," Lucy replied. She drew the girls to her side, circling each one's shoulders with her arms. She stared up at Ivan, trying to understand his irritation. Was it concern for her or for his child? Or was it jealousy at the affection she showed her nieces?

She decided to find out.

She ruffled Charity's hair, then stroked Gracie's plump cheek. "Children are wonderful, don't you think? So fresh and new. So unformed. They want only to be loved. Give them your love and you may shape them into whatever sort of person you want them to be." She paused, then spoke to the girls. "Run along and tell your mother that Uncle Ivan and I shall be there directly."

She stared after them as they caught hands and skipped off in an uneven cadence. Then she turned back to Ivan. "I wonder what sort of person our child will turn out to be."

"It will be a good while before we know that," Ivan said—dismissively, she thought. "Meanwhile, your family awaits." His voice lowered to a husky, mocking whisper. "You don't want your sister-in-law imagining us doing anything sexual—and during the daytime, no less."

The very idea of Hortense censuring such behavior made Lucy laugh. She was immediately mortified to be amused by such things. When Ivan grinned in response, however, her embarrassment eased. He smiled so rarely.

He still had hold of her arm and Lucy decided to take advantage of his good humor. Laying her palm against his cheek, she reached up on tiptoe and pressed a quick kiss to his mouth.

The kiss caught him unawares, which pleased her. He needed to be surprised now and again, she decided. He was always so controlled, so fixed in his opinions and goals. It would do him good to occasionally be shaken up a bit.

When he pulled her closer, as if to prolong the kiss, she resisted. "Not now. They're waiting for us," she reminded him.

She tried to pull out of his embrace, but he wouldn't let her. "Then why did you kiss me? Are you trying to tease me?"

"That was not a teasing kiss."

One of his brows lifted. "What kind of kiss was it?"

Lucy tried to think clearly, but it was hard with Ivan holding her this close. His hands were so warm on her. His dark eyes so alive with desire. She fairly vibrated from the power of his aura.

She took a slow breath. "That was my way of saying thank you."

"Thank you? For what?"

"For worrying that I'd hurt myself—or our child—when I tipped over."

A muscle in his jaw jumped. "Do you think so poorly of me that such a response on my part comes as a surprise to you?"

Lucy smiled up at him. He was so easily wounded. That unfeeling façade he'd perfected hid such a fragile heart. "I didn't say I was surprised. I was just pleased at your thoughtfulness. Now, shall we go in?"

Lucy took it as proof of his sensitive nature that he did not argue further. She'd taken him aback when she'd noticed his show of concern. He'd probably not been aware how much of himself he'd revealed to her. But she was aware and she meant to build on it.

So they went arm in arm into the dining room. With her mother beaming at them, Hortense fussing over them, Graham catering to them, and the children noisy, but generally well behaved, it turned out to be one of the pleasantest meals Lucy had ever eaten at Houghton Manor.

Ivan also found the evening a far more enjoyable experience than he would have expected, and that fact made him uneasy.

He'd spent the entire day fishing with his new brother-in-law and nephews, and had come away with a better of understanding of Lucy as a result. She was definitely the more intelligent sibling, and he could see why she'd felt so stifled in this household. That she'd wanted to return here still did not sit well with him. But for all Graham's bluster and Hortense's nervousness, there was a warmth of feeling in their family that was unmistakable.

What had Lucy once said? That she'd grown up in the bosom of a loving family. He could see that now, and he could see why she wanted the same for their child.

Their child! Every time he thought of her carrying his baby, he began to sweat. He didn't want a child; he never had.

But he would not shirk his responsibilities to it—to her or him, he amended. Whether or not he could love the child, as Lucy wanted him to, he could not say. But he would care for the child just as he cared for his wife.

He stared at Lucy from across the table. Her chestnut hair gleamed in the lamplight. Her eyes sparkled like green glass. Like emeralds. Even her skin, so soft and pink, seemed to glow with vitality, as if the tiny life growing within her had filled her with renewed vigor.

God, she was exquisite! He'd always thought her beautiful, but her pregnancy seemed to make her even more so. More feminine. Softer. Warmer.

She laughed at something young Derek said, then insisted her mother have another portion of vegetables. "It's good for your digestion—as is a walk after the meal is done," she told her mother. "We'll go together." She turned to Ivan. "Will you accompany us on a stroll around the garden?"

With her mother there? An intense wave of emotion assaulted Ivan. Possessiveness? Jealousy? He tried to repress it but was not entirely successful. He wanted to walk with her in the garden, but not with her mother accompanying them. He wanted Lucy all to himself, without anyone else to make demands on her attention.

"Perhaps another time," he answered, forcing himself to sound offhanded and unconcerned. When she just stared at him as if trying to probe the darker recesses of his mind, he deliberately looked away. "I'll have more wine." He signaled the servant standing next to the door.

But he could feel her eyes on him and he had the sinking feeling that she knew his every thought. She knew how she affected him and she knew the power she held over him. He hadn't meant it to happen—nor, once it did, for her to find out. But it had happened, and she did know, and if he wasn't careful, she would figure out how to use it against him. He'd vowed long ago never to let anyone wield that sort of power over him again—especially a woman.

He stood up abruptly. "If you'll excuse me?" he said. He took the bottle of wine from the servant. "I've business to tend to, something urgent that I just recalled."

He heard their querulous voices as he strode from the room.

"What on earth?"

"What could possibly be that urgent?"

"Lucy? Really, but this is—"

"Ivan!"

That last was Lucy. But Ivan kept going. A team of draft animals could not have dragged him back into that scene of familial harmony. Though he knew his reaction was not rational, he could not stop himself. He strode for the back door and out into the late-summer evening, sweating all the way.

Young Derek caught up with him in the stables.

"Are you going riding?"

Ivan stared around the small but well-maintained stable. Anywhere but at the nine-year-old boy. "I haven't decided."

"Oh. Well, if you do, may I go with you?"

"I'm not going riding," Ivan snapped.

"Oh."

That small, subdued response made Ivan feel like an ogre. Cursing himself for his perverse reaction to Lucy and her entire family, he turned to face the boy. "I'm not going riding," he repeated, but in a more reasonable tone this time. "What are you doing out here?"

The boy shrugged. "I dunno." He ran a hand restlessly along the gate to one of the stalls. "Just wanted to see what you were doing."

Ivan wanted to send the boy back to the house. The last thing he needed was some brat trailing him like a lost puppy. But when he looked down at Derek, that's exactly what he saw: a lost puppy looking for attention from anyone who would give it.

For a moment Ivan recalled what Sir James Mawbey had said about Britain's feudal system of primogeniture, about the relationships between fathers and sons, and between brothers. Derek was the quintessential younger son, and while his lot was considerably better than Ivan's had been, he was still a lonely little boy, stumbling along trying to figure out his place in the world. His father's preference for the older Stanley had been obvious on their fishing expedition today. From tying a fly to applauding a catch, Graham Drysdale had shown considerably more interest in his heir. As a result Derek had gravitated toward Ivan. He was still doing so.

Though Ivan did not want to get involved, he found now that he couldn't just send the boy away. After all, he'd been a lonely little boy once.

Ivan cleared his throat. "Actually, I was wondering about the horses you keep. Do you know anything of their breeding?"

He was rewarded by a brilliant, gap-toothed smile. The boy's eyes were green, like Lucy's, he noticed as Derek began with the pony in stall number four.

"This one here is my favorite . . ."

Twenty-three

*I*van had been gone ten days. He'd left with little-enough explanation, saying only that he had business awaiting him in town.

At first Lucy had been crushed. She'd thought they were making such good headway. After rushing off after that last dinner, he'd returned to their room, and instead of sleeping on the chaise longue as he had before, he'd come to bed. They'd made love, sweetly, silently, with neither anger nor desperation between them. She'd gone to sleep in his arms and awakened in his arms, an experience she'd sincerely hoped would become a habit with them.

But she'd been careful not to profess her love to him. Such emotional displays and declarations always seemed to send him fleeing.

But he'd fled anyway, or so it seemed to her. He'd said good-bye to the entire family and even given her a farewell kiss. But the result was the same. He was gone and she was miserable. At least his posts were more informative, and more frequent. She didn't feel quite so abandoned by him as she had before. But she missed him all the same.

Oddly enough, Derek had become her most constant companion. "There's a post for you," the boy called out now. He trotted across the lawn, waving a thin missive in one hand. "It's from Dorset this time," he announced, thrusting it at her. "Is it from Lord Ivan?"

Lucy threw down her knitting and snatched the letter. Her hand shook as she tried to break the seal without ripping the thin parchment to shreds.

"It's from Lady Westcott," she said, unable to hide her disappointment.

"Drat." Derek plopped down cross-legged in the grass beside her chair. Then he brightened. "Does she say anything about Lord Ivan?"

Lucy scanned the letter, then shook her head. There was no news of Ivan, only Antonia's congratulations about the coming baby, and later, her indirect hint that Lucy should repair to the Westcott estate in Dorset.

> . . . my own health is not as good as I would like. The ague or its twin has taken hold of me and I am unable to leave my chambers.

The ague! The elderly did not easily survive a bout with such an illness.

"Is he coming back soon?" Derek asked, distracting her momentarily from her concern for the aged countess.

Lucy focused on the boy's hopeful face. Some bond had formed between Derek and Ivan. She wasn't sure when or how. She hated to disappoint the child now.

"He's not been to Dorset so I cannot say." Derek's crestfallen expression mirrored Lucy's own feelings. She folded the letter, frowning. Ivan gone and his grandmother ailing. Perhaps there was something she could do regarding both situations. She stood abruptly and extended a hand to Derek.

"I believe I shall write to my husband at his city residence and inform him that I am departing for the Dorset countryside right away."

"You're leaving too?"

. "Yes. Would you like to come with me?"

Graham was more disappointed that Lucy was leaving than he was that Derek would accompany her. Lucy knew it was because she was the Countess of Westcott now, whereas Derek was still merely a second son.

If Derek noticed his family's casual attitude about his departure, it was well disguised by his excitement over the trip. "How long will the journey take?"

"A good day, if the roads are dry."

"How long shall we stay?"

"That's hard to say, Derek. I suppose we shall have to see how things go."

"Will Lord Ivan come there too? When his business in town is done?"

Lucy gnawed on her lower lip. "Eventually," she answered. Soon, she suspected.

Ivan would be furious at her for going to attend his grandmother, for he did not want the dowager countess to derive any joy from this pregnancy. But Lucy had explained everything in her post to him. Just because he could not understand that family members looked out for one another was no reason for her to abandon the ailing woman to the care of her servants. If Ivan expected ever to be happy with his wife, he would have to learn those lessons he'd had no chance to learn in his childhood, the ones about love and family and responsibility. She was more than willing to help him with those lessons, but he would have to meet her halfway.

They left at dawn and arrived well after dark. For the duration of that endless day Lucy suffered unceasing nausea. Derek was happy to ride up top in the driver's box, much to Lucy's relief. By the time they arrived, she was as limp as a dishrag and wanted only to fall into bed.

Unfortunately, she'd had to send word ahead that she was en route. She was not surprised, therefore, that Antonia was awake and waiting for her.

"You should be abed, else you'll fall ill again," Lucy scolded.

"Nonsense," the old woman said in a hoarse voice. "Your news was the best medicine I could have received. And now you're here." She held Lucy by the shoulders and her aged face creased in a smile, the sort which Lucy had never before seen on her. Then the smile turned to a frown. "You look dreadful. Haggard. Come. To bed with you. Fenton. Fenton! Help her to her room."

Yes. To her room. Then Lucy spied Derek standing small and forgotten beside the carriage.

"Lady Westcott. You have not greeted our guest. Derek?" Lucy signaled for him to approach.

Though it was apparent that Lady Antonia was not much interested in a nine-year-old great-nephew by marriage, Derek was very correct in his greeting to his hostess. Lucy smiled at him and gave him a proud hug.

"I'll come to your room to say goodnight," she told him. "Make sure his room is near mine," she added to Fenton. Then she turned herself over to Ivan's grandmother and, moving just as slowly as the old woman, trudged wearily up the stairs.

To her credit, the dowager countess waited until Lucy's trunks were delivered to her room, her nightclothes laid out, and warm water brought in for her wash. Then with an imperious gesture she dismissed the two servants and fixed her expectant gaze on Lucy.

"So tell me. You are well? No ailments or problems?"

Lucy had collapsed into a slipper chair. One of the maids had unlaced her boots and now she kicked them off and flexed her stockinged toes. There was no avoiding this inquisition. Better simply to get it over with.

"I have no complaints at all save for the nausea."

Antonia nodded. "In the morning only or in the afternoon as well?"

"Always in the morning. Sometimes in the afternoon."

"A boy. That indicates a boy," the old woman stated with a gleam in her eye.

"If it's a boy he must not like carriages very well," Lucy muttered.

"The traveling made you ill?"

"All day," Lucy admitted. "That's why I'm so exhausted."

Again the old woman nodded. "You must get into bed right away, then. I'll call for a maid. But one more question."

She paused, but Lucy knew what the question was and answered before the countess could continue. "He was shocked at first. But I believe he has recovered."

"You mean he was furious," the dowager countess corrected her. "You needn't pretend otherwise, at least not with me. He was furious that you are pregnant with his heir because this child will also be my heir, one that he knows I have anticipated a very long while." She sighed, and where before there had been excitement and joy in her face, Lucy now saw only a resigned sort of sadness. She decided to be blunt.

"Can you honestly blame him for feeling that way?"

The other woman's chin jerked up and for a moment a fierce blue light glittered in her aged eyes. But then it went out, and that fast Lucy watched as the dowager countess wilted.

"No," the old woman answered. "I do not blame him. But I wish . . ." She trailed off, shaking her head. Then she rallied. "It does not matter what I wish or whether he is angry or not. The fact remains that you carry the next Earl of Westcott."

"But it does matter," Lucy countered, forcing herself to a more erect position in the chair. "He is no longer angry over the child, but he will be furious when he learns I am here."

Again the woman sighed. She gripped the head of her cane tighter. "I am aware that he does not want me to have anything to do with this child, and I know all his reasons why. He thinks I neglected him by providing him with a superior education. He thinks I was wrong to make him heir to a fortune. He thinks——"

"You neglected him when you tore him from his mother's arms and gave him no one to love in her place. And no one to love him back."

"She was a whore," Antonia muttered. "A filthy Gypsy whore who tried to blackmail my son."

"But that was never Ivan's fault!" Lucy cried. "It was not his fault, and yet he is the one who has most suffered. You were two grown women who should have looked out for his well-being, but neither of you did. Nor did his father."

"He was well fed, well clothed, and well educated!"

"None of that will ever make up for not being loved. Even now—" She broke off, then reconsidered. She swallowed hard and continued in a more subdued voice. "Even now he will not let me love him. Physically, yes. But not emotionally. I think he is terrified that he might have to love me back. *Terrified.* And that he will love this baby we've made."

Her hand moved to cover her stomach, to caress the place where their child lay, quietly growing inside her. "Would it have been so hard for you to have loved a frightened little boy? Of all the things he needed from you, that was by far the most important," she finished, her voice trembling.

In the silence that followed, Lady Westcott sat stone-faced, as if impervious to Lucy's words. Lucy's heart ached for her almost as much as it did for Ivan. They were two proud, stubborn people—and two of the loneliest people she'd ever known.

Lucy pushed to her feet. "I believe I'd like to retire to my bed now. Could you send in a maid to assist me?"

Lady Westcott rose slowly. Lucy could read nothing in her face; she could see nothing in its fixed expression. How alike they were, Ivan and his grandmother. Just as he'd inherited her ice-blue eyes, so had he inherited her iron will, her arrogance, and her inability to love those who most needed it from her.

Tears stung her eyes and she turned away from the dowager countess, not wanting her to see. She heard the woman leave. She heard a maid enter and with a minimum of discussion Lucy cooperated with her. But once she was tucked into the high bed—the one she'd shared so briefly with Ivan—she could no longer hold back her emotions.

She rolled onto her stomach, buried her face in the soft linen-encased pillow, and cried as she'd never cried before. Hard tears. Bitter tears. Sad tears that were wrenched from the deepest part of her heart. She cried for Ivan and his grandmother, and the love they were unable either to give or receive. She cried for herself, for her loneliness and unrequited love.

But most of all she cried for her unborn child, her unborn child whom she already loved but whom she feared would always suffer for the lack of his father's love and attention.

Lucy felt wretched in the morning, even more so than usual. As on the previous day, her nausea would not relent, and she spent most of the morning in her room, trying desperately to relax so that the dizzying waves would recede.

When that did not help, she resolved to go outside, to sit on the terrace and read. But that made it even worse. Her stomach was in such a tenuous and unsettled state she feared she could not control it, and that she would embarrass herself in front of everyone. Antonia, though sympathetic, understood the trials of impending motherhood. Young Derek, however, could not hide his worry.

"Can I bring you a pillow?" he asked, his face screwed up in concern. "Would you like something to drink?"

"Thank you, dear, but no. I'm surprised you are not down at the stables," Lucy added. She bit her cheek as a particularly cruel spasm left her dizzy and wanting to retch.

Derek's expression turned to alarm. He whirled toward Lady Antonia, who sat in a chair in the afternoon sun, just beginning to doze off. "Lady Westcott! Help her. Please, help her!"

"God in heaven! Help who?" the old woman cried, startled awake. "Oh. Lucy. Do you need help, girl?"

A chill ran through Lucy and she shuddered. "Perhaps

. . . Perhaps I should return to my room. If I lie down a while . . ."

By dusk Lucy began to fear the worst. The nausea had ended, to be replaced abruptly by severe stomach cramps. Lady Antonia sent for her doctor, as well as the village midwife. Derek was banished from the sickroom, but Antonia never left Lucy's side.

Lucy was more grateful for the older woman's presence than she could properly express. Whether for the right reason or wrong, here was one person who cared just as much as she for the tiny baby inside her. Here was one person who would grieve just as deeply as she should something happen . . .

"Am I losing him?" Lucy whispered. She'd tried not to put words to her fears, but she could no longer hold them back. The pain in her womb was nothing compared to the pain squeezing her heart at the thought of so dire a possibility.

"We don't know. We can't be sure," Antonia said, gripping Lucy's hand with surprising strength. The old woman hesitated before adding in a cracked voice, "I've sent for your mother."

Lucy closed her eyes and turned her face away. A chill crawled down her spine. It must be very bad if the dowager countess had sent for her mother. But there was someone else whose presence she wanted even more than her mother's. She wanted Ivan. She needed him to be here with her.

"No need for alarm, Lady Westcott," the doctor said, trying to sound encouraging. "This is regretful, I know. But you are young. There will be other children."

"No," Lucy whispered, then was unable to continue. *No, I am not young, and there will be no other children. Ivan didn't want this one. He certainly will take precautions to ensure there will be no others.*

Suddenly a cramp worse than all the others, a sharp slicing pain, ripped through her, banishing all thoughts save that of surviving it. Something wet seeped between her legs—her child's lifeblood, she realized in horror. In that moment, Lucy wanted to die also.

She'd wanted this baby so much. She'd wanted to love him and guide him, and hoped that he or she would teach Ivan how to love. But that pretty dream was gone, shredded by the pains that racked her now, drowned in the warm blood that gathered beneath her and pooled in the bed linens.

The doctor and midwife worked together to clean her and staunch the bleeding. Antonia never budged from her bedside nor released her hand. Maids rushed in and out of the overheated room carrying in hot water and fresh linens, carrying away bloodied sheets and towels, and then, sometime around midnight, the tiny wrapped bundle that Lucy knew was her child.

She knew because of the way the midwife held it so respectfully, how she looked at it so sorrowfully, then looked up at Lucy with tears running down her face.

Again Lucy closed her eyes and turned her face away. The pain was over—at least the physical pain. But a new sort of pain, one formed of emptiness and loss, filled the space where the other pain had been. She'd lost her child, the miraculous being she and Ivan had created. But she'd also lost Ivan, she knew. Not that she'd ever truly had him. But she'd lost what little chance she'd had with him.

Sorrow welled up inside her, filling every portion of her being until she could hardly breathe. More than anything she needed to cry, to let loose all the awful emotions that clawed at her insides. But the tears would not come. She was like a stoppered bottle, and all she could do was shake. She let go of Antonia's hand and rolled onto her side, facing the wall.

"She needs her rest," the doctor said. "Just let her be. She feels awful now, but in a few days she'll be better."

"Someone should sit with her," the midwife told him. "She shouldn't be alone right now."

"Nonsense. She's young and strong, and she did not hemorrhage. What she needs is sleep."

"Her heart is broken," the midwife argued.

"I shall stay with her." The dowager countess's tone brooked no argument. With only a bit of grumbling the doctor collected his bag and left. The midwife followed but only after leaning over Lucy to whisper, "Go ahead and grieve, child. Go ahead and grieve for your little boy. God took him up to heaven because he needed him more than you do. It don't seem that way right now, I know. But God will bless you in another way. At another time."

Lucy nodded. But inside she didn't believe the kind-hearted woman's words. She couldn't.

The lamps were lowered. The door closed behind the last maid, and a grim silence settled over the room.

Lucy felt drained, and moving was a torture. Thinking was even worse. But she made herself roll onto her back and look at Antonia. The old woman's face was devoid of any color save, perhaps, for gray. She'd never looked older or frailer, and it gave Lucy a fright.

"You need not sit with me any longer. Go and seek your own bed," she murmured, patting the woman's hand. "As the doctor said, I'll be all right."

The old woman stared at her, and in the other woman's eyes Lucy saw a sorrow to match her own. It was a comfort, but it added also to her own pain.

"I'm sorry, child," Antonia whispered. She shook her head back and forth, slowly, as if it were too heavy to balance on her birdlike frame. "I'm so sorry."

"I know," Lucy said. "But we cannot undo what has been done. Sitting here with me . . . making yourself ill over what has happened . . . will change nothing. Go to bed. You need your rest."

Antonia gripped her hand even tighter. "Don't you worry yourself over me. I'm just going to sit here a little while longer. Just a little while longer."

Ivan stood in the foyer, staring up the broad stairs. He'd just arrived after riding like a madman all the way from town. He'd been furious when he'd received her post, stating that she was departing for Dorset—and his grand-mother's sickbed. But as he'd come storming in the doctor and midwife had been leaving.

Now, horrified and drained of all emotion, he could only stare up the stairs. Lucy was up there somewhere. His wife, who needed his comfort. The thought of seeing her so help-less, though, so sad and heartbroken as the midwife had said she was . . . It terrified him to imagine it.

He stood there, knowing he should go to her, knowing he should rush to her side and let her cry in his arms, but he couldn't do it. His legs shook too much to manage the stairs. His hands trembled too violently to offer her any comfort. And he was sweating like a man being marched to the gallows.

She wouldn't want to see him anyway, he told himself. She needed a woman's comfort. But not his grandmother's. That one didn't know how to offer comfort to anyone. Lucy needed her own mother. Why in blazes wasn't the woman here?

A movement in the shadows alongside the stairs drew his attention. It was Derek, Lucy's nephew, and he ap-peared to have been crying. The boy looked fearfully at Ivan as he swiped his eyes with the cuff of one sleeve. "Is Aunt Lucy . . . Is she all right?"

A tremor rippled through Ivan, a tremor of fear and sad-ness and self-revulsion. "She's better," he managed to say.

An expression of relief rushed over the boy's face. Then he frowned. "What of . . . you know, the baby?"

An acute pain, unlike anything Ivan had ever known, squeezed his chest. The baby. His baby. Their baby.

"The baby did not . . . survive."

Derek approached him, his footsteps echoing hollowly in the empty foyer. The dim light from the one wall lamp still burning made him look younger than he was, yet somehow also even older and wiser than Ivan himself.

When the boy stretched out his hand, Ivan took it. "I'm sorry about your baby. Lucy would've made a very good mother—" His young voice broke and tears filled his eyes.

"She's always been good to me. And more than fair."

Something seemed to break in Ivan's heart. He could barely speak. "She's been good to me too. And more than fair. Much more than fair." Then he pulled Derek into his arms and held him while the boy cried.

"She's going to recover," he murmured into the boy's silky fine hair. "The doctor and the midwife both said so. In just a few days she'll be up and moving about," he added, praying he did not lie.

"Yes, but . . . but when this happened to my mother, she . . . she was sad and cried for a long time."

"Then it's up to us to try to make Lucy happy," Ivan said.

Derek pulled out of his arms, sniffling and wiping his eyes. "How do we do that?"

Ivan looked past the boy and up the darkened stairwell to where Lucy lay. His Lucy.

"I'm not sure, Derek. For now, let's get you to bed. Then I'll go see her."

"Can I see her too?"

Ivan wanted to say yes. He wanted some buffer between him and Lucy, for the idea of seeing her alone terrified him. He'd never had to comfort a woman who'd just lost her child. He'd never known a woman who cared particularly for children. Not his mother or his grandmother, anyway. But Lucy did. Still, he forced himself to turn down Derek's request.

"Tomorrow, if she's up to visitors, you can see her. For now, go to bed. You need to be strong for her in the days to come," he added when the boy yawned.

They went up the stairs together. The boy's room was near Lucy's room, and once the door closed behind Derek, Ivan had no further excuses. He stared at Lucy's door, at the weak light that flickered beneath the tall oak panel, and sucked in a harsh breath.

When he'd received her letter saying she was leaving Houghton Hall, he'd been outraged that she would turn to his grandmother during her confinement. He'd meant to pack her right back to Somerset and her parents' home, with strict orders that she stay there.

To learn that she'd lost the child . . .

He was stunned. Devastated.

He should feel relief, he told himself. But he didn't. Whether this unexpected sorrow was for the lost child or for his grieving wife, however, he couldn't say. Nor did he want to examine his feelings too closely to find out.

He took another breath and forced any stray emotions back into the recesses of his heart. He needed to be calm and strong for her. That's what she needed from him. As for the future . . . The future would be upon them soon enough.

Lucy was dreaming, and in her dream Ivan was there. She heard his voice whispering in her ear. She felt his hand twining with her own.

Her fingers twitched and a hand immediately covered them. But it was a small hand, not Ivan's larger one. And it was cold and frail, not warm and strong.

She struggled to right the dream, to make it better. Happier. But Ivan's voice intruded and it was angry, not kind.

"Get away from her. Get the hell away from my wife."

The hand clenched hers tighter, almost painfully, and Lucy startled awake. Through bleary eyes the room came into focus. Ivan stood just inside the door, glaring at his grandmother who sat beside the bed, still holding Lucy's hand as she had throughout the long, torturous evening.

For one intense moment Lucy was overcome with joy. He was here. She wanted to fall into his arms, weep with thankfulness, and never let go of him.

But that moment disappeared when the old woman's hand began to shake. Lucy could not mistake that emotional trembling. She tore her eyes from Ivan to stare at the countess.

Antonia was old and exhausted, and no match for Ivan's furious temper, Lucy realized. Neither was she. But still, Lucy could not allow Ivan to destroy the one person who had stood by her in this, the worst ordeal of her life.

"No, Ivan," she said, though it emerged as a weak croak. "No. I want her here. I need her here."

He flinched. It was almost as if she'd slapped him, and Lucy regretted that her words must hurt him so badly. But she couldn't bear being the bone they fought over, like two fierce dogs.

"Please. For once . . . For me . . . Can't you put aside your animosity?" Her eyes fell closed and tears leaked from beneath her lashes. She couldn't bear any more today.

Antonia squeezed her hand, then released it. "I'll leave the two of you alone," she said in a voice cracking with emotion. "If you need me you have only to ring."

Lucy watched through blurry eyes as the old woman walked away. Hobbled away. She was bent over her cane and moved slower than ever. When she passed Ivan, she paused.

"I'm sorry," she whispered to her unrelenting grandson. "So sorry." Then, when she had no response from him, she shuffled from the room.

Lucy started to cry. She couldn't help it. After a moment Ivan approached the bed. But he didn't touch her. He seemed frozen in indecision.

"Are you all right?"

Lucy shook her head. She couldn't speak.

"Is there anything I can do for you?"

Hold me. Love me. That's what she wanted to say, and for a moment she almost did. But a part of her knew that would not be fair to him. He would take her in his arms because he would have no other choice. And though it would be heaven to have Ivan hold her, it would be hell knowing he saw it only as his duty.

"Lucy?" He moved nearer the bed, then, after a moment, sat down in the chair his grandmother had vacated. He reached out, and when his hand covered her knotted fist, she cried all the harder.

"I'm sorry," he whispered, leaning close to the bed. "I'm sorry, Lucy. I should have been here with you."

She scrubbed her already damp sleeve across her face

and tried to catch her breath. "You couldn't . . . couldn't have known."

His thumb rubbed across her knuckles, a movement at once both soothing and unsettling. She blinked and looked up at him.

He was more disheveled than she'd ever seen him. His dark curls were rumpled and wild as if he'd run his hands distractedly through them. He wore no coat, his waistcoat hung open, and his collar was missing. The shadow of a beard emphasized the deep lines of weariness in his face. And of worry.

Had he been worried for their child? For a moment hope flared in Lucy's heart, like a tiny light in the darkness. But it was snuffed out when a grimmer reality struck her. He hadn't been worried for the child, but for her. He'd never wanted their child. But though he might not love her, he did feel something for her, and he would not wish her ill.

She found little comfort in that knowledge, however. She needed him to mourn their child with her, to share this terrible sense of loss with her. But she knew he could not.

Somehow she managed to speak. "I'm tired. I want to sleep." Then unable to continue, she turned away, closed her eyes, and prayed for sleep. For oblivion. For anything that would provide a reprieve from the reality of her unhappy existence.

Twenty-four

*I*van sat with Lucy until dawn. She lay perfectly still, and her hands were cold. But her pulse was steady. Still, her breathing was so shallow, he had to lean forward to check the rise and fall of her chest.

And the whole time he was tortured by images of his life without her, of long, lonely years with no one to give a damn about him. He'd lived that way all his life. He didn't want to live that way any longer.

Not that she loved him—especially now. Not that he wanted her to. But she was softhearted and she would only want the best for him. That much he knew. With time—and luck—he hoped he would be able to restore her faith in him.

But he would have to make some concessions to her. He would have to find a place in his life for her, a regular place in one of his houses—but one that his grandmother had no rights to.

He clenched his jaw. He would take a house for them, just the two of them. Yes, once she was well enough to travel, he would take her away from here, from the bad memories they both had of this place, and of the woman who was the cause of it all.

The room brightened slowly, and as it did, so did Ivan's spirits. Lucy's cheeks held a hint of color now. Her hands were no longer so cold. He stared at her, at the dark crescent her thick lashes made on her pale skin, at the tangle of hair that fanned across the pillow.

He'd been the worst sort of husband, neglectful and cruel. But he meant to do better. He meant to make her happy.

But what if she wanted another child?

A chill ran through him. It was not because he didn't want children, though, much to his own surprise. He could live with the idea of children, he realized. But the thought of Lucy chancing this sorrow again, this pain . . . Women died trying to give birth.

Once more he shivered. He couldn't bear the idea of Lucy taking that risk again.

A soft rap sounded at the door. But it was not the maid, nor young Derek. It was his grandmother's face that appeared around the door, and his mood darkened at the sight.

"How is she?" she asked without venturing into the room.

Ivan stood and advanced on her. "She seems all right, no thanks to you," he added bitterly. "What were you thinking, summoning her here when you knew she was in so delicate a condition? Damn you," he hissed. "Have you ever in your entire life considered anyone's needs but your own?"

It was a curious thing, after all these years, to see her flinch at his words. To know at last that he'd hurt her. As a hot wind fed a fire, so did that knowledge fuel his anger to greater heights.

"You summoned her here and now she has lost the very child you've wanted for so long. Or perhaps you didn't want it at all. Perhaps you didn't want me wed so that I could provide you with an heir—a legitimate heir. Perhaps all you really wanted was someone new to make miserable. Someone new to torture. Behold, madam, the results of your handiwork."

He gestured toward the bed, toward his sweet Lucy who deserved none of the misery that had been heaped upon her. His hand began to shake so he tightened it into a fist.

"You have killed my child. You have very nearly killed my wife. Are you content now? Will you ever be content!"

Lucy woke to hear the last of Ivan's tormented words. She was groggy. She felt heavy and compressed, as if she were weighted down on the bed. Something was wrong, that was plain. Then she remembered where she was, and why, and sorrow constricted her chest.

Her child was gone. And Ivan blamed his grandmother.

"No." Lucy's voice was weak and cracking, but Ivan heard and turned abruptly to face her. She could not make out his expression, for he was backlit by the window. But his voice, when he addressed her, was as gentle as it had been cruel when he spoke to his grandmother. His face was wary and hopeful and oh, so welcome to her. Last night she had needed him desperately. But at least he was here now.

"How are you feeling? Can I get you anything?"

Lucy stared up at him. "Don't blame her, Ivan. I beg you. This is not of her doing."

He shook his head. "Don't defend her, Lucy. You don't know her as I do. When she learned you were expecting a child—her heir—she wanted you here. She wrote you and you came."

"She wrote me, yes. But she didn't summon me. I came because she was ill—"

"As she knew you would." He broke off with a curse. "I don't want you to think about this, Lucy. We'll have time to discuss things after you're well. Until then . . ." He turned to stare coldly at his grandmother, who stood in the doorway still, leaning heavily on her cane and holding a candle in her other, trembling hand. "Until then, you will keep your distance from her." He bit the words out to the dowager countess.

"Ivan, no," Lucy begged.

But he did not heed her words. He glared at his grandmother until she backed from the room, an old, beaten woman he'd finally managed to best. Even when the door closed with a hallow metallic click and he turned finally back to face her, Ivan would not hear Lucy's words.

"You mustn't blame her for this."

"She deserves none of your worry. I don't want you to concern yourself with her any more."

"But Ivan—"

"No," he stated, frowning at her. "We're not going to discuss her further. You're the one who's ill. You're the one we have to strengthen."

He rang for a maid and in the ensuing hours Lucy had no opportunity to talk with him at all. Instead she was bathed, dressed in fresh nightclothes, and had her hair combed. A breakfast was brought up to her, along with a selection of books and newspapers to read. Ivan left her to the maids. When the doctor arrived around noon to examine her, Ivan came into the room as well. But when the doctor departed, with assurances that a week of bed rest was all she needed, Ivan departed too.

Lucy was left clean and well fed—though she had no interest in food—and given strict orders to rest. But she feared she'd never be able to sleep, so consumed was she by unhappy thoughts. She stared around the elaborately painted bedchamber, at the gold leaf and elaborate tapestries and portraits of former inhabitants, and felt even worse.

She didn't belong here. She was not meant to be a countess. Nor was she meant to be a mother, it seemed. At that thought she began silently to weep. No child. No husband either, at least not one who truly wanted the role.

Eventually she did fall asleep on her damp pillow. She dreamed of birthday parties, of a little boy turning five and a little girl who was two. And for a short while, at least, she was happy.

When she awoke she was completely disoriented and her head ached. Stronger than those ailments, however, was a profound need to get out of her bed and out of this room.

She sat up and swung her legs over the side of the high bed. When she tried to stand, however, her knees nearly buckled beneath her. She'd never before felt so weak. Still,

she persisted. She found her dressing gown and managed
to put it on. Then moving slowly, on legs that felt none too
secure, she made her shaky way to the door.

To her surprise, young Derek sat on the floor just outside
her door, playing with a half-grown kitten. When he spied
her he jumped to his feet, a relieved grin on his face.
"You're better, then?" he asked hopefully.

Lucy managed a smile. "Better, yes. But still a little
weak. Will you help me?"

At once he slipped an arm around her waist. He was only
nine but he was sturdy, and Lucy was grateful for his assistance. "Do you know where Lady Westcott is?"

"Taken to her bed."

She'd feared that very thing. "And Ivan?" she asked
after a brief hesitation.

Derek's face screwed up in a frown. "He took one of
the hunters out, the strongest, fastest one, the stablemaster
said. I hope he doesn't run it too hard."

Lucy hugged Derek a little closer. "He's very good with
horses," she whispered, past the lump in her throat. "You
needn't worry over that."

At Lady Westcott's door Lucy bade Derek wait outside.
There was no answer when she knocked, but she went in
anyway. The room was dim, with no candles lit and the
curtains drawn against the day. Despite the poor light and
the fact that the bed linens swallowed the old woman up,
Lucy made out her frail form in the bed. She looked very
nearly dead.

Alarmed, Lucy's hand went to her throat. "Lady Antonia?"

The old woman turned her head. When she recognized
Lucy she struggled to sit upright. "You should not be up.
The doctor said a week of bed rest."

"I was worried about you. And about Ivan," Lucy added
as she lowered herself gingerly into an arm chair beside the
bed.

Antonia sank back into her pillows. "Don't worry about
me," she said in a tired voice. "I am old. I'm ready to die.

As for him.'' She paused to control the quaver in her voice. ''As for him, he has his hate to give him sustenance.''

For a long moment Lucy did not reply. Then she sighed. ''Is that so very surprising? It's all he's ever had to give him sustenance.''

The dowager countess turned her face away, and Lucy didn't think she would respond. But she was mistaken. ''I don't blame him,'' the woman murmured. ''But I don't know how to undo what I have done. I don't know how to repair the damage I have wrought. It's too late,'' she finished in the barest of whispers.

''Tell him you are sorry,'' Lucy urged. She leaned forward and laid a hand on the old woman's arm. ''Tell him you are sorry.''

This time there was no reply. Lucy sat there a while in silence, her hand resting on the old woman's arm. When it seemed that she slept Lucy finally left, more exhausted that before, and in no better spirits than when she came. There was such sadness in this house—in this family. And now there was a new sadness.

Derek helped her back to her room then, at her invitation, sat with her a while. He read to her—good practice for him and a distraction for her. She didn't want to be alone. When a clatter of hooves in the yard heralded Ivan's return, however, she nodded at Derek's hopeful look.

''Go on, then. But Derek—'' She hesitated. Still there was no avoiding what must be done. ''Ask him to come to me, would you? He and I . . . We need to talk.''

It was twenty minutes before Ivan came. Twenty minutes that felt like twenty hours. She wasn't sure what she meant to say. No, that was not precisely accurate. She was sure what she had to say. She just didn't know how she would say it.

He came in without knocking, startling her with his sudden presence. She sat in the bed, propped up with pillows, looking perfectly pathetic, she realized, in contrast to his overwhelmingly masculine vitality. He was windblown and disheveled from his ride, of course, and dressed more like

a groomsman than master of the house. A Gypsy groomsman, with his diamond earring glinting at her.

He was neither Gypsy nor lord though, but rather an
uneasy mix of the two. As she stared longingly at him, she
feared that he would never be entirely happy. Most certainly she was not the person who could make him so.

"Thank you for coming," she said when he did not venture any farther into the room. "I thought we needed to
talk."

He flexed his gloved hands. "Derek told me you went
to her room. If you plan to plead her case, save your
breath."

Lucy shook her head. He was so filled with hatred it
made her want to weep. She swallowed the lump of emotions caught in her throat. "I want to talk about us. About
our marriage."

If anything, he became even more wary. "What about
it?"

Lucy could feel herself wavering. Even though it would
be the best thing for everyone concerned, she didn't want
to say it.

"We should never have wed," she finally blurted out.
"You know it; I know it. Now that . . . Now that I am no
longer pregnant, I release you. You no longer need stay
wed to me."

A bitter smile curved his lips, a cold, brittle grimace.
"You can't divorce me so easily as that."

"I know that, Ivan," she whispered. "But I also know
that you do not love me."

"Since when is love a prerequisite for marriage?"

"Nor do you want to be loved," she said, ignoring his
question.

"Again, I ask, what does love have to do with marriage?"

"Oh, God! Must you always be so cynical! Do you want
me to concede that you're the only person in the entire
world who needs no one, who is perfectly content in being
alone? Then I do. I concede it. You need no one at all,

least of all a wife. But as for me, I need people. I need a family. And since you cannot be that for me, since you have never wanted to be that for anyone, then I . . . I am going back to Somerset, to live with my family. You need not concern yourself with me any longer. I relieve you of that loathsome responsibility,'' she finished in a whisper.

His expression might have been carved from stone, he looked that hard and unyielding. His leather gloves stretched taut over his knuckles, he clenched his fists so tight. But his face betrayed no emotion. ''I told you I would not abandon you, and I meant it. There is no reason we cannot manage as before. Better than before,'' he amended.

He took a step nearer and his tone softened. ''I know this . . . this loss hurts you grievously. But you will recover Lucy. We can recover.''

Something in Lucy's heart seemed to twist and tear, and she shook her head helplessly. They would never recover so long as he held his emotions in check and expected her to do the same. ''I can't,'' she whispered. ''I just can't.'' She couldn't live with a man who wouldn't love her, a man who wouldn't hold her when she need to cry. A man who wouldn't cry with her.

I can't. Ivan heard her softly uttered words, and he wanted to run away from them, for they cut him deeper and more cruelly than any words ever said to him.

Go with the nice old lady, Ivan. You'll be better off, his mother had said, then turned away and left.

Ugly Gypsy bastard, his grandmother had said. *Take him to Burford Hall.*

Filthy little heathen, the headmaster's wife had called him.

But none of them—all those insults he'd hoarded in his heart to steel himself against an unfeeling world—none of them cut him so fiercely as did Lucy's tearful whisper. *I just can't.*

He could hardly breathe. His chest hurt and he feared for a moment his legs would give out, the pain was so intense.

But he didn't fall. He stood there not moving, not able

to move, and stared at the woman who'd gained more power over him than any other. He was a man, fully grown, with money and influence, and more power than any man should have. But with those few words she brought him to his knees. She slew him and yet wept as if she were the one pained by it.

He shuddered and struggled for breath. If nothing else he would keep his pain from her. She would not know what she had done, how much she had hurt him. How much power he'd let her wield over him.

"As you wish," he said, his voice steadier than he'd dared hope. More nonchalant.

She bowed her head. Only then did he dare blink. His eyes stung. Tears? No. But on the remote chance it was tears, he'd better leave.

"As you wish," he repeated. "The traveling coach is at your disposal." Then he turned and stalked to the door, terrified to leave, but even more terrified to stay. If he stayed he might break down and beg her not to go. He might beg her not to leave him. He might tell her that he needed her more than he needed anything else in his life.

Outside the door he stopped. His heart thundered and his stomach churned. Would she stay if he confessed how much he needed her? It was not love, but it was the best he could do.

What if it wasn't good enough?

He turned back to her door, then froze at the sound of a step in the hall. Looking up, he spied his grandmother leaning heavily on her cane. She looked thin and frail, almost as tiny as the seven-year-old he'd been when she'd bought him from his mother.

Bought him. Yes, his mother had sold him to his grandmother. But for once he could muster no fury toward either of them. There was no room for fury against either his grandmother or his mother, not when Lucy was set on leaving him.

"I would have a word with you. Just a moment or two

of your time,'' she said. Her voice was hoarse and low as if it pained her to speak.

Ivan's first instinct was to turn away, simply to ignore her, to leave. To get the hell out of this house and all the misery it meant to him. But he stayed because he knew leaving would bring him no reprieve. Still, he did not want to talk to her. Then he spied Derek standing just beyond her, his young face worried and confused.

Unaccountably Ivan recalled something Sir James had said in one of his lectures—it seemed like years ago. Children learned from the adults around them: whether to be honest or not, to be generous or not. To be good or not.

His grandmother didn't matter, but Derek did. Every child did.

Ivan took a slow breath. ''Perhaps you should sit down first.''

She stared at him, but not with the cold glittering glare he'd always associated with her. At some point the blue of her eyes had faded; the steady stare had become cautious and blinking. But where once he would have gloated, he seemed now to have lost the ability to do so.

He followed her into her sitting room. Derek would have slipped inside with them too, but Ivan stayed him with a hand on the lad's arm.

''Don't send me off,'' Derek pleaded. ''Everyone's always sending me off, only I haven't anywhere to go.''

Ivan patted the boy's shoulder. ''Don't worry, I won't be long. I promise.''

Derek sighed, then nodded, and Ivan felt an unaccustomed pang of guilt. But he would make it up to the boy, he promised himself. All Derek wanted was a little attention. In the future Ivan vowed to treat Derek as he'd wanted to be treated as a child, assuming he still had the opportunity. For now, however, he had to deal with his grandmother.

He turned to face her, steeling himself to reveal no facet of his emotions to her. ''I'm waiting. What is it you wish to say?''

He saw her swallow as if she were nervous, and her bony fingers clenched again on her stick. Did she think to plead with him to be allowed to stay here after all she'd done to ruin his life and now Lucy's? He raised a hand to forestall her, but her words were not what he expected.

"I'm sorry."

His hands curled into fists but he forced himself to relax them. "You're sorry? Do you think saying you're sorry will bring my child back?"

She flinched as if he'd struck her, and she swayed on her feet. If she'd not gripped the cane so tightly, she would have fallen. But she didn't fall and she continued. "I'm sorry for the way I treated you all those years ago. For the way I abandoned you at that school."

Ivan went rigid. He could not believe his ears. She was apologizing now? But it was too little, too late. Far too late.

"Apology accepted. Is that all?"

She sat down, a stricken expression on her time-ravaged face. "You have every right to hate me."

"I don't hate you," he said, and it seemed actually to be true. He didn't have enough emotion left to hate her. "I don't give a damn about you."

"But you do give a damn about Lucy."

"Leave her out of this. If you'd just left her alone none of this would have happened. She would still be expecting our child."

"If I had left her alone the two of you never would have met."

"No doubt she would have preferred it that way," Ivan muttered, more to himself than to her.

But though time had ravaged the old woman in other ways, it had not adversely affected her hearing. "Has Lucy said that? Has she?" she repeated when he did not immediately respond.

The last thing Ivan wanted to admit to anyone was that Lucy had rejected him once more. That she had released him from his husbandly duties. That she would rather resign herself to the boredom of her brother's household than remain with him. Most especially he did not want to admit it to this woman, this woman who had never cared at all for his happiness but only demanded that he do his duty to her.

But she'd pricked him in the one place that he was most vulnerable: his feelings for Lucy.

He looked away from her. She would know soon enough anyway. She would learn the truth from Lucy.

He looked back at her, forcing himself to an outward calm. Inside, however, he was shaking. He was dying.

"She wishes to live apart from me. With her family."

He waited for her angry response, for her harsh beratement. Instead she bowed her head, pulled a mangled handkerchief from her sleeve and dabbed at her eyes.

Ivan's belligerent glare turned to confusion. The mighty Dowager Countess of Westcott in tears?

She raised her head and her damp eyes confirmed it. But if that fact shocked him, her words set him back on his heels. "Don't let her slip away, Ivan. I beg you. Don't make the same stupid mistake I made. Don't throw away your one chance for happiness out of pride. You will regret it every day of your life if you do."

"It's not pride," he choked out. "She doesn't want me for her husband. She never did."

Antonia rose to her feet. "She's *always* wanted you for herself," she vowed.

He laughed, but there was no mirth in it. "Yes. Your plotting saw to it that we would collide. But that's all we've done. Collide." He let loose a weary sigh. "There is no more to it than the physical attraction you so accurately predicted."

"Are you saying she does not love you?"

Ivan thought back to the one time she'd said she loved him. Had it been true? He would never know now. "At one time she thought she did."

"And you? Do you love her?"

He did not answer. He could not. But his silence seemed

to energize his aging grandmother, for she approached him
with renewed vigor.

"If you love her, you must tell her, Ivan. She is a romantic. For all her intellectual interests, she is nonetheless
a romantic. If you want to keep her, you must tell her so.
You must tell her you love her."

"And you, of course, are an authority on that nebulous
emotion," Ivan bit out. "A loving mother whose son grew
up to be a spineless, self-centered worm. A loving grandmother who couldn't bear the sight of her only grandchild.
But perhaps you were a loving wife. You'll understand, of
course, if I don't believe that either."

She winced at his sarcasm, but it did not entirely deter
her, for she faced him still, though she trembled beneath
the onslaught of his scorn. "I have made many mistakes in
my life," she said. "And none of them can I undo—most
especially the cruel way I have dealt with you. You were
only a child. A frightened, lonely child," she admitted in
a whisper. "I hurt you and I am heartily sorry for it. I can't
undo the past. But I can try to change the future. Your
future."

How many years had Ivan waited to hear just such an
admission from her, just such an apology? And yet it roused
a new sort of anger in him. It was far too late for her to
be sorry. "You can't undo the past," he echoed. "As for
the future . . . I want nothing to do with you in the future.
Nothing whatsoever."

She nodded and swallowed. "Yes. I understand that. But
. . . But I caution you not to confuse your hatred of me with
your treatment of your wife."

Ivan bristled. "The two have nothing to do with one
another."

"No?" She seemed to rally and her eyes glittered with
emotion. "Then why can't you love her? Why can't you
tell her you love her, as she needs to be told?" She watched
him in the silence that separated them. "I can see the depths
of your feeling for her. Everyone can."

Ivan could feel himself beginning to sweat. He glared at

her, wanting to cut her with some scathing retort. But all he could say was, "If it's so obvious, then why can't *she* see it?"

"You have to tell her," she said, punctuating her words with one knotted fist. "You have to trust her with the truth in your heart. It's all she lacks from you. It's all she needs."

Ivan didn't want to hear it. He didn't want to believe anything she said, least of all this. What if she was wrong? What if Lucy didn't love him at all? What if he bared his heart to her and she still wanted to go?

Then again, she was already set on leaving him. What did he have to lose?

Only his dignity. His self-respect. What little was left of his pride. And yet that risk was nothing compared to what he might gain: Lucy's love.

Before he could turn for the door, his grandmother spoke once more, her ancient voice low, cracked—and earnest. "I have thought many things of you, Ivan, most of them unwarranted and unfair. But I have never thought of you as a coward. Not once."

"Then you don't know me very well," Ivan muttered to himself. He'd been a coward for so long, not risking his feelings for fear he might be hurt. But he could be a coward no more.

He gave her a brief nod and turned away. Once in the hall there was only one direction he could go. To Lucy.

Twenty-five

*L*ucy sat in the window. Summer still kissed the land with green. But here and there the first hints of autumn showed. The sycamore leaves had begun to fall. The daisies had long ago faded and now one of the gardeners was digging and dividing the clumps. The boxwood topiary that flanked the entrance to the garden had been newly trimmed and would hold their obelisk shapes through the dormant season until spring brought new growth to the towering pair.

Lucy's hand moved to her stomach, to cover her empty womb. Would spring bring new growth to her? A new baby to grow inside her? A child to deliver and nurture, to love and shape for the rest of her life?

The answer hung like a grim shadow over her, making her shiver beneath its weight. Not if she left Ivan. Not if she returned to her family.

She looked at the door, hoping. Praying. But it remained still and solid. A six-panel oak door, easily twice her height. Ivan had left through that door. Once again she'd rejected him and he would not be coming back.

Tears stung her eyes. She'd sent him away, and why? Because she wanted more from him than he was able to give. Was that fair? Was that even reasonable? If he didn't love her it was because he didn't know how. But if she would just be patient, if she would just try harder, perhaps she could teach him, if only by example.

She swung her gaze back to the pastoral scene beyond the curtained window alcove. Since when had love become a prerequisite for marriage anyway? Ivan had asked that very question of her. Now she asked it of herself. Mutual respect and friendship had been all she'd wanted from Sir James. Why couldn't that be enough from Ivan?

Because it wasn't. She loved Ivan with every fiber of her being. With her heart, her body, and her soul. And she desperately needed him to love her back.

But until he did, she simply could not let him go.

She flung back the curtain and rose from the deep window ledge. At almost the same moment the door to the hall jerked open and Ivan burst into the room.

"I don't want you to go." He stood in the doorway, his stance belligerent, but his eyes tortured. "You're my wife and I won't let you leave me."

Joy surged through Lucy, joy and love and an overwhelming certainty that he could learn to love her as she loved him. Perhaps he already did, at least a little. After all, he was here, wasn't he?

"I'm not leaving," she whispered, unable to repress a happy smile. They had a long way to go but together they would manage. And together they would make another child—and a family—for them both. "I'm not leaving," she repeated. "I was just coming to tell you that."

Ivan stared at Lucy. He wasn't certain he'd heard her right. She gave him a trembling smile, a beautiful, hopeful smile, that held in it all the warmth of the sun, the serenity of the moon, and the enduring promise of the constellations. She wasn't leaving!

He took a step into the room, then halted. He wanted her so badly it hurt. His need for her was so pure, so all-enveloping, that it left no room for anything else.

"I love you."

He started to hold his arms out, then let them fall to his sides. The words came out so easily. Too easily. They didn't begin to convey the depth of his feelings for this woman who had challenged him, then charmed him. Who was both brilliant and naïve. Who was like no other woman. Why had he feared to say those three little words, when they didn't began to describe the depths of his feelings? How could he ever find the words powerful enough to explain how he felt about her?

Her smile had faded at his profession of love, confirming in his mind the inadequacy of his statement. She shook her head. "You don't have to say that, Ivan. I'm not leaving you. I'll stay even if you don't love me."

"But I do love you. You have to believe me, Lucy. I love you. I was an idiot before, a fool not to realize—"

"Shh." She moved up to him and pressed a finger to his lips. "Don't say anything else."

Their eyes met and held. Hers were a vivid green, so clear they seemed to shimmer with life—and with love.

Ivan was humbled by the love he saw in their luminous depths, love for him, a man who'd done nothing to deserve that love. He made a silent vow to do everything in his power to deserve it in the future. And the most important thing was to open his heart to her completely, to hold nothing back from her ever again.

"I want to make love to you," he said, and rejoiced when she blushed then smiled. "I want to love you always, in every way. I want you to live and breathe every moment of your life secure in the knowledge of my love for you."

She reached up and cupped his cheek with one palm, and he covered her hand with his larger one. "That's the vow I should make to you," she said. "You missed out on so much love as a child, but I promise you, Ivan, that you shall never be denied love as a man. As my husband."

She drew him toward the bed, and like a man mesmerized, he followed her. She loved him! How could he ever have feared that love—or the love he'd tried to repress for her?

She backed toward the bed and he followed, beckoned by her trembling smile, glistening eyes, and open arms. She sat down on the bed and he began to descend over her. Then reality intruded and he hovered over her, wanting her desperately but knowing he could let this go no further.

"The doctor says we may not have marital relations for at least a fortnight. You need time to recover from . . ." He let the words trail away.

Her eyes clouded for only a moment. When she smiled again it was with a new serenity. "Then come lie here with me and we shall say a prayer for the baby we have lost and all the ones we have yet to conceive."

Again Ivan hesitated. More children? He shook his head. "I couldn't put you through that again. It's too dangerous. I don't need to have children to be happy. I only need you."

She laughed, though a hint of tears showed in her eyes. "It's far too late for you to back out of this arrangement now, Ivan. You married me. You have professed your love to me. Now you must take everything that comes with it. For I plan to give you blue-eyed Gypsy boys and green-eyed Gypsy girls, whether you want them or not. More than anything in the world I want to bear your children."

Ivan gathered her in his arms. He could not speak for the tears that suddenly choked him. He'd never felt so loved. He'd never been such an important part of anyone's life. "If that's what you want."

"What I want is you," she whispered, curling against his chest, with her hand resting upon his cheek. "And I want no more misunderstanding between us. No more running away from one another." She lifted her head to stare straight into his eyes. "We have to run toward each other, not apart. Especially when things are not going well."

"Nothing can ever go wrong again, not now," Ivan vowed, and in that moment he believed it. But to his surprise, she laughed.

"You say that now, but I wonder what will happen the first time I disagree with you." She arched one brow, giving him a knowing smile.

Ivan grinned. "I'll kiss you into submission."

''What if I kiss you into submission?''

His smile faded and he stared at her, not believing his incredible good luck at finding and marrying this woman, not believing the miracle that had made her love him. He pulled her close and held her tight, wanting to crush her to him and never let her go. ''Anything, just so long as you love me,'' he whispered into her hair.

As the two of them lay entwined upon their bed, with bright sunshine streaming across them, Lucy heard the message of his heart. He needed her love, just as she needed his. And she knew without a doubt that he would love their children, more than he could possibly guess. Together they would build a family, a circle of love so strong and enduring that he would never go without love again.

Neither of them would.

Epilogue

*T*he dining room glittered with light. The two candelabras had been lowered, cleaned, and now gleamed
with the flames of a hundred candles. Every wall sconce,
lamp, and candlestick contributed to the glow, and the
sweet smell of beeswax competed with the savory scents
of the meal just completed.

The table was crowded with people. His family, Ivan
realized, as he gazed in turn at each of them. From being
alone to being surrounded by family—more family than he
sometimes wanted—he'd come a very long way in the past
five years. And all on account of his Lucy.

He stared down the long table at her and his heart
swelled with love and pride. She was beautiful, both inside
and out, and she'd brought him a contentment he could
never have foreseen. Even this, a dinner in honor of his
grandmother's seventy-fifth birthday, could not dim his
happiness.

"A toast to long life," Sir Laurence said, rising with
some effort to his feet. He lifted his glass and so did everyone else.

"Here, here," Sir James said. He and Valerie sat side
by side, as they always insisted they must. Ivan had never
seen Sir James tipsy before, and he chuckled at the sight
of the somber scholar grinning like a fool.

Lucy's brother and his family were here, the nieces and

nephews each with their own glass of wine. Derek and
Stanley would soon be as tall as their father, and in the past
year Prudence had matured into a lovely young woman.
But Lucy would not be the one chaperoning her in town
next spring when she had her first season. He had no intention of giving his wife up for so long a period of time.

Alex had come from town for tonight's party. He was a
favorite with the dowager countess, so Lucy had insisted.
Giles was here too, though Elliot could not get away. That
was just as well, for Ivan still felt a twinge of jealousy
whenever the man greeted Lucy. Elliot was not a man to
trust with any woman, even his best friend's wife.

And no wonder, for what a wife she was. Tonight, with
her hair swept up, her gown cut low, and her favorite
shawl—his shawl—draped across her shoulders, she was a
sight that would give pleasure even to a blind man.

A tug on his sleeve drew Ivan's attention and he looked
down at Raphael, who sat to his right. "May I make a toast,
Father? May I?"

Ivan grinned at the image of his four-year-old son struggling to cover a yawn. It was well past his normal bedtime,
but tonight they'd made an exception. He rumpled the
boy's dark hair. "Of course you may." He tapped his knife
against his wine goblet, then helped Rafe to stand on his
chair.

The boy raised his glass of apple cider as he'd seen the
adults do. He grinned at his father and then down the table
at his mother. Finally he turned his impish attention on his
grandmother, who sat in the middle of the table opposite
him.

"Happy birthday to the best great-grandmother in the
whole wide world."

Amidst the laughter and shouts of "Hear, hear!" Ivan
waited for the familiar bitterness to set in. He hadn't wanted
his son to love her. He hadn't wanted a child of his to have
anything to do with the old crone. But Lucy had insisted
and he had relented. Now he couldn't deny the true

affection that lay between the old woman and her innocent great-grandchild.

When the dowager countess smiled at the boy, however, what little there was of Ivan's bitterness melted away. She loved his son, almost as much as he did. For that matter, the old woman seemed to love Lucy too. And she would undoubtedly love the new child growing beneath his wife's heart.

He lifted his glass in response to his beloved son's toast and drank with the rest of his guests. Happy birthday to the best great-grandmother in the world. For as terrible a grandmother as she'd been, even he had to admit that she'd proven to be a doting great-grandparent.

Around him the room resounded with happy chatter. Servants moved about, refilling glasses. Derek and Stanley begged to be allowed a second glass of wine, and with a shrug their father agreed.

But Ivan's eyes were drawn to his wife's brilliant gaze. Twelve feet of polished mahogany, glittering crystal, and shining silver separated them, but he read the message in her eyes. She had seen his raised glass. She'd seen him quaff the remainder of his wine. And somehow she knew that he'd made peace with his past.

Then she smiled and the warmth of it flooded him, as always, with love—her love, and as a result, the love of this big, noisy family. Yes, the past was past. Lucy had seen to that. He would never be able to thank her enough.

"Come, give me a kiss, lad," Antonia called to Rafe, and the boy jumped to do his bidding.

Ivan watched him go. He saw how the feeble old woman embraced his son. Then she looked up at him and for a moment their eyes held.

It lasted only a moment, for Rafe said something to her and her gaze shifted back to the child. But it was long enough for Ivan to know that she regretted the past. She'd told him as much, but that look said so much more. A title was convenient. Wealth was most definitely an asset. But family was everything.

A lump lodged in his throat and he sought Lucy once more with his eyes. She was smiling at Rafe in his great-grandmother's arms. But as if she felt the touch of his gaze, she looked back at Ivan.

I love you, she said in that silent way she had of communicating with only her eyes and a smile. *I love you.*

And yes, family is everything.